"You made all this?"

Kathryn ducked her head shyly. "I even hooked the rug."

Impressed, Jake lifted his eyebrows. This was a woman of immense talent. "I suppose you painted the cabinets in the kitchen, too."

"Who else? There's no one here but me."

"I thought you lived with your mom."

Kathryn dipped her chin, dropping her gaze. "I—I did. She passed ten months ago, and before that she was far too immobile to stencil cabinets."

Jake let that sink in. After a moment, he muttered, "We ought to get on our way."

He mused that, if things went well with the shop, maybe he and Frankie could find their own place and hire Kathryn Stepp to decorate it.

Suddenly an idea sprang into his mind. What if he could convince his brother to hire Kathryn? Jake would benefit from this, too.

At least that was what he told himself.

It was a far more comfortable thought than the idea that he might like having Kathryn Stepp around the ranch.

Arlene James has been publishing steadily for nearly four decades and is a charter member of RWA. She is married to an acclaimed artist, and together they have traveled extensively. After growing up in Oklahoma, Arlene lived thirty-four years in Texas and now abides in beautiful northwest Arkansas, near two of the world's three loveliest, smartest, most talented granddaughters. She is heavily involved in her family, church and community.

Multipublished bestselling author **Ruth Logan Herne** loves God, her country, her family, dogs, chocolate and coffee! Married to a very patient man, she lives in an old farmhouse in Upstate New York and thinks possums should leave the cat food alone and snakes should always live outside. There are no exceptions to either rule! Visit Ruth at ruthloganherne.com.

Rancher
to the Rescue

Arlene James

&

A Cowboy in
Shepherd's
Crossing

USA TODAY Bestselling Author

Ruth Logan Herne

LOVE INSPIRED
INSPIRATIONAL ROMANCE

LOVE INSPIRED®

INSPIRATIONAL ROMANCE

Recycling programs for this product may not exist in your area.

ISBN-13: 978-1-335-46280-0

Rancher to the Rescue and A Cowboy in Shepherd's Crossing

Copyright © 2021 by Harlequin Books S.A.

Rancher to the Rescue
First published in 2019. This edition published in 2021.
Copyright © 2019 by Deborah Rather

A Cowboy in Shepherd's Crossing
First published in 2018. This edition published in 2021.
Copyright © 2018 by Ruth M. Blodgett

This edition published by arrangement with Harlequin Books S.A.

For questions and comments about the quality of this book, please contact us at CustomerService@Harlequin.com.

Love Inspired
22 Adelaide St. West, 40th Floor
Toronto, Ontario M5H 4E3, Canada
www.Harlequin.com

Printed in U.S.A.

CONTENTS

RANCHER TO THE RESCUE

Arlene James

For Pattie Steele-Perkins.
You've always had my back,
and I can't thank you enough.
God bless you, my friend.

As for God, his way is perfect;
the word of the Lord is tried:
he is a buckler to all them that trust in him.
—*2 Samuel* 22:31

Chapter One

Glancing at his three-year-old in the rearview mirror of the double cab pickup truck, Jake cranked up the air-conditioning.

"Sorry, son. It's just too hot to ride with the windows down."

Frankie made a face, but said nothing as Jake hit the buttons that rolled up the windows. The boy loved the wind in his face, even the scorching wind of an August morning, which was one reason he'd taken off at a heady gallop on his pony across the field after his six-year-old cousin yesterday. Tyler was a more experienced rider than Frankie, and Jake's heart had leaped into his throat as he'd watched his son's dark head bouncing behind his nephew's horse. Thankfully, Jake had caught up to him before the boy had lost his seat.

Determined that both the boy and the pony would receive further instruction before being allowed out of the corral again, Jake had brought Frankie along with him while he ran errands. He didn't have any other option. His brothers, Wyatt and Ryder, and Wyatt's son, Tyler, were out on horseback checking the least-accessible water holes on the ranch, and Wyatt's wife, Tina, had a doctor's appointment.

Given the size and population of his native Houston, Jake had always thought that in Texas, it was a long drive to get anywhere, but Oklahoma was proving its equal. Its many small towns and few big cities were separated by long stretches of empty road. Consequently, Oklahoma felt rather lonely to Jake, even more so since Wyatt had married Tyler's mother in June.

Tina and Tyler were good for his brother, and Jake wished them only happiness, but now that Wyatt had his own family, Jake had started to feel out of place at Loco Man Ranch. He and his two brothers had spent many joyous summers running wild over the two thousand acres of the ranch on the outskirts of tiny War Bonnet before inheriting the place from their uncle Dodd a few months ago. More and more, though, Jake felt like an interloper in his sister-in-law's house and an unnecessary dependent on the ranching enterprise. As a mechanic, trained by the army, Jake felt the ranch simply did not need or maintain enough vehicles to keep him busy or justify his take of the profits, which were irregular.

On the other hand, the nearest mechanic to War Bonnet was at least thirty miles away. Jake figured he could pull in enough business from the surrounding countryside to turn a profit. So, right after the wedding, with the blessings of his brothers and sister-in-law, Jake had the foundation poured for a shop that he was building at the very edge of the road fronting the ranch property, only a few hundred yards from the house. While doing much of the building himself and keeping a close eye on his budget, he was quickly acquiring building materials and inventory. If the shop was up and running within the next month or so, he should have enough of his dwindling savings left to see him through until the business fulfilled expectations.

With his mind full of lists and plans, he didn't notice the old car beside the road until he was right on it. A woman was bent over the front fender of the little coupe, her head hidden by the raised hood, one tennis shoe kicked up into the air and her long full skirt rising to the backs of her knees. Jake knew instantly that he had to stop. Already hotter than ninety degrees with a high in triple digits predicted, it was too hot to be stranded on the side of the road, and out here the next vehicle might be long in coming.

He brought the big pickup truck to a grinding halt beside the two-lane pavement, well ahead of the stranded car. Shifting the transmission into Park with one hand, he rolled down all the windows with the other before killing the engine. "Don't you get out of your seat," he instructed Frankie. "I'll be right back. I'm just going to help this lady."

Frankie leaned forward and craned his neck, looking behind them. "What lady?"

"Don't know," Jake replied, reaching for the pale straw cowboy hat on the passenger seat. "Looks like her car broke down."

He got out, settled his hat on his head and pushed his sunshades farther up on his nose, wishing he'd taken the time to shave that morning. The coal-dark dusting of beard on his cheeks, jaws and upper lip always made him look rough and undisciplined, or so his late wife, Jolene, had said. He didn't want to scare this poor woman any more than she likely already was.

Jolene, like him, had been military. If she hadn't died

in a training accident, they'd still be soldiers together, army from the tops of their heads to the soles of their feet. That was a tough life for a single father, however.

He approached the hissing car with a smile for a greeting, only to find that his damsel in distress had retreated into her vehicle. Lifting his eyebrows, he casually strolled up to the driver's window and tapped on the glass.

"Howdy." He gestured to the raised hood of her car. "Got a little trouble, I see. How about I take a look?"

For a long moment, she just stared at him with wide, forest green eyes. Then she folded in her lips and bit them. Finally, she rolled down the window a half inch or so.

"I don't know you."

He put out his hand. "Jacoby Smith, from Loco Man Ranch. Most folks call me Jake."

She didn't lower the window. Instead, she stared at him, biting her lips in what was obviously a nervous habit. He gestured toward the hood of her car again.

"I'm going to take a look." Without giving her a chance to object, he stepped to the front of the car and began to take stock. "Can you start it?"

After a moment, she turned the key. It didn't take long for him to diagnose the problem. He went to the window again, finding that she'd lowered it all the way, finally.

Fanning herself with her hand, she spoke before he had a chance to do so. "I suppose you're Dodd's kin."

"That's right. He was our uncle."

She stopped fanning and squinted up at him. "I was sorry to hear he'd passed."

"Thanks. My brothers and I were fond of the old boy."

"You'd be one of those three nephews who used to spend summers with him, then."

"Right again. And you are?"

"Fine," she said quickly. "I'm fine." Her dusky pink lips formed the words even as her gaze cut to the hood of her car. "Just need some water for the radiator, I think."

Jake shook his head, irritated that she wouldn't give him her name. Unlike so many others he'd met in the area, she wasn't exactly a friendly sort, but she needed help. More than she knew.

"I think you've blown a head gasket. At least."

"You can't possibly know that for sure," she scoffed, a hint of desperation in her voice.

"I've seen it many times. I happen to be a mechanic."

She made a face, as if to say that only made his opinion more suspect.

"Look," he snapped, "I'm not out here trying to drum up business."

"Then why'd you stop?" she shot back, turning her head away. "You don't know me."

Recognizing the sound of impending tears, Jake pulled in a slow, calming breath. "I stopped," he said evenly, "because no one should be left stranded beside the road in this heat. Is there anyone you can call for a lift?"

She thought for a minute, biting her lips, and shook her head.

He raised his hands, palms up, in a gesture meant to convey that they were out of options. "My son and I will be glad to give you a ride."

Sniffing, she eyed him suspiciously. "I didn't see anyone else in the truck."

"He's three," Jake gritted out, reaching deep for patience. "You ought to be able to see the top of his car seat at least."

She stuck her head out the window and studied the truck. Her thick, dark gold hair parted in the middle of her head and swung in a jaunty, ragged flip two or three inches above her shoulders. Sinking into the car again, she tucked the sun-kissed strands behind a dainty ear and muttered, "Oh, yes. I see that now."

Heat radiated up off the pavement in blistering waves. Jake pushed back the brim of his hat. "We can take you wherever you need to go."

She lifted her chin, swallowing hard and exposing her long, sleek neck and the delicate skin of her throat in the process. Jake's chest tightened. He told himself it was concern, the fear that she was going to send him away, though he was her only immediate source of help. During his first deployment, he'd developed the habit of speaking silently to the Lord in moments of need, and this was one of those moments.

Lord, You'd better zap some sense into her. It's not safe for her to sit out here in this heat. Even worse if she tries to walk wherever she's headed.

To his relief, she slowly opened the car door and got out, slinging a large fabric bag over one shoulder. She was taller than he'd expected, and her blouse, worn over a full gray skirt, was of the medical variety, like the top half of a scrub suit. A muted green, it crisscrossed in front and tied at the side, creating a V neckline that exposed a dainty but prominent collarbone.

"In case you forgot, my name's Jacoby Smith. Jake."

"Jake," she whispered in acknowledgment. "Kathryn Stepp."

"Nice to meet you, Kathryn, despite the circumstances. Now, shall we?" He nodded at the truck. Reluctantly, her arms folded across her middle, she began to walk in that direction. Shortening his steps to keep pace with her, he asked, "Where can I take you?"

She bit her lips before saying, "I—I need to get to a client's house. Sandy Cabbot. He'll be wanting his lunch soon."

"Don't know him. How do I get there?"

"Just head on east to the county line, then go left. It's only a few miles."

"No problem. You'll have to point out this county line to me, though."

She seemed surprised by that. "Oh. All right."

They drew alongside the truck. Jake opened the front passenger door for her and jerked his thumb toward the back seat. "That's my boy, Frankie."

Frankie waved at her. She waved back, smiling timidly, before climbing into the truck. Jake walked around, tossed his hat onto the back seat next to Frankie and slid behind the steering wheel in time to see her pass a trembling hand over her forehead.

He started the engine and rolled up the windows, sitting for a moment to let the cool air from the vents flow over them. "Tough morning, I take it."

She nodded. He waited. After a long moment, she softly said, "Without that car, I can't work, and if I can't work, I can't fix the car or…" She shrugged morosely.

"I find things usually look better if we give them some time," Jake told her, getting the truck underway.

Muttering something about time running out, she pulled a cell phone from the pocket of her voluminous skirt. "I have to make a phone call." He listened unapologetically as she placed the call and spoke into the phone. "Sandy, this is Kathryn again. I've got a ride. See you in a few minutes."

She replaced the phone in her pocket then jerked when Frankie yelled, "Hey, lady!"

Jake briefly closed his eyes. His outgoing, energetic three-year-old didn't take well to being ignored, and he habitually spoke at the top of his lungs. Tina claimed that was perfectly normal. Applying patience, Jake prepared to remind Frankie to use his "inside voice." Before he had the chance, Kathryn Stepp twisted and gazed into the back seat.

"Hello."

"Hay-ell-o!" Frankie repeated happily, mimicking her Oklahoma drawl.

Jake winced, but she laughed. "You're a cutie."

"You a cutie!" Frankie bellowed back at her.

"Take it down a notch, please," Jake instructed.

She glanced at Jake but went on speaking to Frankie. "Are you having fun, riding around with Daddy today?"

"No," Frankie said bluntly, moderating his volume a bit. "I wanna ride my pony."

She frowned. "That sounds dangerous. Doesn't your mama worry you'll get hurt when you ride your pony?"

Jake leaned forward slightly, watching his son's face in the rearview mirror.

Frankie replied matter-of-factly. "No. She in heben."

"Heaven," Jake corrected gently, relaxing into his seat again.

"Oh," Kathryn said, sobering. "I'm sorry."

"She like it," Frankie said, sounding unconcerned.

"That's nice." Turning to Jake, she asked, "He's only three?"

"About three and a half."

"He seems big for his age," she commented, as if that were a worrisome thing.

"Smiths are big men," Jake muttered defensively.

At the same time, Frankie asked, "S'wat her name?"

He often got his contractions backward, substituting *s'wat* for *what's* and *s'that* for *that's*.

"It's Miss Stepp." Or so Jake assumed. Surely if she had a husband, she'd have called him for help. On the other hand, maybe the man was out of town. Glancing at her, he asked, "Or is it missus?"

She bit her lips before answering coolly, "Miss."

Couldn't say he was surprised. She didn't seem to trust men. Or was it that she just didn't like or trust him?

She was a pretty woman, though, with that long, long neck and those intense green eyes and rosy lips. Obviously, she didn't take much stock in her appearance, given her mismatched garb, straggly hair and utter lack of cosmetics. Even Jolene had known how to get dressed up.

His late wife had been the perfect soldier, but once the uniform had come off, she'd tended toward sparkles and slinky fabrics. He'd often wondered if that had been her way of making up for her dedication to all things military. This quiet, nervous female hardly seemed of the same species. If Jolene's transportation had broken down beside the road, she'd have commandeered the first vehicle to cross her path.

He supposed that most women would be more cautious. Few had Jolene's training and confidence, and too many men were willing to take advantage of a woman alone, especially a timid one. Glad that he'd stopped, even if this unexpected passenger was prickly, Jake smiled at her. Instantly, she leaned away from him, her eyes going wide.

So much for chivalry.

Kathryn had never known how to behave around men, especially the good-looking ones, and Jake Smith definitely fit into that category. With his rumpled black-coffee-colored hair, chiseled features and straight white teeth, he was movie-star handsome, and that dark, prickly shadow practically shouted masculinity. It was the way he moved that made her so nervous, however. Every motion proclaimed him a confident, capable man who had never met an obstacle he couldn't overcome.

Before getting into the vehicle with him, she'd reasoned that no man with a three-year-old in tow would truly present a threat, but old habits died hard. Since the age of seventeen, Kathryn had been virtually on her own, apart from the wider world, tied to her mom's bedside by that woman's debilitating physical condition. Always shy, Kathryn had never been very brave or confident, and from the time of her mother's accident, she had diligently taken every precaution, especially after her father had abandoned them.

As usual, thoughts of Mitchel Stepp brought a world of worry down on Kathryn. How was she to keep him from forcing the sale of her home when she couldn't come up with the money to buy him out? And now her car was broken down. If only she could find her mother's insurance policy. It wouldn't pay much, but it might be enough to satisfy her father for at least a while. Her salary as a home care provider covered her bills and allowed her to put aside a bit every month to cover the property taxes that would come due at the end of the year, but Mitchel expected thousands, half the value of her house.

As Jake pulled the metallic olive-green truck to a stop in front of Sandy Cabbot's lonely little farmhouse, he glanced around. "Can someone here give you a ride back to town when you're finished? I don't see a car anywhere."

Shaking her head, she opened the door. "I'll manage. Thanks for your help."

"It's no problem," he said. "If you want me to look at your car—"

She cut that off right away. "I can't afford to pay you, Mr. Smith."

He balanced a forearm against the top of the steering wheel. "Jake. I didn't ask for payment. And the fact is you can't go walking far in this heat."

Stepping out onto the running board, she replied, "We do what we must." That was one lesson she'd learned early and well.

"What time are you through here?" he asked.

She reached the ground and turned to face him. "Why?"

He pulled off his mirrored shades and tossed them onto the dash, fixing her with a hard stare. His eyes were such a dark brown they were almost black. "What time?"

"Six." The reply was out before she could stop it.

"Then I'll be back at six."

Kathryn bit her lips. She knew she shouldn't get in that truck with him again. He made her feel...well, not frightened really, but completely inadequate, and she did not need help with that. She cleared her throat anxiously. "That's not—"

He reached across and pulled the cab door shut.

"—necessary," she muttered, watching as he backed the truck around and drove away in a cloud of red dust.

Confident, capable, commanding—and apparently not used to taking no for an answer—he was exactly the last sort of man she should find attractive, and that she did find him attractive, wildly so, was reason enough to avoid him. She didn't know how to deal with a man like him, but then he wouldn't be interested in a plain, shy, unsophisticated woman like her, anyway. At least she wouldn't have to walk back to town tonight. How she'd manage tomorrow, she couldn't imagine, but she'd worry about that, and everything else, later. Moving toward the house, she thought of the boy and smiled.

Hey, lady.

Frankie certainly wasn't shy. She didn't know anything about children, but despite losing his mother at such a tender age, he seemed to be happy and well-adjusted, if a bit loud. Nevertheless, with her own mother's death still fresh in her memory, her heart went out to him.

She wondered what had happened to the late Mrs. Smith. Illness or accident? Mia Stepp's death had been a combination of the two, her illness a direct result of the automobile accident that had battered her body and left her paralyzed and brain damaged. Kathryn missed her dreadfully, but Frankie's confident, carefree words concerning his own mother came back to her.

She in heben. She like it.

Kathryn prayed that was so. For both his mother and hers.

As she greeted Sandy, her elderly client, and began checking his vital signs before starting his lunch, she couldn't help wondering how long ago Mrs. Jake Smith had passed on. And how many women were already lined up to take her place.

It made no difference. She would never see Jake Smith again after this evening.

She certainly would not think of him as her rescuer.

Even if he was.

Chapter Two

Despite Frankie's many questions, Jake couldn't get Kathryn Stepp off his mind. *You'd think no one had ever done that woman a favor before*, Jake mused as he wandered around the auto parts store, waiting for the clerk to bring up his supplies from the warehouse. It cost less for the supplier to ship his goods to the auto parts store in Ardmore than to the ranch.

"S'wat that?" Frankie pointed at a rotating display rack.

"Air freshener. It makes the car smell good."

"I wan' it." Frankie reached out his hand.

Jake took the inexpensive air freshener from the display. In the shape of a fir tree, it smelled of evergreen. He scratched the odor patch on the back of the package and held it to Frankie's nose. The boy inhaled deeply, smiled and nodded.

"Okay, but after it's opened it stays in the truck. It's not a toy."

Nodding, Frankie reached for the package. Jake handed it over. Frankie immediately reached for another. "Ty'er want one," he said.

Jake picked up another air freshener for Tyler. They continued wandering the store until the clerk signaled them a few moments later.

After loading boxes into the bed of the truck, they stopped for lunch then ran two more errands before heading home. As Jake turned toward the ranch, he thought of Kathryn Stepp again, of the tears she'd tried to hide from him and the worry in her voice.

Without that car, I can't work, and if I can't work, I can't fix the car. I can't afford to pay you, Mr. Smith.

Mr. Smith.

The contrary woman didn't like him much, though he was just trying to help her. She did like Frankie, though, and vice versa. That counted with Jake. Besides, how could he not help when he had the skills to do so?

For most of the drive, he mulled over how to convince her to accept his assistance. Maybe Tina could talk Kathryn into letting him work on her car. Or the Billings sisters. The Billingses were a prominent ranching family around War Bonnet, greatly respected for their honesty and generosity. He wondered if he could get Tina to ride with him when he went to pick up Kathryn that evening. It would be an inconvenience. Six was the dinner hour in the Smith household. Why couldn't Kathryn Stepp just accept his help and let that be that?

Before he could decide how to handle the problem, he came upon her old car. Instinctively, he whipped over to the shoulder of the road and got out. A quick look told him that the little coupe had a standard transmission and the door was unlocked. Jake kept a sturdy chain handy for emergencies such as this. It was the work of minutes to hook up the chain, flick on the flashers and move the car's transmission out of gear so he could tow it.

"The lady's car!" Frankie exclaimed gleefully as Jake slowly tugged the little old coupe into motion.

"Yep. The lady's car," Jake confirmed, feeling the snap and tug of the chain.

Towing a car like this was risky business, but if he slowed properly he could bring both vehicles to a halt without causing damage to either. He guided the truck and coupe into a slow, arcing turn and made his way to Loco Man Ranch on the outskirts of War Bonnet, where he coasted to a stop in the middle of the compound yard. The coupe came to a rest right behind Tina's old car.

Tina was driving a brand-spanking-new SUV now, and Ryder was supposed to be driving Tina's car, but Jake had noticed that his little brother found lots of excuses for driving his brothers' trucks instead. He couldn't blame Ryder. All the Smith brothers stood three inches over six feet, and Ryder was by far the biggest, most muscular of the trio. A small car wasn't a good fit.

Jake took Frankie and their purchases into the house, where Frankie instantly announced, "We got a lady an'er car!"

Tina, who was removing the lunch dishes from the newly installed dishwasher, straightened in surprise. "I need to go shopping more often. What size lady did you get?"

Jake chuckled. "We stopped to help a lady whose car broke down beside the road. I towed it into the yard so I can take a look at it."

"Oh. Good thing you happened along. Where's the lady?"

"I took her to work. Gotta go back and get her at six."

"Ah. I can go get her if you want," Tina offered lightly. "If you don't mind eating early."

He shrugged as if it didn't matter. But somehow, it did. "I'll take care of it. Besides, I need to talk to her about her car." Tina nodded, but for some reason, Jake felt as if he needed to defend himself. "She doesn't seem to have much money."

Tina smiled. "Naturally you'll help her."

He didn't know what to say to that, so he changed the subject. "Frankie's got something for Tyler. To go in the new SUV."

"Christmas tree!" Frankie declared, holding the two small packages aloft.

"So that's why you had to have it." Jake chuckled. "You're four months too early, pal."

Smiling, Tina went to take Frankie's arm. "Tyler's in his room. Let's carry it up to him. Okay?"

Frankie nodded happily, and they moved toward the hallway.

"If you don't mind keeping an eye on him for a little while," Jake said quickly, "I'd like to get Kathryn's car into the barn and go over it."

Tina shot him a smile over one shoulder. "Sure. And thanks for picking up those things for me."

"No problem."

As he headed to the door, Jake heard her say to Frankie, "Kathryn, hmm?"

"*Miss* Kat'ryn," Frankie corrected.

Tina's soft *hmm* made Jake wince.

Newlyweds always thought everyone around them was trying to couple up. Well, he'd been there and done that already. Besides, even if he dared reach for such happiness again, he suspected that once in a lifetime was all anyone could expect. Maybe it was all he could endure.

* * *

"Where's Frankie?" Kathryn asked, trying not to sound as nervous as she felt.

"Playing with his cousin."

The truck engine idling, Jake waited patiently until she buckled her seat belt before backing the truck around and heading it down the dirt road.

Kathryn watched Sandy's little house recede in the side-view mirror of the truck and wondered if she'd ever be back, and if not, what would become of the gaunt, pleasant old man. Nearly ninety, he got around with the help of a walker and in the average week saw just Kathryn and a rural nurse. With his family far away, he depended on professional caregivers.

Out of the blue, Jake Smith said, "I towed your car to Loco Man."

She gasped. "You did *what*? I told you, I can't afford—"

"Yeah, yeah, I get it," he interrupted, shaking a hand at her. "But I couldn't leave it sitting on the side of the road. It could've been hit. And I don't know where you live, so I couldn't tow it there. Besides, I can fix it for the cost of the parts. My shop's not operational yet, but I've got everything I need to work on it in the barn."

Hope welled up inside her. "You'd do that?"

"Sure. I can give you wholesale prices on the parts, too, but it's still gonna cost in the hundreds," he warned. "The engine has to be completely rebuilt."

Her hope of a moment before waned. If only she could find that insurance policy, but she'd looked everywhere she could think to look. The company insisted that they had no record of the changes they'd agreed upon more than a decade ago. Kathryn bit her lips, no-

ticed him watching and stopped. A moment's thought
told her she really had no other choice.

"Put together an estimate then," she told him uncertainly. "I'll try to figure out something." Hopefully,
her tax savings would cover it. If not…she didn't want
to go there.

"I'll calculate the estimate tonight," he promised.
"Now, where am I taking you?"

"Oh. It's Sixth Street. Number eleven. In War Bonnet, of course."

They drove along in silence for some time before
he abruptly announced that Frankie had begged for
air fresheners for himself and his cousin because they
came in the shape of Christmas trees. Kathryn had to
digest that.

"You mean those evergreen car fresheners?"

"Yep."

"You know those could be dangerous, don't you? He
shouldn't put it in his mouth."

"Relax, worrywart," Jake said, grinning. "The air
fresheners are still in their packages, and once they
come out, they'll be used for their intended purpose."

"Oh. Well, you can't be too careful."

"Really? You mean like accepting rides from strangers on isolated Oklahoma roads?"

She started to say that she hadn't had any other
choice, but suddenly every murder mystery she'd
ever read, every cop show she'd ever watched, flitted
through her mind.

"Oh, come on," Jake said. "You're perfectly safe with
me. It was a joke."

Kathryn caught a swift breath and provided him
with a weak smile. "I'm sure I am. It's just that this

has never happened before, and I can't help worrying. A-about the car."

"Want me to stop off at the ranch and ask my sister-in-law to ride the rest of the way with us?" he asked, clearly not fooled.

She considered it, but Sandy knew where she was and who she was with. He spent a great deal of time on the phone with his few remaining friends, and word had filtered through the grapevine that the Smith brothers were regular attenders at Countryside Church and friends of the Billings family. Besides, Jake had been very generous with his time and concern thus far. She shook her head, feeling a little foolish.

"No. Thanks for offering, though."

He smiled, nodded and fell silent again.

It's just that he's so handsome, she told herself, *and so big*.

She was used to standing as tall as most men, or nearly so. Those she met in the grocery store and at the gas station weren't usually as tall as him. Plus, she knew them, at least by sight or name, and if they spoke to her, she just nodded and moved on. Glancing at Jake's broad, long-fingered hands, she wondered why none of those other men seemed as strong, capable or dangerous as him. She felt a keen sense of relief—and a puzzling disappointment—when they turned onto Sixth Street.

"This is a lovely part of town," he remarked, slowly navigating the tree-shaded lane.

"Yes. Our house is the smallest on the street, but it's so pretty here."

"Our?" he queried. The word came out sharply.

"It's my mother's house," she murmured, deciding not to mention her mother's recent death. Of course, he

could find out from anybody in town, but why would
he? Whether he was a Good Samaritan or merely drum-
ming up business, his only interest would be in her car.
He was no threat and couldn't have any interest in her
personally. Still, she owed him no explanations.

He brought the big truck to a halt in the narrow drive,
glancing around. "This is really nice."

Kathryn couldn't help smiling. She was proud of
her flower beds, and she thought the green trim, which
matched the shingles on the roof, made a pretty contrast
to the white siding.

"About the car," he said, abruptly switching subjects.
"When should I drop off the estimate?"

She didn't stop to wonder why he didn't offer to call
with the estimate. "I have to be at a client's house every
morning by ten and don't get off until six."

How she was going to get to her clients, she had no
idea. Sandy had suggested she rent a car from a facil-
ity in Ardmore, but a quick telephone call had revealed
that even a few days' rental fee would consume more
of her income than she could afford, and it wouldn't fix
her car. Maybe the agency for which she worked could
offer a solution. Hopefully, one other than firing her.

Jake nodded. "I see. Okay, then."

She grappled for the door handle, found it and let
herself out of the idling truck. "Thank you so much
for your help."

Smiling in acknowledgment, he nodded again. She
shut the door and stepped back. Within moments, he
and his truck had disappeared the way they'd come. As
Kathryn turned toward the house, she spied old Mrs.
Trident glaring at her from the front steps of the house

next door. Kathryn waved, but Mrs. Trident simply turned and went back inside.

She'd avoided the Stepp household since Kathryn's father had stumbled up the wrong steps, drunk and belligerent, one night more than a decade ago. Soon after, realizing that Mia Stepp was never going to recover from her accident, he'd abandoned his handicapped wife and seventeen-year-old daughter, but that didn't seem to matter to Mrs. Trident. In all those years, Kathryn hadn't heard from her father until about six months after her mother's death, when he'd sent a letter demanding that Kathryn sell the house and split the profit with him.

Kathryn started toward her own front door, sighing heavily, but as she traveled along the walkway flanked by daylilies and Shasta daisies, she felt a familiar sense of peace and belonging settle over her. This place had always been her sanctuary, the one safe spot in the whole world. She loved this old house. Living anywhere else seemed unimaginable. Somehow, she had to keep her father from forcing her to sell it. If only she could find that missing insurance policy.

Shaking her head, she pushed aside such thoughts and went indoors to telephone her employer and inform them of her changed circumstances. It wasn't as if that insurance money could save her house, after all. She simply would not think of everything else it could do.

"Pretty!" Frankie declared the next morning, pointing to the wreath hanging on the front door of the Stepp house.

Frankie had said the word half a dozen times since they'd pulled into the driveway. While they waited for someone to answer Jake's knock, Frankie gestured toward the prim white wicker rocking chair on the porch. The ruffles on its flowered cushions fluttered in the breeze.

"I know," Jake said wryly, smiling down at his son, "pretty."

The door opened, and Kathryn Stepp gaped at him with obvious alarm. "What are you doing here?"

Wearing a loose, flowered dress that hung almost to her ankles over slender bare feet, she folded her arms, trying—and failing—to fix a stern expression on her face. She looked like a girl playing dress up, a very pretty if somewhat bedraggled girl.

Jake removed his shades, tucked them into his shirt pocket and doffed his pale straw cowboy hat. "Morning."

Frankie, who knew nothing but exuberance, lurched forward and threw his arms around her, bellowing, "Mording!"

After shooting a shocked, puzzled glance at Jake, Kathryn softened. She leaned forward slightly and returned Frankie's hug as best she could, shuffling her feet to keep her toes from being squashed by his athletic shoes.

"Good morning. What brings you and your daddy here today?"

"We're here to give you a ride to work," Jake answered. Wasn't it obvious? He removed a folded sheet of paper from his hip pocket. "The ride will give you a chance to look over this estimate."

Her rosy lips turned down in a frown. "I'm not sure I have a job to go to. It depends on if they've found someone to replace me already."

"Shouldn't you find out?" Jake asked.

She turned her head, glancing into the room. For the first time, Jake looked past her. The living area was larger than he'd expected, with gleaming wood floors and a painted brick fireplace set against a sage-green interior wall. Colorful throw pillows and a basket of flowers in the center of the coffee table gave the room a cheery note. Clean and bright, the room felt peaceful and welcoming.

Frankie broke free of Kathryn and ran to climb up onto the sofa. "Look, Daddy! Pretty." He patted a throw pillow.

"Very pretty," Jake agreed, chuckling.

Kathryn waved a hand absently. "Uh, come in while I… Come in."

She waited until he stepped inside. Then she closed the door and rushed off down a hallway on the right, calling, "Have a seat! Won't be long!"

Jake removed his hat, but instead of sitting he waited until he heard a door close, then he glanced into the open doorway of what might have been a den but was now a bedroom. Curious, he walked past the hallway and through a dining area filled with dark, ornate furniture. Peeking into the kitchen, he saw Formica countertops, worn white in places, and rusty chips in the enamel on the sink. The appliances had certainly seen better days, and a few of the stenciled doors on the cabinet hung at a tilt that made him want to reach for a screwdriver and hammer. A vase of daisies stood on the windowsill above the sink.

Jake suddenly thought of his mom, how she had placed feminine little touches all around their Houston home. Those delicate, homey traces had gradually disappeared over the years after her death. Jake walked back into the living room and sank down in the easy chair, his hat in his lap.

"Mizz Kat'ryn gots lotta flowers." Frankie pronounced *flowers* as flou-hers.

"Yes, she does."

"I like flowers."

"Me, too."

"Mizz Kat'ryn gotta dog?"

"I don't know."

Frankie had been lobbying for a dog of his own ever since Tyler had gotten his pup a couple months earlier. Recently, Stark Burns, the local veterinarian, had shown them a promising litter. Anxious to acquire his own dog, Frankie didn't understand that the puppies still needed weeks before they could be weaned.

A door opened and footsteps sounded, growing louder until Kathryn appeared, dressed in comfortable blue jeans and a filmy, flowered blouse worn beneath the familiar scrub suit top. Frankie flew toward her and threw his arms around her hips, knocking her back a step.

"Whoa." She still looked sad and worried, though she patted his back.

Frankie beamed up at her. "You gotta dog?"

"Uh, no, afraid not." She looked to Jake and changed the subject. "I can work today. They haven't reassigned my clients yet."

Yet.

"Sounds like you could be out of a job."

"I'm afraid so. At least until my car's fixed."

Jake got to his feet. "Ready when you are."

She went to a closet, opened the door and removed the familiar fabric bag.

Meanwhile, Frankie ran and hopped on the couch again, bouncing slightly. "S'let stay here, Daddy."

Jake shook his head. "Can't. We have to take Miss Kathryn to work."

Leaning back against the pillows, Frankie whined, "I wanna stay."

Nodding, Jake glanced around again. "I understand. It's very nice."

Kathryn closed the closet door. "Thank you, but it's just homemade, secondhand stuff."

"Homemade?"

She shrugged. "Doesn't make good sense to throw away things when a little time and effort can turn them into treasures. A torn sheet makes a fine slipcover or set of throw pillows."

"You made all this?" Jake asked, swirling a hand to encompass the room.

She ducked her head shyly. "I even hooked the rug."

Impressed, Jake lifted his eyebrows. This was a woman of immense talent. "I suppose you painted the cabinets in the kitchen, too."

She looked a little taken aback that he'd seen her kitchen, but after a moment she said, "Who else? There's no one here but me."

Surprised, Jake tilted his head. "I thought you lived with your mom."

Kathryn dipped her chin, dropping her gaze. "I—I did. She passed ten months ago, and before that she was far too handicapped to stencil cabinets. Or do much of anything else."

Jake let that sink in, frowning at the implications. After a moment, he lifted a hand, muttering, "We ought to get on our way."

Nodding, she followed him and a reluctant Frankie from the house. As he got Frankie settled in the truck, Jake mused that if things went well with the shop, maybe he and Frankie could find their own place and hire Kathryn Stepp to decorate it.

Hire Kathryn Stepp.

An idea sprang into his mind. What if he could convince Wyatt and Tina to hire Kathryn? Tina could certainly use the help getting the ranch house ready for guests. She'd intended to open a bed-and-breakfast in the ranch house from the beginning, and they were already turning away those who wanted to visit relatives in the area. Even if they would only agree to take on Kathryn part-time, that would give her some income.

Realizing that he could say nothing to Kathryn until he'd prayed about this and talked to his brother and sister-in-law, Jake began to marshal his thoughts and put together his arguments. Excited to think that he might have found a solution to Kathryn's problems that would also help Tina prepare the ranch house for guests, he bit back a smile.

He would benefit from this, too. One way or another, he had to fix Kathryn's car. Donating his labor was no issue, but paying for the parts himself would take a bite out of his savings, if she would even let him do it. He doubted she would accept that much charity.

At least that's what he told himself.

It was a far more comfortable thought than the idea that he might like having Kathryn Stepp around the ranch.

Chapter Three

Kathryn folded the list of parts needed to repair her car and slipped it into the bag at her knee, biting her lips. Jake drove in silence for several moments, waiting for her to comment.

"I—I can cover some of this," she admitted shakily, "but I'd have to pay out the rest."

"We can arrange that."

"It could take some time."

"We'll figure it out."

"How long do you think the repairs will take?"

"Depends on how much time I have to work on it and how quickly I can find all the parts. Three, four weeks, at least." He'd hoped to be well on his way to opening his shop by then, but now he'd have to divide his time between building the shop and working on her car. Seeing the tears that shimmered in her eyes, he said nothing of his own concerns.

"I asked the agency to hold my job, but I doubt they will. Reliable transportation is part of the employment contract."

"Things will work out. We can arrange rides for a while."

She shifted uncertainly in her seat. "Oh, I couldn't ask—"

"In fact," he went on, as if she hadn't spoken, "I'd be pleased to offer you a ride to prayer meeting tonight."

Eyes wide, mouth ajar, she looked as if he'd reached out and slapped her. "Uh, no thank you. That is…" She turned red in the face. "I d-don't think it's a good idea."

For *him* to take her to prayer meeting, she meant. At least that was his assumption. He couldn't figure out why she disliked him so much. He'd done his best to be gentlemanly and helpful. Well, if she didn't like him, she didn't like him. So be it. Still, she needed help, and Frankie was absolutely taken with her, so Jake would do his best.

This second client lived even farther from town than her first one. After they arrived at the elderly woman's house, Kathryn thanked him, shouldered her bag and got out of the truck. Frankie began slapping his palm against his window and calling to her.

"Mizz Kat'ryn! Mizz Kat'ryn!"

Jake rolled down the window. Kathryn leaned inside, saying, "Bye, Frankie."

To Jake's surprise, Frankie smacked a big kiss on her cheek. "Bye-bye!"

Smiling, Kathryn threaded an arm through the window and hugged him. "Have a great day."

"Hab gread day!" Frankie called as she hurried into the house. He sighed as if quite satisfied with himself.

Shaking his head, Jake rolled up the window and drove back toward the ranch, wondering why Frankie was so fixated on her. His sudden affection seemed out of proportion, especially given how much she disliked Jake. Kathryn had made it very clear that she didn't want anything more to do with him than she must. That being the case, he hoped she wouldn't turn down any job offer that came from the Smiths. Then how would she manage the repair of her car?

Jake decided to ask Tina to pick up Kathryn that evening. Maybe Kathryn would be more comfortable dealing with a woman, and getting to know Tina might make her more amenable to him. That way, even if Wyatt and Tina decided against hiring her, maybe Jake would ask her to watch Frankie for a few days. That would give Kathryn a little income and let Frankie spend some time with her.

If only she would agree.

Kathryn stared at the empty road and bit her lips. She'd assumed Jake would return to pick her up at the end of the day, but now that she thought of it, he hadn't said as much. Instead, he'd offered to give her a ride to prayer meeting. Had her refusal to attend the prayer meeting left him with the impression that she didn't need a ride home from work?

Unfortunately a ride was the least of her needs. The agency had called earlier to inform her that they had re-assigned her clients. She was welcome to reapply once she had secured transportation again, but until then, she would be removed from their roster. The fact that she'd expected to lose her job didn't soften the blow.

Suddenly, she spied a trail of dust being thrown up by a vehicle headed her way. She muttered a quick prayer of thanks and waved. To her surprise, as the vehicle barreled closer she saw that it was a large burgundy-red SUV, not the familiar olive-green pickup.

The SUV came to an abrupt stop near her, and a shapely woman with short, stylish, reddish-brown hair leaped out. Wearing jeans and a simple checked blouse with the tail tucked in and the collar turned up, she plucked off her sunshades and smiled.

"Kathryn?"

"Yes."

"I'm Tina Smith. Sorry I'm late. If Jake had given me a little more lead time, I'd have had dinner on the table early enough to keep you from standing out here in the heat."

"Oh. Uh. So Jake isn't coming?"

"He and the rest of the guys are on their way to prayer meeting. I didn't see any reason for all of us to be late."

"Prayer meeting," Kathryn murmured. "I'm sorry. I didn't realize how much I was imposing."

Tina waved her words away. "No, no. Don't worry about it." With that, she got back into the vehicle.

Kathryn didn't know what to do except slide in on the passenger side. "I hate putting you out like this."

Tina waved a hand dismissively and put the SUV in motion.

"I—I don't suppose Jake told you that I live on Sixth Street in War Bonnet, did he?"

"In War Bonnet?" Tina echoed. "Nope. He left out that little detail." She shrugged. "Well, it won't hurt me to miss one prayer meeting."

Katherine winced. "I hate to be the cause of that."

"Well," Tina said cautiously, "you could always go to prayer meeting with me."

Kathryn immediately shook her head. "I'm still in my work clothes."

"You're dressed as well as I am," Tina pointed out.

Kathryn bit her lips. It was just that she hadn't been to church in years. Her mother had required almost constant care, allowing breaks of only minutes to do the shopping and household chores. Years earlier they'd attended Countryside Church together, but Kathryn doubted she'd know anyone there anymore. Still, keeping Tina Smith away from church seemed selfish and ungrateful. At least, Kathryn mused, she'd surrendered to impulse that morning and worn the flowered blouse.

"I guess I'll go to prayer meeting with you. I can remove the uniform top."

Tina beamed at her. "Great! We just might make it on time then."

Kathryn struggled out of the uniform top and stuffed it in her bag before pulling out a brush and going after her hair, raking it back from her forehead to the ends.

"That's a very pretty blouse," Tina said.

"Thanks. It was my mom's."

"It looks new."

"She never got to wear it. Right after she bought it, she was in a serious car wreck."

"I'm so sorry. That's awful."

Kathryn nodded and softly said, "She was paralyzed from the chest down."

"How sad."

For some reason, Kathryn found herself going on. "She had partial use of her left arm, but there were neurological issues, too. She couldn't speak more than the odd word, and for the rest of her life she suffered terrible seizures that choked her and cut off her air."

"Poor thing. I take it she's passed."

"Ten months ago."

"Was she ill for a long time?"

"Just over eleven years."

Tina shook her head. "I can't imagine how difficult that must have been."

"Very difficult," Kathryn admitted, "especially after my father left, but I learned what to do."

"Your father left, so you cared for her yourself?"

"Every day."

"How old were you?"

"Seventeen when the accident happened. You'd be surprised how much I miss her. But at least caring for her gave me the skills to find work after she was gone. Honestly, I have no regrets."

"You shouldn't," Tina said fervently. "What a wonderful daughter you are. Your mom had to know that."

Blushing, Kathryn dropped her gaze. "That's nice of you to say."

"No wonder Jake is so concerned for you."

Kathryn's gaze zipped right back up to Tina's profile. "Oh, Jake doesn't know. I mean, we haven't discussed it."

"No? Huh. Well, he is concerned, and he'll help if you let him." She glanced at Kathryn. "But that's the Smith brothers for you."

For the rest of the drive, Tina regaled Kathryn with the story of how she'd met the Smith brothers and married the eldest one. Clearly, she was wild about Wyatt Smith. "Jake's the most wonderful father," she enthused as she parked the SUV in the church lot. "We can thank Frankie for that. Isn't he the most adorable kid?"

"He is," Kathryn agreed, getting out of the vehicle when Tina did.

"I think Frankie is why Wyatt so easily accepts my son," Tina went on, coming around to meet Kathryn. "Wyatt took care of Frankie when Jake and Jolene were deployed."

"Deployed?"

Taking her arm, Tina turned Kathryn toward the building. They fell in step as they moved toward the door. "They were both career army. Didn't you know? I don't think Jake would ever have taken discharge if his wife hadn't died."

"I see." The poor man. Kathryn bit her lips, but she couldn't keep herself from asking, "What happened?"

"Training exercise."

"Oh. Wow."

Kathryn pondered that as they walked through the wide church foyer and into the sanctuary. Perhaps half-full, with the congregants gathered near the front of the space, the long, bright hall with its pale woods and white, padded pews felt foreign to Kathryn. The last time she'd been here, the room had been dark and shadowy, making it much easier to slip in unnoticed. As they moved toward the front of the sanctuary, a tall, handsome, solidly built man with dark, curly hair stood and started up the aisle to greet them, a smile on his face. Jake got up and followed along behind him.

"You made it."

"Kathryn was kind enough to come with me. Kathryn, this is my husband, Wyatt."

Wyatt Smith put out his big hand and gave Kathryn's a hearty shake. Like Jake, Wyatt had dark brown eyes and the shadow of a heavy beard on his square jaw and chin.

"Nice to meet you, Kathryn."

Tina looked to Jake then smiled and said, "She'll do."

Before Kathryn could ponder that statement, the Billings sisters rushed up to greet Kathryn with exuberant hugs.

"It's so good to see you!"

"KKay! How marvelous you look!"

Ann Billings swept a hand across the ends of Kathryn's hair. "You used to have the longest, thickest ponytail I've ever seen."

"All the boys called you Rapunzel," Meri said, laughing.

"I remember," Kathryn murmured, overwhelmed by the greeting.

The pastor entered through a door at the rear of the auditorium just then, and the piano started playing. Wyatt urged the women forward. "Better sit."

Jake held out a hand. Kathryn nodded, smiling weakly at the Billings sisters, and quickly entered the pew. Jake followed, with Tina and Wyatt bringing up the rear.

"KKay?" Jake murmured into her ear. She crossed her arms to quell the shiver that rushed over her skin.

"An old nickname," she whispered. "My middle name is Kay."

"Ah."

She sat down next to a big, muscle-bound man with sleek black hair and the dark Smith eyes and beard shadow. He nodded at her.

"My baby brother, Ryder," Jake said softly. He placed

a hand on her arm, saying to his brother, "Kathryn Stepp."

At Jake's touch, Kathryn again fought a shiver.

Ryder Smith smiled. "Hi."

"Hello."

Someone passed Ryder several papers then. He handed one to Kathryn and the rest to Jake, who passed them on. Glancing down, she saw a list of names and prayer requests. She'd requested prayers for her mother while Mia had languished in the hospital in Oklahoma City all those years ago. Would it have made a difference if she'd come to pray in person?

After the music, the pastor said a few words then prayed not only for those on the printed list but also for those who turned in request cards that evening. After the pastor, others began to pray aloud. Kathryn kept her head down, but every second she felt Jake's warm presence at her elbow. Again, she wondered if she'd offended him earlier by initially refusing to attend this meeting. She should've explained how uncomfortable big groups of strangers made her.

As the service came to a close, she glanced around her while waiting to exit the pew. She didn't know the current pastor, but to her surprise she knew quite a few of those present.

Tina was already at the door at the back of the sanctuary before Kathryn made it out to the aisle. Slipping around Jake, Kathryn quickly followed the other woman.

The Billings sisters waylaid her again in the foyer, chatting about the changes in their lives. Both had married and borne children. Their husbands soon joined them, little ones in tow. Kathryn looked on with sharp, silent envy. Meri commented on the bag that Kathryn carried, but before Kathryn could reply, something hit her from the side so hard that she stumbled. Out of nowhere, Jake steadied her, his hands at her shoulders.

"Frankie!" he scolded. "You nearly bowled her over."

Kathryn felt the boy's arms hugging her even as she looked down.

"I sorwy," he said, his eyes huge in his little face.

Smiling, Kathryn smoothed his dark, shaggy hair. "No harm done. Hello again."

He grinned at her. "Hello."

"KKay has an admirer," Meri observed, chuckling.

Frankie's brow wrinkled. "KKay?"

"It's an old nickname," Kathryn told him. "Something my friends used to call me."

"KKay my fren!" Frankie announced.

Chuckling, Kathryn said, "Yes. We're friends."

Conversation continued for several more minutes. Terribly aware of Jake at her back, Kathryn struggled to pay attention, saying little. Finally, the Billings sisters and their families began to leave. Glancing around, Kathryn realized with a start that only she, Jake and Frankie remained. When had Tina left?

"Come on," Jake said, his hand against the small of her back. "We'll take you home."

Kathryn tried not to tremble at his touch or look into his eyes for fear he would see how he affected her. Instead, she simply allowed him to escort her from the building, Frankie at his side.

"What did you think of Tina?" he asked, pointing to his truck.

"She's nice. I like her."

"I talked to her about you. If you're interested, we have a place for you at Loco Man."

Shocked, Kathryn came to a halt, bleating, "Whaa-t?"

"A job," Jake explained. "Tina's got her hands full with her son and the B and B." Stopping in his tracks, he turned to face Kathryn. Beside them, Frankie listened to the conversation with interest.

Kathryn shook her head. "B and B? As in bed-and-breakfast?"

"That's right. She's planned to turn the ranch house into a bed-and-breakfast ever since Uncle Dodd left it to her."

Kathryn shook her head again, confused. "I—I thought he left the place to you and your brothers."

"He left the *ranch* to me and my brothers. The house is Tina's. But it's all worked out for everyone. The thing is, Tina could use some help, and you seem well qualified. You cook, right?"

"Why, yes."

"And you clean."

"Of course."

"And you obviously sew and like to decorate. Tina's at the decorating stage now, and she won't rent rooms until she has the house looking like she wants it. Oh, and I might ask you to watch Frankie. I dump him on her too often. When I have to take him along with me, he misses naps and playtime."

Kathryn tried to wrap her mind around this. "You want me to cook, clean, help Tina open a bed-and-breakfast and watch your son. Is that right?"

"That about covers it."

"But why?"

"I told you. Tina needs the help. And Frankie thinks you're great. If you can watch him at least some of the time, it'll free me up to work on your car. Seems like a win for everyone."

Kathryn tried to formulate a reply, but her mind was reeling. Had that conversation on the ride here with Tina been a kind of job interview? Did she dare work for Jake Smith and his family? She could cook and clean, no problem, but as for the rest, she just didn't know. Despite her need for income, her natural caution wouldn't allow her to accept without thinking through this offer.

They reached the truck. Jake picked up Frankie and settled him into his seat while Kathryn let herself into the cab. Suddenly so burdened with concern that she felt on the verge of tears, Kathryn couldn't speak. In the charged atmosphere, even Frankie remained silent on the drive to her house. She just kept wondering how this had happened.

She'd liked her job. All three of her clients were sweet, harmless, elderly folk, and she knew she'd made positive differences in their lives. What did she know about children? As adorable as Frankie was, she had no experience with little ones, boys especially. And the idea of seeing Jake on a daily basis made her insides quake.

The man rattled her in ways she couldn't even describe. He'd hit her life with all the force of a whirlwind, a tall, dark, handsome whirlwind that somehow threatened to blow her careful, tidy existence to pieces. Everything familiar and comfortable in her life had disappeared since she'd met him.

Everything but her home. She still had that. For now.

Without income, she'd never be able to fix her car, let alone buy out her father.

When Jake and Frankie dropped her off at home, Jake said, "Just think about it."

Nodding, she let herself out of the truck and trudged inside to consider her options. She made a list of all the businesses in town within walking distance, but she already knew that those employed locally tended to hang on to their jobs. Calling other home care companies in the area would do no good. They'd all require proof of transportation, just as her last employer had. So it was sit at home for weeks without pay until Jake Smith got her old car running, and then hope she could get hired on with the agency again. Or accept his job offer. Seemed odd to let him pay her so she could afford to pay him for fixing her car, but she didn't see any other choice.

Despite her emotional exhaustion, she slept little that night and rose early the next morning to prepare herself to accept the job at Loco Man Ranch. With no idea when Jake—or Tina—might reach out to her again, she made a second cup of coffee and carried it out to the porch where she sat and waited, long enough that she finally resorted to prayer.

Lord, can't anything ever be easy? Can't You help? Are You even there? What if Jake's thought better of hiring me? What if I never get my car running and lose my house? I don't understand what's happening. I'm afraid.

She was so tired of being afraid.

With the temperature climbing to an uncomfortable level, she decided to go inside, but before she could get up, she heard the sound of tires on pavement and looked around to see a familiar olive-green truck turning into her drive. Correction, *army* green. So great was her relief that she feared collapsing if she tried to stand, and that kept her in her seat as Jake got out and came to her. Without a word, he crouched in front of her and pushed back the brim of his hat before removing his sunshades. Offering her a swift smile, he balanced his forearms atop his knees.

"You really should give me your phone number," she said crisply, foregoing a greeting and keeping her gaze on his chin. The man was just too handsome.

As if he knew exactly what she was thinking, he dropped his head. She suspected that he was hiding a grin, but when he looked up, he appeared perfectly composed.

"I can do that. We'll need yours, of course. Meanwhile, Tina would like for you to join us for lunch. She'll show you around the house and give you a feel for what needs doing."

Kathryn pulled in a deep breath, ignoring the way her heart sped up when his deep brown eyes met her gaze. "You should understand two things. One, I know nothing about children. Two, as soon as you get my car running again, I'll find a real job."

"You'll do fine with the kids," he said. "You're careful and protective. Besides, in case of an emergency, there are four other adults around the place. And this *is* a real job."

"This is pity," Kathryn scoffed softly, dropping her gaze, "however well intended."

"No, no, no. Tina really needs the help. The duties are many and varied. Once the B and B opens, I suspect she'll even want you to help with the guests."

That surprised Kathryn. Didn't he see how uncomfortable she was dealing with strangers? "Oh, I'm not sure I'm cut out for that."

"How will you know if you don't try?" he cajoled gently. "You might surprise yourself. Anyone who can do what you did for your mother ought to be able to manage just about anything."

Obviously, Tina had reported their conversation to him. Kathryn found, to her surprise, that she didn't much mind, especially given the sound of respect in his voice.

"We'll see."

"Then you'll take the job?"

"Yes. And thank you."

"No need for that." He pushed up to a standing position and slid his glasses back into place before tugging down the brim of his hat. "We need the help. You need the job. It's that simple."

It might be that simple for him, but Kathryn wasn't so sure about her own part in this. Oh, why did he have to be so handsome and generous? She rose and squared her shoulders, preparing for an uncomfortable day.

Eventually, she told herself, she'd lose this strange, hopeless attraction. Meanwhile, she'd have income. Then, once her car was repaired, she could put as much distance as necessary between herself and Jacoby Smith.

Please, God, she prayed. *Let it be soon.*

Hopefully before she made a complete fool of herself.

Chapter Four

As Jake walked her up the steps to the back door, Kathryn could hear Tina admonishing someone.

"I told you to get that off the table."

"Aww, Mo-o-m," came the whining reply. "We're still playing."

Frankie's little voice echoed the complaint. "We still playin'."

Jake reached around Kathryn and shoved open the door, hurrying her inside and following, right at her back.

"Francis Jacoby Smith," he barked, "apologize to your aunt Tina this minute."

Startled, Frankie paused, his hand on a tiny bright red car that he was pushing through a jumble of small toys on the terra-cotta tile tabletop. His eyes big and bright, Frankie looked to his aunt.

"I sorwy, Aunt Tina."

Tyler also apologized, bowing his strawberry blond head. "Sorry, Mom."

"Thank you, boys. Just clear away the toys, please."

Tyler got up and grabbed a plastic tub, while Frankie,

beaming now, waved at Kathryn and called out, "Hi, KKay!"

She returned his smile. "Hello, Frankie."

The boys raked the toys off the table into the tub.

"Now upstairs with you two until lunch is ready," Tina ordered. "March."

Frankie got down from his chair, and the two boys ran toward the front of the house, jostling the tub between them. Tina turned to smile at Kathryn.

"Welcome to Loco Man."

A pot simmering on the stove punctuated that statement by beginning to boil over. Tina rushed to turn down the burner before checking the contents. Kathryn ventured closer, recognizing the black-eyed peas and ham cooking in the pot. What captured her attention, however, was the stove.

"I've never seen anything like your range."

"That's because they don't make them like this anymore," Tina told her proudly. "Six burners, three ovens and storage. Our grandmothers sure knew how to do it, didn't they?"

"But it looks brand-new," Kathryn said in surprise.

Tina waved a potholder at Jake. "You can thank him for that."

Jake chuckled. "Now, if I could just cook, I'd be of some real help around here."

"I can cook," Kathryn said quickly. "I like to cook."

Tina smiled. "In that case, mind breading some okra? I never seem to get it right. I just wind up fouling my frying oil."

"No problem," Kathryn said, aware that she was likely being evaluated and hoping her voice didn't waver too much.

Tina opened a drawer and took out an apron, passing it to Kathryn. "I'm going to watch you do it so I'll know how."

Kathryn's hands shook at first, but she'd worked in enough strange kitchens under watchful eyes to manage. Tina had already poured oil into a large skillet and washed and cut the okra pods into bite-size pieces. Now she heated the oil as Kathryn worked.

"So it's three-fourths flour and a quarter cornmeal," Tina noted a few minutes later as she dropped the okra into the frying pan.

More relaxed now, Kathryn shyly gave her a piece of advice. "The key to breading just about anything is to dust it with flour *before* dredging it in the egg. Then you can coat it evenly with your breading. One of my elderly clients clued me in."

"There you are," Tina quipped. "The older generation does know best."

They both laughed. Only when she turned did Kathryn realize that Jake was leaning against the table, watching. That both pleased and unnerved her. She found her feelings toward him to be terribly confusing. As a girl, she'd liked certain boys and had even harbored a few fantasies, but she'd never really been attracted to anyone. Then again, she'd never before known a man like Jake. As if sensing her discomfort, he lurched to his feet.

"Think I'll check on the boys."

Tina bowed her head, a small smile curving her lush lips. Kathryn felt plain and spare next to Tina, but at least she wasn't uncomfortable around this particular Smith. In fact, she'd meant it when she'd told Jake that she liked Tina.

At Tina's direction, Kathryn helped prepare the remainder of the meal. When Wyatt came in to kiss his wife and clean up, Kathryn busied herself setting the table. Ryder arrived just moments later, brushing white dust from his shoulders and his hair.

"That's usually my job," he said to Kathryn, grinning. "Does this mean I'm off kitchen detail permanently?"

"Oh, I don't know about that," Kathryn murmured hesitantly, glancing at Tina, who rolled her eyes at Ryder.

"Leave the woman alone. She's cooked half your meal. Now you're asking her to take over your measly kitchen chores."

Ryder just grinned and went to the refrigerator for a huge pitcher of iced tea. "If she can hang drywall, I'll gladly trade my job for hers."

"As a cook, your drywall-hanging skills are exceptional," Tina quipped dryly.

Chuckling, Wyatt said to Kathryn, "Truth is, Tina's been doing just about everything around here on her own, and it's held up her plans for the B and B."

"I hope I can be of help," Kathryn remarked uncertainly.

"Can't imagine you won't," Jake said, ushering Frankie and Tyler back into the room. "We're looking forward to that fried okra."

Blushing, Kathryn helped get the meal on the table then sat in the chair Tina pointed out to her. Placed between Frankie and Jake, Kathryn felt the latter at her back as he helped slide the heavy wrought-iron chair under the table. The moment the chair was in place, Frankie leaned over and wrapped his arms around her neck, squeezing mightily, his booster seat bringing him almost to her height. He then beamed at Tyler, exclaiming, "My KKay!"

Tyler looked confused, but all the adults started laughing—except Kathryn.

Jake explained. "Frankie is famous for assigning ownership of the people in his life. Not long ago he 'gave' Wyatt to Tyler for a father."

"Worked, too, didn't it?" Wyatt teased, winking at Frankie and mussing Tyler's reddish blond hair. Tyler beamed. Clearly he was pleased with Wyatt Smith as a stepfather.

Finally, they were all gathered at the long, rectangular table. To Kathryn's shock, Jake reached for her hand. Only when Frankie tapped her on the arm and held out his hand for her to take did she understand that everyone was linking hands around the table.

"We do dis," Frankie instructed, bowing his head.

Kathryn obediently bowed her head, biting her lips to hide a smile. Jake squeezed her hand. She cut a glance at him from the corner of her eye, but he sat like stone next to her. She wondered if she'd imagined that squeeze.

Wyatt said, "Jake, why don't you bless our meal?"

Jake cleared his throat and began to pray. "Lord God, we thank You and praise You for Your many blessings and Your boundless generosity. Every time we have need, You provide. Thank you for this food and especially for those who prepared it. Amen."

He released her hand as if it were a hot potato. Quietly glancing around the table, Kathryn tried to concentrate on the fact that he'd just given thanks for her, in an oblique, impersonal fashion. Letting her gaze move from face to face, she told herself that it didn't matter if he felt uncomfortable holding her hand. These were good, kind people, and she was here to work, nothing more. To work and, apparently, to pray.

Come to think of it, she'd prayed earlier that day in sheer desperation, and now here she sat, employed and welcome, her car being repaired. Was that not God meeting her needs? It occurred to her that she had also prayed that morning when her car had broken down, and along had come Jacoby Smith. Why would any man go to such extremes to help someone he didn't even know? Her prayers hadn't even been good prayers, as much complaint as entreaty, but she couldn't deny that her needs were being met.

Ashamed for thinking that God might have abandoned her, she listened to the easy banter of those around her and filled her plate as the dishes were passed to her. Before long, she recognized an unusual feeling rising within her.

It was gratitude. And just a whisper of sweet, sweet hope.

"This is so nice," Kathryn said, taking in the beautifully tiled bathroom. "I love the antique look of the vanity. Forest green would really make the most of all this bright white tile. I confess I'm partial to greens."

"Ooh, that would be gorgeous."

Kathryn swept a finger over the green-and-tan motif pressed into the accent tile. "I'm thinking natural wicker for smaller accents."

"Brilliant!" Tina exclaimed. "I can actually see it all coming together now."

A small hand tugged on hers. "KKay, see my room." Tyler had gone to play, but Frankie had been following them from room to room, watching and listening, sometimes beetle-browed.

Smiling down at the boy, Kathryn nodded. "Okay. Show me."

Obviously delighted, he tugged her out of the bathroom and along the hallway to his small room. The walls had been painted a buttery gold. The furnishings were all constructed of gleaming golden oak. A practical rug in a warm, medium brown lay beside the narrow bed. Short curtains of the same color flanked the single window where several colorful light catchers had been hung. Kathryn watched, smiling, as he opened his closet door to reveal neat shelves stocked with toys and a few articles of clothing hanging from a short rod. A series of stuffed animals, all dogs except for a teddy bear and a rabbit, lined the top of his tall dresser.

"What a great room," she enthused, remembering his desire for a real dog. "You know what it needs?"

Staring up raptly into her face, he shook his head.

"Puppies."

"Puppies!" Frankie cheered, hopping up and down and clapping his hands.

"I have a stencil," she said to Tina, holding up her hands to demonstrate its size, about one-by-three feet. "Would you mind if I painted some puppies on the walls?"

"What a fun idea," Tina said. "I don't mind, and I'm sure Jake won't, either."

Kathryn bit her lips. She hadn't even thought of consulting Jake. She would remember to do so in the future.

"Now," Tina said, "about the master bedroom…"

Kathryn followed Tina downstairs, leaving Frankie in Tyler's room, gushing about puppies. After several minutes in the master bedroom, Kathryn said, "I think you need a contrasting print in here, but the colors need to be exact. I have some swatch books I can bring over for you to look at."

Tina cocked her head, studying Kathryn. "I get the feeling that you intend to make a lot of the items we've talked about. Jake says you made everything in your house."

Worried that Jake had misrepresented her qualifications, Kathryn shook her head. "I may have said that, but I didn't mean it literally. It's not like I built the furniture or anything."

"You just upholstered and slipcovered it all," Tina surmised with a grin. "And apparently, you made a remarkable rug."

"It's just an oval rug for the coffee table to sit on."

Laughing, Tina shook her head. "You have no idea how talented you are, do you?"

Both pleased and mortified, Kathryn bit her lips and said nothing.

"I wish I had a sewing machine here for you to use."

More excited than she wanted Tina to know, Kathryn quickly offered to bring over her machine. "It's old but portable and makes a fine stitch."

"That's a wonderful idea. Bring anything you like. You can set up in the laundry room."

"Perfect. There's plenty of space in there, and the counter is just the right height. Plus, I saw several electrical outlets."

"We'll have to move some things so you can get a chair under the counter, but that shouldn't be a problem."

"I don't want to be a bother."

"A bother? Pfft. I already know you're going to be a huge asset."

Thrilled, Kathryn dipped her head and bit her lips. Tina let her know that she was ready to move on by pointing toward the door. They walked out into the hallway and turned toward the kitchen, where they found Jake and Wyatt nursing glasses of iced tea and talking quietly.

"Once the parts start coming in, you can split your days," Wyatt was saying. "Ryder will help."

"You need him to finish up the bunkhouse and take care of the horses," Jake said.

"He can split his days, too. Besides, the bunkhouse can wait. He doesn't care that the walls aren't painted yet or whether the baseboards are down. I suggest the two of you work on the garage in the cool of the mornings and save the afternoons for—"

Jake waved a hand, cutting him off midsentence. He nodded at Kathryn and Tina, calling Wyatt's attention to them. Wyatt got up and pulled out a chair for Tina. At the same time, Jake stood and pulled out a chair next to him for Kathryn. The women sat, and Tina leaned forward to address Jake.

"You were so right about her." Tina straightened, looked at her husband and gushed, "Wait until you see what we have planned. Thanks to Kathryn, I've finally got a real vision for this place."

"Oh, no," Kathryn said quickly. "You've established the style very well. I've just suggested some decoration."

"It's going to be beautiful," Tina told Wyatt.

"You mean it isn't already? All I see is beautiful. No, wait. That's my wife."

Laughing, Tina half rose and kissed him, leaning on her forearms. Jake glanced at Kathryn, pushed back his chair and rose.

"I think that's my cue to leave."

"Why don't you take Kathryn home now?" Tina said. "I think I picked her brain clean this afternoon. She's probably ready to kick back for a while."

"But shouldn't I start dinner?" Kathryn asked anxiously.

Tina patted her hands on the tabletop. "Nope. I've already planned to pull a casserole out of the freezer. Just needs heating up. You're welcome to stay and eat, but you've done enough for one day."

"Guess I'll see you tomorrow then." Kathryn stood as Jake pulled out her chair. "What time should I be here?"

Tina considered. "We'll discuss lunch and dinner tomorrow. I'll need you here for cleanup after the evening meal, so say…about ten? Half past maybe."

Kathryn looked to Jake. He was her only transportation, after all.

"Ten thirty it is." He nodded at Kathryn. "I'll be there a quarter after."

Tina got up and slipped around the table to quickly hug Kathryn. "I think working with you is going to be fun." To Jake she said, "We'll look after Frankie until you get back."

"I appreciate that."

"Have a good evening."

Nodding, Kathryn let Jake steer her toward the back door, his hand resting against the small of her back. It was a meaningless gesture, she knew, but she was keenly aware of that gentle hand as they moved together out the door, down the steps and along the concrete pad of what Wyatt, according to Tina, intended to be a massive carport. Kathryn climbed up into the cab of Jake's pickup truck, surveying the house as Jake walked around and got in behind the steering wheel.

The big old house had been freshly painted the color of aged parchment and trimmed in a medium grayish brown that looked good with the shiny metal roof. Kathryn thought the house needed decorative shutters in that same brown and green window boxes filled with flowers. Painting the rocking chairs on the porch and adding a pair of planters would dress up the place, too.

"So, you and Tina settle all the particulars?" Jake asked, interrupting her reverie.

Kathryn nodded, then shook her head. "Just about. Tina didn't mention salary."

"Didn't she?" Jake started the engine and checked his mirrors before backing out the truck. "Well, we discussed it. She must've assumed I'd told you." He shifted the transmission into Drive and headed the truck toward the highway. "How does this sound?" Just before he turned the truck onto the pavement, he named an hourly figure that made Kathryn gasp.

"Are you sure? That's almost twice what I made in my last job."

"You'll be doing more than you were in that job," he pointed out casually.

Kathryn bit her lips for a moment, thinking. "I suppose that's true." She beat down tears of relief, struggling to remain impassive. "Maybe I can afford to fix the car, after all. Doesn't seem right, though, to pay you for fixing my car with money you're paying me."

"Believe me, no one's complaining about this arrangement. Least of all Frankie."

Frankie. Struck by the thought that she should have taken her leave of the boy, Kathryn began apologizing. "He doesn't know I've gone. I didn't think to say goodbye. Maybe we should go back so I can."

"Oh, man." Jake chuckled. "You're going to spoil my kid rotten, aren't you?"

"No. I—I just don't want him to think I'm abandoning him."

"That's the last thing I worry about. You didn't abandon your mom when most girls your age would have."

Kathryn smiled, but then she winced. "In a way, though, I did abandon my former clients."

"That wasn't your fault. You were fired after your car broke down. That's not abandonment by any stretch of the imagination."

Warmed by his defense of her, she fought a smile. "They depended on me. They won't know the new helper, but I'll try to keep in touch with them. It's the least I can do. So is saying goodbye to Frankie."

"When Frankie notices you're gone, everyone will tell him that you'll be back in the morning. Wish I could say that about the puppy he's expecting."

Kathryn snapped her fingers. "That reminds me. Is it okay with you if I stencil puppies on the walls of Frankie's room? I sort of promised him."

"Yep," Jake said. "Spoiled rotten." He flashed her a quick smile. "I don't mind at all."

In the silence that followed, Kathryn closed her eyes and mentally thanked God. *Now if You can just do something about my house...*

Maybe her father would accept monthly payments.

She'd figure out what she could afford to pay with this new job and make him an offer. But what if this job didn't last? Only this morning she'd told herself this job was temporary, and now she was worried it wouldn't last. What foolishness. If the Smiths weren't pleased with her or she couldn't get over this silly infatuation with Jake, she'd go back to home healthcare. Or maybe she'd babysit full-time.

That brought up another concern. She jerked her eyes open to see that they were almost to her house.

"We didn't discuss my duties concerning Frankie."

Jake turned the truck into her drive and brought it to a stop. He rubbed a forefinger over his eyebrow. "Well, if you can just keep an eye on him. Maybe get him down for his nap when I'm not around. Manage his snacks." He shook his head, smiling. "That boy can eat his weight in sweets, so keep those to a minimum." He spread his hands. "You know, just sort of step in when I'm not around."

"I can do that. With Tyler, too, if needed."

Nodding, Jake said, "I'll be sure to let Tina know."

"Okay then." Kathryn released her seat belt and opened her door, but then she paused to meet his gaze. She'd thanked God, but Jake deserved her gratitude, too. "Thank you, Jake. For everything. I don't know what I'd have done if you hadn't stopped to help."

Shrugging, he said, "Seems to me it's all working out for the best."

"I hope so. From the bottom of my heart, thank you."

Shifting in his seat, he lifted his hands and gripped the steering wheel, his jaw hardening. Taking that to mean he was ready to get home, she slipped out onto the ground.

"See you tomorrow."

"A quarter after ten," he confirmed, his voice oddly strangled.

She hurried to the porch, paused to wave and let herself into the house. Only after she closed the door did he back out the truck and drive away. For the first time since her old car had begun to lurch and sputter on the way to Sandy's house, she wasn't worried. Well, not too much. Her father's claim on the house still had to be settled. But first things first. Once her car was repaired, she'd contact her father and try to work out something. Meanwhile, things were looking up.

She had a job. And maybe friends, too.

Strangely, despite the breakdown of her car, that was more than she'd had in a long time.

Chapter Five

Had he lost what remained of his tiny mind?

Horrified with himself, Jake could barely manage not to squeal his tires on the pavement of Kathryn's street.

He'd very nearly kissed the woman! She'd looked at him all soft-eyed and trusting, and he'd instantly, desperately wanted to kiss her. Only by throttling the steering wheel had he managed not to haul her into his arms and show her that he was less Good Samaritan than interested male.

And that salary! What had possessed him to name such a figure? The rest of the family would think he was crazy. Maybe he was. God knew he couldn't afford to burn through his money before the garage was up and running, but he was obligated now. He was appalled to realize that he might have been acting out of unrecognized attraction all along.

Kathryn Kay Stepp was as prickly as a wounded porcupine, but the first time she showed the slightest inclination to fold her spines, he'd wanted to leap at her and drag her into his arms. She'd just barely relaxed her guard around him, and he'd come within a heartbeat of pushing their feeble, casual relationship to a new—and probably fatal—level.

Idiot.

Kathryn was right to distrust him, and that upset him as much as the thought of Jolene. Not even two years since his wife's death, and he was jumping at the first woman he'd come across in this state. And she was nothing at all like Jolene!

That alone felt like a kind of betrayal. It was as if he'd stumbled into some ugly bog of emotions, and before he knew what was happening, he'd blown right past the ranch. He didn't begin to calm until he drew near the place where he'd first seen Kathryn's car broken down beside the road. A few hundred yards beyond the spot, he finally slowed to a stop and ran a hand over his face.

"Lord, how do I get myself back on solid ground?" he asked.

He didn't know why she affected him so. She was timid and guarded and generally uncommunicative, while Jolene had been the opposite in every way. Yet Kathryn was also courageous, dedicated, capable, lovely…

Okay, he needed to keep his distance, at least until this fascination wore off. He didn't have the time or money for a relationship right now. He'd do well to get the garage operational and repair her car before he exhausted his funds.

Frowning at himself, he turned the truck around and headed back to the house. As he brought the vehicle to a stop in its customary spot, he prepared himself for the scrutiny of his brother and sister-in-law. Maybe his envy of those two had as much to do with his attraction to Kathryn as anything else. If so, it would play itself out soon enough.

Meanwhile, he'd keep as much distance between himself and Kathryn Stepp as the situation allowed and clamp down on his personal expenses so he could afford to pay her the difference between what he'd promised and what he, Wyatt and Tina had agreed to. Remembering the surprise and delight in Kathryn's big green eyes when he'd told her what her pay would be, he smiled. Then he sternly told himself to cut it out.

He could manage this, and it wouldn't be for long. Kathryn had as good as told him that she would be looking for another job as soon as possible. Relieved, he congratulated himself on reasoning through the situation. When he walked into the house, he felt calm and unconcerned.

Tina's casserole heated in the oven, filling the kitchen with appetizing aromas. He found Wyatt and Tina in the den, snuggled up on the couch watching cable news. Both looked at him.

Wyatt asked, "Get Kathryn home okay?"

"Sure."

"Tina's been talking nonstop about Kathryn's ideas for decorating the house."

Jake tried very hard not to acknowledge a swell of pride. He had no business taking pride in her talents. "That's good."

"Kind of funny," Wyatt remarked, "such a plain woman being such a whiz at decorating."

Both Jake and Tina spoke at the same time. "She's not plain!"

"She just hides her light under a basket," Tina added. "Get her into some fashionable clothes, shape up her hair a bit, give her a little confidence, she could be a knockout."

"If you say so," Wyatt muttered.

Jake wanted to growl at his brother. What nonsense. Kathryn, plain? Hardly. And she was just fine as she was. Wyatt laid his head back on the sofa and smiled meaningfully. Jake didn't even want to consider what that smile meant, but it reaffirmed his decision to keep his distance from their new employee. Jake changed the subject.

"Where's Frankie?"

"Upstairs playing," Wyatt said. "When he realized you and Kathryn were gone, he asked for his pony. I took him out and let him pet the pony in its stall." Wyatt tossed Jake a pointed look. "He promised the horse they'd go riding real soon."

"Yeah, I've got to do something about that." One more drain on his time. Still, his son needed instruction. The problem was, he didn't know what to do. "Nothing Uncle Dodd taught us about horses has settled down that critter or helped Frankie keep control of it."

"Maybe we ought to talk to Stark about it," Wyatt suggested. He and the busy veterinarian had become fast friends. "According to Rex, the man knows more about horses than anyone around." Rex Billings was a local rancher and attorney, and Stark Burns was his brother-in-law.

"Good to know," Jake replied. "I'll go check on Frankie now."

Surprised to find his son playing in his own room, Jake took a seat on the narrow bed, smiling.

"What's up? You and Tyler have a little falling-out maybe?"

Frankie just looked at him. "Ty'er room cars. KKay gettin' puppies on my wall!"

"I know. She told me. Won't that be fun?" Apparently to Frankie, just the promise of puppies was more fun than Tyler's car-themed room. Nodding, Frankie got up, came over and crawled into Jake's lap.

"Where KKay?"

"I took her home, but she'll be back in the morning."

"S'let go her."

"No, we can't go to her. She has other things to do tonight."

Frankie huffed and laid his head on Jake's chest. What a pair they were, both wrapped up in a woman they barely knew.

"Hey, want to watch some TV in Dad's room? We have some time before dinner."

Frankie nodded, so Jake stood with the boy in his arms and carried him into his bedroom. He wondered if Tina had shown this drab, utilitarian room to Kathryn, and if so, what her suggestions might have been. Mentally closing off that thought, he dropped Frankie onto the bed and smiled as Frankie bounced, laughing. Jake vaulted over him, jostling the mattress again just to make his son laugh.

They settled onto the pillows. Picking up the remote control on his bedside table, Jake aimed it at the flatscreen TV on the wall and pressed the On switch. After quickly finding Frankie's preferred channel, Jake tossed aside the remote and folded his arms behind his head, grinning as Frankie copied the action.

They watched the kid's program until Tina called them down to dinner a few minutes later. Baths, books and bedtime followed. As Jake drew the curtains over

Frankie's bedroom window—summer days in Oklahoma were long and bright—he felt his own weariness. He shouldn't be so tired. He'd worked on Kathryn's car for a few hours that morning, but he hadn't even gotten to the difficult part yet. So far it had been about loosening and disconnecting stuff under the hood so he could get to the motor mounts. He hadn't even made it over to the shop site today, and if he was going to get up early enough to get anything done over there, he'd have to turn in early.

Settling in to sleep, he closed his eyes. And saw Kathryn gazing at him with that soft, pleased look on her face.

After tossing and turning for what felt like hours, he finally drifted off, only to wake groggy and stiff before dawn the next morning, having slept too heavily for too short a time. He dressed and quietly left the house.

When he arrived at the shop site mere minutes later, he found Ryder already there, mixing mortar for the cement blocks with which they were building walls. Wyatt must have spoken to him about helping out, because Jake had not. Smiling, he clapped Ryder on the shoulder.

"Thanks, man."

"Let's get to it," Ryder said, slapping mortar onto the top of the last row of cement blocks that Jake had laid.

Working together, they put up almost an entire row of blocks before Jake's phone told him it was time to knock off so he could make it to Kathryn's at the specified time. He hated to leave the row unfinished, but Kathryn, Tina and Frankie were depending on him.

"Time to grab some breakfast."

Ryder didn't argue. Back at the house, they strode

into the kitchen together and hung their hats on two of several pegs on the wall. Ryder headed to the bathroom in the back hall to wash up, but Jake decided a quick shower was in order.

He stopped by Frankie's room ten minutes later to find it empty. As soon as he stepped into the kitchen, Frankie waved his fork in the air, yelling, "KKay comin'!"

Obviously, his weren't the only thoughts constantly hijacked by Kathryn. "She'll be here soon, so you better finish up there."

Frankie began wolfing down his breakfast. Jake, on the other hand, had to make himself eat. He often lost his appetite in moments of stress. He tried not to think about all he had to do that day, but that just gave him space to think about Kathryn. Did she know he had almost kissed her? He prayed not.

The boys finished eating and ran upstairs to dress for the day. Ryder carried his plate to the counter and headed out to care for the horses. Wyatt announced that he was going over to see a bull that Stark was holding for the owner.

In a sense, the veterinarian and his family were the Smiths' closest neighbors. Their place was across the road, loosely referred to as a highway by the locals, and a mile or less east, past Stuart Westhaven's farm supply store and grain silos. All three establishments—the Loco Man compound, the grain yard and the Burns home and veterinary practice—were located well outside the city limits.

"I'll ask Stark what we should do about that pony," Wyatt commented, taking his hat from a hook by the door.

Irritated that Wyatt seemed to think he was the ultimate authority where Frankie was concerned, Jake shook his head. Frankie was *his* kid, and *he* would take care of this issue. "I'll stop by there on my way to pick up Kathryn."

"Suit yourself." Wyatt kissed Tina, put on his hat and left.

"I should tell you that Kathryn is bringing her portable sewing machine today," Tina said. "I expect there will probably be some other things, sewing notions at least. Oh, and we'll need to move the boxes we've stashed under the counter in the laundry room." She started to turn away but stopped. "A chair. We'll have to find a decent chair for her."

"My old desk chair is out in the barn," Jake said. "It should fit nicely under the counter. I'll haul those boxes out there and bring the chair in."

"Excellent."

He quickly toted several boxes from under the laundry room counter to the barn then found the chair and hauled it inside. Frankie and Tyler waited for him in the kitchen.

"We get KKay," Frankie insisted happily.

Remembering what Tina had said about Kathryn bringing her sewing machine, Jake realized that the boys could easily get underfoot. Strangely relieved to have a reason to deny them, Jake shook his head. He told himself it was because he didn't have time to add Tyler's car seat to Frankie's in his truck, but he worried that he might enjoy those moments when he had Kathryn to himself a little too much. Imagine how he'd feel if the woman liked him. What then?

For a moment, everything about the current situation weighed on Jake. What if he ran out of money before he got the garage open? What if the business he expected never materialized so the garage failed? Maybe he and Frankie would be better off back in Houston. He could get a job there. He wouldn't have to worry about building his own shop, running out of money or failing at business, and Kathryn Stepp would be just an interesting memory. But he and Frankie would be living far away from their only family, and Jake had already given up his military career to raise his son with the uncles he adored. They'd added stability to Frankie's life when Jake and Jolene hadn't been able to do so themselves.

He felt a pang of guilt at resenting Wyatt's penchant for assuming responsibility for Frankie. That was just Wyatt, and Jake had no doubt that if anything ever happened to him, Wyatt and Ryder would step in to raise Frankie without a heartbeat's hesitation. He couldn't take Frankie away from them. No, he had to see this plan through, no matter what.

"Sorry, son. I'm going to be moving some things for KKay," Jake said. "You boys stay here out of harm's way. I'll be back soon. With KKay." Frankie's bottom lip plumped, but Tyler slid an arm across Frankie's shoulders and suggested they go play with his dog, Tipper. Jake let Tina know that the boys had gone outside and set off for Kathryn's.

On the way, he impulsively decided to stop at the Burns place. Maybe he could catch Wyatt and Stark and include Wyatt in the conversation about Frankie's pony. The clinic was closed up tight, though, and Wyatt's truck was nowhere to be seen. A bull stood by itself in the pen out back. Jake drove around to the house, a large, modern brick affair that completely dwarfed the small clapboard clinic. Meredith, Stark's wife, said that

Wyatt and Stark had gone over to speak to the owner of the bull Wyatt was considering.

"They won't be long. You're welcome to come in and wait."

"Thanks, but I have to go pick up Kathryn."

Meredith Billings Burns smiled and tilted her head. "Do you mind if I ask how you met Kathryn? She's been the next thing to a hermit for years. After her mom died, several of her old friends reached out to her, invited her to dinner, things like that. She was polite, but she refused, so we backed off. Then suddenly I see her at church with you and your family."

"Church was Tina's doing," Jake said, still smarting because Kathryn had refused to accompany him to the midweek service. "All I did was stop and help her when her car broke down beside the road."

Meredith considered that. "Interesting. I'd expect to have a difficult time getting her to let me help her, and I've known her since kindergarten."

"Huh. Well, the thing is, I'm a mechanic, so—"

"Really? We could use a good mechanic around here."

"That's why I'm building a shop. Already poured the foundation and started putting up the walls."

"So that's what's going on. We saw the cement mixer come by but just assumed the driver was lost. Who's your builder? Lyons and Son?"

"No. Lyons is good, but my brother and I are doing most of the work ourselves. Takes longer, but it's cheaper, and I'm hoping not to borrow any money."

"Sensible."

"Hope so. Well, Kathryn's expecting me, and I'm late." He started to leave then thought better of it. "She's working for us now. Working for Tina, I mean. That's why I'm picking her up. It's not…her car's not running."

"Ah. Well, I'm just happy to know that she's around people her own age for a change. It's been years, you know, ten at least."

"More like eleven or twelve," he corrected automatically. Meredith's smile made him wish he'd kept his mouth shut. "Since her mother's accident, anyway. I don't know anything about her life before that. Or even since."

"She was well liked in school," Meri informed him, "but her shyness kept her apart somewhat. She never went to the slumber parties or football games. Then, of course, her father left her to care for her mom when she was just seventeen. I doubt she's ever even been on a date."

"I can't believe that," Jake retorted, aware as he said it that he was giving himself away. "Not that it's any of my business." He chuckled to show that what Kathryn had or had not done was of no importance to him. But he was shocked to think that Meredith might be right. No. Couldn't be. "Well, I'll stop by to speak with Stark later."

"You do that," Meri said with a smile. "He'll be opening the clinic shortly."

Jake nodded to show that he understood, waved a farewell and was standing at Kathryn's door five minutes later. He didn't have to wait long for her to answer his knock. She greeted him with the brightest smile he'd seen from her yet.

"Sorry I'm late."

"Are you late? I've been so busy I didn't notice." Sweeping an arm at the pile of boxes, bags, sewing machine and plastic tubs, she added, "I have some things to take with us." Looking over the accumulated stuff, her smile wilted. She bit her lips, as if fearing she had assembled too much. Something in him rebelled at that.

"We made space this morning." Jake rubbed his hands together. "Let's get loaded."

She brightened at once and began gathering what she could carry. "I know it's a lot, but I have whole bolts of fabric and books of swatches that I picked up when the fabric store here closed. You remember when Gladys Page had her shop downtown? Oh, no, you wouldn't. That was years ago. My mother was still in the hospital. Gladys let me have a lot of stuff for free because I helped her clear out the place. I always wondered what I'd do with some of it, and now I know. I've even got an idea for the bunkhouse." Having gathered up the smaller items, she paused. "I hope I've got something that'll work for the master bedroom. If not, we'll have to go shopping."

"I know how you women love to shop," Jake commented absently, turning to follow her with an armload of fabric in bolts. Shopping had been one of Jolene's favorite pastimes, and Tina seemed to spend more time shopping online than anything else.

Kathryn stopped in her tracks and looked over her shoulder at him with a worried expression. "I hate it. But then since my mom's accident, I've never had any money to shop or anyone to go with me." She brightened. "I do like a good antique store, though. It'll be fun to look for things for the ranch house with Tina. We're hoping to find some wicker accessories."

She went on in that vein as they trooped out to the truck and stowed the items. Bubbling over with ideas, she talked nonstop. Jake was shocked by such a babbling, animated Kathryn, but he found this enthusiastic, happy woman breathtaking. It was a good thing he had so much to load. The impulse to hug her made him dizzy. He wondered what she'd do if he tried it. Then he realized abruptly that she might not be the only one to object.

No matter what Meredith Billings Burns said, Kathryn could well have a boyfriend—or several—for all he or anyone else knew. Every man in the whole county couldn't be blind. Besides, what did he really know about her? If she were as private as Meredith said, she could be seriously involved with none the wiser, except the guy himself. But if such a fellow existed, why wasn't *he* here helping her? Why wasn't *he* driving her around?

Could be he worked out of town, or drove a semi. Frowning, Jake silently contemplated the possibilities as Kathryn climbed up into the truck cab, still chattering.

"Oh, and I have the perfect fabric for place mats. They'll work beautifully with that terra-cotta tabletop."

Jake closed the door and walked around the front of the truck, only to realize that she was bailing out before he could even get in.

"I almost forgot to lock up!"

He watched her race into the house and return with her bag. She slung it over one shoulder, getting it out of the way while she used her key. The notion struck him that she'd probably made the bag herself. He remembered Meredith mentioning something about it as the women had chatted in the church vestibule on Wednesday.

What self-respecting man, Jake asked himself, would watch his woman do without the things that other women took for granted, like handbags and new clothes and a dependable car? He remembered what Tina had said about

Kathryn's father abandoning the family after his wife's accident. With an example like that, Kathryn might be willing to accept far less from a man than a woman like her was entitled to.

Someone should show her different. Not him, though. Even if she didn't dislike him, he was in no position to provide for her. It would be all he could do to pay the wages he'd promised her, get her car running and open the garage without bankrupting himself.

He handed her up into the truck once more, resisting the urge to let himself touch her more than absolutely necessary. He couldn't help thinking, *Lord, this is not what I call solid ground. On the other hand, You've been known to help others walk on water.*

He just hoped he wasn't about to find himself in over his head.

They were halfway back to Loco Man when Kathryn suddenly remarked, "You're awful quiet."

He shifted in his seat. "Lot on my mind. First, there's Frankie's pony. That's why I was late. I tried to talk to the veterinarian about it earlier. Hopefully, he can help me figure out how to tame that contrary little beast."

"The pony, you mean," she clarified.

"Yes, the pony," Jake said, grinning. Shy and private she might be, but she couldn't help those protective instincts, not when it came to Frankie, anyway. He'd called her a worrywart that first day, but she was more of a polite Mama Bear. "I'm perfectly aware that my son is no beast. He is, however, fearless on the back of a horse, even though he's not as in control as he needs to be."

"He'll figure it out," Kathryn assured him. "You'll keep working with him, and he'll figure it out."

"Yeah. Eventually."

"So what's next?"

"Huh?"

"You said you had a lot on your mind, and first thing was Frankie and his pony. I just wondered what was next."

"Right." He waved a hand. "Well, there's the shop."

"What shop?"

"I told you I was building an auto repair shop."

"Oh. That's right. Where is it?"

"A few hundred yards from the house, fronting the road."

"Sounds convenient."

"That's the idea. We're putting up the concrete block walls now. Meanwhile, I'm buying all the stuff I'll need to get operational."

"And working on my car," she said apologetically.

He shrugged. "Ryder's helping out."

"I'm sure you'll be glad when you no longer have to drive me everywhere. That'll be one thing off your mind."

As if, he thought, *I haven't been able to get you off my mind since I met you.*

He said, "Aw, that's no big deal. It's just a few minutes each way."

"I guess you'll need me to look after Frankie even more once your shop opens."

Now, why hadn't he thought of that? She was entirely right. "I will," he told her, hoping he didn't sound as surprised—or dismayed—as he felt. So much for temporary situations and keeping his distance.

Lord, help me, he prayed.

Why did he think this was one prayer that wouldn't be answered as he hoped?

Chapter Six

Frankie greeted Kathryn with hugs. While he towed her off to see Tyler's dog, Jake unloaded her stuff and hurried away. Afterward, despite Frankie's "help," Kathryn was able to organize and settle her sewing materials into the laundry room before Tina sent the boys upstairs to play so she and Kathryn could look through fabrics and talk decor. Frankie soon returned to usurp Kathryn's attention, however.

"My puppies," he pleaded.

Kathryn pulled out the stencil and took him upstairs to begin the process. He lay on the bed, his little chin propped on the heels of his hands, and watched as she drew a level line around three walls of the room. She taped the stencil to the wall to show Frankie where the puppies would go, but she couldn't paint without first sanding the area smooth. Before she could begin that, Tina called her downstairs to talk about lunch.

They'd barely discussed the menu when a contractor arrived to consult with Tina about the massive carport that Wyatt had planned just outside the back door. According to Tina, Wyatt wanted the door, steps and

stoop covered, too. That meant connecting the roof of
the carport to the house. Tina's main concern was that
the carport look period appropriate and not detract from
the house. While Tina and the contractor pored over architectural styles on the computer, Kathryn made lunch
on her own. Tina had told her that the guys would eat
almost anything but loved Mexican food in particular.

By the time Ryder came in, followed within minutes
by Wyatt, Kathryn had an enormous chicken-and-rice
dish on the table, along with a spinach salad, sliced
melon and flour tortillas. After seeing out the contractor, Tina stood with her hands on her hips and shook
her head.

"Beats the stuffing out of ham-and-cheese sandwiches." She shook a finger at Kathryn. "I need to pick
your brain about the breakfast menu for the B and B."

Pleased, Kathryn said she'd look through her cook-
books. "I've got a bunch of old ones that belonged to
my grandmother. There's some good stuff in them."

Tina waved a hand at the table against the far wall
that she used as her personal desk. "There's the computer, too."

"I don't know much about computers. Anything, really."

"You'll get the hang of it," Tina promised, just as
Jake came through the door.

"I'll do the cooking and leave the computer to you,"
Kathryn replied happily.

The boys clambered down the stairs and soon appeared in the kitchen. Tina swept them into the bathroom to wash up, while Kathryn went to the refrigerator
for salsa and iced tea. As they all took their places

around the table, Wyatt announced that he'd bought another bull and turned it into the south pasture.

"Hopefully we'll grow the herd and have a few head ready for market by this time next year."

"That's good news," Tina said, clasping his hand.

Everyone else linked hands then. Kathryn noticed that Jake held her hand loosely. Tyler was deputized to lead the prayer this time. He showed no signs of self-consciousness but kept it brief. Wyatt, Tina and Ryder chatted about their mornings as they filled plates.

Last to serve himself, Jake neither looked at anyone nor spoke. A whisper of unease filtered through Kathryn. Wyatt also seemed to sense Jake's withdrawal and tried to bring him into the conversation.

"Did you get to talk to Stark?"

"Yep."

"And did he have any ideas about what to do with that pony?"

Jake nodded, his attention fixed on his plate.

Wyatt pushed him a little. "What did Stark say?"

"He thinks we're using the wrong tack, and he had some advice on training."

"Which is?"

"We can discuss it tonight. I have to eat and get back on that car."

Kathryn's unease increased. "I—I can start paying you back for the parts next week," she told him softly. "My last paycheck from my previous employer should be in the bank by Monday." Jake responded with the barest of nods, prompting her to speak further. "A-and, of course, I'll recompense you for your work, too."

"We can discuss that later," Jake said briskly, stirring his arroz con pollo in such a fashion that she worried he found it unappetizing. She had made it on the mild side because of the boys, but the salsa should have added enough spice for him.

"As long as you know that—"

"Later," Jake snapped.

An awkward silence followed. Tina cleared her throat and launched into a description of what she and Kathryn had planned for the master bedroom.

"Sounds great," Wyatt said, smiling. "Ought to be very pretty."

"It won't be too feminine," Tina promised. Tina had been adamant about that. Some sort of silent communication sizzled between husband and wife. Kathryn looked away, a little embarrassed by the cozy, affectionate air that so often surrounded the couple.

Ryder forked up a bite of food and waved it at Kathryn. "This is really good."

Kathryn smiled and said, "Glad you're enjoying it."

Talk turned to Tina's visit with the contractor that morning. Kathryn ate in silence, casting glances around the table. All the Smith brothers were handsome men, but something about Jake drew her and had done so from the beginning, so much so that she'd felt nervous and wary around him. This morning, she'd thought they were becoming more comfortable with each other, but now he seemed to be sending off waves of...it felt like disappointment or hostility. Or maybe it was just indifference. He seemed completely detached.

Ryder pushed back his chair and addressed her. "Can I help you with anything this afternoon, Kathryn? Tina said you wanted to do some stenciling in Frankie's room."

She automatically hesitated. "Oh, I wouldn't want to interrupt your schedule."

"It's too hot at this time of day to work on the shop, and I'm waiting for the baseboards and paint we ordered for the bunkhouse to come in. Don't need to tend the horses 'til evening, so if you need some prep done, I'll be glad to help."

Once, Kathryn would have turned down his help for fear she'd be criticized or somehow disappoint him, but that wasn't true now. She knew exactly what she wanted to do on Frankie's walls, and she knew that she could do a good job of it, just as she knew that she could do a good job with the rest of the house and be of real help to Tina. Why should she turn down help when it was offered?

She looked at Ryder and said, "I'd appreciate that. I've marked off the border on the three walls I want to paint, but the space has to be taped and sanded."

"Consider it done," Ryder said, getting to his feet.

Jake also rose. Looking down at Frankie, he ordered, "Stay out of the way and let Uncle Ryder work. And do whatever KKay tells you."

Frankie nodded meekly, watching, along with everyone else, as Jake strode to the door, yanked it open and disappeared.

Tina sat back in her chair and raised her eyebrows at her husband, who reached for the serving spoon and dipped it into the arroz con pollo. "Mighty good lunch," he said, nodding at Kathryn. Glancing at Tina, he added, "Interesting."

What that meant, Kathryn didn't know, but she felt a little sick, as if the ground had moved unexpectedly beneath her feet. Silently, she rose and began cleaning the kitchen.

* * *

Jake strode out to the barn, his mind whirling with doubts and confusion. He felt like a surly old dog with a bone that he kept burying and digging up. It just wouldn't leave him alone.

Or rather, she. She just wouldn't leave him alone. He'd kept his distance all morning, tracking down Stark and badgering him for advice about Frankie's pony when he should have been working on her car. Through it all, she hadn't left his mind for a moment.

Did she have some man in her life that no one knew about? Or was it possible, as Meredith Burns believed, that Kathryn had never even been on a date? He couldn't accept that at first, but now the idea haunted him, so much so that he feared he'd do something stupid if he spent much more time in her company.

Jake had done some math and figured out that Kathryn had to be in her late twenties. If it was true that she'd never been on a date, someone should do something. Otherwise, he feared that she would spend the rest of her life alone, and what a tragedy that would be.

Someone should definitely do something. But not him.

Resolutely, he turned his thoughts to her old car. A platform of planks laid on the dirt floor of the barn created a firm foundation for his portable lift. He'd moved Kathryn's car onto the lift the very day he'd towed it in. The car now rested about eighteen inches off the ground. The lift would raise the car to a maximum of forty-one inches when he needed to work beneath it, but the current height allowed him to work under the hood without straining his back. He opened his tool chest and started going through the drawers, choosing the tools he'd need and arranging them on a pullout tray. All the while, Jake's thoughts kept circling back to Kathryn.

As he tackled a particularly stubborn bolt, he thought about her father. What kind of man abandoned his handicapped wife and left his quiet, shy, teenaged daughter as her only caregiver? The selfish jerk had to have known how narrow of a life he'd condemned his daughter to, but apparently he hadn't cared.

It wasn't fair. The kind of life she'd led just wasn't fair.

With that thought, he threw his whole weight onto the bolt, which promptly broke off. He knew without even looking that he didn't have a tap bit big enough to move that bolt. Disgusted with himself, he threw the wrench against the wall. What was wrong with him?

Kathryn Stepp's life, including her social life or lack thereof, was none of his business. Still, someone should ask her out. Someone, but *not* him.

He couldn't afford to be dating right now, and even if he could, Kathryn wasn't the right woman for him. She was nothing like Jolene. Besides, it had only been a little over two years since his wife had died. Even if sometimes it felt like forever, another lifetime ago, it was too soon for him to be interested in another woman. He was just missing Jolene. And Houston. And anxious to get his new shop built. He wasn't ready for another serious relationship, and he wasn't sure he ever would be.

Realizing that he could do nothing more until that bolt was drilled out and replaced, he leaned against the fender of Kathryn's old car and wiped his hands with a rag. His throat burning, he dropped the hood of the car and walked out to his truck. Briefly, he considered going into the house, but he didn't want to see Kathryn or anyone else right now. He felt raw and vulnerable. Better to keep his distance until he felt more himself.

He got into the truck and escaped. When he reached the outskirts of Ardmore, he called Tina from his cell phone, in case she needed anything he could pick up on his way to the auto parts store—and because he felt guilty about taking off without a word to anyone. Tina gave him a list so long that she elected to text it to him before she'd even finished talking. He was glad for it. Shopping for her justified his actions somewhat.

After purchasing the correct drill bit for tapping that broken bolt, he started on Tina's list. Nearly everything could be purchased at the home improvement store, but she wanted him to find a particular pair of work gloves for Wyatt at the ranch supply store. After he tried on the gloves and settled on the right size, he picked up a pair for himself and another for Ryder. Then he went to the tack section. Stark had suggested a particular saddle for Frankie, and a certain type of bridle for the pony. Jake could see right away why. The new saddle and bridle would give Frankie greater control of his mount. Jake bought the saddle and bridle, trying not to think about the cost.

Despite his money worries, he was in a better mood by the time he'd arrived back at the ranch house, but then Tina ambushed him the instant he walked through the door with her purchases.

"Listen," she said excitedly, "why don't we let Kathryn drive my old car until you get hers repaired? She wouldn't have to depend on anyone else for transportation that way."

A mobile Kathryn would be a lot easier to avoid. He might never see her again except in passing. Convinced it was a good idea, Jake nodded, but then he heard himself ask, "What about Ryder? That car's *his* transportation. And besides, you still haven't registered the car in Oklahoma. How would you feel if Kathryn got pulled over for having Kansas plates?"

Tina blinked. "I didn't think of that. You're right. I need to take care of getting that vehicle properly registered. Until I do, even Ryder could have a problem."

"Kathryn's shy and skittish, but she's proud, too," Jake went on thoughtfully. "She wouldn't want to let us pay a fine for her. Come to think of it, how do we offer her the car without making it seem like an act of charity?"

"Maybe we could say the car is part of her compensation."

At the rate they were already paying her? He grimaced. "I don't want her to think she's a burden to us."

"No, we don't want that," Tina agreed. "I guess as long as you don't mind driving her around, we ought to just leave things as they are."

"I don't mind," he said quickly, in what he hoped was a casual tone.

Tina suddenly beamed at him. "She's a sweetheart, Jake, a real blessing. You were right about her."

"I'm, uh, glad it's working out," he murmured, feeling oddly exposed all of a sudden. And foolish. What was wrong with him? He knew what he should do. Why couldn't he do it?

Movement at the periphery of his vision caught his attention. He turned his head to find Kathryn standing near the refrigerator. The look on her face hit him like an arrow to the chest. Shyly pleased, guardedly hopeful, she gazed at him with such warmth that he knew instantly she'd overheard the conversation and put the worst possible connotation on his objections to giving her Tina's old car to drive. The worst possible connotation and the right one. Before he could think of anything to say, she aimed a smile at Tina.

"I've been thinking," she said a little too brightly. "What if we attach the bed skirt to the box springs with Velcro? It won't move around, can be easily removed and will present no problems when you turn the mattress."

"Wyatt will love that idea." Tina turned a gleeful smile on Jake, explaining, "We're going with a simple bed skirt, pleated at the corners. You know, so it's not too frilly." Jake made a humming sound, and she hurried on. "The bed's so big Wyatt worried a bed skirt that completely covered the box springs would make turning the mattress difficult."

"Problem avoided," Jake said, tossing a congratulatory smile around the room while managing to avoid direct eye contact with Kathryn, who muttered something about getting back to work and slipped away.

He quickly handed over Tina's goods then escaped to the barn again, where he began drilling out the broken bolt. Every time he thought of the look on Kathryn's face when he saw her standing there by the refrigerator, he dredged up memories of Jolene and forced his mind back to the job at hand.

He had the broken bolt out and a hoist and chain rigged to take the weight of the engine when Ryder showed up.

"Dinner's on."

"Already?"

"It's past six."

Jake pulled out his phone and glanced at it. He never wore a wristwatch anymore. He'd broken too many crystal watch faces and demolished too many watch-bands. His eyebrows shot up when he saw the time.

"Wow. Okay. I'll straighten up here and be in."

"Can I help?" Ryder asked.

"Nah. Won't take a minute."

"Kathryn's made fajitas. Beef and shrimp." He rubbed his flat belly with the palm of one hand before wandering over to lean against the tool chest, his arms crossed over its smooth top. "Thanks for the work gloves. They're good ones."

"You're welcome."

"Apparently, Rex told Wyatt about them, and he mentioned them to Tina."

"She sure takes care of him, doesn't she?"

He assumed that Ryder nodded, but he didn't look until Ryder suddenly said, "I'm a little envious." Jake shot a surprised glance at his brother. Ryder smiled sheepishly. "When you and Jolene married, I thought it was the dumbest thing you'd ever done."

"What?"

"Well, I didn't understand how marriage could be back then," Ryder admitted.

Jake sometimes forgot that Ryder was five years younger than him, just as Jake was five years younger than Wyatt. He chuckled. He'd married at twenty-three. Ryder hadn't turned eighteen until a few weeks after the wedding. Strange, it felt a lot longer ago than seven years.

"Jolene adored you," Jake said, smiling. "Thought you were the cutest thing she'd ever seen. And it embarrassed you to no end."

Ryder grinned. "She liked to embarrass me."

"She did, but just because she was so fond of you. I thought for sure she was going to pair you up with that cousin of hers."

Ryder rolled his eyes. "No way!"

"She was a pretty little thing."

"With blue hair. And what was with all that eye makeup?"

Grinning, Jake said, "Sometimes I think you're the most conservative Smith of all."

Ryder shrugged. "I just always wonder, what would Mama think?"

Sobering, Jake nodded. He was never sure how much Ryder remembered about their mother. He'd only been five when they'd lost her.

"Mom would be proud of you," Jake told him.

"I hope so." Ryder's gaze slid away, and Jake feared he was thinking about the death of his former sparring partner Bryan Averett. Though it had been nothing more than a freak accident, Jake suspected Ryder still blamed and condemned himself for what had happened.

"Mom would like Tina," Ryder announced. "And Kathryn, too."

Jake's gaze zipped over to his brother again. Ryder gave him a lopsided smile.

"You found a good one there, bro."

Shocked, Jake struggled not to react more than he should. "I think she'll be a big help around here."

Ryder gave him a knowing look. "Uh-huh."

With that, he turned and strolled away. Jake gaped at his little brother as he exited the barn. Had Ryder just let him know that he'd recognized Jake's interest in Kathryn and approved? But Ryder didn't understand.

Kathryn wasn't anything like Jolene. Besides, he wasn't ready. Maybe if he were stable financially, not solely dependent on the ranch and Wyatt's efforts, he could think about…he didn't know what he was thinking or doing anymore, let alone what God was doing.

Jake passed a hand over his face. Part of him wanted to run back to Houston. Part of him wanted to watch Kathryn's eyes soften again and her lips curl into a shy, hopeful smile.

It's only been two years, he reminded himself. She was nothing like Jolene, and he didn't have the money or the time for romance.

Resolved yet again, Jake put away his tools, walked to the house and took his place at the table next to Kathryn.

Chapter Seven

Tina rebuffed Kathryn's efforts to clean up the kitchen. "You've been here long enough today. Go home. Relax. We'll see you on Monday."

Frankie didn't share Tina's sentiment. "KKay, do my bath."

Wyatt scooped up Frankie and tossed the boy over his shoulder, sending Frankie into shrieks of delight. "Doesn't old Uncle Wyatt get a turn to splash water in your face? Besides, we need to clean up your nose. Maybe then you can smell your stinky self."

Frankie clapped both hands over his nose, laughing and protesting at the same time. "Don' clean by nodes!"

Wyatt carted the boy off to the bathroom, shouting at Tyler to join them. Kathryn laughed and waved. Frankie waved back with his free hand.

Overhearing Jake's comments earlier had made Kathryn rethink her behavior. Did she act as proud and skittish around Jake and his family as he'd implied? She very much feared that she did, but no one and nothing in her experience had prepared her for the casual openness and generosity with which this family treated her.

Even before her mother's accident, Kathryn had been shy and careful around others, unwilling to join in group activities. She'd always felt that taking care of things herself was often easier than depending on others. Easier and safer. Kathryn had an abhorrent fear of appearing foolish and incapable. The more she kept to herself, the less reason she had to fear making a misstep. Like Jake, her mother had seen that as pride.

In the past, her fear and pride had driven her to refuse help even when she'd needed it. These Smiths had taught her a thing or two about that. She couldn't imagine a more informed or capable person than Tina, but even she needed help, and Kathryn knew she could be that help. So did Jake. He'd known it before she had.

Kathryn retrieved her bag and looked to Jake. "Ready when you are."

He stuck his left hand in the front pocket of his jeans and pulled out his keys. Kathryn called a farewell to Tina and walked through the door ahead of him, feeling his hand settle into the small of her back as they moved down the outside steps. Her stupid heart flip-flopped inside her chest, but she did her best to ignore it. He meant nothing with his small touches and polite smiles. In fact, sometimes she thought he barely tolerated her. He'd been quick to spare her feelings, though.

"My mother used to tell me I was too proud," she blurted as Jake reached around her to open the passenger door of his truck.

He looked as shocked by her comment as she was. "Hey. Listen. I—I didn't mean anything negative by what I said to Tina earlier. I was just concerned that we not, uh, offend you."

Kathryn smiled wryly at that. "Embarrass me, you mean."

"No. That's not—"

"You got it right," she interrupted gently, bolstering her courage. "I couldn't in good conscience accept the use of a vehicle from your family, not after all you've already done for me. I mean, unless it would benefit you. A-all of you. I mean, you're the one who drives me everywhere. Y-you and Tina."

He pulled the door open, concentrating on the handle as if it required a complicated maneuver to make that happen. "Ten minutes here or there. No big deal." As she climbed up into the passenger seat of the truck, he added, "Besides, it's only right that we help you out when you're doing so much to help us. Tina and Frankie, I mean. Well, me, too, when you think about it, I guess."

Kathryn shook her head. "It's not the same. You're paying. It's my job to help you. Besides, I could walk back and forth to the ranch. It's not that far."

He settled a stern look on her, his face turning to stone. "I won't hear of you walking, not in this heat. And not when the drive takes so little time."

She nodded, telling herself not to feel so pleased as he closed the door and moved around the truck. He was a good, kind, Christian man. His care and generosity meant nothing except that he tried to follow the precepts of Christ Jesus. It felt *personal*, though, which meant that she was likely having personal feelings about him. Oh, who was she kidding? She'd be mooning over Jacoby Smith day and night if she didn't watch herself.

She'd daydreamed about boys in the past, wondered how it would be if they'd liked her as much as she'd liked them, but she'd always backed away when they'd gotten too close. She was sure that if they'd truly come to know her, they'd have found her as boring as dishwater. That, sadly, hadn't changed.

"So," he said in a conversational tone, sliding behind the steering wheel, "got any plans for the weekend?"

Kathryn nearly laughed. When had she ever had plans for the weekend? She went nowhere and did nothing. She couldn't even call herself a wallflower because she'd have to go somewhere social before she could wind up hiding in a corner. She wasn't pathetic enough to say that, however, so she settled for a negative shake of her head.

His expression blank, he concentrated on backing around the truck and moving it out onto the highway. After several minutes of silence, he abruptly said, "Thought maybe you'd have a date or something."

"Uh, no. Fact is, I've never been on a date."

He looked… She couldn't decide if he was stunned or angry. The next moment, his brows drew together and his lips flattened as if he were in pain, but then he blew out a breath and nodded crisply.

"Oh. Well. You must not see too many movies then."

"Nothing you can't find on TV. I haven't been to a movie theater in years."

"Uh-huh," he said. "You should go with me, then. Us. Me and Frankie, I mean."

Frankie. Ah. She would be overseeing Frankie at the theater, making sure his father could enjoy the movie. Or something. Refusing to acknowledge her disappointment, she pondered the situation. Would Frankie be content to sit still and quiet through a whole movie? She doubted it. Even when he was sitting quietly he was moving, swinging his legs or twisting his body in time to some tune only he could hear, and he naturally spoke in a near shout. Tina had told her that children whose linguistic skills hadn't yet fully developed often did that in a misguided effort to make themselves understood. Shouting, after all, usually drew a quick response. Kathryn figured she'd probably wind up walking him around the theater lobby while his dad enjoyed the movie. Still, even babysitting at the movie theater would be a welcome change from her usual weekend routine.

Her mind began whirling. She needed to look as presentable as possible. Jake, after all, was her boss. One of them, anyway. She didn't want to embarrass him or herself.

"What do people wear to movies these days?"

He shrugged. "Uh, I don't know. Pretty much anything and everything, I guess. Jeans, dresses…date clothes, I suppose. That is, anything you'd wear, like, on a date."

And there was the problem. At this point in time, she had work clothes and little else. She'd had no need for anything more. Still, given enough time, she could devise something. With her sewing machine at the ranch, however, she'd have to start the alterations by hand and finish them during work breaks.

Gathering her courage, she meekly asked, "Would it be possible to put it off a week or so?"

"Oh, sure," he said quickly, nonchalantly. "I just meant we should go sometime. Taking Frankie to the movies by myself is an exercise in futility. But it can wait."

"So, next weekend then?"

He waved a hand. "Next weekend's fine."

"Fine," she echoed, already going through her wardrobe in her mind. Or rather, her mother's wardrobe.

Kathryn had grown taller and filled out since she'd left school, so she could no longer wear the clothes of her youth, not that they'd have been appropriate now. Her mother had owned a lot of nice things, though, and they were close enough in size that she could alter them, even update them a bit. Often, she didn't bother to make the alterations. Who cared how she looked when she was cleaning or cooking anyway? This time, she cared. This time it was more about style than utility.

Date clothes.

"Should I pick you up for church on Sunday?" Jake asked casually.

She startled at the thought. Church clothes. She didn't have any of those, either—nothing appropriate for a Sunday service, anyway. Maybe date clothes could do double duty as church clothes.

"Um, not this week. I—I'll be better prepared next week."

He accepted that easily, nodding. "Right." He lifted a hand, spreading his fingers as if to say he was all out of questions, and they finished the trip in silence.

"See you Monday morning then," he said, bringing the truck to a stop.

Kathryn reached for the door handle. She slid down to the ground and grabbed her bag off the floorboard before backing up a few steps, but then she just stood there awkwardly before blurting, "Have a good weekend!"

"You, too!" he called heartily.

She shut the truck door and hurried up onto the porch. Okay, so it wasn't an actual date, but it was still the first opportunity she'd had in years—decades—

to dress like it mattered. Somehow, it did matter, very much. She wasn't even sure she wanted to know *why* it mattered. If she dwelled on that too long, she'd lose her nerve and find an excuse to just stay home.

Her mind filled with possible plans and designs, she didn't even hear the truck back out and drive away or remember unlocking her door and going inside. Suddenly she found herself standing in front of a closet, her gaze roaming over the garments crammed in there. It shouldn't be anything too dressy or ornate, but of course it should be flattering. Very flattering. And contemporary. She didn't want to look like she didn't belong.

She began pulling hangers off the rod and assessing each garment before either tossing it into a pile on the bed or returning it to the closet. A week. She had a week to knock Jake's eyes out. Pausing, she corrected herself.

She had a week to make herself presentable.

Then Jake was taking her to a movie.

She simply could not wipe the stupid grin off her face.

"K-Kay!"

Kathryn quickly swept the dress she was working on into a rumpled heap of fabric when Frankie and Jake appeared in the laundry room. For two days, she'd been quietly working on the garment during her breaks and free moments. Hopefully they would think it nothing more than another pillow sham or slipcover. She felt guilty for working on the dress at the ranch, but she couldn't ask Jake to tote her heavy old machine back and forth every day. Besides, she made sure to do everything Tina asked of her first. She'd tried to decide if she should cut the long sleeves out of the dress entirely or shorten them, but she remained uncertain. She thought about asking Jake his opinion, but it seemed too much of a personal decision. Maybe she could ask Tina.

"Come out, KKay," Frankie pleaded, drawing her attention back to the present.

"He wants you to come out to the corral to watch him ride his pony," Jake explained apologetically. "I tried to tell him you're too busy, but we're breaking in a new saddle, and he's been working very hard."

Kathryn tried to hide the spurt of alarm that came with thinking of Frankie on horseback, but Jake saw right through her.

"And, yes, we've taken all safety precautions."

"Oh." Pushing back the wheeled desk chair, Kathryn leaned forward, bringing her face down to Frankie's level. "What's your pony's name?"

"Good Boy!" Frankie declared at the top of his lungs.

Perplexed, Kathryn drew back.

"You don't have to shout," Jake admonished. "Remember what we said about using your inside voice?"

Frankie leaned toward Kathryn and in a voice barely above a whisper repeated, "Good Boy."

Still puzzled, Kathryn looked to Jake, whose lips wiggled suspiciously. "Good boy is something Tyler often says to his dog, Tipper. It's an affectionate kind of thing, so Frankie has adopted it as his pony's name."

Disciplining her own smile, Kathryn quickly bit her lips before calmly saying, "Good Boy is an excellent name for a pony. Or a dog."

Frankie turned to his father, clearly making an effort to moderate his volume, and asked plaintively, "S'when doggy?"

Jake rolled his eyes. "When it's weaned. Dr. Burns

will let us know as soon as the puppies can leave their mother. They have to stay with her until they can eat solid food and get all their shots. Remember?" Shaking his head at Kathryn, he added, "I never should have taken him to see that litter."

Clearly dissatisfied with that answer, Frankie folded his arms. It was a gesture of Tyler's that Kathryn often saw. Apparently, Jake recognized it, too. Reaching down, Jake brushed Frankie's arms back to his sides.

"Pouting won't make the puppies grow any faster."

Clearly chastened, Frankie bowed his head.

Kathryn shared a glance with Jake then reached out and turned Frankie by his shoulders, saying brightly, "Puppies are such fun. What are you going to name your pup?"

"Doggy," Frankie said, as if that ought to be obvious.

"We'll work on that," Jake commented dryly.

Kathryn bit her lips again to keep from laughing.

"Your pony's waiting," Jake reminded Frankie.

Kathryn quickly stood and offered her hand to the boy, who immediately grasped her fingers and tugged her toward the hallway.

They walked out to the hot, dusty corral. Someone had disked up the dirt to cushion the hard surface, which the heat was busily baking hard again. The little round white pony with brown patches huffed and shifted its weight as Jake led Frankie into the pen. Kathryn stayed outside to lean against the metal-pipe fence.

Jake tightened the girth on the saddle and buckled a helmet onto Frankie's head, but instead of lifting Frankie into the seat, he had the boy grab the saddle horn and hop high enough to get the toe of his left shoe into the stirrup. He then assisted as Frankie threw his right leg over the pony's back and settled in. The boy had some trouble finding the right stirrup, so Jake walked around, always keeping a hand on the little horse, and placed Frankie's foot in the stirrup. Next, Jake simply reached out and untied the reins from a lower rail of the fence and handed them to Frankie.

Her heart pounding, Kathryn noticed that the reins were knotted and Frankie grasped the leather strips on each side of the knot. He laid one side of the reins against the pony's neck and clucked his tongue. When that didn't produce the desired result, he slid his hand down and pulled on the opposite side of the reins. The pony reluctantly turned and plodded along the fence line.

"Good job," Jake called out.

Frankie tried to push the animal to a faster pace. Eventually, the pony picked up its feet. By the second time around the fence, the pony was trotting. Frankie bounced along in the saddle but looked firmly in control. Kathryn relaxed somewhat.

Jake rested his elbows on the top rail of the fence right next to Kathryn, watching Frankie ride. "Stark Burns was sure right about the new rig. Frankie couldn't use his knees properly with the old saddle."

"Frankie seems to know what he's doing now."

"He's getting there."

After a few more rounds, Jake moved into the arena and called out instructions to Frankie, who responded with clear efforts. "Good job, son," Jake called after a few more minutes. "Bring him in now."

Frankie obediently turned the pony and walked it to a halt next to his father. "Get your horse, Daddy?"

"I don't have time to ride out with you today, son.

I'll be working late tonight as it is. Maybe tomorrow, though, if you promise not to take off on your own again."

"I pwomise!" Frankie pledged loud enough to make the pony sidestep. Quickly tugging on the reins, Frankie stilled the little horse and turned a beaming smile on Kathryn. "I ridin' good."

"You are," she agreed, "and your pony is very well behaved, too."

Frankie leaned forward and patted the pony's neck. "Good boy, Good Boy."

Kathryn laughed. Grinning at her, Jake told the boy to ride around the corral once more before they rubbed down the horse.

As Frankie turned his mount, Kathryn said to Jake, "I've been meaning to ask you what movie we'll be seeing next weekend."

Glancing at Frankie, Jake folded his arms atop the corral fence and leaned close. "Uh, I haven't said anything to Frankie yet. Kid has no sense of time. You saw how he is about the puppies. If he knows what we're planning, he'll get up every day thinking it's *the* day, and then I'll just have to disappoint him over and over until the time finally comes."

"Right. Should've thought of that."

"Anyway, Frankie seems to generate his own mental movies, no matter what's showing."

That sounded a little alarming to Kathryn. "What do you mean?"

Jake turned and waved over Frankie. He trotted his pony back to the fence and brought it to a stop.

"Son, tell KKay what your favorite movie is."

Frankie put his head back and exclaimed, *"Big Puppy 'n Princess Fly Horses to Moon!"*

Kathryn blinked. "I don't think I've ever heard of that movie."

"No one has," Jake said softly, chuckling. "The big puppy, princess and flying horses are characters from some of his favorite cartoons. He's developed elaborate stories around animated TV characters, and if you make the mistake of letting him tell you about them, you'll be listening *forever*."

Chuckling, Kathryn nodded. "Got it."

"Big puppy hold wings," Frankie began. "She climb on. Woosh! Up, up, to—"

"There's a reason we don't let Frankie choose our movies," Jake interrupted, sending a droll grin to Kathryn. Turning toward Frankie, he reached for the knot in the reins. "Your pony's hot and tired. He needs a rest. You, too. Besides, KKay should get out of this hot sun." As he spoke, he pulled the reins down over the pony's head and began to lead it, with Frankie still in the saddle, toward the barn. "Tell Kathryn thanks for coming out to watch."

"Thanks you, KKay!" Frankie yelled before smacking a kiss into the palm of his hand and throwing it toward her with a broad, exuberant sweep of his arm.

"You're welcome," Kathryn called, blowing her own kiss to him as she moved toward the house.

Only as she sat down at the sewing machine again did she realize that Jake hadn't answered her question about what movie they would be seeing on Saturday evening. What difference did it make, though? As long as she was with Jake—and Frankie, of course— she'd have a good time. Even if she wound up walking Frankie around the lobby while Jake watched the movie undisturbed, she wouldn't mind. She'd have almost as much fun people watching as movie watching. And she'd look good doing it, too.

Even as she mentally prepared herself for the least enjoyable experience, though, a vision planted itself in her head, a vision of sitting next to Jake in the dark, Frankie snuggled into her lap, Jake's arm spanning her shoulders as the movie played out on the screen in front of them. She wouldn't have the nerve to lay her head on Jake's shoulder, but maybe they would share popcorn and smiles from time to time.

Maybe he'd even hold her hand.

She shook her head.

And Jake thought Frankie's mental movies were farfetched!

Chapter Eight

Jake repositioned his hat and straightened a crooked belt loop on the waistband of his dark jeans before lifting his gaze to the wreath hanging on Kathryn's front door. He still couldn't believe he was doing this. He'd surprised himself as much as her by suggesting this outing, but when she'd confirmed Meredith's suspicions that she'd never been on a date, he'd wanted to smack every man who'd ever known her. What was wrong with the men around here?

At the same time, Jake knew he shouldn't be the one to ask her out, to let her know she was worthy of a date, which was why he'd brought Frankie into it. Somehow he'd thought he could have his cake and eat it, too, but how did you date a woman, make her happy and still leave her with the understanding that absolutely nothing could come of it? In a few months, maybe, if everything went his way and the garage was turning a profit, he could think about dating, but this was the worst possible time in his life for romance.

Still, he couldn't bear the idea of her sitting home alone weekend after weekend. If only he'd thought it

through before he'd opened his big mouth, he might
have come up with another way to resolve her situation,
but he couldn't seem to control his impulses where she
was concerned. Yesterday, in front of the whole family,
Tina had presented Kathryn with her first paycheck and
mentioned that Kathryn had agreed to attend church
with the family tomorrow. Jake had told himself that he
would cancel their date when he drove Kathryn home
and slipped her his check—he still hadn't told the rest
of the family about her raise in pay—but instead he'd
arranged the time to pick her up tonight!

To make matters worse, his family had to know it
was happening. When he'd asked Tina to tend Frankie
tonight, she'd agreed without even asking why or where
Jake was going. No one had commented or so much
as cracked a smile when he'd come downstairs in his
best jeans and long-sleeved, button-up shirt. He'd left
the collar open and rolled up his cuffs in an attempt
to present a casual image, but everyone had to have
known he was going out for the evening and who was
going with him.

Squaring his shoulders, Jake lifted his hand and
rapped his knuckles against the door. It swung open
immediately, as if Kathryn had been standing on the
other side waiting for him to knock. The thought made
him smile. Then he got a good look at her, and his smile
died in astonishment.

She wore a simple navy blue closely-fitted dress with
a slightly scooped neckline, short sleeves and a hem
that frothed around her slender calves. He thought he
recognized that fabric from somewhere, but he couldn't
think where. He could barely think at all. She'd pulled
the sides of her hair up and back, emphasizing her del-

icate ears and long, graceful neck. She didn't seem to be wearing makeup, except for some gloss on her lips, but the overall look was sleek and polished, as if she could walk into a boardroom or fancy luncheon with panache and confidence.

Or as if she was ready to go out on a date.

"Wow. I—I mean, you look fantastic."

"Why, thank you." Blushing, she smiled and picked up a small handbag from the arm of the sofa. Moving forward, she caught the doorknob with one hand, pulling it closed as she passed through the opening. Jake stood there like a dumb lump while she took out her keys, locked up and dropped the keys back into her purse. His hand found the small of her back again as they walked across the porch and down the steps side by side. He walked her around to the front passenger door of the truck and assisted her as she climbed up into the seat. Suddenly eager to start their evening, he ran around to the driver's side with long, loping steps and hopped in.

She glanced into the back seat and asked, "Where's Frankie?"

Jake lifted a hand to the back of his neck then got busy starting the truck and backing it out. "Uh, Frankie seemed happier staying home with Tyler, and I thought…" Bringing the truck to a stop, he briefly spread his hands. "You have no idea how long it's been since I saw anything but a kid movie."

She looked at him with a completely blank expression, but then she laughed, prompting his own laughter. Relieved, he drove on.

"I can't even remember what movie I saw last," he admitted.

"I can," Kathryn said.

She named the last movie she'd seen in a theater. He tried to place the title, and it finally clicked.

"That was…" Ten years ago. At least. But he didn't say that because he didn't want to risk sounding as shocked as he felt, so he simply went with "a good one."

She smiled. "It was. I can't wait to see how everything's changed. And I think Frankie's well looked after by his aunt and uncles."

"You don't mind the two of us going on our own?" Jake asked.

She shook her head, eyes shining, and that was enough for him. He'd been right to do this. Nothing meaningful could come of it, of course, but at least she could say she'd been on a date. Besides, he really couldn't remember the last time he'd seen a first-run movie, let alone one made for adults. He couldn't think of anything else to say, so he said the obvious.

"You're right about Frankie being in good hands. Wyatt, Tina and Ryder treat Frankie like he's their own."

"Well, he's a great kid."

"Yeah, I know." For some reason, Jake felt compelled to confide in her. "It bothers me, though, that Frankie sometimes doesn't seem to draw much distinction between his dad and his uncles."

"Oh, but he does," Kathryn insisted. "Do you know what he told me when I tucked him in for his nap after lunch the other day?"

Jake shook his head.

"He told me that his dad is a hero. And his mom, too. He is so proud of that. He called his uncle Wyatt a cowboy and said Ryder was strong." She bent her arms at the elbows, her fists in the air, showing him the gesture that Frankie had made. "Then he said, 'My dad's a soldier. He's a hero.' That boy couldn't be more proud of you."

Pleased, Jake chuckled. "I doubt he worded it exactly like that. We're still working on his sentence structure."

"He got close enough. I certainly had no problem understanding him."

Warmth spread through Jake. He supposed all dads worried about their relationships with their kids to a certain extent, but maybe he didn't have to worry about Frankie preferring his uncles to his father. In fact, he was putting that one little concern aside. Permanently.

"Thanks," Jake told Kathryn. Impulsively, he reached across to squeeze her hand. Smiling, she squeezed back, and that small gesture sent excitement rocketing through him, followed swiftly by doubt and alarm.

Oh, Lord, he thought, *what am I doing? And why haven't You stopped me?*

The last thing he wanted to do was get her hopes up and then disappoint her.

Just this one night. Then he'd level with her. He wasn't looking for a wife. He'd been down that road already. Besides, he couldn't afford even a courtship right now. He might not ever be able to, not so long as he stayed here. Those were just the facts of his life, whether he liked them or not.

Kathryn could not believe the size of the theater. Jake couldn't believe how limited their choices were. Only when they stood in front of the box office window did either of them realize that the one upcoming showing of the film they'd both most enjoy was sold out. Jake sheepishly admitted that he hadn't figured on the whole county turning up for a Saturday night movie.

The only other suitable film would not begin for another half hour, so Jake bought their tickets, and they went inside to sit on a bench while they waited. At first, Katherine used the time by looking around, then a poster featuring a soldier coolly striding out of an explosion caught her eye, and she found herself asking Jake how he'd liked being in the military. Soon they were in deep conversation. Talk naturally progressed to his late wife.

"Jolene was something," he said, smiling. "All woman and all soldier. In some ways, she seemed indestructible. I mean, I thought about getting killed while I was away on deployment. You have to. And I even thought about her getting killed, but not really. You know? It just didn't seem possible. Or maybe I just didn't want to think about it."

"I can understand that," Kathryn told him, thinking how different Jolene must have been from her. Irrationally, she hoped that Jake wasn't thinking the same thing.

"Is her death why you and your brothers moved to Loco Man rather than let someone run the ranch for you?"

He shook his head. "It was another tragedy that prompted our move, but that's a long story." He pulled out his phone then and checked the time. His eyes went so wide that Kathryn instinctively looked up at the clock on the wall of the theater lobby. The movie had started nearly thirty-five minutes ago!

Jake jumped to his feet and threw up his hands.

"What do you want to do? Go in late? Try another movie?"

She didn't know what to do. "How bad do you want to see a movie?"

He just looked at her, then he started to laugh. "I don't, really. Other than our original choice, I'm not sure there's anything showing that wouldn't embarrass us with bad language and other junk. These days you can't tell unless it's G-rated, though."

"I'm definitely a G-rated kind of girl," she said, not at all disappointed. It wasn't about the film for her, anyway. It was about… Finally, she faced the facts squarely. It was about spending time with Jake, getting to know Jake, and it always had been.

He reached down to take her by the elbow and help her to her feet. "Let's just go, then. We can, I don't know, grab a couple of milkshakes maybe?"

She could've danced out on air because he hadn't said he'd just take her home, but she made herself nod serenely. "Sounds good."

He drove her to a chain restaurant famous for milkshakes. They sat in a booth, sipping the deliciously indulgent drinks, laughing about their lousy timing and discussing the general state of modern movies.

After a while she said, "You never did explain what brought you and your brothers to our little corner of the world."

He told her about Ryder then, about the freak accident that had killed Ryder's sparring partner. Kathryn was shocked and saddened by the story, but not disturbed. Ryder, in fact, disturbed her the least of all the Smith brothers. He was big and strong, yes, but less grizzly bear than teddy bear, all cute and no bite. Wyatt, on the other hand, as the eldest brother, was definitely the boss at Loco Man Ranch. He'd have intimidated Kathryn terribly if she hadn't witnessed firsthand how caring and indulgent he was with his wife.

"Ryder must've been horrified by what happened," she mused. "He's a gentle giant. I can barely see him as a martial arts enthusiast, let alone a fighter."

"I know. Right?" Jake shook his head, as if still puzzled over how it had happened. "It's not at all like him, but he let himself get talked into competing by a promoter. He didn't want to hurt anyone and was determined to be a skills fighter. He believed that if he honed his skills enough, he'd win on the basis of technique alone. And it worked until that kid, Bryan—he was just barely twenty-one—broke his neck while they were practicing a new move. I can't tell you how deeply it affected Ryder. The press wouldn't leave it alone, even after an investigation proved Ryder had done nothing wrong."

"So you brought him to Oklahoma to get away from all that," Kathryn surmised.

Jake swirled the inch or two left of his milkshake, nodding. "Moving was Wyatt's idea, but it felt like God was pointing us this way when we found out Uncle Dodd had left us the ranch. I considered staying behind in Houston, but for what? Who? We don't have much family left, just some distant cousins and each other. And Frankie loves, needs, his uncles."

"I'm not surprised about Wyatt. As for Frankie, his uncles and you must be all the family he remembers. Of course, now he has Tina and Tyler, as well."

"True. But I'm not sure what you mean about Wyatt."

Kathryn thought about it before carefully answering. "Wyatt's the decisive, authoritative, take-charge type. I'm not surprised he drove the decision to move here. I imagine he can be, well, forceful when it comes to getting his way about something."

Jake chuckled. "He's more reasonable than you seem to think. Granted, he's the big brother to his bones, and he's used to running a business. Several, actually. He took over for our dad, in more ways than one, well before Dad passed on. And it's true that he didn't want me and Frankie to stay behind, but he wouldn't have pressured me on it. Too much."

She laughed at that, repeating his words for emphasis. "Too much."

Jake grinned. Then his gaze shifted to meet hers evenly, and he folded his arms against the tabletop, dropping his voice a notch. "So if Ryder's the gentle giant, and Wyatt's the authority figure, what does that make me?"

The last words she'd said fell out of her mouth again of their own volition. "Too much." Knowing that sounded ridiculous, she dropped her gaze and softly added, "Too much of everything. Handsome, kind, generous, hardworking. Masculine."

For a long moment, she could neither lift her gaze nor breathe. Her heart seemed to have stopped beating. She couldn't believe she'd found the courage to say all that. Then he reached across the table, picked up her hand and pressed it between both of his. Suddenly, she could function again. Looking up, Kathryn found him smiling tenderly.

The waitress chose that moment to drop off their check. Jake sat back, picked up that little slip of paper, glanced at it and looked to Kathryn.

"Guess it's time to go."

Disappointed and at the same time absurdly happy, she nodded, made sure she had her handbag and slid to the edge of her seat as Jake moved to his feet. This time, when Jake reached down, she gave him her hand, thrilled beyond words when he kept it until they reached his truck.

Too much.

Jake continually pondered her words as he drove them back to War Bonnet.

Too handsome. Too kind. Too generous. Too hard-working. Too masculine, whatever that meant.

He didn't think it was bad, any of it. He thought that perhaps he had misread her early on. She didn't dislike him. She liked him *too much*.

For a woman like her, that must be unsettling, and it made this little outing a very bad idea. That being the case, he shouldn't smile about it, but he couldn't help himself, so he tried to focus on just how badly he had fouled up the evening.

"I'm really sorry about the movie."

She sent him a gentle smile. "Don't worry about it. The milkshake was compensation enough. I shudder to think how long it's been since I last had a simple milk-shake. Besides, you were under no obligation to take me to a movie after Frankie dropped out."

Increasingly uncomfortable with that fiction, Jake shifted in his seat and came clean with her. "About that. I never really intended to bring Frankie. I just said that because I didn't want you to think this was…"

"A date?" she finished for him.

He shot her a surprised glance. "Yeah, I guess.

Sounds stupid, I know. But, look, I'm not in a position to get serious about anybody. It's only been a couple years since Jolene. A-and the truth is, the shop is eating my lunch. I've got to get it up and operational before..."

"Before?"

"I don't want you to take this the wrong way, but I have to get the business established before I run out of money."

"And working on my old car is putting a crimp in things."

"No, no, I'm not losing anything but time working on your car, and Ryder is helping me with the construction on the shop to make up for that. But what it if doesn't work out? I think there's enough business in the area to pay the bills, especially if I don't have to borrow to finish the building, but it's not a given. I could wind up supporting the shop instead of the other way around. Frankly, I shouldn't even be spending money on movies, let alone kids' saddles and special bridles, not until I know the shop is going to be at least self-supporting. I—I just shouldn't be dating right now."

"So if you didn't want me to think this was a date, why didn't you bring Frankie?" she asked.

Grimacing, Jake said, "He's a disaster in a movie theater. He talks to the screen at the top of his lungs, and half the time he's on his feet. I just said I was including him because..." He tried to think of the least embarrassing way to say this. "I didn't think you'd go if it was just the two of us."

"And why would you think that?" she drawled wryly. "Just because I locked myself in the car when you stopped to help me? Or was it how long it took me to look you in the eye?"

Jake realized with a shock that she was teasing, but that she was also well aware of how her behavior must have come across. He had to smile. At both of them.

"Let's just say it's been a long time since I asked a woman to go to a movie with me. Or anywhere else."

She laughed softly and admitted, "I probably wouldn't have."

Jake shot a glance at her and caught her self-deprecating grimace.

"Go to a movie with you, I mean. Or anywhere else. Your fiction about including Frankie allowed me to make peace with my desire to go by telling myself that it was work related. I think I always knew you hadn't originally intended to include him, but I did expect you to bring him along after you added him to the equation."

Surprised again, but also pleased, Jake asked, "Then why did you come with me after I showed up without him?"

Again, she gave him that wry smile and tone. "Because sitting at home alone isn't nearly as much fun as I pretend it is."

A bark of laughter burst out of him. She laughed, too. Within moments, they'd settled into a comfortable silence.

Then abruptly she said, "I take it this is your first date since your wife died."

He blinked at that, his smile fading. "You know, you're right. I've met a few women, called them up on the phone, chatted with them, even flirted a little. I just didn't…" He looked at her, realizing what the problem had been. "I just wasn't ready. I'm not real sure I am now either. Or that I ever will be."

"So I guess it was a first for both of us," she said softly, ducking her chin. "And the last."

The sound of disappointment in her voice cut Jake to the quick. He wished he'd made a real date of it, an actual invitation, dinner and a movie, maybe even flowers. At the very least, he should have put some serious thought into the event, especially if it was to be the only one. And it ought to be. He had no right to usurp any woman's time and emotions until he knew they had a chance for something more.

The silence grew increasingly thick, not strained exactly but rife with…awareness. Thankfully, they reached her house before the atmosphere became unbearable.

"I'll get your door," he announced, bailing out on his side. It was the gentlemanly thing to do, after all. She waited while he rushed around to open the door for her. He backed up, giving her room to get out. As he followed her up onto the porch, properly seeing her right to her door, he kept that distance, his nerves jittering beneath his skin.

Without a word, she took her keys out and unlocked the door. Then she turned to him, smiled and said, "Can I ask you something else?"

"Sure."

"If, as you say, you're not in a position to be dating, why did you take me out?"

He did not know how to answer that. If he gave her the same excuses he'd been giving himself, it would sound like pity, and he couldn't let her think that. For one thing, it wasn't true. Maybe she hadn't dated, but Kathryn had made a life for herself all on her own. She had a kind of strength he'd never before encountered, and he was only just realizing it.

He stood there, staring at her, his tongue glued to the roof of his mouth, and wrestled with what he knew to be true. He'd asked her out because he'd wanted to be the first man ever to do so and because she needed to know that she was lovely, completely worthy.

When she mumbled a farewell and started to turn away, he couldn't let her. She deserved more than that, better than that. His hand at her waist, he turned her back to him. She looked up with those big, deep green eyes, and he knew what had to happen next.

Shifting closer, he brought his other hand to the center of her back, between her shoulder blades, but he didn't pull her against him as he wanted to do. Instead, he simply bent his head and kissed her. She closed the small distance between them, leaning forward until she met his chest, her arms at her sides. Thrilled, he tightened his embrace incrementally until she lifted her arms and slid them about his neck.

It was the sweetest kiss ever, as tender and pure as his very first. He'd been about thirteen and so nervous he'd shaken like a leaf in a gale. That girl's face had long ago faded from his memory, but he did recall that there had been about a foot between them and they'd both blushed furiously afterward. Still, that first kiss had been one of his sweetest, most sentimental memories. It paled in comparison to this.

Everything will pale in comparison after this.

That thought jolted him, breaking the kiss and shoving him back several inches. Kathryn looked as stunned as he felt, her eyes wide, fingertips hovering tremulously over her lips. Before he could even blink, she bolted, disappearing into her house. He stood for several moments staring at the wreath on her door before he realized that the evening was at an end and he should go. Still, more seconds ticked away before he could make himself draw breath, turn and walk back to his truck.

Frowning, he told himself that he'd just done the most stupid thing he'd ever managed in his entire life, but he couldn't seem to stop the pleasure that filled him. All the way home, he vividly relived every instant of that kiss. She'd bolted afterward, yes. As shy, skittish and careful as Kathryn was, he had expected no less, but before that, she'd kissed him back. She had kissed him as much as he had kissed her.

And his head was still spinning because of it.

Chapter Nine

Looking at her reflection in the mirror the next morning, Kathryn wished once again that she had not agreed to attend church with the Smith family.

The kiss had kept her awake all night. As a girl, she'd dreamed and dreamed of her first kiss, but she'd never come close to imagining the sensations or emotions that Jake's kiss had evoked in her. She'd felt cherished and beautiful, as if she'd been made for that exact moment, that one man. To him it had undoubtedly been nothing more than a good-night gesture. To her, it was nothing less than a wonder.

Now, in the light of day, she didn't know how she was going to face him. He'd been frank about the fact that they had no future, but that didn't keep her from wishing it could be otherwise. Would he be able to read her foolish sentiment in her eyes? After all, he was a mature, experienced man. He'd been married, for pity's sake. A spinster's first kiss couldn't mean to him what it meant to her. Even if he didn't see how she felt, Tina surely would.

She and Tina had quickly become good friends. Kathryn was glad for that, but she worried Tina would take one look at her now and *know*. Not that she had anything to be ashamed of. A woman her age could reasonably be expected to have been kissed.

But no woman could be expected to have had a first kiss like *that*.

Oh, how she wished she hadn't agreed to attend church with the Smiths this morning.

She thought briefly of feigning illness, but she didn't want to lie, so she was ready and waiting at the appointed time. To her relief—and disappointment— it wasn't Jake at her door. Instead, Tina, smiling and lovely in a summery print dress, looked approvingly at Kathryn's, the same one she'd worn last night with Jake. She hadn't had time to refashion anything else, but she was already planning her next project, if only to have something different to wear to church in the future.

When she got to the SUV, Kathryn found that the boys occupied the third-row seat. With Tina and Wyatt in the front, that left the second row for Kathryn alone. Frankie greeted her enthusiastically.

"KKay pretty!"

She smiled at him. "Thank you." She hoped his father would be of the same opinion, instead of wondering why she'd chosen this particular dress again. Then she silently scolded herself for even thinking about Jake. He'd made it clear that he wasn't interested in romance at this point in his life. She couldn't let herself think of anything more than friendship with Jake. And she dared not allow thoughts of *the kiss* to enter her mind.

That proved even more difficult than expected when they arrived at the church. Jake and Ryder stood outside, waiting for them. Wyatt stopped the SUV right in front of them. Ryder opened Tina's door while Jake did the same for Kathryn. He smiled impersonally as she exited the vehicle, then he ducked inside to free Frankie from his safety seat and pull him out of the automobile. Tyler managed for himself, and Jake moved back to allow Ryder to shepherd the boy toward the church. Tina followed, while Wyatt parked the vehicle.

Kathryn couldn't keep her gaze off Jake. He looked impossibly handsome in his dark jeans, white shirt and tan suit jacket, a brown tie knotted at his throat. He wore a cowboy hat as if born to wear it, and every time she looked at him, she remembered *the kiss*.

With those memories came awkwardness, but she didn't know what to do about it. Running away was not an option this time. Thankfully, no sooner did Jake set Frankie's feet on the ground than Frankie grabbed her hand, drawing her attention away from his father.

"KKay come to me," he said, tugging her toward the church.

Jake strode after them, speaking to Frankie. "Come *with* me. Kathryn doesn't need to see your classroom, though."

"I don't mind," Kathryn countered quickly.

Without another word, Jake followed her and Frankie into the church foyer, Ryder and Tyler holding the door for them. Frankie tugged Kathryn down a hallway flanking the sanctuary. Behind her, she heard Jake say, "I'll take Tyler. Y'all save us seats."

They reached Tyler's classroom first. He went in with a quick parting wave. Frankie's room was tucked into a corner near the nursery suite, and he insisted on showing Kathryn every corner of the colorful space. She made the appropriate noises of approval and appreciation, until Jake impatiently swept her out of there and back the way they'd come, his hat in his hand. Music was playing by the time they slipped into the end of the pew next to Wyatt and Tina. That didn't stop Wyatt from leaning forward, looking past Kathryn and speaking to Jake.

"So where did you get off to last night? You ran out before I could ask this morning."

Tina jabbed Wyatt with her elbow. At the same time, Jake shushed him, a finger lifted to his lips. In that moment, Kathryn realized that the family knew nothing of the evening she'd spent with Jake. Tina might—probably did—suspect, but she couldn't know for sure. Kathryn had told Tina that the dress she was working on was for Sunday, and it was. However, it was also for the movie, which Kathryn hadn't mentioned for fear Tina would assume a context that didn't exist.

Beside her, Jake fixed his attention on the front of the sanctuary and kept it there, which allowed her to focus somewhat on the service. To her surprise, the music, message and familiar rituals calmed and comforted her. She knew that Jake would not be asking her out again, and her disappointment was keen, but she couldn't be angry or resentful with the one man who had taken her out on a date.

Jake Smith had unknowingly brought change to her life, change for the better. She had a job she enjoyed, good friends and more financial security than she'd known in a long while. Plus, her car would soon be running again.

And she'd been on a date, or as close to one as she was likely to get.

She would be forever grateful.

After the service, Tina hurried off to collect the boys while everyone else stood around the crowded foyer and chatted. The Billings family joined them, patriarch Wes with his bride, Alice, on his arm, along with Rex and his wife, Callie, and Meri and her husband, the veterinarian Stark Burns. Kathryn knew Alice best of all. The only time Mia had ever left their house after her accident was by ambulance or to visit the office of Dr. Alice Shorter, now Billings. Those visits had proved so arduous that Kathryn had been discouraged from attempting any other outings, but upon occasion, Kathryn herself had used the services of Dr. Alice.

"It's so good to see you, Kathryn," the doctor said warmly, "and in such good company."

Kathryn smiled and nodded, desperately trying not to be aware of Jake at her side. It was enough that she didn't feel out of place, out of her depth. The sense of belonging, of being part of group, was a novel sensation for her, but she knew very well that she wasn't part of a *couple*. Even if Jake hadn't leveled with her, his cool, casual demeanor would have told her that their one date would not be repeated. Even as they left the building and Jake's brothers teased him about his "mysterious disappearance" the night before, Jake remained calm and impassive.

"You know, what I do is none of your business," he replied easily to their prods.

Kathryn was glad for his circumspection. Had his behavior or tone implied any intimacy between them, she would have been hard-pressed to maintain her composure.

Finally, Wyatt announced that everyone should "load up." The whole family trooped out into the parking lot. While Jake crawled into the back of Tina's SUV to buckle Frankie and Tyler into their safety seats, Kathryn waited outside, Tina next to her, chatting about the service. Just as Jake stepped down onto the ground and straightened, Tina placed a hand on Kathryn's arm and asked easily, "Joining us for Sunday dinner?"

Jake stiffened, prompting Kathryn to refuse. "Oh, no, thank you. I have a lot to do."

Flashing her another impersonal smile, Jake moved off toward Ryder. "See you in the morning then."

Both relieved and disheartened, Kathryn got into the SUV and buckled up. She told herself that she'd gotten through her first meeting with Jake and his family after *the kiss* and her secret was safe. No one ever needed to know that she'd developed a killer crush on Jake, not that anything could come of it. He'd made that very plain.

After carefully thinking over all he'd said and done, she had concluded that she'd been a safe first date for him after his wife's death, a way to test his readiness to begin again. No doubt he had asked her out precisely because she could have no expectations where he was concerned. He'd been up-front about it. Besides, a man like Jake could spend time with any woman he wanted. He certainly didn't need a plain gal like her. It was enough that her first kiss had been the stuff of legends. Even if it proved to be her only kiss, she would treasure the memory always.

After Sunday and the way that kiss had affected him, along with his tendency to act on impulse with her, Jake decided that keeping his distance would be best for both of them. It spared him temptation and her the idea that he was ready for more in a relationship than he was. He still didn't understand what drew him to her, given how different she was from Jolene, but it didn't matter. He was in no position to pursue any woman now, and if the garage wasn't a success, he might never be.

As the oven that was August cooled into the slightly more tolerable temperatures of September, school started. Jake asked Ryder to take over driving Kathryn back and forth to the ranch, telling everyone who would listen that he was too busy to drive her himself. Kathryn hadn't turned a hair. She privately accepted a check from him every Friday with downcast eyes and a silent nod of thanks. During meals, she remained quiet and subdued, saving her smiles and conversation for Tina and Frankie, who missed Tyler dreadfully during the day. Jake told himself that Kathryn was fine.

They were both fine, even if he felt hollow inside.

As September moved along without any rain, Jake's composure felt as dry and fissured as the landscape, and his brutal work schedule—mornings and evenings on the shop, afternoons on Kathryn's car—wasn't helping. Kathryn's car was slow going, mostly because he was determined to spare her every penny he could, and that meant searching out the cheapest parts and sometimes opting for used ones, which often required reconditioning.

By the second Monday of the month, he felt ready to shatter. After a couple hours of cleaning an old part, he was ready to install it, but then he realized he'd mislaid his work gloves. Those gloves gave him a sure grip and helped prevent busted knuckles. He'd taken his extras to the shop site so he didn't have to manage those concrete blocks with bare hands. He went to his truck to see if he'd left his new gloves, or even an old pair, in there. All he found was a pair of heavy, mangled cotton gloves. Making a mental note to buy a few extra pairs of leather ones to stash around the place, he paused to think where his good leather gloves might have gotten to. Suddenly, he had a clear memory of leaving them atop his dresser.

Despite the need to avoid Kathryn, Jake quietly entered the house and climbed the stairs. Neither Kathryn nor Tina was anywhere in sight. He went first to Frankie's room. His son napped peacefully beneath the ceiling fan in his bedroom. Jake tiptoed to his own room and found the gloves exactly where he remembered leaving them the night before. Congratulating himself on accomplishing his task without inadvertently walking into the lion's den of Kathryn Stepp's gentle presence, Jake slipped downstairs and headed for the back door, only to freeze when he heard Tina's voice coming from the master bedroom.

"So he did kiss you."

"All right, he kissed me," Kathryn confirmed softly.

Jake had no doubt about which *he* the two women were speaking. He told himself not to listen, that eavesdropping was wrong and dangerous, that nothing good could come of overhearing their conversation. Like so many other times, he ignored his own best advice where Kathryn Stepp was concerned.

"I knew it!" Tina crowed. "And?"

"And what? It meant nothing."

"Oh, please," Tina scoffed. "I know these Smith brothers. Everything means something to them."

"Not in this case."

"What was it like?" Tina asked.

For several seconds, Kathryn said nothing, then she spoke again. "Unique."

Jake frowned. *Unique?* His kiss was unique? What

did that mean? He folded his arms and leaned his head forward slightly in the hope of hearing better.

"That's it?" Tina prodded.

"I don't know what to tell you. I have nothing to compare it with."

Jake pressed back against the wall, imagining Tina's shock.

"You're telling me that you can't compare Jake's kiss to any other because you've never had any other?" Tina demanded.

"Jake was my first date. If you can even call it a date."

"What do you mean?" Tina sounded indignant, almost angry. "A date is a date."

Jake waited for Kathryn to reveal that he had tricked her into going out with him. Instead, she said, "We meant to go to a movie, but we wound up just having milkshakes."

"Milkshakes!" Tina squawked. "What is this, 1950? Were you wearing bobby socks and a poodle skirt?"

Jake squeezed his eyes closed in a grimace. Tina was right. He hadn't even given the woman a proper first date. Hearing Kathryn's laughter didn't ease his mortification one bit.

"No, I was wearing a very nice dress. You saw it. The blue one."

"He took you for milkshakes in *that*?" Tina demanded. "What is wrong with him?"

Jake rather wanted to know that himself.

"It didn't mean anything," Kathryn said again, her voice breathy and hushed. "I think I was a safe choice for his first date since the death of his wife. That's all."

A safe choice? It was all Jake could do not to snort in derision.

"What a dope!" Tina exclaimed.

Kathryn ignored that, asking, "Where did Wyatt take you on your first date?" Jake got the feeling the answer was important to her.

Tina stammered for a moment. "It—it was…well, w-we…come to think of it, we didn't actually date at all, not in the strictest sense of the word."

"But you've both dated others, right? So you both knew exactly what you were looking for."

"I dated quite a bit when I was younger, and of course, I was married before," Tina told her. "And Wyatt, well, just look at him. I'm sure he dated lots of women before he met me, but no one ever knows exactly what or who they're looking for, not that either of us was particularly looking for anyone. I, in fact, was definitely not looking."

"But you must have known what you didn't want, at least," Kathryn pressed.

"Absolutely. I didn't want anyone like my ex. I guess, now that I think about it, I wanted someone like my stepdad."

"Dodd Smith."

"That's right."

Kathryn seemed to consider that before slowly saying, "I don't want anyone like my father. Beyond that…"

"Have you even known anyone else to compare your father to?" Tina asked.

"Beside the Smith brothers? Not really. Well, a little. Teachers and people like that."

"But you haven't been in school in years," Tina pointed out.

"It has been a long time," Kathryn agreed, "and I was awfully shy back then. I didn't know anyone well."

"Back then?" Tina chuckled. "And now?"

"Now I know you," Kathryn pointed out, and Jake could hear the smile in her voice.

"And I know you," Tina responded warmly. From the sound of it, they were hugging.

Jake hurried away before they discovered him. Tina was correct that Kathryn deserved much better than Jake had given her, but he didn't dare try to offer her anything more. If he took her out again, let alone kissed her again, she'd expect more than he could give her. It wouldn't be fair, to either of them.

Sick at heart, Jake went back to the barn, but he couldn't concentrate on the work. He recalled how she'd looked this past Sunday in a simple gray knit dress with hardly any sleeves. The knit had hugged her curves lovingly, its gently bowed neckline resting just below her pretty collarbone. He hadn't been able to take his eyes off her. Memories of his "unique" kiss had kept him awake that night. It wasn't the first time.

Suddenly, he felt as if he were drowning. The lingering heat, the frustratingly slow process of building the shop while working on Kathryn's old car, the uncertainty of his financial future and this nameless ache inside of him poured out in a flood of frustration. He had to get away, if only for an hour or two.

Resolved, Jake returned to the house, glanced casually at Kathryn and Tina, who were preparing the evening meal, and reached for his hat.

"Sorry, ladies, I won't be home for dinner. Tell Frankie I'll see him soon as I get back."

"If you're going into Ardmore—" Tina began sharply, parking her hands at her waist.

"Not this time," Jake interrupted apologetically. "There's a guy with a bunch of junked cars in a gully on his place. I'm going to see what I can find there. I'll make a run to Ardmore for you later, though."

"Don't bother." Tina looked at Kathryn. "Want to take a drive into Ardmore tomorrow?"

Kathryn bowed her head, her lips clamped firmly between her teeth, but then she nodded. Tina waved a hand at Jake, dismissing him. Clearly he had sunk in his sister-in-law's esteem. He couldn't blame her. He wasn't thinking too highly of himself just then.

Jamming his hat onto his head, he went out the door. A couple hours later, he had removed several small parts from the rusting jumble on a property east of town. It was almost dinnertime, and he needed to get something into his stomach. He drove into War Bonnet and walked into the diner, where he took a seat on a stool at the counter.

A vaguely familiar-looking man soon claimed the stool next to him. He smiled at Jake and said, "You're just the fellow I've been wanting to see."

Jake didn't place the guy until he removed his hat and laid it, crown down, next to his elbow. "It's Goodell, isn't it? With the Cattlemen's Association."

"That's right. Clark Goodell. And you're one of the Smith brothers."

"Jake."

The two shook hands. The waitress dropped off glasses of water, slung menus at them and said she'd be back. Jake opened the small bill of fare, but Goodell didn't reach for his menu, his gaze fixed on Jake.

"I hear that KKay Stepp is working for your outfit now."

Shocked, Jake frowned at the other man. "Yeah, so?"

"I'm just wondering…is she seeing anybody?"

Ice water suddenly poured through Jake's veins. "And what concern is that of yours?"

"Look," Goodell said with a slight smile, "Kathryn is highly thought of around here."

"Not surprised by that," Jake growled.

"She was completely devoted to her mother," Goodell went on, "but I'm told that she was seen recently at the movie theater in the company of a man."

"And that would be your business how?"

Clark Goodell looked away. "We went to school together."

"Okay. And?"

Goodell fixed him with an implacable gaze. "And I want to know if you or one of your brothers has a claim on her."

It took every ounce of Jake's willpower to keep his fists tucked beneath the counter. "My oldest brother is married."

"So that leaves him out," Goodell prodded. "What about you and the other one?"

Jake took a long drink of water. Looked like the joke was on him. The men around here weren't blind and stupid, after all. For Kathryn's sake, he was glad of it, but knowing that her options were about to explode crushed him in a way he hadn't expected.

"She's not seeing anyone," Jake made himself say before draining his water glass. With that, he got up and walked out of there.

His appetite had vanished, and he was starting to feel sick to his stomach.

He had the feeling that would get worse before it got better.

Chapter Ten

Exhaustion pulled at Kathryn as she dropped down onto the sofa in her living room the next evening. After their trek to Ardmore that morning, Frankie had run rampant all afternoon. Kathryn had done her best to distract and entertain him, but Tina had finally reached the end of her tether and sent him to his room. He hadn't even taken a nap. He'd just lain in his bed babbling some fiction about horses, dogs and talking cars. Dinner had been a tense affair, with Tyler whining about homework, Frankie pouting, Wyatt distracted with the beginning of construction of the carport and Jake silent and brooding throughout.

Kathryn was starting to think Jake resented her presence. In fact, she'd begun to wonder if she could continue as an employee at Loco Man Ranch. In answer to a pointed question from Wyatt, Jake had estimated that her car would be ready within another week or so. Kathryn had told herself that it might be best if she went back to the home care agency as soon as her car was drivable. Then she'd come home just now to find a letter from her father in her mailbox.

He warned her that he had consulted an attorney. Though declaring that he didn't want to force her hand, he revealed that he'd had the house evaluated by a Realtor. All he was asking was that she put the house on the market—as if that wouldn't destroy her world. Her plan to offer him monthly payments to buy out his interest in the house would be completely unworkable if she went back to the home care agency. What was she going to do? Work two jobs, perhaps? If she could find two jobs around here.

She needed to work up some numbers, but before she could do that, a knock sounded on her door. Her heart in her throat, she jumped to her feet.

Had her father come in person to demand that she accede to his wishes? His mail had come postmarked from Tahlequah, but that was only a little over four hours away. With the second knock, Kathryn lurched toward the sound.

Seeing a cowboy hat through the high, narrow window in the door, she threw the bolt and yanked the door open, only to find herself staring at a stranger. Of average height, with a blocky build and dressed in the standard cowboy fare of boots, jeans, button-up shirt and hat, he smiled at her, displaying dimples. He swept off the hat, revealing short, sandy hair atop a squarish face with twinkling blue eyes.

"Hello, Kathryn."

Something clawed at the back of her mind, a memory long abandoned. With it came a name—and complete shock. Only the dimples and the blue eyes remained of the classmate she'd once known.

"Clark Goodell!"

The dimples deepened. "The same. How you doing? It's good to see you. You look great, by the way."

Her hand went instinctively to her hair, the top part of which she had pulled back in a short, thick ponytail. She had decided to grow it out again and was trying her hand at various styles in the meantime. "I do? I—I mean, I just got home from work, so…"

He leaned a forearm against the doorframe. "Loco Man Ranch, right?"

"Yes."

"How's that going?"

She shrugged. "I cook and clean, help with the kids, do some decorating. I like it."

"Glad to know it. I also hear you're getting out and about."

"Oh. Uh. Yeah, I guess."

"I know you've been seeing someone," he said softly.

"What?"

"Weren't you at the movie theater in Ardmore with someone a while ago?"

Kathryn's jaw dropped. "Oh. That." She didn't know how to explain her outing with Jake, so she retreated into silence.

"I was just wondering if it's exclusive," Clark said smoothly. "Jake Smith didn't seem to think so, but he looked kind of stumped when I brought it up."

Kathryn's heart thumped. "You spoke to Jake about me?"

Clark had the grace to appear abashed. "I figured if you were seeing someone it was probably one of the Smith brothers."

Her chest ached so deeply that she could barely

breathe. "No," she whispered. "I'm not seeing anyone exclusively."

"I'd like to ask you out for dinner, then," Clark said, smiling.

Kathryn blinked, beyond speechless.

"You were always so sweet and shy," he went on. "I can see that hasn't changed. So, dinner? Would Friday work for you?"

For some reason, she wanted to cry, but that would be foolish. Clark had only confirmed that Jake wouldn't be asking her out again. She had tried not to let Jake's rejection hurt, but it did. She knew herself well enough to know that if she retreated now, she'd spend the rest of her life grieving what could never have been. Lifting her chin, she pasted on a smile.

"Friday will be fine."

Clark hung around for several more minutes, setting the time and place for their dinner together. He gave her a card with his phone number on it. Kathryn saw that he worked for the local cattlemen's association. He was probably a friend of Jake's. Her disappointment escalated. How many ways did Jake have to tell her that he lacked interest in her? She supposed it would be the same with Clark. He'd discover how dull and unexciting she was, and that would be that. Still, she couldn't find the strength to take back her acceptance of his invitation. She had never learned how to be that rude.

Over the next two days, she hastily made over another outfit and resigned herself to an uncomfortable evening in the company of Clark Goodell. Clark had always been a polite, well behaved boy in school, with a strong desire to attend Oklahoma State University. She hadn't even realized he'd returned to War Bonnet after college, but then she hadn't thought about it one way or another. And now she was going to dinner with him. Belatedly, she realized she should've made the date for Saturday rather than Friday. Had she done so, she wouldn't have had to explain to Tina why she needed to leave early, and Tina wouldn't have announced the same at lunch on Friday.

"Kathryn has to get ready for a dinner date, so we'll be eating frozen pizza tonight."

The boys cheered. Tina fixed them with a stern look, adding, "And salad that Kathryn will prepare before she leaves."

Frankie sighed. Tyler said "Yum," but the curl of his nose revealed his true feelings.

Kathryn couldn't help smiling. These boys were a constant source of joy to her. She would miss them. The thought brought her up short, but she knew then that she would leave Loco Man and everyone on it. For her own peace of mind, she must. From now on, she would concentrate on saving her home, as she'd done before she'd met Jake Smith.

"Kathryn will need to leave earlier than usual," Tina said.

Everyone instantly looked to Jake. Ryder was texturing the walls in the bunkhouse, as the smears of white on his clothing attested, and Wyatt had scheduled a teleconference with a tax consultant. Tina would be busy with the kids and the evening meal. Jake, after all, was the logical choice to drive Kathryn home. He was working on her car. It was only right that work for her be delayed for her convenience. Yet Jake said nothing until he finished his meal and rose to leave the table.

"Back to work," he muttered, striding for the door, as if he hadn't heard a word Tina had said.

Kathryn's face flushed, the breath catching in her lungs.

Ryder gave her a sweet smile. "I'll be happy to knock off early enough to get you home in time for your date."

"Thank you," she managed, but she couldn't look anyone there in the face. Rising from the table, her appetite gone, she began cleaning the kitchen.

Behind her, Tina said, "I have a better idea. Kathryn, why don't you drive my old car? I got it registered and tagged recently."

Kathryn paused. "But that's Ryder's transportation, isn't it?"

"Oh, I don't mind," he told her. "There's plenty of transportation around here."

"It's settled then," Tina decreed. "You'll drive the sedan until your car's ready."

Tears burned the backs of Kathryn's eyes. Yes, she must leave this job as soon possible. She told herself that she would miss Tina most of all, but she knew that wasn't so. It was Jake—just the loss of the dream of Jake—that would inflict the deepest cut.

She managed to get through the rest of the day and drive home in Tina's little sedan. It had been weeks since she'd last driven a vehicle, and Tina's car was a definite step up from her small, bare-bones coupe. She told herself how pleased she was to have some measure of independence returned to her, but she was no good at lying to herself. As she dressed and prepared for the coming evening, she tried not to think of anyone or anything except what she was doing at that very moment.

Clark arrived right on time, and she found herself in

yet another pickup truck. He drove her to Healdton for catfish—excellent catfish, as it turned out. Clark was an entertaining conversationalist and a gentleman. He put her at ease early on, and that didn't change even when he confessed that he'd had a crush on her in high school and was sorry when she'd dropped out.

It was a surprisingly pleasant evening, and after he drove her home, he kissed her good-night standing on the porch of her house, just as Jake had done. Except it wasn't the same at all. Clark promised to call her and left her smiling, despite the depression that had settled over her. She'd expected to be relieved at the end of the evening. Instead, she wanted to cry. She finally had a social life, and Clark was a very nice man. Still, she hoped he wouldn't ask her out again, at least not for a while.

To Kathryn's surprise and puzzlement, she had two more invitations that weekend, both by telephone and both of which she turned down. It was easier to refuse when the invitation came by phone. One of the men was younger than she was and complained about the dearth of women his age around War Bonnet. The other was several years older and the divorced father of three. She was flattered at the sudden interest, but dating now seemed like a lot of bother for no good reason. Maybe later, when she was over Jake, she'd feel differently.

She'd never been able to talk to anyone else the way she could talk to Jake. Even with Tina, she felt foolish and inadequate at least part of the time. With Jake, she hadn't just been at ease, she'd been herself. Her true self. Obviously, her true self hadn't been engaging enough to hold his interest. She should just accept that. She would accept that.

Clark was waiting for her when she arrived at church on Sunday. She'd considered not going, but when she'd refused Tina's offer to pick her up, Tina had laughed and hugged her.

"What am I thinking? You can drive yourself. We'll meet you there."

Kathryn hadn't known how to tell Tina that she didn't want to be anywhere Jake might be, but with him ignoring her like she didn't exist, it didn't make much difference, anyway. When she saw Clark, she almost turned around and left again, but then he smiled and hurried toward her.

"Thought we might sit together."

At least she wouldn't have to sit next to Jake while he looked at everything and everyone but her. Kathryn smiled at Clark. "I'd like that."

They took a seat several rows ahead of the Smiths and on the other side of the aisle. After the service, Clark offered to drive her home.

"Oh, I drove myself," she said apologetically.

Just then, Frankie ran up and threw his arms around her. "KKay! We fishin' today!" Frankie reported. "You come."

"It sounds like fun," Kathryn began.

Before she could say more, Clark kissed her on the cheek and said, "I'll call you."

She nodded, and he went on his way. Focusing entirely on Frankie, she refused to so much as glance in Jake's direction. "I'm afraid I can't go fishing with you today. I have things to do at home."

Frankie dropped his head, but then he snagged Kathryn's hand and towed her toward the door in Tina and Wyatt's wake. She was aware of Jake trailing along behind them, but neither acknowledged the other. When they reached Tina's SUV, Frankie urged her to get in.

"Sweetie, I'm not riding with you today. I drove myself here, and I'll have to drive myself home."

"Come on, son," Jake said, sweeping around Kathryn to pick up the boy. "I'll belt you into your seat."

"No!" Frankie bawled, shoving at Jake's hands. "KKay do it!" Jake made an exasperated sound and plopped the boy into his safety seat. "KKay do it!"

Jake backed out of the vehicle and walked away without another word. Kathryn had helped Tina buckle in the boys the previous week, so she had little difficulty getting the restraint system in place. Again, Tina invited her to Sunday dinner, but again Kathryn declined. It had become something of a ritual.

"I'm sure you've had enough of me for one week."

"Are you sure it's not the other way around?" Tina asked softly, frowning.

Kathryn couldn't let Tina think that. "Not at all. You're like family to me now."

"And even family needs some personal time," Tina remarked, smiling.

Kathryn nodded, but home had never felt quite so empty as it did that hot Sunday afternoon in mid-September.

Jake didn't like to work on Sundays, but he couldn't seem to relax that afternoon. Watching Kathryn with Clark Goodell had told him that her date with the local cowboy had gone well. They seemed at ease together, and Kathryn had never looked finer. Jake suspected that Tina either knew the details of the situation or soon would, but he didn't dare ask. He told himself that it didn't matter, that it was all for good, but something more than curiosity gnawed at him. He tried to think of Jolene, to call up the old grief and feelings of loyalty. That didn't help. Memories of Jolene left him with a sense of gratitude and melancholy but did nothing to blot out the vision of Kathryn sitting beside Clark in church.

Desperate for distraction, Jake went over every detail of his business plan. He looked at his estimates and adjusted the numbers to reflect the additional outlay of Kathryn's salary. That reminded him that he still hadn't informed the rest of the family of her raise in pay. Today he wondered why he bothered to keep it a secret.

At first, he'd feared that the extra pay would betray his interest in Kathryn, but now that she was dating Clark Goodell, that was no longer an issue. No one could say that Goodell let moss grow under his feet. He must have beat a path straight from the diner to Kathryn's door. And she obviously hadn't turned him away.

Suddenly, Jake wanted to throttle someone, but the only villain in this piece was him. He'd tricked her into going out with him, then told her in no uncertain terms that he wouldn't be dating her or anyone else again any time soon. And then he'd kissed her. He'd tried to convince himself that they could be friends without expectations of more in the future, but that friend stuff would only work if he could maintain a safe distance, and after that kiss he wasn't at all sure he could. God knew he'd tried, but the best he could do was to skulk around her wishing it could be different and feeling like a ghost.

He tried to imagine some way to make it work, but what if the garage failed? If the garage failed, he and Frankie would wind up back in Houston, or they'd have to move to some other big city where he was sure to find work. How could he ask that of Kathryn, knowing how difficult she found it to meet strangers and make friends?

Good grief, he was thinking of marriage. The very idea shocked him, but what other option did he have with a woman like Kathryn? She deserved marriage and would remain alone for the rest of her life before she'd settle for anything less. He didn't want her to live her life alone, so he had to accept that she'd wind up with another man, probably sooner rather than later. She was entitled to every happiness, and he wanted that for her. Still, he couldn't seem to keep a civil tongue in his head when he saw Kathryn on Monday.

She served up a massive submarine sandwich for lunch. He took one bite and complained, "Did we run out of mustard? This is as bland as cardboard."

Kathryn silently set the mustard jar in front of him. He proceeded to drown his portion of the sandwich in the tart yellow stuff, then he had to choke it down with everyone glaring at him. Later, when Ryder asked to borrow Jake's truck, Jake started digging out the keys and grumbling.

"Man, I'll be glad when that stupid car is finally running so we can get back to something like normal." He tossed the keys onto the table.

Stiffly, Kathryn turned from the sink and walked over to the peg where she'd hung her bag that morning, saying, "That's not necessary." She pulled out the keys to Tina's little sedan and carried them to Ryder. "It's your car," she said. "I only need it for twenty minutes a day, and even driving it for that long makes me uneasy."

Ryder glowered at Jake then took the keys from

Kathryn. "Thanks, Kathryn. I'll return the keys to you later, or drive you home, whichever you prefer."

Nodding, she smiled wanly and went back to the sink.

Ryder sent Jake another hard look, shaming him to the point that he called her that night and apologized.

"It's all right, Jake," she said in that soft, shy voice that made him want to reach through the phone and wrap his arms around her. "You're under a lot of pressure." Then she changed the subject. "Tina and I have been talking about taking Frankie to the lake to swim. I don't know how much help I'd be, though. I never learned to swim myself."

"You never learned to swim?" Jake yelped. "Well, you must. Everyone needs to know how to swim." He opened his mouth to say he'd teach her, only to remember at the last moment that he was keeping his distance. And Clark Goodell was not. "Maybe Clark will teach you," he heard himself say, then he wanted to bite off his tongue. She said nothing to that, so after a moment of sheer agony, he asked, "How's that going, by the way?"

"I don't know what you mean."

"I saw you sitting with Clark Goodell in church on Sunday."

"Oh. That went just fine."

She wasn't willingly going to give him anything more. He should have expected that, given how introverted, cautious and closed off she could be.

"How about your dinner date? That go okay, too?" He had to ask.

She was slow to answer. "It was very good. If you like fried catfish."

"I love fried catfish." And yet he hadn't been the

one to take her to dinner. "Apparently not as much as old Clark, though."

"How did you know Clark was the one to take me to dinner?"

Stunned that it might have been someone else, Jake stuttered. "I—I j-just assumed. You had a dinner date on Friday and you were sitting with him in church on Sunday. Seems logical the two are connected."

"I know he spoke with you," she said.

Jake closed his eyes. He could've warned off Goodell, could've staked his own claim, but that wouldn't have been fair. To anyone. "Yeah, Goodell spoke to me at the diner."

"The diner? You discussed me at the diner?" Her voice shook. "That's gossip central. And what else did you discuss at the diner, Jake? My father the drunk who can't keep a job? How my mother had to drive to Duncan and back every day for work to support us? That she crashed her car one rainy night and would need constant care from that point on? Maybe how he walked out on us."

"It wasn't like that," Jake said, grimacing at the thought of all she'd been through. Her family must have been the subject of much gossip at one time, and a shy woman like Kathryn would find being the talk of the town mortifying.

"Oh, of course. That's old news," she retorted. "Maybe this time you heard that he's threatening to sue me for *his* half of *my* house!"

Good grief. No wonder she had despaired when her car had broken down. After all he'd done, her father had some nerve trying to get money out of her for her house. She must be worried sick about that.

"No," Jake told her quietly. "I didn't hear any of that. Clark only wanted to know if you were seeing someone. Apparently, whoever saw us at the movie theater recognized you but not me. I knew by the way Clark reacted that he would be calling you, then when I saw you sitting with him in church yesterday…"

"You naturally assumed it was Clark who took me to dinner on Friday night."

Jake forced a light, congratulatory tone to his voice. "Apparently, he knows all the good places to eat around here."

"It was good," she said, adopting his tone. "Maybe I should take you there after you're finished with my car. To thank you."

Part of him rejoiced. Part of him quailed. But what harm could a meal do? They had eaten many meals together. Before he could accept her invitation, she spoke again.

"Oh, no. That's no good. That would just be me doing what you did. I'll give you the address of the restaurant. Then you can go whenever you want. With whoever you want."

Jake closed his eyes, fighting with himself. He considered saying that they could go together once the shop started paying off, but that took for granted that the shop would provide income and that she would wait.

What if she waited and it didn't happen? What would that cost her? A chance at happiness? A chance for marriage and a family of her own? He couldn't do that to her.

Resigned, he put away his justifications.

"I'll have your car ready soon," he told her softly.

A moment later he ended the call, as depressed as he'd ever been in his life.

Chapter Eleven

Looking up from the sewing machine, Kathryn glanced at her phone sitting on the counter at her elbow. She'd set a timer then ignored it, and now Tina had to come in, probably to tell her that she needed to start lunch.

"I'm so sorry. I was just going to finish this one row of stitching then get back to work, but I got caught up in the project and lost track of time."

Tina chuckled, waving away her concern. "No need to apologize. What are you working on? Another gorgeous dress, I see."

Kathryn shook out the silky brown fabric, holding the garment by the narrow sleeves, which she'd shortened to elbow length.

Tina fingered the fabric. "Oh, my. Your mom had excellent taste."

"I always thought so, especially with her work wardrobe."

"What did she do?"

"She was an insurance agent. She started as a secretary and taught herself the business. She knew everything there was to know about all kinds of insurance—auto, home, health, life… I shudder to think what would have happened to us if she hadn't had excellent health insurance."

"She was a well-dressed insurance agent," Tina said.

Kathryn sighed. "I just wish she'd had some more casual things."

Tina's eyes lit up. "We have to go shopping."

Kathryn threw up her hands. "Never fails. What did we forget?"

"Not for the ranch," Tina declared, pulling Kathryn up by the arms. "I need to buy Tyler a few more things for school, and Frankie's jeans are already too short. He'll never make it through the fall with what he's got now."

"Grows like a weed, doesn't he?"

"He does. So we're going shopping. And we're not taking the boys."

"But—"

"Not taking the boys," Tina repeated firmly. "I have their sizes, and it's easier to choose for them when they're not around. And I want you to have all the time and freedom you need to shop for yourself."

"Oh, I don't know if—"

Tina held up a finger. "I'm pulling rank on you, girl-friend. I'm the boss, and I say we're going shopping."

Kathryn could only smile and say, "Yes, ma'am." She couldn't help wondering what Jake would have to say about her leaving Frankie behind, though.

When Tina informed Wyatt at lunch that he would be staying home to oversee the contractor and watch the boys that afternoon, he glanced around the room and meekly said, "Yes, dear." His brothers laughed, but Wyatt just winked and said, "Feisty little thing, isn't she?"

Tina smirked, ignoring him. "Kathryn and I will put chicken and potatoes into the crockpot, so we can get dinner on in a matter of minutes after we get back. If you'll just have the boys ready, we should make prayer meeting without any problems."

"We can do that," Wyatt said, looking at Jake, who merely nodded.

"It's settled then," she decreed, rushing Kathryn toward the door. Once they were outside, Tina laughed and said, "That was easier than expected."

Kathryn made one more protest. "I should be working, not shopping."

"Shopping *is* working," Tina countered dryly.

Kathryn got in the SUV.

Five hours later, exhausted but the proud owner of three new outfits—all purchased at deep discount—Kathryn desperately wanted a shower. Tina, on the other hand, had resisted buying anything for herself. Once or twice she'd seemed tempted by certain items of clothing, but then she'd just sighed and put them back. When Kathryn asked why, Tina made a face.

"I'll get too fat to wear them. You don't know how good you have it being thin. You're the kind who won't even put on weight when you're pregnant."

Kathryn didn't say that her chances of ever having a child were slim to none. She'd be thirty before she knew what hit her, and it wasn't likely that she'd marry any time soon. Jake's face popped up before her mind's eye, his gaze warm above that gorgeous smile. Mentally shoving away the image, she'd scolded Tina for thinking she was overweight.

"You're not fat. You're shapely. I, on the other hand, have the figure of a stick."

"Rub it in, why don't you?" Tina drawled.

Kathryn laughed and helped Tina stow their purchases in the SUV. When Tina straightened and reached up to pull down the tailgate, all the color drained out of her face and she suddenly collapsed against the bumper. Crying out, Kathryn caught her and lifted her up enough to sit on the edge of the SUV's baggage deck.

"Tina! What's wrong?"

Tina put a hand to her head. "Dizzy. Guess it's the heat."

"Let's get you home."

"You'd better drive."

Tina reached into her handbag for her keys and handed them over. Kathryn walked her around to the passenger seat before hurrying to take her place behind the steering wheel. She turned on the air conditioner full blast and stopped at a drive-through for a cool drink, but halfway home Tina gasped and put her hand over her mouth. Kathryn quickly pulled over so Tina could throw up. Afterward, Kathryn gave her a mint, helped her lie back her seat and broke speed limits getting home to the ranch.

Because the construction crew was working on the carport, Kathryn parked the car in front of the corral, which was directly across from the house.

"Where's Wyatt?" she demanded of the workers, but the voice that answered her was Jake's.

"He and the boys drove into town," he said, striding toward her from the barn. "What's wrong?"

"Tina's ill. Help me get her in the house."

"I can manage on my own," Tina said, sliding down

to the ground. She did look better, but Kathryn wasn't taking any chances, and neither was Jake. He rushed to Tina's side and would have carried her into the house if she hadn't threatened him. "I'm fine. Put your hands on me, though, and I'll kick you in the shin."

She wouldn't have hurt him, of course, and he did put his hands on her, but he settled for wrapping an arm around her back and escorting her inside, Kathryn hurrying along beside them. Tina insisted on brushing her teeth. Kathryn followed her, standing outside the bathroom door in case Tina felt faint again. They returned to the kitchen, where Jake waited anxiously. Tina sat at the table.

"How about a cold glass of iced tea?" Kathryn offered, feeling Tina's clammy forehead with the palm of her hand.

Tina made a face. "I think I'd rather have a soft drink. And crackers." Always worried about her weight, Tina seldom drank anything sweetened with sugar, and lately she'd stopped stocking colas and soft drinks with artificial sweeteners.

"Are you sure?"

"I think it might settle my stomach."

Kathryn went for the crackers while Jake retrieved the soft drink.

"I think I should call Wyatt," he said, delivering the cold, canned beverage to her.

Tina shook her head. "No. I'll be better in a minute."

"After you finish that, go lie down," Kathryn urged. "I can manage dinner."

"I'll help her," Jake volunteered.

Kathryn shook her head. "It's mostly ready. I'll just open some canned vegetables and call it done."

"Well, I'm not leaving until Wyatt returns," Jake said, pulling out a chair.

Kathryn went about getting the dinner together, while Tina munched crackers and sipped her clear, sparkling beverage. Wyatt and the boys came in just as Kathryn was pulling plates from the cupboard.

"Tina is ill," Jake announced immediately.

Concern stamped on his face, Wyatt went to her, tossing whatever he'd bought in town on the table. She got to her feet as he approached, smiling.

"I'm fine. Just a little upset stomach. Probably the heat."

He wrapped his arms around her. "You sure, sweetheart?"

"Absolutely."

Wyatt smiled down at her, seeming to relax. "I love you," he said, and the two kissed.

Jake shot to his feet and out the door. Obviously, Kathryn reflected sourly, he couldn't wait to get away from her. At least he'd stayed put until Wyatt came.

"Dinner in ten minutes," Kathryn called after him.

"We got popslickels for 'zert!" Frankie declared to Kathryn.

She pulled her attention away from Jake's retreat and focused on his son. "That's wonderful. Let's put them in the freezer so they don't melt."

"Yeah," Frankie said, adding emphatically, "I want red."

Kathryn chuckled. "I'll remember that." She sent both boys off to wash their hands and went back to preparing dinner.

Tina asked Wyatt to go out to the SUV and bring in the shopping bags, then insisted on setting the table before separating their purchases into two piles. Ryder came in and went to wash up. Kathryn was putting the food on the table when Jake came in again and went to the kitchen sink.

"When we're done here," Tina said to Kathryn, "Wyatt and I will clean up so you can get home. I know you probably want to shower before prayer meeting."

"Are you sure you should go to prayer meeting tonight?" Kathryn asked, concern tugging at her.

Tina chuckled. "I keep telling everyone, I'm fine. I'll feel even better *after* prayer meeting."

Kathryn smiled. "That's always how I feel, too."

"Oh, wait," Tina said. "Why not just get ready here? You can use one of the guest rooms upstairs."

Kathryn glanced at the parcels on the floor. "I can do that, I guess." No one would have to drive her back and forth this way or pass her the keys to Tina's old sedan again.

They finished the meal, Jake again as silent as stone. Kathryn carried her shopping bags upstairs and dropped them on the bed in the room at the end of the hall before going straight to the shower. Just feeling clean again cooled and reinvigorated her. Tina brought up a blow dryer and curling iron, as well as a few other essentials. She seemed almost fully recovered from her earlier bout of sickness.

After drying and curling her hair, Kathryn pulled out a newly purchased sundress, removed the tags and put it on. Thankfully, she'd worn sandals that morning. She loved the way the dress swirled around her legs, falling to midcalf. Tying the string belt at her waist, she tossed the faded denim jacket that came with the dress over her shoulders and went downstairs to join the others.

Everyone commented on how pretty she looked in her new dress. Everyone but Jake. He barely glanced at her before heading outside.

She felt frostbitten, his cold indifference a kind of death of all her hopes and dreams. Determined not to cry, she pasted on a smile, stiffened her spine and filed out with everyone. Once again, Jake and Ryder traveled in Jake's truck. Kathryn rode in the SUV with the others. At the church, Kathryn found herself sitting between Tina and Ryder. She told herself she was glad. It made it easier for her to ignore Jake. He certainly had no trouble ignoring her.

Kathryn was surprised that neither Wyatt nor Tina asked for prayer after Tina's bout of illness that afternoon. Ryder also seemed bothered by that, leaning forward at one point and sending his brother a meaningful look. Wyatt's response had been to take Tina's hand in his. Well, Kathryn certainly understood the desire for privacy. Perhaps Tina was not quite as fully recovered as she pretended, however, for as soon as they reached the foyer, Wyatt announced that he was taking Tina and the boys straight home. That left Jake and Ryder to drive Kathryn to her house.

She rode in the back seat, staring at the text message that had come in while her phone was silenced in church. Clark had written to say that he was out of town and hadn't had a moment to call due to constant meetings but didn't want her to think he was ignoring her. Kathryn knew that if not for Jake Smith, she'd be thrilled, but it was difficult to swoon over Clark when the man who had alternately enthralled and wounded her sat within her immediate line of sight.

Arriving at her house a few minutes later, she was

surprised to see an unfamiliar luxury sedan parked in her driveway. Jake pulled up on the passenger side of the other vehicle.

"You've got company," Ryder said needlessly.

"So I see," she murmured, opening her door. "Thanks for the ride." She quickly alighted and walked around to the car, wondering who her visitor might be and fearing the worst. Perhaps it was her father. More likely his attorney. Mitchel Stepp had never owned a luxury anything.

A tall, slender man with very little blond hair and a nervous smile got out on the driver's side to greet her. Wearing a short-sleeved sport shirt, pleated slacks and black dress shoes, he looked distinctly uncomfortable.

"Kathryn?"

"Yes."

He put out his hand. "Jay Wilson. I was just about to leave."

Jay Wilson, the divorced father of three who had called her some days ago. As an introvert herself, she knew one when she saw one. She shook his hand.

"You won't remember me," he said, as if that explained everything. "I was several years ahead of you in school. I called on Saturday."

"Oh, yes." She forced a smile.

"I was wondering," he said, "if you'd reconsider going out with me. There's…there's a recital. My daughter's a piano student. She's only eleven, but she's quite good."

"You must be very proud of her," Kathryn said quickly. She heard a door open and glanced over his shoulder in time to see Jake get out of the truck. Frowning, she switched back to Jay Wilson. "Normally I would be happy to go with you to your daughter's recital, but I'm…" She lowered her voice, quickly adding, "I'm, well, I'm interested in someone else."

Jay Wilson glanced back at Jake. "Ah. I see. Sorry to have bothered you."

"Not at all," she hastened to say, smiling apologetically. "I should have told you when you called. I was just so flattered by your invitation…"

Bobbing his head, he took swift leave of her, flags of color flying across his cheekbones. His car was halfway down the drive before Jake reached her side.

Scowling at the sedan, Jake asked, "Who was that?"

"A nice man," Kathryn answered tersely, starting toward the house.

Jake kept pace with her. "That's not Clark."

"No, it's not. Clark is out of town."

He stopped at the bottom of the porch steps. "That guy asked you out, didn't he?"

Kathryn just smiled and went up the steps. She had no desire to go out with Jay Wilson. He was attractive enough, and she couldn't deny that his persistence flattered her. Moreover, she was thrilled to think that men, some men, found her attractive, but it was unfair of her to go out with anyone, Clark included, until her heart was her own again.

That didn't mean her social life was any business of the one man who'd made it clear she was not for him. She went into the house without another word.

Jake sat silently beside Kathryn at church on the following Sunday and mentally kicked himself for the thousandth time. He'd opened a proverbial Pandora's box by denying his interest in Kathryn. He'd answered the question of just one man, and now suitors were coming out of the woodwork. For days now, he'd tried to be glad for her but could only be miserable for himself. Would every single man within driving distance be on her doorstep now? At this rate, she'd be married by winter.

He tried not to look at her, but she was so stunning, elegant and sophisticated in a formfitting brown dress with a flat bow on one shoulder. He couldn't help himself. Of course, she wasn't sitting beside him so much as she was sitting beside Tina. He'd just managed to get between her and Ryder. Another stupid move on his part. He couldn't concentrate on anything but her, and she wouldn't even be sitting here next to him if Clark Goodell had attended church this morning.

His own jealousy and possessiveness shocked Jake. He had no right to such feelings, and silently confessing them did little to alleviate his gloom, especially when a man whom Jake didn't know approached Kathryn immediately after the service and received a warm welcome. Tall, blond and muscular, he seemed a little young for Kathryn, but the two hugged and stood talking animatedly together. Trying not to glower, Jake fetched Frankie from his classroom, only to find the pair still talking when he returned to the foyer.

Jake had sense enough to recognize his own jealousy and fight it. Surely his preoccupation with Kathryn was not healthy. It bordered on obsession, and that bothered him. He'd never had these issues with Jolene.

He and Jolene had come across each other in the course of their assignments. Rank being no issue, they'd both flirted a bit. They'd been comfortable together from the very beginning, and Jake had never known a moment's concern about Jolene liking him. In fact, she had asked him out the first time, rather than the other way around. Neither of them had dated anyone else from that point on, and their mutual affection had quickly become so obvious, a superior officer had suggested that marriage would be best for their careers. They'd gone shopping for a ring the next day and were married in uniform by the base chaplain just over four months later.

Jake reflected morosely that Kathryn seemed more comfortable with Clark and this new fellow than she was with him. Knowing it was all his fault didn't help a bit. The whole thing made Jake's head and chest ache.

"Grinding your teeth won't make her yours," said a voice at his shoulder. Jake spun on his heel, turning his glare on his big brother. Wyatt lifted both hands. "Just saying."

Jake turned away, scoffing, "You don't know what you're talking about."

"No? Wasn't that long ago that you and Ryder advised me to go after Tina."

The fact of that made Wyatt's words no less galling. Both of his brothers obviously read him much more easily than he'd assumed, but neither of them understood his turmoil.

"It's not the same," Jake hissed. "Kathryn is nothing like Tina or—"

"Jolene?" Wyatt finished for him. "What difference does that make? You're not trying to replace Jolene. The people we love aren't replaceable. You're moving on to a new relationship, something unique. Unless you let yourself get beat out by a college kid."

Ignoring the rest of Wyatt's words, Jake seized on

what felt most pertinent. "College kid?" Jake glanced at the man talking to Kathryn. He was muscular and fit but quite young.

"Rex says his name is Derek Cabbot. Apparently, he plays college football in Texas."

Cabbot. The name flitted through Jake's mind, lodging in a specific memory.

"Is he any kin to a Sandy Cabbot?"

"Rex said he's Sandy Cabbot's grandson, but I have no idea who Sandy Cabbot is."

"He's a former client of Kathryn's."

"Ah. Sandy probably misses her," Wyatt remarked casually. "We would if she left us."

She'd said she might go back to the home care agency once her car was repaired, and it was drivable now, though the brakes felt spongy to him, and the clutch was slipping. Plus, he thought she could have an exhaust leak. That was all beside the point, however.

He shook his head at his brother, his gaze on Kathryn. "I can't get involved with anyone right now."

"I don't see why not."

"My finances are stretched to the limit," Jake admitted, finally looking at his brother. "If the shop doesn't quickly turn a profit, I... I don't know what I'll do."

Grinning, Wyatt clapped him on the shoulder. "Try a little faith."

At the rate he was going, Jake thought glumly, it was going to take a *lot* of faith. Heaps and tons of faith.

More than he could find.

Chapter Twelve

"I'm taking Tina and Tyler home now," Wyatt said. "Ryder and I will see to lunch. Want me to take Frankie with us?"

Jake nodded, preoccupied with Wyatt's advice. Faith. Was it faith to expect that God would give him what he wanted when he wanted so much? He wanted Kathryn, but he wanted the financial stability to support her, too, and he wanted it here, near his brothers. On the other hand, how was he to know if he didn't take at least a few steps in the direction he wanted to go? *I'll understand if You slap me down, Lord*, Jake prayed silently, taking his son by the hand and walking straight toward Kathryn and her friend.

"Guess Frankie will go with you," Wyatt muttered, chuckling.

Jake barely heard him, his troubled mind trying to make sense of what he knew, what he felt and what he wanted. Kathryn might well bring him up short. God knew she had no reason to feel kindly toward him after the way he'd alternately ignored and grumbled at her.

Frankie, as usual, showed no restraint. He threw his

arms around Kathryn as soon as they reached her. She stooped to hug him then rose to split a smile between Frankie and Mr. Athletic.

"Frankie, this is my good friend Derek. Derek, this is Frankie."

Derek went down on his haunches, smiling at Frankie and offering his hand. "Nice to meet you, Frankie."

"S'it nice mee' you!" Frankie practically bawled into Derek's chiseled face, shaking his hand.

Looking up at Kathryn, Derek quipped, "Kind of like talking to Grandpa. He thinks everyone is as deaf as him."

She laughed. Apparently, Frankie didn't like the attention Derek was paying her any more than Jake did. Grimacing, he gripped two fingers on Derek's hand and pumped it again. Derek grinned and pretended to shake blood back into his fingers.

"Wow. That's quite a grip you've got there. How old are you?"

Frankie held up three fingers.

"You're a big boy for three. Maybe you'll play football in a few years. What d'you think?"

Frankie shook his head. "I can't frow."

"No? That's okay. You'll be able to knock over the guy who does throw the ball, and that's the most fun part."

Both Frankie and Kathryn laughed as Derek pushed up to a standing position once more. That was all Jake could take. It was bad enough Derek Cabbot could charm Kathryn; he didn't have to charm Frankie, too. Jake stepped up next to Kathryn. For a fraction of a second, he hesitated, then—like Frankie—he did exactly what he wanted to do. He slid an arm loosely around her shoulders and placed the other hand on top of Frankie's head, effectively claiming both. Kathryn stiffened and shifted slightly away from him but otherwise did not react.

Jake nodded at Cabbot and said to Kathryn, "About ready to go?" He patted Frankie's head, smiling down at him. "We need to get this one fed so he doesn't miss his nap."

Derek Cabbot's eyebrows rose halfway to his hairline. Kathryn bit her lips then made the necessary introductions.

"I hope your grandfather is well," Jake said, after Kathryn had told him what he already knew.

"As well as he can be, I guess," Cabbot replied.

"He always rallies when you're around," Kathryn said to Cabbot. "He enjoys your visits so much. Tell him I'll call soon."

"He'll like that," Derek said to her. "You know how he loves the telephone."

They laughed about Sandy Cabbot's fondness for the telephone. Irritated, Jake put on a smile. Finally, Kathryn said farewell to Derek and moved toward the door, out of Jake's reach. He and Frankie followed close behind.

"When did you meet Derek Cabbot?" Jake wanted to know.

"When he visited his grandfather. He's such a thoughtful grandson," Kathryn said brightly, but her arms were as stiff as rods at her sides. "Sandy lives for that boy."

Boy. Suddenly Jake could breathe a little easier. He reminded himself, however, that Clark Goodell was no boy, and Kathryn clearly preferred Clark to him at the moment.

Tina hailed them as soon as they stepped out the doors, insistently waving them over to join the group around her. Mentally sighing, Jake followed Kathryn to Tina's side. Tina stood with Wyatt, Tyler, Ryder and Ann Billings Pryor's family.

"Ann and Dean are inviting everyone over to their place for dinner next Sunday," Tina announced.

Ann looked at Kathryn and Jake. "It's cooled off some, and the new school year's started. We thought an end-of-season cookout was in order. Is 6:00 p.m. too late for y'all?"

Y'all. As if they were a couple. Him and Kathryn. Jake tried not to take that as some sort of validation. Instead, he simply looked to Kathryn, keeping his expression bland. "Fine by me. What about you?"

Kathryn seemed to struggle for a moment. Being the center of attention would always make her uncomfortable, but he suspected this was less about that and more about him. He couldn't blame her. He'd done a very good job of keeping his distance and discouraging any connection between them. He probably ought to keep on doing that, but he just didn't have the energy or the heart for it anymore. Besides, what difference would one evening in the company of others make?

All the difference he could squeeze out of it, he decided abruptly.

To his relief, she finally nodded and said to Ann, "I look forward to it."

Ann beamed a smile all around the group. "It's a date then. Next Sunday. Six o'clock."

"Let us know what we can bring," Tina said. "Kathryn's a marvelous cook."

As color rose to Kathryn's cheeks, Wyatt said to Tina, "Now will you go home?"

She rolled her eyes and trekked off toward the SUV, followed by Wyatt, Tyler and Ryder. Jake walked Frankie and Kathryn toward his truck.

"Tina's right," he said. "You are an excellent cook."

Kathryn bit her lips and bowed her head but said nothing. She didn't speak again until they reached her house, and then she merely murmured her thanks before getting out of the truck and going inside.

Faith, Jake thought.

Would faith put money in his bank account? Or make up for the damage he'd already done? Or keep Kathryn's father from forcing her to sell her house? He'd been worried about the latter, and the truth was that if he should somehow overcome all the barriers he'd erected and win Kathryn's heart, he'd be adding one more overwhelming financial responsibility to his already overburdened budget. Yet somehow, he just couldn't find the sense to care about that anymore.

Now if only he could undo the damage he'd done.

"It's running," Jake said the next morning, "but you'd better test-drive it before we call it done." He opened his fingers to show the key lying on his palm.

It had been so long since Kathryn had seen her own car parked in her driveway that she had to laugh as she swept the key from his hand. Smiling, he opened the driver's door for her. She tossed her bag into the back and got in. By the time she had her seat pulled forward enough to reach the pedals, he'd come around and squeezed himself into the passenger seat.

"Good grief, who were you driving around before your engine conked?"

She chuckled as he let the seat back as far as it would go. "No one."

"No one must be short."

Grinning, she started the engine then paused to marvel at its silence. "It was never this quiet before."

"Well, it had problems."

She put the transmission in Reverse and backed it out of her drive. "The clutch is different."

"I adjusted it. The transmission should shift more smoothly now."

It took a few moments for her to acclimate herself to the new tension, but by second gear, she had it. "Very nice."

When the stop sign came within sight, she automatically shifted to a lower gear.

"Do you always downshift?"

Surprised by the question, she glanced at him. "Yes. The fellow who sold the car to me told me that I should."

"It's not bad advice," Jake said. "It's what I'd tell anyone driving a car with iffy brakes."

"You mean my brakes are bad?" she asked, dismayed at the possibility.

"Not anymore. As if I'd send you out in an unsafe vehicle."

She bit her lips but couldn't keep back a smile. "It wasn't part of our deal. The clutch, either."

"What's the difference? It needed to be done. I did it. Cost me nothing but time."

Maybe the added repairs had made no difference

in cost, but something had made a difference in him. She tried to keep her hope in check as she drove them through town, out onto the highway and to the ranch. No doubt his improved, more relaxed mood was the product of having finished, at long last, the repairs to her car. She didn't dare think that it could be anything else. She told herself to guard her heart, but a relaxed, congenial Jake was difficult to resist, and the longer he hung around, the more difficult—and alarming—it was.

She couldn't help wondering why, after avoiding her like the plague, he suddenly seemed to seek out her company. Monday, it was the car. On Tuesday, he told her that Frankie wanted her to watch him ride his pony again.

"We're headed to the barn. Won't you come out with us?"

Frankie jumped up and down in excitement. "Yeah, KKay, come out!"

Jake's mercurial moods were troublesome, but she couldn't say no, and the trip to the barn proved very enlightening. Jake introduced her to the other mounts in the stable before giving her a detailed tutorial on saddling a horse. Watching little Frankie fearlessly clean his pony's hooves was eye-opening. And terrifying. Kathryn managed to keep her mouth shut only because Frankie displayed an expertise and familiarity far beyond his years. The twinkle in Jake's eyes told her that he was well aware of her struggle, and that helped ease her fears, too.

"You know," Jake said, as he led the pony from the barn into the corral, "wouldn't hurt you to learn to ride."

Kathryn wasn't so sure about that. She glanced warily at the horses in the stalls behind her. They were enormous animals—beautiful but enormous. "Frankie," she asked, deadpan, "will you share your pony with me?"

Jake burst out laughing, though Frankie appeared to think it over before shaking his head. "You ride Mouse wif Daddy."

"Maybe Mouse is a better choice," she agreed, glancing at Jake, who had explained earlier that Mouse, a gelding, was named for the color of his coat, not his size. Mouse was huge, so riding lessons would have to wait until Kathryn gathered her courage. For riding and for trusting Jake again. Or maybe the issue was trusting herself. She didn't know anymore.

Frankie acquitted himself ably. He'd seemed well instructed before, but he was quite the little expert now. By the time they were all parched, Kathryn was suitably impressed. Jake sent her to the house to pour cold drinks for the three of them. After they'd cooled down, he kept her at the table for a good half hour, basically lecturing on horsemanship.

On Wednesday, as soon as Frankie went down for his nap, Jake asked Kathryn to take a look at his shop. He wanted advice on choosing paint colors and general organization, he said. Though afraid that her wariness concerning him was waning dangerously, she was too curious not to accompany him.

The shop walls were up, but the roof hadn't been put on yet, and windows and doors were missing. Jake pointed out the two pits where the lifts would go in the work bays and the four spaces in the blocks that represented doorways into the customer area, as well as the small restroom in the back far corner of the customer area and the storage space next to it.

"I thought the cash drawer and counter should go on this side next to the service bays, between the two doors. What do you think?" he asked.

"Hmm. Shouldn't the counter enclose that back door and access to the storage space? That way, you could come in directly from the service bay and everything could still be kept secure if you were here alone."

"Makes sense." He swept an arm to indicate another area. "What about the waiting area? What should I do there?"

She saw it all in her mind's eye. "Paint the floor black. Go army green about halfway up the wall, white over that with red and blue stars scattered everywhere. Paint your benches the same green as the wall."

Jake looked around as if picturing it all and broke out in a grin. "All right. What else?"

She paced off the length of the counter. "Put your coffee bar here and leave it open to both sides. That way, you can make fresh coffee from behind the enclosure." She pointed to the wall beside the restroom door. "Hang a TV right there."

He threw up his hands. "And *that's* why I brought you here. You have an uncanny ability to see how best to utilize spaces and put together colors. Have you ever thought of opening a decorating or consulting business?"

"Oh, no. I don't have the education."

"You can go to college online, you know."

"I can't afford that."

"But if there was a way, would you consider it?"

"I'd consider it," she said dismissively. But no way existed, not until she could pay off her father. *If* she could pay off her father.

The rest of the week passed in similar fashion. Jake seemed to be around the house frequently. When he wasn't working on the shop, he was drinking glass after glass of iced tea at the kitchen table or helping Tyler and Frankie teach tricks to Tyler's dog, Tipper. Several times he sought out Kathryn to ask how her car was behaving or if she knew when to have the oil changed and how to check the tire pressure.

During his absences, Kathryn could easily remind herself that nothing had really changed. Jake might seem more relaxed and pleasant, even a little flirtatious at times, but neither of their situations had changed. He still had a business to establish and a late wife Kathryn knew she could never measure up to, and she had her father's claim hanging over her head. If she couldn't find a way to settle that, she'd be selling and moving because she certainly wasn't going to find anything to rent around here, or any other work that paid well enough to afford it.

By week's end, Kathryn very much feared she was well on her way to falling under Jake Smith's spell again, but she couldn't forget the pain of his indifference and the feeling of rejection. Could she bear that again? And again? Even if Jake decided that she would suffice as a girlfriend, who was to say that it wasn't a cycle she would have to endure from now on? She'd never survive a hot-and-cold Jake, content with her one minute, disappointed in her the next.

On Friday, she swallowed her building grief and applied for a position with every home care agency in the tri-county area. She'd take two jobs, if she could get them, and work day and night, seven days a week, until she had her father paid off. And Jake out of her heart.

* * *

Jake's heart sank when he saw Clark Goodell waiting in the church foyer that next Sunday. A quick glance around showed him that Kathryn had not yet arrived, but before he could get Frankie to the hallway that led to the children's wing, Goodell's face brightened. Jake could feel Kathryn's presence even before he turned to greet her, only to find her smiling at Goodell.

"I'm sorry I haven't called," Goodell said as soon as he reached her. "They've had me running all over the country."

"Oh, that's all right," she told him. "I understand. How was your trip?"

Frankie naturally headed in her direction. Jake caught him and tugged him down the hallway. "Hush now. We'll see Kathryn tonight. Remember? We're going over to the Pryors' for a cookout."

"S'let take KKay," Frankie said, staring wistfully behind him.

"That's exactly what we'll do," Jake answered.

Kathryn and Goodell were nowhere in sight when Jake returned to the foyer. Heavy of heart, he started down the aisle, spying them sitting side by side near the front and across the aisle from his family. He hadn't made arrangements with Kathryn to take her to the Pryors' tonight. He'd meant to do that this morning, to approach it as a given and simply ask her what time she wanted him to be there. Now he wished he'd done the thing properly and actually asked her to accompany him. Why was it, he wondered, that he could never seem to do the right thing with her?

He'd been a coward about her from the first. All along he'd told himself that he was just being prudent and fair. All the difficulties he'd used as excuses still applied, but he couldn't hide the truth from himself anymore. The way he felt about her scared him half to death. He'd already lost Jolene. The idea that he could go through that again…he couldn't think about it. Yet, he also couldn't let go of Kathryn.

Faith.

He had to trust that this was all happening for a reason. If only he didn't mess it up.

After the service, Jake hurried to the foyer, but instead of immediately going after Frankie, he hung around, chatting with one person or another, his hat in his hand, until Kathryn and Clark reached the already crowded space. Tina swung by on her way after Tyler and asked if Jake wanted her to pick up Frankie, too.

"That would be great. Thanks."

As soon as she disappeared down the hallway, he made his way over to Kathryn, who stood speaking to Clark and Wes Billings. Stepping up next to Kathryn, Jake took advantage of Billings's presence.

"Wes, you going to be joining us tonight?"

"You know it." Wes slid a glance at Clark, smiled and moved away, going to his wife, who stood laughing with some other women.

Fully aware that he'd rudely brought up a social engagement to which one of their party had not been invited, Jake felt a stab of guilt, but he wasn't backing down. He tried to think of the least objectionable way to accomplish his goal. It came in the form of his son, who suddenly appeared and threw himself at Kathryn.

"KKay! S'let go pardy now."

Jake chuckled. "That's not until tonight, son, and you've got to have a good, long nap first." He lifted a hand to the small of Kathryn's back, asking softly, "Can we pick you up about five-thirty?"

She glanced at Clark, color rising in her cheeks. "Oh, uh—"

"Earlier? Later?" Jake asked patiently.

Biting her lips, she glanced at Clark again then quickly, quietly said, "Five-thirty will be fine."

Smiling, Jake took Frankie by the hand, nodded at Clark and got out of there.

Would the day ever come, he wondered, when he could simply, formally ask the woman for a date? Maybe it was time to step up his game.

"Dese for you!" Frankie called, thrusting the bouquet of flowers at Kathryn with both hands.

As wide as he was, the colorful mixed blooms had been wrapped in the waxy, green paper that she recognized as coming from the local grocery. She'd never received flowers before, but then she'd never had so many invitations, either. First Jake, then Clark and two others, now Clark and Jake again. At least Clark had the good manners to make an actual request for her company. She just wished she could be as happy about that as she ought to be. Instead, it was Jake's high-handed assumption that she considered him her escort for the evening that both infuriated and thrilled her. The flowers just intensified the thrill.

Even if Frankie had delivered them, she had no doubt who had thought of and purchased them. He shouldn't have done it, not with the drain on his finances that the shop was making, but she couldn't be upset with him.

Her first date. Her first kiss. Her first flowers.

She didn't dare carry the thought further. She

couldn't, wouldn't, let Jake Smith be her first love. If Jake was her first, she feared she would never know another. Taking the flowers in hand, she backed away from the door and smiled down at Frankie. She made a show of sniffing the blossoms.

"Mmm. Beautiful. Thank you so much."

Frankie swung his arms, obviously pleased with himself. "We gots 'em for Mizz Ann, too, an'..." He screwed up his face as if trying to remember. "Mizz Billie!"

"Donovan's great-grandmother," Jake informed Kathryn. "She lives with them."

"How very kind," Kathryn managed, busily tweaking one blossom after another. Finally, she looked at Jake.

He regarded her steadily, his hat in his hands, his folded sunshades poking up out of his shirt pocket. He'd shaved again since church, and her heart flip-flopped inside her chest. Flustered, she suddenly couldn't seem to breathe properly.

Oh, she was in trouble.

Big, big trouble.

Chapter Thirteen

Turning, Kathryn fled toward the kitchen, saying, "I'll put these in water and get the cake." Frankie ran for the sofa. Behind her, she heard Jake step into the house and close the door.

She was standing on a stool and pulling a vase down from an upper cabinet when Jake came into the kitchen. He tossed his hat onto the counter and reached around her, wrapping his long, strong fingers around the dusky green vase and taking it out of her hands. He stayed where he was as she backed down off the low stool. Slowly lowering the vase to the countertop, he momentarily surrounded her with his arms, his chest scant inches from her back. Kathryn closed her eyes, taking in the aroma and heat of him.

He smelled of shaving cream and mint, and though no part of him touched her, she felt warmed, embraced. After a moment, he backed away. Her heart hammering, she quickly turned to place the vase on the island beside the flowers and pulled open a drawer to find scissors.

"You could get the cake out of the fridge," she told

him, beginning to trim the flower stems. "I put it in there to set the icing."

Ann had tasked the Loco Man contingent with dessert for their cookout. Kathryn had proposed a strawberry cake. Tina had volunteered to provide homemade ice cream. Kathryn had placed the cake, on her mother's crystal cake plate, on the lowest shelf of the refrigerator. Bending, Jake carefully pulled it out.

"Wow. Chocolate-covered strawberries." He set the cake on the end of the island and licked a tiny blob of pink icing from his thumb. "Mmm, strawberry and cream cheese. Forget the steaks. This is my main course."

Dropping stems into the vase, Kathryn glanced at the cake, smiling. Chocolate-covered strawberries were her favorite indulgence. She'd covered the top of the cake with them. Jake apparently shared her affinity for the sweet, red fruit dipped in waxy chocolate.

"The cover is on the counter behind you."

He turned, spied the domed cake cover and picked it up by the glass knob on top. Carefully, he settled the glass dome over the cake. Folding his arms, he backed up to lean against the counter behind him and watched her arrange the flowers.

"That must be a new outfit you're wearing."

Keeping her head averted, she nodded and turned with the vase to carry it to the sink, where she began filling it with water. She'd told herself that her choice of deep, olive green had nothing to do with Jake's preference for army colors. Green, after all, was always her color of choice. She had passed over similar loose, comfortable capris and matching tops in two other shades of green, however.

"I like it," Jake said. "But then, you always look good, no matter what you wear."

Kathryn froze in the act of lifting the vase out of the sink, her pulse pounding. "Thank you." The words came out softer and more husky than she'd intended. Perhaps if she could breathe, she could speak normally.

Jake stepped up next to her and picked up the flowers. "Where would you like these?"

"I-island, for now." Later, she would move them to her bedroom, where she would see them the moment she awakened.

He carried the vase of flowers to the island and placed them in the center of the countertop before picking up his hat and fitting it to his head. "I'll get the cake."

Kathryn caught her breath and followed him into the living room. Frankie went nuts over the cake, hugging Kathryn and pretending to gobble the dessert with his hands.

"Um-um-um-um."

His antics eased Kathryn's hyperawareness of Jake. Laughing, they trooped out to the truck. Jake secured the cake in the back seat, and Frankie kept pretending to eat it as they drove to the Pryor farm. They were still getting out of the truck when Donovan Pryor and Tyler came running around the house. Donovan's red hair glowed like a flame against the sinking sun.

"We got ice cream!" Tyler called happily.

"An' cake!" Frankie shouted as Jake lifted him down to the ground. "Wif s'rawburries! Candy ones!"

"Strawberries," Donovan repeated, licking his lips. "Yum."

Jake handed Frankie the wrapped roses, and the boy ran toward the older ones, calling, "I gots flou-hers!"

Shaking his head, Jake instructed Frankie to deliver the roses. All three boys took off, yelling about strawberries, cake and flowers. Chuckling, Jake reached into the truck for the cake and carried it toward the house, Kathryn at his side.

"Looks like I'm going to have to fight off the hordes to keep my cake."

"*Your* cake?"

"My girl, my cake," he said silkily, dropping a warm, lazy look on her. Kathryn's heart stopped, her jaw dropping.

Before she could get her mouth closed, Dean Pryor, Ann's husband, came out onto the porch, calling to them. "Good to see y'all! Come on in." He reached for the cake as they climbed the steps, saying, "I'll take that."

"Oh, no, you won't," Jake said, twisting to keep the cake out of Dean's reach. "If you're real nice, I might let you have some, though."

Dean laughed. "It's like that, huh? I can see we're going to have to bribe you to share." Laughing, he pulled open the screen door for them.

"That might work," Jake conceded, winking at Kathryn. "Let's see what you've got to trade."

They walked through the old house, with its charmingly outdated furnishings and many family mementos, to the kitchen, where Ann and an older woman whom Dean quickly identified as his grandmother Billie were accepting Frankie's roses with smiles and exclamations of delight.

"KKay gots more," Frankie reported, holding his arms wide. "S'lot more. Huh, Daddy?"

"Lots more," Jake corrected, while Kathryn bit her lips to conceal a smile and tried to hide her blush.

"What's the occasion?" Ann asked.

Jake shrugged, grinning. "Steaks and strawberry cake. What else do you need?"

The two roses were deposited in matching vases and sent out the door with the boys and Dean.

Ann came and took the cake. "Thanks for the roses. That was so sweet. Oooh, the cake does look good. I'll put it over here next to the ice-cream freezer."

"I'm gaining weight just thinking about it," Tina drawled, entering the room from another part of the house.

"Me, too," Billie Pryor declared. "Let's get some exercise." She headed toward the door, waving for the others to follow. "I want to show y'all the garden before it gets dark, and I'll need some help gathering the corn."

Kathryn followed Billie and Tina out the back door, Jake on her heels. A couple of wood picnic tables, covered with checked plastic cloths, stood just beyond a large, shiny grill, where Ann's father, Wes Billings, tended a full grate of thick steaks while Dr. Alice arranged plates, napkins, flatware and plastic tumblers for iced tea and lemonade. A bud vase with a single long-stemmed rose rested in the center of each table.

A cooler of ice squatted between two folding lawn chairs occupied by Rex Billings and Wyatt. Several other chairs stood beneath the overarching limbs of an enormous hickory tree. Dean Pryor rose from feeding wood to a fire in a hole in the ground. A grate covered the fire pit, and a large, heavy pot of water sat atop the grate. He walked over to a lawn chair next to Ryder beneath the tree and dropped down into it before picking up a tall tumbler of iced tea from the ground. He gulped down a long drink, then waved at Jake.

"Grab a glass and a chair."

Tina set off up a small rise after Dean's grandmother, who now carried a pair of baskets. Jake leaned close to Kathryn and whispered, "I'll save you a seat."

Her heart in her throat, Kathryn merely nodded and went after Tina. Behind her, she heard Ryder teasing Jake.

"Can't the woman even walk up a hill without you ogling her?"

Despite the burn in her cheeks, Kathryn couldn't help looking back. Jake stood right where she'd left him, watching her. He slid a finger around the front curve of his hat brim in a kind of salute. Despite telling herself that it didn't mean anything, Kathryn felt as if she could float up that hill.

To her surprise, Kathryn found Billie Pryor's vegetable garden to be very interesting, especially the part planted in straw bales. While Billie gently lectured on growing vegetables, Tina and Kathryn followed her to the cornfield and helped her look for the remaining ears of corn and snap them off the stalks. When Billie decreed that they'd gathered enough corn, they carried the ears toward a water bib, where the boys washed and stripped them. Soon the ears went into the big pot heating over the fire pit.

Kathryn felt uncomfortably warm, despite the slowly sinking sun. Tina fanned herself with her hand and started toward the lawn chairs, saying, "I hear a tall, cold glass of iced tea calling my name."

"Funny, I thought that was my name I heard."

"If you did," Tina teased, tossing a grin over her shoulder, "it was Jake calling."

Kathryn caught her breath, but then all she could see was Jake smiling at her. Somehow, she managed to make it down the hill without breaking anything. Jake waved her over to a chair at his side. Conversation had already turned to Tina's plan to put in a vegetable garden at Loco Man Ranch.

"Dean will till the ground for us," Tina explained, Dean nodding in agreement. "We just have to decide where to put our garden plot. It should be close to the house. I was thinking out past the storm cellar." She turned to Kathryn. "What do you think?"

"Unless you're planning to take down trees, that's not much space," Kathryn said, saddened to think that she wouldn't be there to see the garden take shape. She dared not linger at the ranch with Jake in this happy mood. It was bad enough when he was ignoring or snapping at her, but this attentive, flirtatious Jake was a great danger to her heart, and now that her car had been returned to her, she had no excuse for staying on at Loco Man.

"We'd have to push into the pasture to enlarge the area otherwise," Tina mused.

"We've got two thousand acres, sweetheart," Wyatt said. "We can give up a few yards of pasture for a garden."

"But you'd have to deal with the barbed wire and the cattle, then," Kathryn pointed out.

"Don't worry about that, honey," Jake said casually. "I'll build you a fence to keep the cattle out, one with no barbed wire."

That word, *honey*, exploded like a grenade in Kathryn's mind. Apparently, it had quite an effect on everyone else listening, too. She saw knowing smiles and glances being exchanged everywhere she looked. Her face flamed red, and a lump formed in her throat. Why now, when it was too late? She couldn't trust him, dared not trust that he'd always be this Jake. The one she couldn't seem to help loving.

As night fell and the food disappeared, along with copious amounts of tea and lemonade, laughter rang out and conversation spun from one subject to another. Katherine sat next to Jake and mostly just listened, wondering what it would mean to truly be Jake's girl. Delight followed by heartache followed by delight followed by heartache? Or love and security without fail?

Rex and Callie Billings created considerable excitement by announcing that they were expecting a third child. Kathryn saw Tina and Wyatt exchange glances and smiles. Rex and his family left soon after, Callie saying she was exhausted all the time in the early weeks of her pregnancies. Rex, an attorney as well as a rancher, explained that he had paperwork to catch up on and needed to get an early start.

Perhaps half an hour later, Frankie crawled up in Kathryn's lap and went to sleep on her shoulder. He was a lead weight against her chest, a sweaty one, but she held him close, treasuring the feel of him in her arms, until Jake rose a few minutes later and gathered up the boy.

"We should be going, hon. Way past his bedtime."

Those endearments seemed to roll off his tongue with careless ease lately. If only she could trust in them.

The party began to break up in earnest, with Tyler

whining that he didn't want to go and Tina herding the exhausted six-year-old toward the front yard while Wyatt fetched the ice-cream freezer. Wes had cleaned the grill as soon as the last steak had come off it, so he and Alice began helping Billie carry leftovers into the kitchen. Ann brought Kathryn her cake plate and dome, clean now. The cake had been a big hit.

"I hate to leave you with a mess," Kathryn said.

"No, no. Dad and Alice will help us finish up while Billie gets the kids down for the night. We'll be done before you get home." She hugged Kathryn around the covered cake plate clasped to her chest, adding, "It's so good to have you in our lives again."

Even as she murmured her agreement, Kathryn wondered if she would see any of these people anymore after she stopped working for the Smiths.

They arrived at her home fifteen or twenty minutes later. Sucking in a deep breath, Kathryn started to thank Jake for the flowers and the evening, but he lightly pressed a finger to her lips, whispering, "Don't want to wake Frankie."

Twisting to look into the back seat, where Frankie slept with his head lolling to one side, Kathryn nodded and reached for the door handle. She was going to miss that little boy fiercely. Jake got out on his side and started around to meet her. He'd turned off the overhead light in the cab, so Frankie slept on.

She still cradled the cake plate and its cover in her lap. Jake took them from her, and she slid out onto the gravel of her drive. Jake carried the empty cake plate and its cover with one arm and hit the lock with the other hand before gently closing the door. They walked in silence to her front steps and climbed them to the porch.

Kathryn took out her keys and unlocked the front door. To her surprise, Jake brushed past her and set the cake plate on the small table just inside the door. Kathryn reached for the trio of light switches on the wall above the table, but Jake's hand got there first. Instead of turning on the living room lights, however, he turned off the porch light. Then, there in the open doorway, he pulled her into his arms.

She shouldn't do it. She knew she shouldn't do it, but a growing sense of urgency filled her, an impatience which she recognized despite never having felt it before this moment. This was the end, her final chance to feel his arms around her. Turning up her face, she slid her arms around his neck and kissed him.

After the first time, she hadn't imagined that his kisses could improve, but she found herself moved in profound ways. This kiss shifted her reality.

She was lost now. She had no choice but to love him.

Sadly, it changed little. Just her.

Only his kiss could simultaneously ground her and fling her to the stars.

Only his kiss.

And this was the last one.

Jake woke early on Monday morning, as usual. He shaved, slipped downstairs and made coffee, but he didn't go to the shop. He wanted to see Kathryn as soon as she came in. After last night, she had to know how he felt about her. They had to talk things through and make a plan. He wanted a bit of privacy, not too much, just enough time to say the things he'd been contemplating. But not enough to allow temptation to get the better of him. The woman was a major temptation to him, though he hadn't wanted to admit it at first.

He'd realized, just before he'd drifted off to sleep, that he'd gotten so good at pushing away what seemed to weaken or threaten him that it had become second nature. With Jolene, he'd had to do it. No one could live in constant fear of losing someone they loved. Everyone had to find a way to cope with the threat of danger. His way was to deny his fears and refuse to think of them. He'd done the same thing with Kathryn. But it hadn't worked.

His feelings for her were stronger than his fear. No matter how hard he'd tried, he couldn't stay away from her. All he'd done was make himself miserable. Eventually, though, he'd seen her hidden strength and independence.

Despite her natural reticence and caution, she'd soldiered on in the face of tremendous difficulty. Her strength was born of love combined with generosity and personal sacrifice. She'd closed out a world that preached self-fulfillment, dependence and monetary success and done the right, best thing, even when all she'd had wasn't truly enough. In the process, she'd honed astounding talents, using them to create comfort, warmth and peace. The woman hadn't been inside a church for years, but she'd walked in and taken her place with the Smiths more of a Christian than anyone Jake knew, himself included. She humbled him. He could only pray that she'd forgive him.

A phone rang. Jake ignored it. A few minutes later, Tina stumbled into the kitchen, Wyatt following in his bare feet, jeans and an undershirt. Jake didn't realize anything was wrong until she started sobbing. He jumped to his feet.

"What's happened?"

"She quit!" Tina exclaimed.

"What?"

"Kathryn quit. She said she's moving."

Astounded, he could think of only one question. "But why?"

Tina swiped tears from her face and folded her arms. "Think about it. I expect you'll figure it out."

"Me? Because of me?"

She threw up her hands. "What else?"

Jake didn't even try to answer that. Instead, he whirled and hit the door, leaving his hat behind. Maybe five minutes later, he whipped the truck into her drive, killed the engine and bailed out, the keys still in the ignition. Just as he raised his fist to knock on her door, he heard an unfamiliar voice, a masculine one, raised in what sounded like anger.

"Don't pretend I'm being unreasonable! You slaved for your mother but can't even share anything with me!"

"I offered you monthly payments," Kathryn said in a tired voice.

"I don't need monthly payments! I need a lump sum. Now!"

"I told you I'd sell the house," Kathryn said tremulously. "That's all I can do."

Sell her house? Jake opened the door without knocking and walked inside, confused and struggling not to rush to her aid without all the facts. One of the hallmarks of Kathryn's character was her calm, deliberate, careful manner. He would try to follow her lead in this, at least until he found out what was going on.

Her head turned at the sound of the door. Sadness mixed with resignation weighted her expression. She sat in the armchair, her entire body drawn into a tight, wary stillness, while a large, intimidating, middle-aged man with an unkempt mop of faded, thinning hair stood over her, bent forward slightly, his thick hands coiled into fists. One of those beefy fists clutched a sheaf of papers.

Jake's first instinct was to knock the bully over, but something, perhaps the dullness of Kathryn's eyes, told him that would be a mistake. She looked ready to shatter. He went to stand beside her chair.

"Honey, what's happening?"

"This isn't your business," the man growled. "Whoever you are, get out. This is between me and my daughter."

Daughter.

It was as he thought. Still, the word jolted Jake. He looked into the angry face of the long-absent Mitchel Stepp, seeing nothing of Kathryn in the bloated eyes, veined nose and heavy jowls.

Laying his hand on Kathryn's shoulder, Jake squeezed, letting her know that she wasn't alone.

If it were up to him, she would never be alone again.

But first things first. One problem at a time.

Faith.

They would work it out. God would help them work it out.

Chapter Fourteen

"Anything that concerns Kathryn concerns me," Jake said calmly. "And my family."

"I don't know you, and I don't care who your family is," Mitchel Stepp sneered.

"Jacoby Smith," Jake said, not bothering to offer his hand.

"Smith," the older man repeated in a considering tone. "There's that Smith on Loco Man Ranch. What's his name? Dodge?"

"Dodd. He was my uncle."

"Was." Suddenly, Mitchel Stepp's belligerence faded somewhat. "Old Dodd is gone, then, and you got the ranch."

"Me and my brothers," Jake clarified.

"He's not giving you money," Kathryn stated firmly.

Mitchel shook the papers at her. "Someone's giving me money! My lawyer says so! I can sell this house on my own, you know. My name's on the deed, not yours."

"Mother's will—" Kathryn began.

"Gives you half. That's all. Just half. And probating

that will to get your name on the deed will cost you a pretty penny. Save us both all the trouble."

Kathryn swallowed, her gaze dropping to the floor. "I said I'd sell the house."

"Oh, no, you won't," Jake declared, tightening his hand on her shoulder. "Not until we talk to our lawyer."

Kathryn tilted her head back, looking up at him. "*Our* lawyer?"

Jake dropped to his haunches, bringing his face close to hers. "Sweetheart, the ranch keeps Rex Billings on retainer. He's a fine lawyer and a good friend. I know he'll help us."

He leaned forward and kissed her forehead before pushing up to stand and again face Mitchel Stepp. "We'll talk to our lawyer and get back to you."

"Don't waste your money on lawyers. No lawyer's going to tell you anything I haven't already," Mitchel insisted. He smacked the papers in his hand with the other. "I got it all right here. Sell and be done!"

Biting her lips, Kathryn looked up at Jake. "I guess it can't hurt just to talk to Rex."

"That's my girl."

Tears filled her eyes. She looked tired enough to pass out where she sat.

"Time for you to go," Jake said to Mitchel Stepp. Leaving Kathryn's side, he pushed the older man toward the door.

"Get your hands off me!" Stepp blustered, smacking Jake with the papers in his fist.

Jake snatched the papers out of Mitchel's hand and stuffed them into the back pocket of his jeans. Mitchel tried to retrieve them.

"Give me those!"

"Not on your life. These are going to our lawyer," Jake decreed, hustling the man out the door. "I'm sure you've got copies."

Mitchel blustered and balked and glared, but he quickly stood on the porch looking in. Jake closed the door in Mitchel's face and threw the dead bolt. Then he simply turned to Kathryn, who surged to her feet. He opened his arms, and she flew to him. Folding her close, he tucked her head beneath his chin.

"It's okay, honey. It's all going to be okay."

"I don't know. I just don't know."

"We'll get through this together. All of us. You're not alone. Remember that."

She bowed her head. "Didn't Tina tell you?"

"That you quit? Yeah, she told me. But it isn't so. You know it isn't so. You just said that because you thought you were going to have to sell your house and move away."

"Jake," Kathryn whispered, "you should know—"

"If it's about the job, Kathryn, we'll discuss it later. Right now, we've got to figure out this mess with the house. Let me call Rex."

Disentangling himself, he took out his phone. Meanwhile, Kathryn went to the window and peeked through the sheers.

"Someone was waiting close by," she murmured. "They're picking him up now."

"Good riddance," Jake said just as Callie answered the call. After hearing why they wanted to consult Rex, she advised them to come over right away. "We'll be there in fifteen minutes or less," Jake replied before breaking the connection. "Can your father get into the house?" Jake asked Kathryn, looking for his hat.

"No. I had the locks changed about a month after he left. He'd been taking anything of value for years to buy his booze. One day after he disappeared, an oxygen tank went missing. I couldn't take the chance he'd help himself to anything else. He'd have sold Mom's wheelchair if he could've gotten his hands on it."

"Addiction is a horrible thing," Jake said, touching his head and remembering that he'd left his hat at home. He patted the front pocket of his jeans, then threw the dead bolt and opened the door. "You drive, hon. I want to call Wyatt. My truck's behind your car. The keys are, uh, in the ignition."

Kathryn lifted her eyebrows at that but said nothing as she snagged her bag from the closet and went out the door. As she drove them through War Bonnet, at a decidedly more sedate pace than he had on his way to Kathryn's, Jake gave Wyatt a blow-by-blow recitation of Mitchel Stepp's words and manner.

"Jake," she began again as soon as he ended the call, "you really should know..." Breaking off, she bit her lips.

He reached across the divide between their seats and smoothed his hand over the back of her neck beneath her thick, silky hair. "You should know some things, too, honey, but we'll talk later. I promise."

She nodded, looking troubled. Jake wouldn't let himself think about what she might have to tell him. Whatever it was, they'd work through it. He would not, could not, believe that it might be insurmountable. That wasn't in the plan.

Impossible was never part of God's plan.

They made good time, but Wyatt was closer and beat them to Straight Arrow Ranch. Kathryn parked behind

Wyatt's truck at the side of the road, and the three of them walked through the trees to the front porch of the ranch house. It was newer by a few decades than either the house at Loco Man or the Pryors' farmhouse, but it wasn't exactly a modern structure. Callie greeted them at the door, looking wan and hollow-eyed, then quickly excused herself.

Rex came out of a room on the right of the foyer, a worried expression on his face. He glanced down the hallway in the direction Callie had gone then smiled at Jake, Kathryn and Wyatt. "Hey. Callie told me y'all were coming."

"We don't want to intrude," Kathryn said, watching Callie disappear through a doorway, "or keep you from other business."

He shook his head. "Naw, not a bit. I'm sticking close to the house for a while because Callie's just so sick with this baby. Dad and Alice are watching the other kids for us so she can get on top of this."

"Tina's having her issues, too," Wyatt commented, "but it's more the afternoons for her. I thought it was supposed to be morning sickness."

Kathryn turned on him in shock.

"Is Tina pregnant?" Jake yelped, his eyes wide.

Wyatt grimaced. "I wasn't supposed to say anything for at least another month."

"Oh, my word!" Kathryn exclaimed. No wonder Tina wouldn't buy any clothes for herself! And all that talk about gaining weight.

Jake clapped his brother on both shoulders. "That's excellent news!"

"Not to mention fast work," Rex chortled.

Grinning, Wyatt said, "Tina's going to kill me, but

how are you supposed to keep something like that to yourself?"

"She won't stay mad too long," Rex teased. "No more than seven or eight months, anyway. A word of advice—learn to change diapers with your eyes closed. Comes in handy in the middle of the night."

"Thankfully, we've got Kathryn to help shoulder that burden," Wyatt said, but then he frowned and turned to her. "I thought we did, anyway."

"We'll talk about all that later," Jake interjected. "Right now, Kathryn's got a crisis of her own to deal with."

"Come on into the office," Rex said. "I want all the details."

Wyatt went across the room and leaned against the windowsill while Kathryn and Jake sank into a pair of wood-and-leather chairs in front of Rex's battered old desk. Jake handed over the papers he'd taken from Mitchel. Rex settled behind the desk and looked them over while Kathryn succinctly explained the situation.

He pulled a sheet of paper out of those on his desk and handed it to Kathryn. "Is this an accurate copy of your mother's will?"

Kathryn scanned the paper, frowning. "Yes. There were several copies, but the last time I looked, I only found one."

Rex passed over some papers. "How about this?"

She recognized the insurance policy. "Thank God! I thought I'd lost those." She shoved the papers at Jake. "My father must've taken these before I had the locks changed."

"But why?" Jake asked, scanning the papers. "He's

not the beneficiary of either the will or the insurance, so what good would this do him?"

Rex spread his hands. "Spouses have certain entitlements in Oklahoma that no will can circumvent. Insurance isn't one of them, but he might not have known that. He might even have shown these to a lawyer, hoping to find a legal way to subvert Mia's wishes. Or he might've just wanted to check out how much Kathryn would get so he could hit her up for part of it. Kathryn was young, after all, and no one knew how long Mia would live."

"Glad I got these away from him," Jake said, laying the papers on the desk.

Kathryn shook her head. "He must've been upset when he realized the amount of the policy had been reduced. We did that because we couldn't afford the premiums. Mom's old boss arranged it so the policy was fully paid with the premiums she'd already sent in, but he retired and the agency had no record of the amendment. I thought I'd misplaced our copy, and the insurance company said they couldn't verify the changes or process payment without solid proof."

Rex folded his arms against the edge of the desk. "Whatever Mitchel's reasons for taking these, the bottom line doesn't change. The proceeds of the life insurance are yours. Period. Other items mentioned in your mother's will are yours. Furniture, household goods, bank accounts…"

"There was just enough in the bank to bury her," Kathryn said.

Rex nodded. "The house, I'm afraid, is half his. Even if they divorced, unless there was a property settlement, he's entitled to half the value of your house."

Kathryn sighed. "They didn't divorce. At least I don't think they did. She never got anything saying he'd divorced her."

"He likely wouldn't have chanced it if he had any hopes of contesting her will," Rex said.

"So what do we do?" Jake asked, taking Kathryn's hand in his.

"I'm sure he has legal counsel. Just the fact that he waited six months after your mother's death to make his first demand tells me that. He doesn't want to look too predatory."

"He looked plenty predatory this morning," Jake put in.

"Sounds like his patience has worn thin, so we negotiate," Rex said. "We try for a buy-out price that you can live with. And we cash in the insurance policy. Maybe he'll take that. Maybe he won't. But we'll cut the best deal we can."

Jake squeezed Kathryn's hand. She gently removed it and smoothed the edge of Rex's desk with her fingertips, thinking through Rex's advice.

"The insurance won't be enough," she predicted. "He told us he has a lawyer, so he knows everything you just told me. I'll have to sell the house."

Jake slid an arm across her shoulder. "No, honey. Wait. We can come up with the cash. I know we can. I have several thousand at my disposal. That and the insurance money ought—"

She cut him off. "What are you saying? I can't take your money. That's for the shop."

"You're more important than the shop," Jake said softly. "Saving your home is what matters now."

"Loco Man looks after its own," Wyatt interjected. "We have funds. We can handle this together."

Confused, Kathryn shot to her feet, moving away from Jake, who also rose. She'd had this all settled in her mind even before her father had shown up that morning. Selling the house was the only real option. The insurance money just meant that she could easily start over again somewhere else. Away from everyone and everything she loved. But how could she stay and die a little every day, watching Jake pull away from her again? In time, he'd find someone else, someone like Jolene. What would she do then? How would she live with that?

"I'm not part of Loco Man," she gasped, barely holding it together.

"Of course you are," Jake insisted, coming toward her. "A huge part."

She shook her head, backing away. "No. Not anymore."

Jake looked at Wyatt, as if for help. Then he rubbed a hand over his face and turned back to Kathryn. "I'm part of Loco Man," he said. "And you're part of me."

Kathryn folded her arms across her middle, shaking her head. Nothing made sense anymore. It hadn't since the first time Jake had kissed her. He reached out, and she backed up a step.

"Please don't." She could barely think as it was. If he touched her now, she'd lose her mind.

"Just listen to me," he said. "I can put off opening the shop for a few months. Or...or sell it to someone who can see it through."

"No!"

"I'll borrow money, then, take out a loan. I'll make

it work. But I can't let you lose your home, not when I can see what it's doing to you."

"Stop trying to rescue me! Don't you understand? It's not about the house. I just can't…" *Be around you anymore.* Having friends was wonderful, but it just wasn't enough with Jake. She turned to Rex. "Do whatever you think is best, but I'm calling a Realtor today."

"Kathryn, please."

She ignored him and addressed Wyatt. "Will you take me ho—" She gulped down a fresh spate of tears. "Back to the house, please."

Wyatt sent Jake a loaded look and nodded grimly. Kathryn turned and walked out of the room. Tears were dripping off her chin before she reached Wyatt's truck. He arrived a few seconds later and let her in.

Kathryn stared blindly out the window, keeping her face averted and swiping impatiently at her tears. They drove quite a while in silence before Wyatt said, "He just wants…he *needs* to help you, Kathryn."

"Everyone's hero," she remarked bitterly. "What happens when I don't need to be rescued?"

"Could be he'll need you to rescue him."

"How could I possibly ever do that?"

"You'd be surprised."

Kathryn sighed and laid her head against the window. "I used to wish for a surprise every now and then, anything but the same old same old. Now I just want a quiet, steady, peaceful life."

"You think you'll find that by selling your house and moving away?" Wyatt asked.

"No," she admitted after a moment. "I don't think I'll ever find that. But maybe at least the pain will stop."

"You pulled away from everyone and everything once before, Kathryn. Did that make the pain stop?"

She closed her eyes, so tired. "No."

Tina pointed an accusing finger. "You'd better fix this, Jake Smith, and fix it fast! You brought her here, and now we can't manage without her."

"If I just knew what to do," Jake said miserably, his head in his hands, elbows braced against the tabletop.

"You can convince her that you love her," Wyatt said, coming through the door.

Jake dropped his hands. "Don't you think she knows that?"

"I do not think she knows that," Wyatt stated flatly.

Angry at the way this whole morning had turned out, Jake shot to his feet, his chair screeching against the floor. "I told her that I was willing to give up the shop and go into debt to help her! Does she think I'd do that just out of the generosity of my heart?"

"Yeah," Tina said, folding her arms. "She does. She thinks you're the kindest, most generous man in the world. Or she did before you started treating her like a leper."

Rocked, Jake felt the color drain out of his face.

"Think about it," Ryder said from his seat at the table. "You rescued her from the side of the road, got her a job here, fixed her car for free. And as soon as all her troubles were taken care of, you treated her like the biggest inconvenience on the face of the earth."

"No. That's not what—"

"And as soon as she's in trouble again, off you go," Tina interrupted, "riding to the rescue. What's she supposed to think? That she'll have to run from one calamity to another to hold your attention?"

"She said it herself just now," Wyatt told him. "Everyone's hero. That's what she called you."

Jake passed a hand over his eyes. "I only want to be her hero, but how am I supposed to convince her of that?"

Tina shook her head, looking at Wyatt. "I thought she was the innocent and he was the one with the experience."

"How did you convince Jolene that you loved her?" Ryder asked.

"I didn't," Jake said. "We just sort of fell into it." He tried to think what to say, how to make Kathryn hear him, but his brain didn't seem to be working. He wasn't sure it ever would again. "I don't know how to make Kathryn listen to me now. I'm not sure she'll even open the door for me."

"Well, you'd better think of something," Tina muttered.

He closed his eyes, silently talking to God. *Is this the end? You have Jolene with You, so I know she's all right. But Kathryn is alone, and if she leaves here, she'll always be alone. And I'll always be alone because I don't know how I'm supposed to live without her now.*

Frankie came stumbling into the room just then, yawning and rubbing his eyes. "Where Ty'er?"

"The school bus picked him up, sweetie," Tina said. "Let me make you some breakfast."

Suddenly, Jake knew what to do. "We don't have time for that," he said, taking Frankie by the arm. "Go to the bathroom. I'll bring down your clothes."

"I'll get them," Tina said, her face brightening as Frankie shuffled off.

"I have something that might help," Wyatt told him. "Let me get it."

Jake nodded, not sure what Wyatt had in mind and not caring. "Ryder, can you find an apple or a cheese stick, something for Frankie to eat on the way?"

They all went in different directions. Tina returned with the clothes, and Jake quickly dressed Frankie.

"We goin', Daddy?"

"Yes, son. We're going after Kathryn."

Frankie smiled and let Jake lead him back to the kitchen, where Ryder waited with a cheese stick and slices of apple in a small plastic dish.

"Here you go, pard. Eat it slow."

"And this is for you," Wyatt said, handing Jake a small box.

"What's this?"

"Mom's engagement ring. It's too small for Tina's hand, and I hated to alter it, but I'm guessing it'll fit Kathryn."

Gulping, Jake opened the box. The diamond was middling, maybe just over half a carat, but the setting was elegant and the slender band platinum.

"You and Jolene bought a ring before we could offer it to you. Dad said God must have other plans for it."

"I hope so," Jake said in a thick voice, hugging his brother. He swept Frankie toward the door, but at the last second he paused and looked back. "Well, start praying. I need all the help I can get."

Chapter Fifteen

❧

*B*oom. *Boom. Boom.*

Kathryn jerked at the sound of a fist applied to her door. She'd finally stopped crying long enough to look for the local real estate agent's number, and now this. If it was another man asking her out, she was going to bodily remove him from her porch; she didn't care if he wanted to take her to Buckingham Palace.

Boom. Boom. Boom. The sound came accompanied this time by lighter sounds that peppered the bottom of the door. What on earth? She finally got up and went to see.

"KKay!"

When she opened the door Frankie threw both arms around her, as usual, knocking her back a step. She glared at Jake. Oh, this was low, unforgiveable. To use his own child against her. What kind of complex drove a man to such extremes?

"I've made up my mind," she told him firmly. "I'm selling the house and leaving here."

"Okay," he said, crowding inside and forcing her back another step. He got her in far enough to reach behind him and close the door. "If that's what you want to do, we'll go with you."

"What?"

He rested his hands on Frankie's shoulders. "We'll go with you. Anywhere you want to go."

She stepped back out of Frankie's embrace. "I can manage by myself."

"I know. You always have. But I can't let you do it this time. I love you, Kathryn. And Frankie loves you, too. It'll kill me and break his heart if you leave here without us. Or if you stay without us."

He loved her? She was too stunned for a moment to do anything but stare. How could that be?

"What? Why? Why hold yourself back? Why make me think—"

"Fear," he admitted. "Sheer terror. I love you more than I've ever loved anyone, Kathryn, but I've been down this road before, and the thought of losing someone else I love…" He shook his head. "I was so afraid that I tried to keep my distance. I made up every excuse for it I could think of, but the truth is I knew…from the beginning, some part of me has known that if I loved you and lost you…" He spread his hands. "I don't know how to survive that. God forgive me, I don't know how I would survive that. My faith just isn't that strong. What I had to figure out is that losing you is losing you, no matter how it happens. But I'm not going to lose you because I was too stupid to tell you how much I love you."

She stared at him, hardly able to believe what she was hearing. Then the tears came again. She couldn't stop them. And with them came all the hope and trust she'd tried so hard to put away.

"Oh, Jake. I've loved you from the very start, and

I hoped you might feel the same, but I didn't dare believe it."

He heaved a huge sigh and stepped to the side, reaching for her. "Thank God. Thank you, God." He pulled her against him.

"It hurt so much when you stopped being nice to me," she said into the hollow of his shoulder. "The silence and the distance. It was unbearable."

"Honey, I'm sorry. You don't know how sorry. If it's any consolation, I was utterly miserable the whole time. And I hated—hated—seeing you with those other men."

She bit her lips, and then she giggled, elation rising up within her at last. "That part was kind of fun," she admitted. Pulling back a few inches, she looked him in the eye, adding, "But none of them could measure up to you."

Smiling broadly, he cupped her face in his hands and kissed her. Suddenly so happy she couldn't contain herself, she started to laugh.

"Hey," Frankie said, elbowing his way between them. "S'that my KKay."

Grinning, Jake put a hand on his head. "Back out, buckaroo. I can handle it from here. And you have to learn to share."

Frankie stepped aside, but he folded his arms and frowned up at his father. Jake ignored him, reaching into his pocket. He pulled out a small box. Kathryn gasped.

"Hold on," he said, taking her hand and going down on one knee. "I've got to do at least one thing right in this cockeyed courtship."

"Jake!" She clapped her free hand over her mouth.

"Kathryn Kay Stepp," he said, smiling up at her, "will you marry me? Please?"

"Yes! Oh, yes!"

Rising, he grinned ear to ear and pulled the top off the little box. "It was my mother's. The diamond's not all that big, but—"

"It's beautiful."

"Let's hope it fits," he said, taking the ring from its bed of cotton. It slid onto her finger as smoothly as silk.

"Later, if you want to," he said, holding her hands and rubbing his thumbs over her knuckles, "we can get a bigger diamond."

She yanked her hand away. "No! It's perfect. Why would you alter something this precious? I won't let you ruin it."

Jake chuckled and wrapped his arms around her. "Kathryn, I love you more than life. Promise me you'll never change."

"You're going to make me cry again," she grumbled. "And of course I'll change. So will you. We'll change together. Until we morph into an old married couple who finish each other's sentences and..." She dissolved into tears again. "Oh, Jake, I'm so happy!"

How could she not be? A man who loved her. A man she loved. Family. Friends. Even a son.

As Jake kissed the tears away, grinning all the while, Frankie shoved in between them again.

"My KKay!"

Laughing, she wiped her face with both hands. "Yes. I'm your KKay." She put her hands on her knees, stooping enough to bring her face level with his. "But now I'm going to be your mommy, too. Is that all right?"

He looked at Jake as if to say, *Well, duh. Like I haven't known that all along.* Then he wrapped his little arms around her again, tilted his head back as far as it would go and very clearly said, "Mama, I'm hungry."

Kathryn and Jake both laughed. Reaching down, he caught Frankie beneath the arms and swung him up onto his hip.

"Neither of us have had breakfast."

She smiled. "I guess I'd better cook then."

As she turned toward the kitchen, Jake slung an arm around her neck, pulling her sideways so he could kiss her temple.

"Let's eat," he said. "Then let's figure out how to save our home."

She nodded, a lump forming in her throat. Suddenly, nothing seemed impossible. They'd figure this out. Together.

"What a ride," Wyatt said the next afternoon, looking at the ring on Kathryn's finger again.

Jake nodded. Yeah, it had been some roller coaster, but he couldn't be happier. Whatever happened, he and Kathryn would face it together. They'd shared their news with the rest of the family yesterday, then talked long into the night about what they hoped for and how many options they might have. He'd slept like a baby afterward, and Kathryn had said much the same thing when she'd come in this morning.

"I still haven't fully recovered from the heart attack you gave me when you called yesterday," Tina said to Kathryn. She pointed a finger at Jake. "If you hadn't fixed this, Jake Smith, you'd be living in the bunkhouse with him." She jerked her head at Ryder.

Jake looked at Kathryn, sure she was thinking the same thing he was. They might both wind up living in the bunkhouse. He hoped not, but he couldn't worry about it anymore. Kathryn was going to be his wife, and whatever happened, he would live in that joy. Besides, if God could arrange that, He could work out the rest of it. Jake just didn't want her to be unhappy if they had to sell the house, after all. As long as they were together, though, they'd be fine.

Kathryn got up from the table to start dinner, but a tap on the door turned her attention in that direction.

"That'll be Rex," Wyatt said, and it was.

Rex came in and hung his hat on a peg. Jake saw the way Kathryn stiffened, as if preparing herself for bad news. He got up and went to wrap his arms around her.

"You saw my father."

"Spoke with his attorney," Rex corrected. "After I did a little research."

"Oh?"

"Can I get you some tea, Rex?" Tina asked.

He shook his head. "Naw. This won't take long."

"Spit it out," Jake said. "We can take whatever you've got to say."

"Twenty-five thousand. He'll settle for twenty-five thousand."

Kathryn turned in the circle of Jake's arms and laid her head on his shoulder. It was less than they'd feared, but still more than they could pull together.

"That's all?" Jake asked, suspicious of the amount. "He'll sign over the deed for a buyout of twenty-five thousand dollars?"

"It doesn't make sense," Kathryn said. "He was so adamant that I sell the house and split the proceeds with him."

"He has no choice," Rex divulged. "It's that or go to jail."

She whirled around. "Jail!"

"He's willing to take that now rather than wait for the house to sell," Rex explained, "because he has a judgment against him in Tahlequah. A restitution judgment. Seems he got drunk one night and entered the wrong house."

"He did that to our next-door neighbor!" Kathryn exclaimed. "Nearly scared her to death. She still hasn't forgiven him."

"Well, this time the homeowner pressed charges. Apparently, there was considerable damage—broken door and windows, some lamps and furniture. And he owes attorney fees. If he doesn't pay up, he goes back to jail, and I'm sure he's running out of time."

"That explains a lot," Jake said. It did, indeed, not that it mattered. It was what it was, and they would deal with it. "The bank should be able to loan us that much, especially if we put down the insurance money."

"Without a steady income?" Kathryn asked softly.

"That's not a problem," Wyatt said.

"We've got income," Jake pointed out, focused on Kathryn. "The ranch makes money, and if the shop turns a profit, we'll have no worries."

"I'll get a job," she said.

"You've already got a job," Tina told her, but Kathryn had told Jake that she couldn't accept money from family for just helping out around the place.

"I've already applied at all the home care agencies," Kathryn went on. "One of them will call."

"Will you two shut up for a minute and let somebody else get a word in edgewise?" Tina demanded.

They pulled apart, staring at her in surprise. She walked over to Wyatt and linked her arm with his. "Jake," she said rather primly, "Wyatt and I have discussed this thoroughly, and we've agreed. You and Ryder have done a lot of work on *my* house. I owe you both."

"Don't be silly. I live here, and we agreed at the beginning that Ryder and I would work on the house in exchange for room and board."

"That was before I married your brother," Tina insisted.

"And truth be told," Wyatt put in, "the division of income we agreed to at that time is unfair, and we knew it even then. Tina and I shouldn't get half while you and Ryder each get a fourth."

"But there are four of us in this," Jake argued.

"And soon there will be five," Wyatt countered, pointing at Kathryn. "And one day there will be six. No, the only way to do this fairly is a one-third split for each of us brothers."

"And the wives share in the husbands' split," Tina said. "Simple."

"That being the case," Wyatt pronounced authoritatively, every inch the big brother now, "we've put cash aside for you and Ryder. You don't have to dip into your savings, and Kathryn doesn't have to give up her insurance money. It's covered, the full amount."

Stunned, Jake walked slowly across the floor and brought his hands up to rest on his brother's broad shoulders. "Wyatt, I love you and Tina for this, but I can't take your money."

"It's *your* money!" Tina exclaimed. "We were going to surprise you with it when you opened the shop. As for Ryder, we kind of figured he might want to buy his own vehicle. We just didn't want to ruin the surprise by giving him his cash before you got the shop open."

"By the way," Wyatt said, "we've got another sod

harvest coming up, and that's another infusion of income that will more than see us all through the winter. Not that we were worried about it at all."

Jake looked at Kathryn. He ran his hand through his hair.

"I don't know what to say."

"I do," Kathryn spoke up. "Thank you. And thank God!" She burst into noisy sobs then.

Jake hurried to gather her against him, chuckling softly. "Oh, honey, don't cry now that everything's fine."

"I've cried more since I got happy than I ever did before," she wailed. "I just can't help it." Sniffing, she looked up at him then. "Thank God you stopped that day. Thank God I found enough courage to go with you." She looked around the room, as if memorizing the moment and every face.

Jake heard Frankie and Tyler laughing upstairs. He tried to see it and hear it as she did. Frankie, who had loved and wanted her from the beginning. And Wyatt, who was the best big brother in the world. And Tina, the sister Kathryn had never had. Ryder, the big old teddy bear. He was right. Their mom would approve. Jake silently vowed to spend the rest of his life making Kathryn so happy they'd have to buy tissues by the truckload.

"I have a family," Kathryn said softly, looking over his shoulder. "And I love you all so much."

Tina rushed them, hugging both Kathryn and Jake, while Wyatt looked on, grinning. Rex crossed the room and reached for his hat.

"Time to go check on my wife."

He turned a bright smile on them and went out the door while they were still thanking him.

Kathryn laid her head on Jake's shoulder. "Thank You," she whispered. "Thank You. Thank You. Thank You."

Jake knew she wasn't thanking him, and that was just as it should be.

"Amen," he whispered.

Jake waited in front of the altar in a brand-new suit. His boots gleamed, and the green tie Kathryn had picked out for him perfectly matched the dresses that Tina, Ann and Meredith wore. Jake had tapped Ryder as his best man because Wyatt had landed the privilege of escorting Kathryn down the aisle.

Despite his misgivings, they'd decided to invite Mitchel to the wedding, but he hadn't bothered even to respond to the invitation. Jake was relieved, and if Kathryn was not, at least she wasn't upset. Her father hadn't been part of her life in a long while, after all.

Rex Billings and Dean Pryor made up the rest of the wedding party, along with Frankie as ring bearer, Tyler as candle lighter and three little flower girls in identical flowered dresses. Dr. Alice herded her granddaughters toward the front of the church. Halfway down, the littlest one turned and demanded to be held. Muted laughter circled the room. Alice picked up the child and carried her to Wes, while the eldest, Callie's daughter, calmly urged her remaining cousin down the aisle, scattering petals as they went.

Jake couldn't smile any wider. October was a good month to get married. The weather had cooled and the leaves had begun to turn. They'd had time to decorate Frankie's room at the house in town, stenciling puppies on the walls.

Stark had finally pronounced Frankie's pup old

enough to leave his mom. Tufts, so named for the tufts of hair on the top of his head and end of his tail, had developed a particular fondness for Kathryn. Who didn't? She'd turned out to be a very able trainer.

Jake wasn't surprised. He firmly believed she could do anything she put her mind to, including make her own wedding dress. She'd insisted, claiming that she couldn't find what she wanted in the stores. He thought she just hadn't wanted to spend the cash. She hadn't learned how to have money yet, or so she said.

She proved once again just how talented she was as soon as the doors opened at the back of the sanctuary. A strapless sheath of white satin overlaid with long sleeves, an off-the-shoulder neckline and a modest train in pure white lace, the dress could not have been more perfect. Her hair was long enough now to be twisted up in a sophisticated French roll, showing off her beautiful neck and collarbone. Wyatt had once deemed her plain, but she looked like a model today, with a bouquet of bright orange roses, the finest of veils flowing down her back and her lovely face smiling at him.

It was all Jake could do to wait for her to reach him. He was ready to start this life as husband and wife. More than ready. But they had the ceremony to get through first and a reception at Loco Man, with a huge cake baked by Callie Billings and decorated with strawberries dipped in white chocolate. He was delaying the opening of the shop for another week so they could take a honeymoon. His worries on that end had dissipated like so much smoke. He already had more work lined up than he could handle and was looking for a mechanic to hire.

They were headed to Galveston on their honeymoon.

Thankfully, Frankie was not a fan of the beach. He'd had enough of it while they were in Houston, apparently. He was content to stay at the ranch for a few days with Tyler and his pup and his pony. Jake would show Kathryn his old stomping grounds and they'd have time alone together, just the two of them.

Perfect. It was all so perfect. She was perfect, or as close as a human being could get.

"Wow," he said, as soon as she reached him.

Their guests laughed, and she blushed, but then her hand was in his, and they were standing in front of the minister. Tina held the bouquet along with her own at exactly the right angle to disguise her baby bump. Ryder helped Frankie deliver the rings, and the next thing Jake knew, he was married. He thought of Jolene and how happy she had made him. He couldn't have been more grateful, but he knew that had just been the prologue for now.

He held Kathryn in his arms, looked down into her beautiful, serene face—this wife of his, the mother his son had chosen, the mother of his future children, the constant source of his delight—and softly said, "I love you."

"I love you, too," she said, loud enough for everyone in the building to hear, and then she kissed him.

His shy, proud, stubborn, talented, beautiful wife kissed him. Until his precocious, self-assured, somewhat territorial son yelled, "Hey! S'that my KKay!"

Laughter, it turned out, was the perfect recessional for a completely joyous occasion.

* * * * *

A COWBOY IN
SHEPHERD'S CROSSING

Ruth Logan Herne

This book is dedicated to Christina,
a wonderful young woman who won my heart
from the very beginning... Thank you for becoming a
true "overcomer." Your story is the kind of thing that
inspires others to do their best. To try harder.
To never give up. I love you, kid.

Judge not, and ye shall not be judged:
condemn not, and ye shall not be condemned:
forgive, and ye shall be forgiven.
—*Luke* 6:37

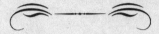

Chapter One

The last thing Jace Middleton wanted was to leave the place he loved so well. The place he knew, the town he'd called home for nearly thirty years and the land that beckoned him like a cow calls a calf. But the town had fallen on hard times, and the choices he wanted no longer existed in Shepherd's Crossing.

He ran one hand across the nape of his neck as he studied the family farmhouse that had been passed down for three generations. Three generations that ended with him.

He shoved emotions aside and studied the old house from a builder's perspective. The faded gray house lacked…everything.

Not the essentials. The modest one-and-a-half-story home was solidly built, and the mid-twentieth-century addition nearly doubled the first-floor living space, but there was nothing about this house that tempted folks to make an offer anywhere near his asking price. The way Jace saw things playing out, he would be left with two choices.

Walk away, begin life anew in Sun Valley and let the Realtor handle it. Or fix the place up, except…

He sighed.

He couldn't do it. He was good at tearing apart other folks' things and putting them back together. The thought made him flex his arms. There was nothing Jace liked better than reconfiguring something old into something new, but every time he went to change something in his parents' home, he ground to a stop. These were family walls. Family memories. They belonged to him and his younger sister, Justine.

These walls held all he had left of his parents, Jason and Ivy Middleton. He'd lost one to cancer and the other one to heartbreak, and he couldn't bring himself to demolish one stinking part of this house, even to increase the resale value. It felt wrong. Plain wrong. But he was slated to begin a new job in Sun Valley by Labor Day, which meant he had a couple of months to get things in order, sell the unsellable house, pay off his sister's college loans and start fresh. With dwindling jobs, cash and population, there was little left in Shepherd's Crossing, and things had grown worse over time.

He needed a fresh start.

He pretended he didn't downright hate that thought as a stylish SUV pulled into the nearby intersection. The car started to turn left, then paused.

It pulled back, onto the main road. Then the driver cranked the wheel in the opposite direction.

She paused again, looking left, then right, then frowned down at something… A map? A GPS?

Jace had no idea but every now and again a stormy day messed up satellite signals so he started her way about the same time she banked a sharp left turn and spotted him. She pulled up in front of the house, climbed out and came his way, leaving her car running in the middle of the road. Not pulled off to the edge like normal folks do, but smack-dab in the middle of the road, hogging the northbound lane. Who did things like that?

Tall, beautiful, well-dressed women who think they own the world, he decided as she crossed the driveway looking way too fine for their humble little town. He'd done a stint with a worldly woman a few years back, and one high-heeled heart-stomping had been more than enough.

"Your car." He pointed behind her as she approached. "You might want to move it off the road."

"I won't be long." Strong. Self-assured. And cucumber-cool. So already annoying. "You're selling this place?"

Was she a would-be buyer? If that was the case, she could leave her car wherever she wanted and he'd be crazy polite. "Yes."

"What's the asking price?"

He told her and she lifted an eyebrow. "How long has it been on the market?"

Longer than it should have taken, but he wasn't about to admit that to her. "A few weeks."

She waited, watching him, as if she knew he was downscaling the time frame.

"Six weeks, actually."

Her look went from him to the house and back as two cars came down the road. She paid no attention to the cars, or the fact that they needed to get around her car to make it into the intersection. She moved forward, toward the house, then paused. "This is your place?"

"Yes."

"Do you want advice?"

"Not if it requires me changing anything." It was a stupid answer, and he knew it, but he couldn't bring himself to pretend.

"I see." She gave him a smile that was half-polite and half something that wasn't one bit polite. "Well, best of luck to you."

She crossed back to her car, waited at the road while another car buzzed by, then took her place behind the wheel. He thought she was going to put it in gear and go, but she paused. Looked back at him. "I'm going to Pine Ridge Ranch. Do you know where that is?"

He shoved his cowboy hat back on his head and choked down a sigh.

He knew all right. He'd spent the last dozen years working there with his friend Heath Caufield. This must be the middle Fitzgerald sister, come to stake a claim on the ranch. He knew that because her sister Lizzie told him she'd be along soon.

This sister was different, though. Smoky gray eyes, dark curly hair and skin the color of biscuit-toned porcelain, a current popular choice in kitchens and baths. Lizzie failed to mention that her sister thought herself a cut above, so his work time on the ranch just got a little more tedious than it needed to be. "I'm heading there right now. I'll take lead. You follow."

"Or just tell me how to get there," she replied in a voice that suggested she wasn't about to follow anyone anywhere.

So be it. He did a slow count to five before he let her have it her way. "Two miles up the road, give or take, a left turn into a winding drive that heads deeper into the valley. There's a mailbox that marks the spot."

"Great. Thanks." She put the car into gear and drove off.

He got into his worn pickup truck, turned it around and followed her, and when he parked the truck at the ranch about five minutes later, her stylish SUV was nowhere to be seen.

"Jace, you want to run the baler now that the dew's burned off? That first cutting of hay looks mighty nice this year." Heath Caufield came his way and Jace nodded as he shut the truck door.

"Glad to. Hey, buddy. What's up?" Jace high-fived Heath's son when the five-year-old raced over to him—the child seemed unhampered by the neon-green cast on his right forearm.

"We're having another baby horse, and a wedding!" shrieked Zeke. He barreled into Jace's arms and gave him a big hug. "And you're goin' to be with Daddy when he gets married and then my Lizzie gets to be my mom like every…single…day." He paused between words to magnify their importance, and Jace understood real well how nice it was to have a mom. And how much you missed them once they were gone.

"Zeke." Heath made a face at the boy. "I'm supposed to *ask* Jace to stand up with me at the wedding. Not boss him around."

Zeke put his little hands over his face and giggled. "Oops. Sorry! Hey, somebody's coming, Dad!" He pointed up the hill as the white SUV made its way into the valley. Dust rose from the graveled drive, blanketing the car, and when it finally made its way into the barnyard, the sleek white paint wore a film of fine Idaho dirt.

The door opened. The woman got out, and waited

for the dust to clear. When it did, she spotted Jace right off. "You beat me here."

He may have smirked slightly. "The turnoff could be better marked, I suppose."

Her eyes narrowed, but then she spotted Heath.

She smiled then, and Jace was pretty sure it was about the prettiest smile he'd ever seen. Fitzgerald eyes, about the only thing she had in common with her uncle Sean and her sister Lizzie.

"Melonie?" Heath started forward. "Gosh, it's great to see you. Lizzie will be over the moon that you're here. And this big guy—" Heath set his hand on the five-year-old's head "—is my son, Zeke."

"We've met over the computer." Lizzie's sister bent to the boy's level and offered him a sweet smile. "But you're even more handsome in real life, Zeke Caufield."

Zeke grinned, clearly charmed in less time than a foolish man takes to ride a rodeo bull. Heath clapped the boy on the back and laughed. "Lizzie's at the horse stables, but she'll be right along. How are you?" he asked as the woman stepped forward and gave him a hug.

"Ask me in twelve months when I can take my career off hold," she told him. She lifted her eyebrows toward the beautiful horse stables just west of the graveled parking area. "If I live that long. You know me and horses—we learned the hard way to stay clear of one another and that's not about to change. Sakes alive, Heath." She gazed around and her eyes softened with appreciation. Her voice drawled now, a nod to the woman's Southern roots. Funny there was no trace of that drawl when she'd stopped at Jace's place. "This has got to be the back door to nowhere, isn't it? And yet… It's real pretty in its own Western way."

Back door to nowhere?

Jace hung back, purposely.

He knew her kind, all right. The sort that kept themselves separate, disparaging the dawn-to-dusk hard work on a spread like this. The kind of woman that found down-home ranching beneath them. His family had helped settle this town. They'd built homes, dug wells and arranged for schooling and libraries, and they'd done it all expecting nothing in return except a chance to grow a town worth living in, so he not only respected the work that went into this town. He admired it.

"Jace." Heath motioned him over and it would be rude to stand still. Rude…but tempting, nonetheless. He rebuffed the temptation and crossed between the vehicles. "Jace, this is Lizzie's sister, Melonie. Mel, this is my friend and right-hand man, Jace Middleton."

"Mr. Middleton." She drawled his name out with all the pomp of a modern day Scarlett O'Hara and if that didn't spell trouble with a capital *T*, then nothing did. "It is a pleasure to make your official acquaintance."

"Mine, too, ma'am." He extended his hand. She met his gaze, straight on, then took his hand. The strength of her grip surprised him but he refused to show it. "Glad you found your way. Eventually."

"As am I." He was pretty sure the Southern drawl was all for his benefit because it disappeared when Lizzie came running across the grass from the stables.

"Melonie!"

"Lizzie!" They hugged and laughed and at that moment he couldn't resent her because he knew what it was like to have family love.

You knew it, you mean.

He choked down a sigh. He started for the baler,

wishing things were different. He wished the town's economy hadn't started to nose-dive two decades back when no one bothered looking. Wished he wasn't the last Middleton in a town built by Middletons.

But he was, and there were no two ways about it. Jace was going to do the one thing he hated to do. He was going to leave Shepherd's Crossing and all his family had built over the years. Built…and lost.

He yanked his cowboy hat onto his head and fired up the baler. He'd longed for a chance to set things right, to make a name for himself in his hometown, but that wasn't about to happen now.

So be it.

He'd do whatever it took to help his kid sister, Justine, get the start she deserved, and to make his way in the world. Even if it meant changing up the old house. He pushed the thoughts aside as he maneuvered the big machine out of the equipment barn to gas it up.

Lizzie's sister looked up. Not at him, but beyond him. Something marked her gaze. Something shadowed and maybe even sad as her eyes swept over the beautiful ranch with a long, slow look. A look that indicated she was in the wrong place at the wrong time. She righted her features before she turned back toward Lizzie, but then she saw him looking her way.

Her gaze narrowed. Her mouth did, too. But the face she showed Lizzie two seconds later was warm and genuine.

Only it wasn't, and right now Jace Middleton was pretty sure only he and Melonie Fitzgerald knew that.

Sparse population, drastically cold winters and a herd of horses probably waiting to trample her senseless.

What on earth was Melonie Fitzgerald doing in western Idaho, when she'd been on the verge of contracting her own home-design TV show?

She knew the answer. Her father. He was a major publishing owner/executive who'd brought down his company, his home and his three daughters when he diverted millions in cold, hard cash into overseas accounts…then followed it there.

She didn't do ranches. She steered clear of horses for good reason. And when her long-term boyfriend realized she was not only broke, but also in a mountain of debt, he'd dumped her like a hot potato fresh out of the coals.

Yet here she was, fulfilling the terms of a bequest on her late uncle's ranch when she should have been on camera, filming the pilot episode of *Shoestring Southern Charm.*

Girl, you make the best of every situation. If it gets dark, you light a candle. If it gets cold, start a fire, or warm a room with your smile. A smile goes a lot further than a frown.

Corrie's words. Succinct and true, always dependable. She turned to ask Lizzie about their nanny/surrogate mother, but caught the cowboy's gaze instead.

He was hot. Not big-city hot, either. Country hot, with his long-sleeved blue thermal shirt, dark blue jeans and a to-die-for real cowboy hat. The black hat showed off his bronze skin and made him look even more rugged, if such a thing was possible.

He'd duped her over the directions.

After you treated him like a back-road hick.

She winced because she'd iced him and she wasn't usually like that. But four years of running part of the magazine's corporate office had affected her. She faced her sister. "Where's Corrie?"

"Up the drive visiting Rosie and the baby."

Was Melonie supposed to have a clue what she meant? Because she didn't.

Lizzie took her arm as the good-looking cowboy busied himself with a fairly monstrous piece of machinery. "You'll get to know folks quick enough. There are a lot of nice people here, Mel."

Mel locked eyes with her. "There are nice people everywhere. Doesn't mean I intend to live there. You know me. This isn't exactly my thing."

"And on that note." Heath slipped an arm around Lizzie, kissed her, then bumped his forehead to hers. "I'll be back tomorrow. Love you."

Lizzie gave him a smile that said more than words. "Love you, too. See you tomorrow."

"Yeah, see you, Dad!" The brown-skinned little boy jumped into his father's arms and gave Heath a big hug. "Maybe we'll make some cookies for you. Okay?"

"Okay." Heath shared a grin with the boy, then took off in a muscled-out pickup truck.

"They're taking the winter lambs to market."

Melonie scowled. "I know what that means."

"Says the steak lover in the family."

Melonie started to acknowledge that, but spotted Corrie coming their way. She dropped her purse and raced off to meet the woman who'd stood by the three sisters for as long as she could remember.

"Have mercy, I've missed you, girl!" Corrie pulled back, looked Mel over, then offered her a sweet, wide smile. "Look at you, all Louisville fancy in the heart of western Idaho."

"Please do not tell me this is overdressed," said Mel. She glanced at Lizzie's blue jeans, barn boots and T-shirt and sighed. "Never mind."

"I've got stuff you can use, Mel. But yeah, even casual silk has no place here. " Lizzie exchanged a grin with Corrie. "And cotton's a must."

"Meaning I might as well leave my luggage in the car, right?"

Corrie laughed. "Let's get your things inside and we'll catch up. Did Cottonwood Productions offer you a contract? And are they willing to wait?"

"Yes and no." Melonie pushed a lock of hair out of her eyes as she trundled a bag up the steps. "When they realized I had to be here, they quietly shredded the whole thing."

"Oh, Mel." Lizzie stopped on the top step. "That could have been a huge step forward for you. Wasn't it worth foregoing Uncle Sean's bequest to give it a shot?"

Melonie shook her head as she climbed the stairs. "Breaking into cable is high risk. Most pilots go nowhere. Only a few make it, but with nothing to live on, the choice became a no-brainer. Ezra is shopping it around, but I've got bills to pay." Ezra had been a photographer for the magazine. Now he was working freelance photography and videography.

"I hear you," said Lizzie. "Come on in, let's get you settled. And I don't know about the two of you, but I'm hungry. Let's make some sandwiches and eat them on the porch with the cute kid. We can play with the puppies."

Cute kid. Puppies. Sandwiches?

Was this her low-carb, former publishing-executive sister talking? The one whose job disappeared along with their swindling father? She reached out a hand to Lizzie's forehead. "No fever, but possible delirium. Who are you and what have you done with my sister?"

Lizzie laughed as Zeke popped in, grabbed a cookie, then headed right back out again. "I'm a rancher, Mel. Welcome to the Pine Ridge Ranch. It is—" she slipped an arm around Melonie's shoulders and gave her a half hug as they moved to the stairs "—real nice to have you on board. I'm hoping you'll be surprised by the reception you get when you meet the locals. I gave all kinds of people the last two copies of your magazine and they loved them. Who knows?" She lifted the suitcase to carry it up the stairs. "You might land some jobs here."

Melonie had gotten an eyeful of what Shepherd's Crossing had to offer when she shot past the farm drive on her first pass through. The small town just north of Pine Ridge featured worn-out buildings, paint-peeling facades and a pervading air of desperation. Not exactly a recipe for success.

She could make a difference. She knew that instantly, but she had no stake, no cash and no reserves to draw on. For a design person like her, Shepherd's Crossing would be a fresh canvas. She'd love to engage her hands in a project like that, to help renovate a run-down community.

But she'd found out the hard way that nothing came from nothing, and without money... Well, there were no options without money.

"Ladies."

That voice. Jace's voice, ringing deep and strong and true. She came face-to-face with him as he crossed the broad front porch. She moved to the screen door and pointed. "They're taking my things upstairs. Can I help?"

"Let Lizzie know we'll be running hay all day. Have her text if she needs me between loads."

"I will. And hey—I was short with you when I stopped by your place. I'm sorry."

"No harm done."

"There was," she insisted, opening the screen door. For some reason she wanted him to understand. "Generally I'm a nice person. Except around horses and dirt and manure."

He didn't smile at the joke. He looked almost sorry for her, then put up his hands. "Apology accepted. Those of us who work around all three on a daily basis will be sure to steer clear."

That wasn't what she meant and only a thin-skinned, stubborn, boneheaded man would take it that way. A man with the greatest set of shoulders she'd ever seen.

He walked away, climbed onto the big machine and started it up. Then he rumbled it past the barns, down a long lane stretching to faraway fields. And he didn't look back.

Chapter Two

Jace parked the baler midafternoon and headed toward the ranch house for lunch. Bob "Cookie" Cook managed the ranch kitchen. He was gone for the day, but he'd texted that he'd left a platter of meat, cheese and sandwich fixings in the kitchen, along with a bowl of potato salad. After five hours of baling the important first cutting of hay, he and the others would get the hay under cover before the predicted overnight rain. Wet hay fostered mold growth, so they'd be running the hay wagons back and forth from the field to the hay barns and lofts until dark…and maybe after. It wouldn't be the first time he'd hauled hay in the dark.

He climbed the steps and met two of the other hands in the kitchen. Harve Jr. was building a sandwich and Wick was already plowing into a monster-sized plate of potato salad. He saw the women on the front porch, laughing together, but the cool reprieve of the kitchen offered more invitation. He'd taken his first bite when the crunch of tires on gravel drew the men's attention. From his seat, he spotted Gilda Hardaway, the grumpy eccentric who lived in a sprawling, decaying house on an empty ranch near the Payette National Forest. She approached the porch, looking testier than ever.

But then the front door opened. Lizzie came in. She spotted him and motioned him forward.

Wick and Harve Jr. exchanged grins, glad they weren't summoned.

He stood, swiped his mouth with a piece of paper towel and walked to the porch. "Ladies." He tipped his head in their direction. "What can I do for you?"

"Not them. Me, young man."

He was afraid of that. He faced Gilda. "Well, how can I be of help, Mrs. Hardaway?"

She looked him up and down as if he was a science exhibit. Then she sighed. "Can I come inside or do I have to air dirty laundry out here where any Tom, Dick or Harry might overhear?"

"Of course," Lizzie answered. She opened the white, wooden screen door and let the old woman precede her. Then she sent Jace a questioning look.

He shrugged, because he didn't know any more than she did.

"We should sit down," said the old woman.

Jace didn't want to sit. He wanted to eat his lunch and get back to work. He was on a tight schedule. One band of sheep was still in the hills, and Heath and two other hands were loading lambs for market on the far side of the mountain. Already he heard noise in the kitchen, meaning the other men had wolfed down their food and were ready to haul. One look at Gilda Hardaway nixed his choices. He sat.

The old woman lifted a magazine from the coffee table. She held it up to Lizzie. "That your sister out there on the porch? This one?" She waggled the magazine.

Lizzie nodded.

"We'll need her in here."

Jace watched Lizzie fight whatever she wanted to say, because Lizzie wasn't the kind of woman anyone bossed around. But she kept her lips pressed tight, then called Melonie and Corrie in. If the old woman didn't want Corrie on hand, she at least had the grace not to show it.

Once the other two women had taken seats, Mrs. Hardaway turned back toward him. "Your name is not Jace Middleton."

Well, that explained the unexplainable visit. She'd gone batty. Clearly batty because he knew who he was.

"Your father was Lionel Tate."

Lionel Tate was his father's cousin. He'd left town a long time ago and died somewhere. Jace didn't remember where because he'd never known the man. "My father was Jason Middleton."

The old woman's frown deepened. "Jason and Ivy took you in as a baby. You were just over a year old, and when they offered to take you in, it was agreed upon because it fit."

Hairs began to rise along the nape of Jace's neck. What was she talking about?

"Your mother was angry when Lionel left. Very angry. She handed you over and went off on her own. As far as I know, no one heard from her until she showed back up nine years later with a baby girl."

"Mrs. Hardaway, I believe you're confused." He kept his voice calm as he offered an explanation. "Justine is six years younger than me. She's just finished her master's in biochemistry and she's doing a paid internship in Seattle."

"Your *other* sister," she told him. "Your biological half sister. She is younger than you by nearly eleven years."

The firmness in her voice—the staunch look in her eye, as if she was the one who was right—unnerved him. "Mrs. Hardaway…"

Lizzie put a hand on his arm. Her sister darted a look from him to the old woman and back, as if embarrassed for him. Or her. Or just plain embarrassed to be there.

"She gave that baby up for adoption, too, because she came here and no one stepped in to take care of that baby girl, and there's plenty of shame to go around about that. When your folks offered to take her in, too, seeing as she was your sister, they were told 'no' because of tough family finances."

She wasn't making sense, and yet… He remembered hushed whispers around that time. He'd been plenty old enough to realize something was going on, but never knew what. Snips of private conversation came back to him, conversations that meant nothing then…and everything at this moment. "That makes no sense, because we weren't poor. My mother was a schoolteacher and Dad was a contractor. He worked all the time. We were always financially solid."

She locked her eyes with his, then said something that tipped everything into sharper focus. "Your sister is white."

And there it was. A divide he'd never personally felt in Shepherd's Crossing because the Middletons had been some of the earliest pioneers in the area. But now—

A mix of raw emotions began churning inside him. "How can that be, Mrs. Hardaway?"

She held his gaze, held it hard, as if this whole thing hurt her more than it pained him. Then she spoke, and

he understood the wounded expression. "Because I am your grandmother, Jace. And my daughter Barbara was…" Her mouth trembled slightly. And her eyes looked sad. "Your mother."

None of this could be true.

It couldn't.

He'd seen his birth certificate. He had it, back at the house. "You're wrong, I'm afraid. I have proof of who I am at my home. My family home, Mrs. Hardaway." He stood, ready to end this nonsense and get to work.

"Your birth certificate," she said.

He nodded. "It lists everything. Mother. Father. Date and time of birth. Place of birth. We're haying today, but if you give me a day or two, I'll bring it by so you can see it for yourself." Whatever had happened back then, he had government-certified proof of who he was. Clearly the old woman was mistaken.

"It is the practice in many states to alter the birth certificates of adopted children, Jace. Adoptions back then were meant to be private affairs for a reason. I have the original certificate here." She reached into an old purse and withdrew a folded, faded sheet of paper. Then she handed it over.

He didn't want to look at it.

What if it was true?

He unfolded the paper and read the information there. And his heart chugged to a slow, draining stop in his chest.

"Jace." Lizzie had stood, too. She gripped his arm gently.

He read his birth date.

The time of birth, the place—all exactly the same as his certificate at home. But the names were different.

He swallowed hard, wanting to shove the paper back at her and walk out the door. Wanting—

"I know this is hard, but there's a reason I'm here today." The old woman hunched forward. "I have things to fix."

Not on his dime.

He set down the paper. He didn't crumple it and throw it back at her, which is what he wanted to do. No. He set it down and started for the door.

"Jace." The old woman stood and began to hobble after him. She looked frantic, but he didn't care. He didn't care one bit, he—

"I'm not looking for forgiveness." She rasped the words and his heart lurched. "I'm looking for help. For labor."

None of this was making sense, but he turned back. "Listen, Mrs. Hardaway…"

"Gilda. Please." She held out a picture of the old, rambling house on Hardaway Ranch. The place must have been a beauty in its time, but that was a generation or two back. Now it was a neglected wreck with a grumpy recluse living inside. "I had to tell you the truth, Jace, because I need you. Your sister's gone off, leaving her two babies. If we don't step in and do something to claim those little girls, they'll end up in foster care. And I can't let another wrong go unchecked."

Now she had his attention. "What do you mean about my sister? About babies?"

"Valencia." Corrie breathed the word softly. She folded her hands tight in her lap, as if praying.

"You know her?" asked Mrs. Hardaway.

"I have met her twice, but it's the children I know best. Two beautiful children, twin girls. Ava and Annie. Rosie watches them here on the ranch. But I believe that Valencia has a mother working at the Carrington Ranch. Correct?"

"She did, but she's left there and gone to Florida. Lora Garcia is her adoptive mother and she wants nothing to do with Valencia or those children," Gilda told them. "She has made that clear. But I cannot turn my back on another child. I've done that three times." She stood and locked eyes with Jace. "I must make amends, but my house is unlivable for children."

"You're thinking of taking these children?" This reclusive woman could barely care for herself. "Impossible. If what you say is true—"

"It is," she interrupted firmly, then waited.

He prayed.

In his head, quiet as can be, he prayed because right now he had no idea what to do. Except he knew he couldn't turn over two small children to an elderly woman with health issues and a laundry list of regrets regarding children already. He'd seen the two little girls at Rosie's house a time or two. He hadn't thought much of it. Now he'd be able to think of nothing else. "I will take charge of the children." He thought he glimpsed a gleam of approval in her eye, but if he did, it was short-lived. "Unless you have objections to their dark uncle taking charge."

She flinched, but then shook her head. "No objections at all. I don't have energy for little children, I'm not what they need, but I've got money."

He didn't need her money. "I—"

She raised a hand "To hire you. And her." She poked a finger toward Lizzie's very surprised sister and Melonie's eyes opened wide. "To make a difference. I want my house to be beautiful again. To be a place I can be proud to leave for these children. It's time I took charge,

Jace. And I've seen your work." She tapped the magazine as she drew Melonie into the conversation. "It's remarkable and inviting. I want you to do the designing." She turned to face Jace again. "I want you to make her designs come true. If you can both look at the project once the hay is in the barn, you can come up with an estimate and I'll give you start-up costs. Then we'll have begun to fix two things. My great-grandchildren will have a place to live. And maybe the ranch won't look sad and lonely anymore."

Renovate her home. Her ranch. Take on the custody of twin toddlers he didn't know.

Six hours ago he'd lamented his lack of family in Shepherd's Crossing.

What a joke. Because now he seemed to have more family than he knew what to do with…

He caught Melonie's eyes across the room. She had the grace to stay quiet, but what choice did he have?

He turned toward Lizzie and Corrie. "I've got to help get the hay in. Rain's expected and my house isn't ready for two little kids. Can I impose—"

Melonie stood up. "It's no imposition. You can have my room here. I'll bunk in the stable with Lizzie." She faced her sister. "There's room, isn't there?"

"Always, Mel. It will be like old times," Lizzie said quietly. "The horses won't bother you?"

"Not as long as they stay downstairs."

They'd thrown him a lifeline. A lifeline he'd gladly take hold of. "I'd be grateful," Jace told them. "Just until I can get things right at the house. And—" he turned toward Melonie and had to eat his words from that morning "—the advice you offered this morning?"

"About your house?"

The sudden addition of two toddlers negated his reluctance to change things up. "I'm ready to take it."

He went through the door and didn't look back. The women would sort things out with Gilda, and they'd be more diplomatic than he could be right now.

He crossed to the hay stacker, climbed in and turned it on. He spotted Wick and young Harve making bales in the far field. He aimed the stacker that way while his mind churned on what he'd just heard.

He hated that it made sense. He hated that the two wonderful, faith-filled people he loved weren't really his parents and had never trusted him enough to tell him. Why would they keep this a secret? It wasn't like there was shame in adoption.

He'd been hoping for local jobs to crop up again. He'd said that often enough, and here was a mammoth one being laid at his feet, a job that hinged on something he'd never much thought of until just now. The color of his skin and the accidents of birth.

His grandmother hadn't wanted him thirty years ago. She'd made sure he was tucked in with a lovely black family because it fit.

And now it didn't.

His phone buzzed. He pulled it out. Glanced down. I scheduled a meeting with Gilda Hardaway for 3:00 p.m. tomorrow. Okay?

It was from Melonie Fitzgerald, telling him what to do and how to do it. Could this possibly get any worse?

He sighed, texted back Yes and shoved the phone away because he was pretty sure it could get worse.

And there wasn't a thing he could do about it.

Chapter Three

Two borrowed portable cribs.

A mountain-sized stack of disposable diapers.

Creams, lotions, shampoos and bottles. Lots of bottles. Two babies had just moved into the ranch house.

Melonie Fitzgerald had never changed a diaper in her life. Nor had she cared to.

By hour three she'd changed two under Corrie's watchful eye. "Done." She set the wriggling girl onto the floor and stood up to wash her hands.

The baby burst into tears. Big, loud tears.

Then the second one noted her sister's agony and followed suit. The babies looked around the room at all the strange faces and kept right on crying.

"Here, sweetie." Lizzie picked up one. Corrie lifted the other. And still they cried.

"Mel, Rosie brought bottles ready to warm. Can you do that for us?"

"Sure." She slipped into the kitchen, took out the bottles and stared at them. Then she picked up her smartphone and asked it how to warm a baby's bottle while the twins howled in the front room.

No answer and they had two screaming babies and a perfectly good microwave. She searched for directions.

Oops. Microwave warming was not recommended… but desperate times called for desperate measures. She followed the non-recommended directions, made sure the formula wasn't too hot, shook it and tested it again, then recapped the bottles.

"Mel?" Lizzie's voice sounded desperate.

"Coming." She brought the bottles into the great room and handed one to Lizzie and the other to Corrie, but Corrie surprised her. "You take charge of this one."

"Me?"

Corrie nodded as she tucked the baby into Melonie's arms. "I promised Zeke I'd take him to play with the puppies. We don't want him to feel left out."

"Corrie, thank you." Lizzie looked up from the straight-backed chair and Melonie was glad she didn't look any more skilled than Melonie felt at that moment. "We'll get the hang of this. Won't we, Mel?"

Don't say what you're thinking. Just smile and nod.

She did and Lizzie grinned, because Lizzie always knew what Mel was thinking. She sat down primly and posed the nipple near the baby's mouth.

The baby… Ava, maybe? Or Annie? She wasn't sure so she peeked at the baby's arm.

Ava. She knew because she'd surreptitiously put a tiny dot on her right forearm.

The baby grabbed hold of that bottle, yanked it into her mouth and proceeded to drink as if starvation was on the horizon. From the looks of the wee one's chunky thighs, Melonie was pretty sure her desperation was vastly overdone.

"Are they supposed to be this big?" she whispered to Lizzie. "They're like monster-sized."

Lizzie burst out laughing. "I was thinking the same thing. But Rosie said they're ten months old, so that's almost a year. And Rosie has been taking wonderful care of them. And she said she's happy to continue being their nanny while we all work."

Work.

Melonie drew up a mental image of the picture Gilda Hardaway had flashed her way. The two-and-a-half-story home was a skeleton of its former self, but with help…

"This is them?"

Jace's voice drew her gaze. He was framed in the screen door, looking every bit as good as he had that morning, which meant she needed to work harder to ignore it. He opened the door and walked in. Once inside, he glanced from one baby to the next and she wasn't sure if he was going to run screaming or cry.

He did neither.

He set that big, black cowboy hat on a small table, crouched down in front of her and Baby Number One and smiled.

Oh, that smile.

Melonie's heart did a skip-jump that would have done an Irish dancer proud. She quashed it instantly. She was here to do her part, whatever that might be, and then leave. Her dream wasn't here in the craggy hills of western Idaho. It resided south, in the warm, rolling streets of Kentucky and Tennessee, where she yearned to show folks how to create a pocketbook-friendly version of Southern charm.

He started to reach out for the baby, but then his

phone rang. He glanced at the display and made a face. "Justine." He turned to face Lizzie. "How do I explain all this to my kid sister?"

"The same way it got explained to us," she said softly. "But first." She stood and crossed the room, then handed him the baby. "Let Justine go to voice mail for a few minutes. Meet your niece. This is Ava."

Melonie frowned. "That's Annie. This is Ava."

Lizzie frowned, too. "No, I'm sure that—"

Melonie shifted the sleeve of the baby's right arm. The tiny black dot showed up.

"You marked her?" Lizzie lifted both eyebrows in surprise.

"Well, we had to do something," said Mel. "Even Rosie said she had trouble telling them apart except when they're sleeping. Annie brings her right hand up to her face. Ava brings up the left."

"Well, let's try this again." Lizzie handed the baby to Jace. "This is Annie. Annie, this is your Uncle Jace and he's a really good guy."

Jace looked down.

The baby looked up. She squirmed into a more up-right position in his arms, then squinted at him. Her right hand reached up and touched his cheek and his face. And then she patted his face with that sweet baby hand and gurgled up at him.

"She's talking to you." Lizzie grinned. "Look at that, Mel. She's talking to Jace!"

Annie looked around, then back at him. She frowned slightly, then touched his cheek again and laughed.

"She likes you."

He met Melonie's gaze across the room. "I think

she finds me an interesting specimen at the moment. They're pretty little things, aren't they?"

"Beautiful. And this one—" she eased up, out of the chair "—is sound asleep. Should we put her in bed? Hold her? What do we do next?"

Rosie came up the front steps just then, carrying two bags. "Don't let her sleep now, or she'll keep you up tonight. Except that once Ava's asleep, she does not want to waken, so good luck with that." She smiled as she said the words, then set down the bags. "What do we do if Valencia comes back? How do we handle this?" she asked. She faced Jace. "The women filled me in on your story. What if your half sister returns? Do we simply allow her to take these babies, knowing she abandoned them once? Should we call the authorities?" Concern deepened her voice. "I can't understand such behavior because the preciousness of life is very important to me. But what do I do if Valencia comes to my door when I'm watching the girls?"

Jace looked down at Annie. She dimpled up at him, then yawned.

He shifted his attention to Mel and Ava. Then he sighed. "I don't know. We'll have to figure that out. I'm prone to putting things in the Good Lord's hands, but we need to put their safety first. And that might cause a ruckus if she comes back. Rosie, I have no idea what to tell you."

"Do you think she'll come back, Rosie?" Melonie asked. The thought of someone abandoning this sleeping baby gutted her, because parents weren't supposed to abandon their children. Ever.

Uncertainty clouded Rosie's eyes. "I do not know.

She is not a maternal person, and yet I feel she loves these babies. In her own way."

"Maybe loves them enough to give them up." Mel kept her voice soft as Ava squirmed in her arms.

Jace turned her way. "Giving up children shows them love?" Disbelief marked his voice and his expression. "I don't buy that. Caring for kids. Feeding them, clothing them, teaching them. That's what love's all about. Anyone can toss something away. It takes a real parent to go the distance."

He knew nothing, Melonie decided. Because she'd been on the other side of that equation and he was wrong. So wrong.

She stood and handed Ava to Rosie. "I've got to get my stuff settled in the stable."

She walked out, refusing to go toe-to-toe with him. The only reason she held back was because he'd been handed a rough reality a few hours before.

By Jace's definition, her father had gone the distance. Wrong.

He'd provided funds to raise her and her two sisters, he'd paid Corrie to mother them and he'd encouraged them to make the grade in good schools. The recent corporate bankruptcy had left her and Lizzie jobless at a time when print media was shrinking. Her father's personal finances had left her and Charlotte with massive college loans to repay. Jobless with massive debt wasn't how she'd expected to face the year, but her late uncle's legacy would help.

As she crossed the sunlit lawn dividing the two arms of the horse stables, she was glad she'd kept silent inside. If tomorrow's meeting went all right, she'd be working with Jace daily. She'd avoid arguments if she could, but she knew one thing for certain: it took a whole lot more than providing food and shelter to be a parent.

No way was he going to take on Gilda Hardaway's job, Jace decided as he steered his truck toward the Payette forest the next afternoon.

He couldn't bring himself to use the term *grandmother*. She'd gotten the title by circumstance only. It might be a biological truth, but it meant nothing to him. And saving her broken-down house meant even less. He was sticking with his plan, one hundred percent. Sell the house. Move to Sun Valley. Take the girls along with him. End of story.

"How'd your night go?" Melonie had been busying herself doing something in her electronic notebook. She looked up as they made a turn. "With the twins?"

"All right."

She whistled softly. "That's not what I heard."

"Well. They're babies. And I know nothing about babies, so let's say it went all right, considering the circumstances."

The twins hadn't loved their new sleeping arrangements. They'd let that be known in full voice several times during the night. Corrie had jumped in to help him, which was a good thing because Jace would have crashed and burned by hour four. This way they both got some sleep. Just not much. The twins woke up babbling and smiling as if they'd gotten a full night's slumber. But then, they got to take naps. Naps didn't happen for grown-ups.

"Were you guys able to get the hay all in?"

"Harve Junior and Wick stayed out late to beat the rain. It's done."

The rain had held off until just after midnight, but it was coming down now. Not a massive storm. A steady gray drizzle, the kind of rain that benefited crops but thwarted farmers needing to access fields.

But the hay was safe. The girls were with Rosie and Corrie. Now, if he could get through this afternoon's interview…

"And you spoke with your sister?"

Justine. He'd told her as gently as he could, but when she burst into tears, he half wanted to cry with her. He didn't, because big brothers hang strong. Always. "She was shocked. Understandably."

"I expect she was. Whoa." Melonie stretched up in her seat as they took the weed-edged asphalt drive leading up to Hardaway Ranch. Tucked behind trees leading to the national forest, he'd never had a clear look at this house. He'd heard of it, of course. Small towns loved to talk about their eccentrics, and Gilda fit the bill.

But as they emerged from the final curve and the once-grandiose home rose up before them, he took a deep breath.

"Did you just get a horror-film vibe?" Melonie whispered. "Because I sure did."

He couldn't fault her comment because the large, moldy two-and-a-half-story structure would have done Stephen King proud. Surrounded by a yard in desperate need of a brush hog, the place sat like a haunted house on a hill, shrouded by three decades of shrub and tree growth. It was an absolute mess from top to bottom. So bad that he was almost tempted to take the job for the challenge it offered, but not stupid enough to do it.

"Here we are." He pulled up to vine-choked steps and stopped the truck. He studied the building, then Melonie. "We don't have to get out. We can head right back to the road and go home."

Genuine surprise made her look quizzical. "Not go in? Are you crazy? I just had to turn down a cable TV contract to come here, and that was tough. That makes this an amazing opportunity. I absolutely cannot wait to get inside. Come on." She opened her door. "Let's go."

She wanted the job.

The anticipation in her voice was reflected in her eyes as she climbed out of the truck. That meant he had to climb out of the truck, too.

He did. Then he studied the house, the choked yard and the sprawling acres beyond it.

Somewhere within him he could almost imagine the beauty it had been thirty years ago. Before he was born, he realized.

He fought a sigh. He was all for getting back into the truck when Gilda's voice called down to them. "I'm here. And I'm waiting. And there's a few things folks my age don't do well. Waiting's one of them. Come on, come on, I'm not getting any younger."

The old saying drew his attention. It struck a nerve or a memory or something… He kept quiet and followed Melonie up the stairs.

Full sensory overload.

Melonie cloaked her excitement as she walked into the big house. She paused inside the door to take in the ruination of what should have been a gracious old home. The classic, wide farmhouse stood as a shell of its former self. Moldings had been damaged by water leaks.

Some were rotted straight through. Others had simply disintegrated. Plaster showed water damage in multiple rooms on the first floor, which meant the second floor wasn't going to be too pretty because that water came from somewhere. The thought of reclaiming this wreck of a home and showing off her talents was a power boost for Melonie. Getting this job would keep her in Idaho, as required, but she'd be working away from the smell of the horses. Sheep she could deal with. She had no violent history with sheep.

Horses were another story altogether.

"You're quiet. Both of you." Gilda pressed her lips into a thin line. "I don't like it when folks get quiet because that usually means they're scared to say what they think."

Melonie had been jotting a note in her tablet. She raised her eyes without raising her head. "This doesn't scare me, Gilda."

The old woman looked skeptical.

Melonie jotted something else before she continued. "It invigorates me. It's rare that a designer gets the chance to walk in and lay out a fresh canvas."

"What does that mean?"

Jace shifted his attention to her, too. She'd seen his initial reaction as he walked into the house. Horror... and interest. And something else. Regret, maybe. As if the decay made him sad.

She stopped making notes and faced them. "It means I'm mentally planning massive demolition and starting new. I think the bones of the house are great."

"Bones?"

"The structure," she explained. "The water leaks have done significant damage. The first order of business will be new roofs. Once that's done we can begin the demo inside. No sense starting anything until we've got a solid roof in place."

Jace stayed quiet. He'd brought a few simple tools with him. He poked walls for plaster rot and found plenty. The ceilings on the first floor were ruined, except in the front parlor. He noted that into his phone, then laser-measured the house dimensions. As they moved from room to room, the magnitude of what the elderly woman was asking became obvious.

"Mrs. Hardaway." He slipped his phone into the leather pouch on his belt and rubbed a hand to his neck. "I'm going to be honest with you."

"I am not paying for opinions," she told him in a craggy voice. She'd been following them with a bright pink cane. She tapped that cane sharply against the water-stained floor.

"I beg to differ." He kept his tone even. "That's exactly what you asked, and I'm telling you that the cost of refurbishing this place is astronomical. Perhaps—"

"I've got a five-hundred-thousand-dollar budget earmarked for this. How much help can I get for five hundred thousand dollars?"

Jace stopped dead.

So did Melonie because that was some serious money.

Jace stared at Gilda, then scanned the house, then looked at his grandmother again. "All I'm saying is that we could start over. Something more practical. We tear this down and build a well-constructed ranch house on the site. Everything would be bright and new and accessible." He noted the cane with a glance. "That's nothing to take lightly."

Melonie didn't like Jace's suggestion, but she understood his reasoning. An old woman in frail health—what was she doing here all these years, living amid the decay?

She stood there, silent, letting the old woman make the choice as offered. And hoped she opted for a complete renovation.

Jace had to shoot fair and square, even with the rich eccentric who had shaken his world to the rafters the previous day. He'd handle that later. This was different.

He didn't pretend to like her as she gazed around the house, considering his words. Growing up in Shepherd's Crossing, he'd heard all kinds of things, and he was pretty sure no one much liked her, but this wasn't about emotion. It was about common sense. "We could have it done before winter."

A small, cozy rebuild made more sense. He knew it. And he was pretty sure the women knew it, too.

He didn't look at Melonie. She'd be disappointed because he could see her mental wheels spinning as she moved from room to room. But who in their right mind would put that kind of money into—

"I appreciate your suggestion, young man. I know it makes sense and it's an honest man that lays out the truth even if it doesn't pay as well. But I need my home back." Gilda Hardaway locked eyes with him, sorrow in her gaze. "From top to bottom." She gripped her cane hard, and her hand shook with the pressure. "I messed up my time, but I can fix this if God gives me the days and if you'll take the job. It's not about money, son."

He wanted to take offense at the familial term, but

he couldn't because she looked too sad and alone to mean anything bad.

"It's about fixing what needs to be fixed. Can you do it?" She turned to include Melonie in the question. "Now that the first hay is in and the winter lambs are off to market?"

She was ranch-savvy. She'd caught him at a good time. They'd have to hire roofers first, and that would give him a couple of weeks to renovate his house to make it safe for the twins. "I can do it."

"But will you?"

There was the crux of the question.

Could he handle this mammoth job, with help, and still make it to Sun Valley as planned? Because as grand as this job was, it was one job and now he had not one, but three mouths to feed. Two babies to raise. And he couldn't even begin to think about the astronomical costs of day care in Sun Valley.

Stop worrying about tomorrow. If the Lord sees fit to take care of the birds of the air and the lilies of the field, He's got you. He's got this.

Jace wasn't so sure, but when he brought his gaze back to Gilda's, something in her eyes, her face…

Something made him say yes.

He was pretty sure he'd regret it. He already did, truth be told, and when Melonie began shooting pictures of each room, he realized something else.

For the next few months they'd be working side by side.

She'd lay out plans and expect him to follow them. Oh, he'd looked at her magazine that morning as research. She liked to plot intricate layouts, but that was for a two-dimensional magazine, where every shot was strategically perfect.

Gutting a place like this was about as three-dimensional—and dirty—as it could get. And the silk-wearing Fitzgerald woman didn't seem like the type to get her hands dirty. Or compromise. Which meant this could be the longest three months of his life.

Then she turned. Met his gaze. Smiled at him.

Something went soft inside him.

He hardened it right back up. No way was he about to let a pretty smile get in his way. Melonie Fitzgerald had *fancy* written all over her. He'd sworn off fancy a few years ago when he showed up at the church…and his bride was nowhere to be found. That was a punch in the gut for any self-respecting cowboy.

But when they got to the truck and Melonie turned toward him, excitement brightened those gray eyes to liquid silver. Distinctive eyes set in one of the sweetest faces he'd ever seen.

Maintain your distance. You've been nailed by a woman with dreams of stardom once. Don't be stupid a second time.

He wouldn't be stupid. Not again. But with her bright floral scent filling the cab of the truck, Jace didn't fool himself that it would be easy.

Chapter Four

"We need to have a meeting." Melonie scribbled notes into her tablet at a furious pace as Jace drove them back to Pine Ridge Ranch.

"You're here. I'm here. Let's have a meeting."

She angled a wry look his way.

His jaw quirked, just a little. So he might have a sense of humor hidden under layers of angst after all. Good. "Are you doing the roofs?"

"No. Contracting them out. There's a couple of great roofing companies between McCall and Council. I'll get some estimates for the job. People around here are hungry for work, so we should be able to line up someone fairly quickly. How much of your designs are you running by Mrs. Hardaway?"

"I want to put together a package and present it to her. My goal is to keep it true to the structure and history, but make it more modern. Less fuss, more open space, but still classic design."

"It must have been something in its time."

"Did people realize how bad it was getting?" she wondered. "Did they just ignore it?"

"Well, it's Gilda Hardaway, and you've met her. She's always been rich and beyond eccentric since I've been old enough to know she existed. But you can't see the house from the road, the weeds and brush are a turn-off and, other than a few old-timers, I don't think she entertains visitors."

"So this is a huge step forward for her."

He didn't answer.

He stared straight ahead, his jaw tight and his hands firmly clenched on the steering wheel. She changed the subject. "I'll come up with an exterior palette so we can pick roofing materials by the time we head up there to-morrow morning. And I'll work on the design this evening. It won't be quick." The fact that she couldn't redo a two-and-a-half-story house in a matter of hours made her feel like she should apologize. "I'll need some time."

"We've got as much time as the roofing takes."

"That might not be enough, even if I don't sleep. How about this, instead?" He glanced her way as they turned into the Pine Ridge Ranch driveway, and she had to re-mind herself that those big brown eyes were off-limits. This guy had "Welcome to Idaho" written all over him. She was headed south once her year was complete. He was staying. "I come up with a quick design for you to fix up your place, you focus on that, roofs get done, my design for Gilda gets done and we move forward in a couple of weeks."

He didn't say anything right away, then he flexed his jaw. "It will have to work."

Have to work?

She climbed out of her side of the truck and shut the door. "'Thanks, Mel, that's a great idea.' 'Glad to help, Jace. Great working with you.'"

She started toward the stables, and it would have been a perfect stomp-off, but then she realized she needed to see his house. Like quickly.

She turned.

He was standing there, stock-still, arms folded, watching her. And a hinted smile softened his jaw and put a sparkle in his eyes. "Forgetting something?"

"You are a particularly annoying person."

"Nothing I haven't heard before." He indicated the house with a tip of his head. "Let's grab sandwiches, head to my place and then you can march off indignantly. Okay?"

"It's not okay at all," she grumbled as they climbed the steps. "It totally loses punch in the delay, so what sane woman wastes a great walk-off when it's already been defeated. No." She turned to face him at the door, and she wasn't afraid to add a slight splash of Southern geniality to her tone. "I will save my stomping for moments of necessity. Right now, we have work to do. You. Me. And my design program."

"So I can expect the cold shoulder at a future time?"

"Only as needed, Jace."

Sassy. Saucy. And strong, despite her diminutive size. Did she know her stuff?

The magazine pictures said yes, but while the pictures looked great, he worried. Did someone have to rein her in and explain bearing walls and structural integrity?

"I smell something amazing."

"Cookie's beef-and-onion soup."

"Be still my heart." She set her bags onto the couch

and inhaled deeply. "Who'd have thought soup would smell so amazing on a summer's day?"

"Cookie makes soup all year round, don't you?" Jace asked as they entered the kitchen. "Are we too early?"

"Give me fifteen," answered the cook. "Bread's in the oven. Nothing like hot beef-and-onion soup with fresh-baked bread. There's sandwich makings in the fridge."

"I'm waiting on soup," Melonie declared.

"I'll call the roofers, see who's available to get on the job quickly."

"Because of the farm timing, right?"

He turned slightly. "Because I'm scheduled to leave town by Labor Day and that's already going to have to be delayed with this project."

"You're leaving?"

"Jobs have pretty much dried up around here. I have little choice."

Doubt clouded her features. "But you stand to make a year's worth of money on this project. Correct?"

"That will all depend on costs and labor, but we should both do all right."

"Then why leave now? Why not take the year God's given you and see what happens?"

Just what he needed, a stranger pointing out the flaws in his logic—logic that had worked until yesterday, when he discovered his whole life was a lie.

"I don't mean to interfere."

He was pretty sure that's exactly what she meant.

"But to become an instant father, tackle a huge project and have your moving time delayed until winter, why not put it on hold? Unless you're precontracted there?"

"I'm not."

She faced him, waiting, then she turned.

He hated that she was right, but it did make sense. He'd have plenty to live on with Gilda's project, and using that as a showcase in his portfolio would make sense during the next building season. "I'll add the Realtor to my list of calls."

She grabbed a cookie from the old-fashioned cookie jar that had a place of honor on the counter. Then she paused, grabbed two more and handed them to him as she went back to the living room for her tablet. "Best appetizers ever."

He made the first calls and wasn't sure what soothed him more, getting the roofers to meet him at Gilda's place tomorrow, canceling the sale of his house, or the two macadamia-nut, white-chocolate-chip cookies.

It almost didn't even matter that she was right. He could relist the house if he regretted the decision, but renovating his house while prospective buyers were coming through would be a lost cause. He only wished he'd thought of it first.

He called Rosie quickly. "How are the girls doing?"

"Fine, as always, so adorable these two and getting busy! Ava is determined to walk, but, of course, that means falling."

"You let them fall?" Babies weren't supposed to fall. Were they?

"I blame this on gravity, Jace. Not ineptitude."

"No, of course, I didn't mean…"

She laughed. "I must go—Annie is crawling faster than her sister is walking along the sofa's edge and she seems determined to trip her."

Sibling rivalry already?

He put off the next roofing call to hop online and order three how-to-raise-your-child books. Then he called two more roofers for scheduled meetings at Hardaway Ranch. He might be in over his head when it came to raising babies, but he knew building and he knew ranching. And with three books slated to be here in two days' time, he'd have a firm handle on raising children, too.

"Soup's on!" Cookie jangled the porch bell. Midday meals were casual. Cookie knew folks couldn't just drop what they were doing and run to the house in the middle of the workday.

Suppertime wasn't formal, but it was more structured. At least it had been. With the arrival of the Fitzgerald sisters, new foals dropping, Annie and Ava staying in the big house temporarily and Rosie's infant daughter, Jo Jo, the plethora of small people meant change. Flexibility. And a mountain of diapers, he'd realized yesterday.

He went inside. And saw Melonie busily making notes into her device. She looked up when the door smacked shut behind him.

She smiled.

Those eyes…like mercury.

Mercury's poisonous, in case you've forgotten.

He knew that, but there wasn't one hint of poison in those pretty gray eyes. "Any luck on roofing estimates?" she asked.

"Two can meet me tomorrow."

"Us?"

"Sure, if you want to be there. But it's roofing," he continued. "Pretty cut-and-dried if you're keeping the original lines."

"I'll come anyway. I like being involved in every step of the process—it gives me the feel for the end product."

"Nine thirty and ten thirty. Then a third one in two days, if needed."

"Got it." She jotted it into her online calendar and stood. "Food. Then your place."

Did she think bossy was cute? It wasn't. But when he let her walk in front of him toward the kitchen, he realized she wasn't just cute…she was beautiful. And curvy. And smelled great.

Doomed.

Except he couldn't allow that to happen, so he focused on the delicious food as Melonie put a bit of the melted provolone onto the bread. "This is to die for, isn't it?"

It was but when she had a second helping, he was perplexed. "How can you eat all that?"

She gazed down at the soup, then up at him. "I honestly don't know. Trucker's appetite. And I don't sit around worrying about being a size zero because I like food. And exercise. And last I knew, women were supposed to have curves."

What was he supposed to say to that? "My sister was on a too-skinny kick for a while. It got better, then we lost Mom after Dad died and she slipped downhill again. I hate that she's over in Seattle, where I can't boss her around. Make her eat doughnuts."

"Weight and eating disorders are tough." She sipped water, and frowned. "We humans are hard to figure out at times, aren't we?"

After what he'd found out yesterday? "Can't argue that."

"How hard do you think that was for her?" She stood

up to clear her dishes, and he appreciated the effort. Some folks thought Cookie was part maid and house-keeper. He wasn't, but it was nice that she didn't have to be schooled on ranch manners. "Your grandmother, I mean. To come here like that and tell you everything?"

"Not as hard as it was on me hearing it." He didn't soften the bitter edge of his voice. He stood, too, then raised his hands. "Sorry. This isn't your fight, and twenty-four hours isn't enough time for me to be wav-ing the peace flag."

"I wonder when it will be time?" she said softly, and when she walked toward the kitchen, he realized she might not be talking about him. "Cookie, that was the best. Thank you so much for making it. I wouldn't have thought hot soup would taste so good on a beau-tiful summer's day."

"You're welcome. Jace said you two are heading to his place to figure things out. You might want to grab a few of those." He indicated the cookies with a glance. "His cupboards are pretty bare. He makes sure the horses have food. He doesn't worry so much about himself."

"The few times I eat at home don't require a lot of groceries." Jace grabbed his cowboy hat from the wall of hooks just inside the back door. "Although if I'm up at Hardaway's place and raising two little girls, I'll have to change that up pretty quick."

"Truth." Cookie liked to wear an old-style fishing cap in the house. He said it was to keep hair out of the food, but Jace figured the older man just liked wear-ing a hat. The cook raised one finger to the hat as they were leaving. "See you at supper."

Melonie grabbed her two bags. He held the screen

door open for her and tried to ignore the sweet scent that came back to him as she went by.

"You have horses?" she asked once they were settled in the truck.

"Two," he answered. "Sometimes I keep them at Pine Ridge. We used to take the sheep into the hills for browsing but we had to stop doing that."

She arched one really well-groomed eyebrow in silent question.

"Government changed up the rules and took away grazing rights."

"Lizzie said something about that but we didn't have time to go into detail. So now the sheep are pretty much being raised in the valley?"

"With more hay, less exercise so less muscle mass."

"Oh, of course. That makes sense."

Now he was the questioner. "You get that?"

"We had fresh-raised turkeys in Kentucky. It was a Fitzgerald thing. We only raised enough for family and friends or esteemed business acquaintances of my grandfather. It was a mark of acceptance to be given a Fitzgerald turkey in November."

"And this relates to sheep…how?"

She laughed. "Good point. When you eat a store-bought turkey, the consistency is different. It's been tenderized. The home-raised turkeys had a much firmer feel."

"That's it exactly." He sent her an approving look. "The sheep will be the same weight and look the same, but the ratio of fat to lean will be slightly different and the texture will vary. Here we are," he said as he pulled into the driveway. "That's Bonnie Lass over there." He pointed to a dark sorrel mare on the far side of the split-rail paddock. "And the black-and-white is Bubba. My dad's horse. Would you like to go see them?"

"No."

He'd started that way. He stopped, surprised.

She took a step back and shook her head. "I can admire them from afar, thanks. Lizzie and Char are the horsewomen in the family. I'm better inside a house than inside a barn."

How did someone with an aversion to animals just become quarter owner of a multimillion-dollar ranching operation? "Good to know." He moved back and led the way to the front of the house. He unlocked the door and waited for her to follow.

She didn't.

She stepped back and snapped several pictures of the exterior.

"The outside doesn't need fixing."

She jotted something into the tablet and shrugged. "I want to envision the whole package, if that's okay? Just like with Gilda's place."

She followed him inside.

He expected criticism because the real estate agent had given him a hefty list of changes—a list he tore up as soon as she was gone.

Melonie surprised him instantly when she grabbed hold of his arm. "Jace, this is charming."

"Is it?" He ran a hand over the stubble along his jaw.

"Well, it needs a little spruce-up, some painting and some crown molding, but look at these built-ins." She motioned to the floor-to-ceiling bookcases flanking the fireplace. "You put a wood-burning insert in here."

"The Realtor told me I should pull it out and redo the fireplace. She said it adds eye appeal to the buyer."

"And then they freeze all winter?" When she rounded her eyes in disbelief, a wave of relief washed over him. "Cold winds, slashing rains, heavy snow? Who wouldn't want a cozy wood-burning stove to come home to?"

"Exactly. It takes the pressure off the heating bill and gave me some extra money to help Justine get through college."

"Jace, what a good brother you are." She'd been jotting quick notes as she moved through the downstairs rooms. Now she turned. Met his gaze. And then she didn't stop meeting his gaze. She brought one hand up, her free one, and touched her throat.

Oh, man.

He wanted to step forward. Smile at her. Maybe flirt, just a little.

He stepped back instead. "There are two bedrooms and a bathroom upstairs."

"Let's check them out." He followed her up the stairs. She paused at the top and snapped a couple of pictures. She didn't say anything.

That kind of unnerved him. A quiet woman was a rare bird in his experience, and as she tapped things into her tablet, he shoved his hands into his pockets. Then pulled them out again. He motioned downstairs. "I can make coffee. I've got a one-cup system so it's always ready."

"Coffee sounds great," she told him. But she didn't look up. She was perched against the short stair rail at the top of the stairs while her fingers flew.

"Okay." He went downstairs. Made the coffee. When she didn't come down, he called up to her. "Coffee's ready."

"Perfect."

She hurried down the stairs, and came really close

to sliding across the hardwoods like he'd done as a kid. "Is it in the kitchen?"

"On the counter. There's milk, too. And sugar. Nothing fancy, though. Sorry."

"Black's fine. If it's great coffee, why ruin it with all that other stuff?" She grabbed the coffee, took a seat at the table and sipped. Then she savored the moment, eyes round, before she lifted the mug like a salute. "Perfect blend."

"Cowboy blend," he told her.

"You made this?" That got her full attention. "Like the actual coffee beans and stuff?"

"No." He didn't sit. Not in the middle of the workday. There was too much stuff to do. "I order it from a place in Boise—White Cloud Coffee. This is one of their signature blends. Cowboy."

She smiled at him, then took another sip of pure appreciation. "It's ideal. Not bitter. Not weak. Great aroma."

"You love coffee." He did, too. Maybe too much.

"I love good coffee," she corrected him. "I will admit to being a coffee snob. It's a fault, I know."

"Then it's one I share because bad coffee shouldn't be allowed."

"Exactly." She smiled up at him again. Did she know how inviting that was? Was she using that pretty smile to break him down before she gave him bad news about the house?

"I'm going to go take care of the horses while you nose around, all right?"

She lifted the ironstone mug. "I've got coffee in a great mug and the info I need. I'm good."

"And cookies," he reminded her. He set the little pack

of Pine Ridge cookies on the table. "It's like afternoon tea, ranch-style."

"Way better," she told him.

He went outside, conflicted.

She dressed upscale and talked hometown-friendly. Until she turned the drawl on to put him in his place.

He smiled, thinking of that, then stopped smiling because he was thinking of it. Thinking of her. That's all he needed, to fall for another woman with big dreams of TV or stardom or anything that wasn't down-home Idaho.

His phone buzzed a text from Justine. Can we talk? Soon? Because I can't get my head around all this, Jace.

Him, either, but he was older. Call me tonight.

Busy now?

Getting house ready for babies.

Unbelievable...but cool. In a weird way. Coming home in a week to meet them. Hug you. Figure things out.

She needed to touch base with reality, just like him. Good. Can't wait to see you. Talk later.

He finished filling the water trough, then opened the grain bin.

Both horses headed his way. Bonnie trotted the length of the paddock, still spritely at ten years old.

Bubba plodded along, an easygoing old fellow. He wouldn't last much longer, most likely. He was ancient in horse years. He snorted toward Jace, spattering him. "Thanks, old man."

The aged gelding nodded as if pleased, then went to his grain bucket.

"A man and his horses."

He turned, surprised to hear her voice. "I thought you didn't like horses?"

"I have enough respect for them to keep my distance," she told him. "They're over there. I'm here." She pointed to her side of the fence. "It's all good. I've got some quick ideas to show you."

"Already?" He stroked his hand along Bubba's neck, reminded the horses to behave, then came her way. "That's quick."

"I kept it basic," she told him as they walked back to the house. "What you could do, what you should do and what must be done. Then I'll work up the design specs on it tonight so you can jump in."

"More coffee?" he asked her once they were inside. He kicked off his boots at the side entry.

"Your mama raised you right, cowboy." She flicked a glance at the boots. "Barn boots don't belong inside."

Your mama.

Funny how a simple term like that had felt so good two days ago. Now it cut deep because he'd found out she wasn't his mother.

Oh, she loved him. Jace had no doubt about that. Ivy Middleton had taught high-school science, raised two great kids and kept a sharp eye on their small holding and his father. She doted on faith and family, one hundred percent.

But she wasn't his mother after all.

"Please say that dark expression isn't heading my way."

He grimaced and pulled up a chair once his coffee was done brewing. "Sorry."

"The adoption thing has you spinning."

He glared at her for being right, but it wasn't her fault

so he made a rueful face. "It's like a weight on my shoulders. Not that they adopted me, because they were the best parents anyone could ask for. If you wanted model parents, Jason and Ivy Middleton were the benchmark."

"Ivy?" Her eyes went wide again. "Oh, I love that name." She sighed softly. "It's so pretty. I love that old-fashioned names are coming back in style." She placed her right hand over her heart. "Dignity and beauty comes with the name."

"That was Mom. But she hated lies. She was honest all the time, so why keep this a secret? It's not as if folks don't adopt children all the time."

"Good questions with no answers you want to hear, I expect."

"Grandparents are raising grandkids all over the country. But not mine. Because I didn't fit the image of a Hardaway grandson."

"Their loss. And not for nothing, cowboy…" She sat back and sipped her fresh cup of coffee. "If they were as mean-spirited as Gilda made herself out to be, they did you a huge favor. I'd be writing her a thank-you note."

He started to glare, but paused when she raised her hand.

"You ended up without any of the negative nonsense that was so prevalent thirty years ago. That's all I meant. How is your sister handling this? Justine, right?"

"She's calling me later. Wants to talk. And she's coming home next week. She's in the middle of an internship in Seattle, and probably can't afford the time, but she wants to see me. Meet the babies. And come to terms with all this. But I'm not sure how to help her do that when I hardly come to terms with it myself."

Chapter Five

Melonie wasn't exactly an expert on forgiveness. Her father had given her more than enough experience with untrustworthy relatives, but she hadn't reconciled any of it. She probably needed to get over the urge to do a full-fledged father-daughter smackdown first, an urge that went against what she believed. What her faith taught her. She frowned. "They say time is the best help. And faith. But in my experience, it hasn't exactly worked like that so I'm no help. Sorry."

"Lizzie said your dad messed you guys over." He ran one finger around the rim of his mug, frowning. "That's got to be rough. I'm sorry you ladies had to go through that."

"Us and a few thousand employees when he embezzled all the corporate funds he could get his hands on." She pretended a bright smile. "And now he and his current significant other are lolling in Dubai, spending other people's money. But here's a lovely and quite notable difference." She opened her notebook and pitched him a smile. "Your parents loved you to distraction. My sweet mama went home to God when my sister Charlotte was a baby. I was a toddler. We never knew her. We have no memories of her, just photographs.

"We had Corrie," she continued. "She called us her babies and she meant it. So we didn't have a mother, not much of what you'd call a father and our grandparents were caught up in Kennedy-esque dreams.

"Through it all we had Corrie. She was there at every event, every recital, every soccer game, every choir practice. And that's what I mean about Gilda doing you a favor, because if it had been my dad in the stands, things would have been quite different. Because no matter how well you did, it was never going to be good enough." She slid a list across the table. "Here's my rundown. Must. Should. Could."

"I organize my jobs and seasons that way." Approval laced his tone. He read the list. "Yes to the must list, and to the should column as well. Why not do it all right now while the roofers give me time?"

"That was my thought, too." She waited a few beats. "And the could list?"

"To pretty up the outside?"

"Yes."

She wasn't asking for the moon, and if he did revisit selling for the following spring, the house would be ready. "Yes."

"All right. Are you fine if we keep the outside classic, like it is? This isn't a historic landmark, but I'd like to keep the historic look. No new siding. The clapboard is perfect, it just needs painting. Vintage-style shutters. Paint the picket fence, which I love, by the way. New gutters. Wash and paint the concrete porch. And we'll pretty up the gardens."

"I meant to keep them up better." He gripped his mug

with both hands. "But then there wasn't time. They were my mom's gardens and she had a sweet hand with them."

"I can see it."

He looked skeptical for good reason. To an undeveloped eye the landscaping was a mess.

She laughed. "I really can, despite the weeds and the old stems poking up through. There are tricks to keeping things tidy now, with little or no weeding. Leave it to me."

"I'm not used to that." He met her gaze frankly and she had to fight the little catch in her throat when he did that. "Handing over the reins on personal things."

"Pretend it's professional."

"Except that we're talking about my house. My home. My parents' house," he added softly, and there was no denying the longing in his tone. A man who loved and missed his parents.

"I'm giving you veto rights," she told him.

"Yeah?"

"Sure. I'll have the design set by morning because we're not doing anything major. The house is wonderful as is. If this was a car, we'd call this a detail job."

"You don't want to change the kitchen cabinets?"

She stared at him, then the classic cabinetry, then him again. "Only a fool would mess with something like that. Do you want new cabinets?" It pained her to even think of these old beauties being taken down.

"No, but the real estate agent suggested a full tearout. She said the kitchen update should be at the top of the list."

"Agreed. But we can work *with* the pretty cabinets. Not against them. The very idea is ludicrous." She stood and took her mug to the sink. "We should switch out the sink and the countertop and do a fresh paint job. And a new light fixture. Then change the appliances as you need to, but watch for sales."

"Easy enough."

"We're in a time crunch. Here, give me your mug, I'll rinse it out for you." She put out her hand.

So did he.

Her hand closed over his on the mug. Then she looked up. Met his gaze.

Eyes the color of rich cocoa with just enough gold flecks to brighten when he smiled. Thick eyebrows. A firm jaw. Corrie told her once that a good man didn't blubber or fuss or fumble much with words. That a good man had a strong heart, well-set shoulders and a firm jaw.

This cowboy fit the definition to the max.

His eyes swept her face. Her mouth.

Then he let go of the mug, withdrew his hand and stepped back. "You can just leave it."

She rinsed it anyway, and set it on a dish rack to dry. A meow sounded outside the door.

"Barn cat. Great mouser. I'll make sure she's got food before we go."

"I'll meet you outside."

She gathered her notepad and camera bag. And her purse. When she walked through the side door, he was waiting.

"My mother loved this little covered entry."

"Quaint and picturesque."

"She called it a proper entry for an old home."

Melonie's heart melted. "She's right. So many old places became add-a-room houses. It's not easy to do additions that keep the integrity of an old place while addressing necessities."

"What made you decide to do this?" he asked as they

walked to his truck. He didn't walk real close to her, but not all that far away, either. "Designing? Homes? Making things pretty?"

"See, that's the common misconception," she told him once she'd pulled herself up into the truck's cab and snapped her seat belt into place. "Function first. Unless I'm working with someone who absolutely doesn't care about function and the sky's the limit. But for us normal folk, it's about function. Make it accessible, safe, keep the flow of people in mind and then make it pretty enough so no one feels engineered."

He backed the truck around and headed for the road.

"My grandmother was the inspiration for our design magazine," she explained. "She loved to see a home come back to life. Not as a profession, but she had an eye for how to make it work. When my sisters were out winning equestrian events, I was designing floor space with graph paper and a pencil. Once I discovered computer-aided drawing, the rest was history. I could create, change, practice and never have to waste another sheet of paper."

"Do you need my help tonight?"

"Are we picking up Annie and Ava now?"

He nodded.

"Then, no. You spend time with those babies so they get to know you. I'll work in the stable apartment."

"Your uncle put a great office on the first floor," he reminded her as he turned into the Pine Ridge Ranch driveway.

"And it's lovely," she said smoothly. "But I like that full flight of stairs between me and the horses. And that apartment is crazy cozy."

"Will you stay out there when Heath and Lizzie get married?"

"An Independence Day wedding and a backyard barbecue reception, two things that I might not have associated with 'Fitzgerald wedding.'" She laughed as he swung the truck into Rosie's driveway. Two small shepherd homes stood side by side along the longer ranch driveway. Aldo lived in one, and Harve and Rosie lived in the other, with their kids. "We'll see. Charlotte's good with animals, your house should be ready for the girls by then, and it might make sense for Char to take the stable apartment."

"The house will be ready." He'd pulled off his cowboy hat and tossed it behind the back seat of the truck. "What about me?"

"One big, strong cowboy and two baby girls? How hard can it be?" She smiled at him, teasing, and moved to the door.

He found out how hard it could be that night.

Annie was teething.

He didn't even know what that meant until Corrie rubbed some sort of salve on the little girl's gums and gave her a pain reliever. "Just rock her," she told him. "Once it takes the edge off, she'll probably go back to sleep."

Her and him both, he hoped.

"Would you like me to do it?" she asked.

He'd love it, but it wasn't Corrie's responsibility. It was his. "Gotta learn, right?"

"And experience is the best of teachers."

He settled into the wide easy chair and rocked the little one. She fussed at first, scowled up at him, withdrew the bottle, put it back, then scowled again. Like it was his fault. Or maybe she was just downright mad that he couldn't make the pain stop instantly. He was kind of mad about that, too.

She struggled to sit up.

He tried to keep her lying down in his arms.

She frowned again, sat up and gave him a trucker's belch.

He stared at her in disbelief.

She patted his cheek, then pulled the bottle back to her mouth with one hand. The other hand played with the wisps of hair along her cheeks, then slowly, rhythmically, she began twisting a tiny hank of hair with her finger.

Sleep stole up on her like a summer sunset. Nothing hurried about it. And when she finally closed her eyes one last time—and the bottle went lax in her mouth— he stared at the absolute miracle he held in his arms.

So small. So dependent. So perfectly beautiful.

Blond wisps framed her face, a face that seemed more pale against his darker hands. Black lashes lay against rounded cheeks. A tiny nose. A little mouth. And not too much chin to speak of, yet.

She wasn't a year old. That meant at least seventeen years of parenting.

She frowned as if the pain was coming back.

He shifted back in the reclining rocker and started humming.

She settled her pretty little head against his T-shirt, sighed and dozed off again.

So did he, and he didn't feel a thing until they both woke up nearly five hours later.

Ava had woken up. She'd come to the side of her por-table crib, spotted them and started babbling something very loud and pretty funny because the little blonde kept making herself laugh.

She reached out, patted his knee, then tugged her sister's leg.

"Sissy is sleeping," he told her. "She had a rough night."

"Bah, bah, bah, bah, bah!" Ava insisted, tugging at Annie's bare leg again. "Bah!"

One man.

Two babies.

One sleeping.

One not sleeping.

And him, caught in the middle. Did he dare try to put Annie down? Would she wake up? Did it matter?

He started to move but the door opened softly. Melonie slipped in and reached for Ava. "I've got her," she whispered.

Ava instantly grabbed two hands full of Melonie's gorgeous dark curls. And then she pulled.

"Hey, baby, that's not how this is supposed to go down." Melonie loosened one of Ava's hands. "You've got a great grip, kid," she added as she unwound the second hand.

Ava's face went sour.

Her lower lip came out.

By the time Melonie got her out of the room, she'd let out a full-fledged wail that grew fainter as Melonie went down the stairs.

How would he manage? How could he possibly do this if he just utterly failed his first test?

Corrie came into the room just then. "Here." She eased the still-sleeping baby from his arms. "Let me tuck her into her bed—that probably wasn't the best night's sleep you've ever had, Jace."

"Compared to cold, hard ground when we're running sheep, I'd say this chair and a sleepy baby were all right. I smell coffee."

"Cookie's got the kitchen ready for action."

He stood and stretched, then watched as Corrie bent low to set Annie into the crib.

He raised an eyebrow when she straightened, and she motioned him out the door, then spoke. "Babies fear falling. If you go down with them, cradling them, it's not scary. It's just plain nice."

"And you kind of kept your hand on her back while she settled."

"Too quick, they wake up. Patience and time are your biggest assets. And a sense of humor."

Her words made him smile. They also made him question.

Could he handle this? Raising two precious children?

He turned the corner at the bottom of the stairs, and paused.

Melonie was tucked along the corner of the couch, feet out, cooing to Ava as she gave her a bottle.

Ava's tiny hand kept patting Melonie's dark curls, as if she was happy to see them. Feel them. Touch them. And when she began to knit her hands into Melonie's hair, Melonie scolded, "Uh-uh. Don't do it, missy."

The baby let the bottle go loose and giggled.

Then she wound her fingers in Melonie's hair again.

Another scolding.

Another giggle. Louder this time.

That baby not only understood Melonie, but she'd also turned it into a game.

"Are babies that smart?"

His voice surprised Melonie. She turned quickly. The

strap of her tank top slid off her shoulder, just a bit, letting her dark hair fan the lightly tanned skin.

She shrugged the strap into place, made a face at Ava, then him, and laughed. "Seems like it. So how are we going to stay two steps ahead of you and your sister, Miss Ava? Because I expect that will be quite a job."

"A juggling act."

Melonie made a face. "It's all in the timing. And sleep deprivation," she added, smiling.

She was beautiful in the morning.

Beautiful at night.

An at-ease kind of beauty that seemed like it was part of her.

She didn't flirt with him.

He grunted at Cookie, poured coffee and kind of wished she would because he wanted to flirt right back.

He shouldn't.

No, make that couldn't. He'd learned his lesson and he understood her goals. She'd practically prebooked her flight back to Kentucky and her cable TV dreams once her year on the ranch was up.

Once burned, twice shy.

But when he went back to the living room, carrying coffee for both of them, the sound of her voice, laughing at that baby...

The joy in her voice made him wish she was laughing at him like that, and they were only on day three. How would he manage to keep his distance for the next several months?

Chapter Six

"Oh, thank you." She gave him a grateful look when he set the mug of coffee on the table. "I stayed up to get the basics done on your house, so this coffee will become my mainstay for the day."

"And Annie is teething, according to Corrie."

"Does that mean you held her all night?" The look on her face made him feel like a hero. He wasn't a hero. He was just a guy with a job to do. Three jobs, he realized as he took his first long sip of coffee. Two precious girls, helping on the ranch and now an unexpected mega construction contract on Hardaway Ranch. Was it only a few days ago he was hoping for a job to fall in his lap? Yep.

He set down the mug. "It kept her happy."

"Oh, Jace."

She lifted her eyebrows and offered a sympathetic smile. "That is so wonderfully kind of you."

"Yeah, well." He scrubbed a hand to the back of his neck. He needed a shower. And a shave. Probably a haircut, too.

"My dad used to do that with Justine," he told her.

"When she was sick. I must have been like six or seven years old. He'd hold her and rock her and she'd fall asleep in his arms. And when I'd get up in the morning, he'd still be there, in that big old rocking chair, holding his baby girl."

He'd glanced away, picturing the image. When he brought his gaze back to hers, there was no missing the sheen of tears in her eyes.

Her eyes glistened.

He reacted instantly.

"Hey. I didn't mean to make you cry. Stop that," he told her. He grabbed tissues from a side table. Since Lizzie had come to live on the ranch, tissues had appeared in almost every room. A woman thing, he guessed. "Here."

"Don't mind me, I get sentimental way too easily, but what a perfect memory, Jace. And what a lovely portrait of your family you've given me."

"They were wonderful." He shrugged. "I only wish I'd told them that more often. I should have made sure they understood how special they were."

"They knew."

He looked up.

"By the kind of man you are. By the beautiful daughter who cares about others. It's not the words that matter, Jace. It's the actions, and you and your sister have shown that again and again. Especially now." She dropped her gaze to little Ava.

The baby tossed her bottle aside, burped and giggled.

"She's not like a *baby* baby, is she? They're almost more like little people now. In diapers."

"Speaking of which." She swung her legs over the side of the couch.

Then she began to stand.

Ava reached for the coffee mug.

Jace jumped forward. He grabbed the baby's arm just before she snatched the mug of hot coffee, and there he was, right there, almost cheek-to-cheek with Melonie, and the tiny trouble-seeking blonde between them.

"Great save. I couldn't dodge backward quickly enough."

"And this time it was two-on-one," he told her. "Upstairs it was one-on-two until you came along. Right now I'm thinking the odds are against me."

"'If God be for us, who can be against us?'" Melonie quoted Paul's verse to the Romans gently. "Parents have been raising multiples forever. It's just that most of them have nine months to prepare, physically and mentally. You got an hour."

The common sense of her words struck him. "You're right."

"Oh, Jace. *Darling.*" She handed Ava to him and smiled, teasing him with the meaningless drawled endearment. And then she drawled the rest of the words, sending his pulse sky-high. "You will find out that I am almost always right."

Heath and Zeke came in from outside just in time to hear Melonie's comment. "While they don't look alike, that is one thing these sisters have in common. They are both *almost* always—" Heath stressed the word almost with intent deliberation "—right. A fact that bears getting used to. Hey, dollface." He plucked Ava out of Jace's arms. "I expect you want a shower," Heath said to him.

"The world around me would certainly appreciate it."

"Zeke and I will take baby detail. He's been like a

big brother to these two girls since they were born. He'll coach me along. Won't you, big guy?" Heath clapped a hand onto Zeke's five-year-old shoulder as they crossed into the dining room.

"I know everything they like and don't like," bragged the boy. "And all their best foods. Mostly Rosie still feeds 'em stuff. But just mostly."

"I believe our young friend here is telling us that while finger foods have their place, these little ladies still like to be waited on." Corrie followed them into the dining room with two bowls of something. She thrust one at Melonie before handing the second one to Jace. "Most nutrition still comes from the spoon or the bottle. I put baby spoons with each. When they are done eating, I will pack them into the stroller and walk down to Rosie's with them. If that's fine with you, Jace?"

He stared at how quickly Annie began devouring whatever was in the bowl. "It's wonderful. What's in this bowl and why does she like it so much? Because it looks dreadful."

Corrie laughed. "Rice cereal, mashed banana and vanilla-flavored Greek yogurt. A full meal in a dish."

"Ava loves it, too."

"All my babies loved this," Corrie told them as she fixed herself a fresh cup of coffee. "Simple good food, high in nutrition and calories that babies need."

"They need calories?" Jace didn't mask his surprise. "Aren't they already on the fat side?"

Corrie stopped moving.

Heath took a long step back.

Melonie stayed absolutely quiet because she was thinking the exact same thing.

Corrie tsk-tsked Jace. "These are perfectly normal,

healthy babies. They are not fat," she assured him. "They are exactly as they should be. If you had been held and fed for nearly ten months, how would you look?"

"Like a barrel?" he suggested.

"Yes. Both babies will soon be walking. Then running. Then climbing. They will barely stop to eat and you'll be scratching your head, thinking they're starving themselves."

"Corrie, for real?" Melonie squeezed Ava's chunky little calf and the baby giggled.

"Nature's way is amazing. It prepares them. And then they keep us running for a long, long time." Corrie aimed a fond look at Zeke. "Little boys sporting casts are just one prime example of how adventurous life becomes."

"I'll hang on better next time I climb a big tree," boasted Zeke. "Dad says they'll take my cast off really soon, then I can play in the water. Or swim in the creek with Dad!" The funny boy raised his casted arm like a badge of honor.

Memories washed over Melonie. Her hands refused to move.

Broken bones.

A broken face. A wired jaw.

Long days of pain in the hospital. Long weeks of liquid food and more pain.

Then the first glimpse in the mirror, of her bruised and battered eight-year-old face. She'd gone off to hide, almost wishing the horse had done her in.

Corrie found her like that. Held her. Whispered to her. Let her cry. And then Corrie went to their hometown library and brought back pictures of people who'd had their faces wired.

And they all looked normal and wonderful and good.

For the first time since being pummeled by hooves, hope had chased fear aside. It came back as she healed, but in the end, Corrie had been right. As usual.

"Did you hear me, Melonie?"

She swung around as Jace came closer. "Sorry. No. I was focused on mush, I guess."

Corrie aimed a look her way from the other side of the pass-through. A look of love and understanding, and maybe a little concern.

"If you bring your notes for my house along this morning, we can swing by the lumberyard this side of McCall and get everything we need."

"I'll show you the plans once the girls are on their way to Rosie's with Corrie, all right?"

He paused by her chair, nuzzled Ava's round, pink cheek and made the little girl giggle out loud. "Yes. Give me an hour in the barn with the guys, then time to shower. Heath said they could use an extra pair of hands."

"An hour works for me." She tried not to notice how good he smelled because ignoring his good looks was impossible enough. The complete package was harder yet. He rolled his shoulders as he moved away.

She bit back a sigh and turned her attention to Ava. "You're done," she exclaimed a few minutes later. "You did great, Ava!"

The baby burbled up at her, lifted her eyebrows and grinned.

"They couldn't be cuter, could they?" Lizzie lifted Annie and washed her little face and hands. "Mel, do you have time tonight to go over wedding plans with me?"

"I will make time. I'm a wretched sister for taking

this amazing job on when I should be helping you plan barbecue."

Lizzie laughed as she gently cleaned Annie's little face. "Scoff if you will, but people around here take barbecue seriously. Not as seriously as Texas or the deep South."

The truth in that made Melonie grin.

"I know this job is important to you," Lizzie continued. "We're having most of the food catered so folks don't have to worry about anything. But you have an eye for placement, and putting things together. I want it to look nice without messing my equine budget."

"It's amazing what I can do with clean Mason jars, wildflowers and two dozen lace tablecloths."

"I love lace tablecloths." Lizzie patted her heart, Southern girl to the max. "I wish Charlotte was here to help plan."

"Me, too. But she'll be here in time for the wedding. And then for at least a year."

Lizzie handed the soft, warm washcloth through the pass-through. "We might have to sneak away tonight so we can plan things."

"Why?"

Lizzie raised one of those perfect Fitzgerald eyebrows her way before she slanted a look toward the door. "These men are a distraction."

"Oh, Heath. Of course." Determined not to blush, Melonie trained her gaze on the baby.

"Not just Heath."

"Lizzie. Stop."

Her sister laughed as she took the baby up the stairs. "I'm going to get clean clothes for each of them. Corrie, can Zeke walk to Rosie's with you?"

"He surely can, and we might just stay and play for a while if he'd like. Or he can walk back here and help in the barn."

"Like all by myself?" Zeke hollered from the front porch. "From Rosie's?"

"Will you stay out of the way of tractors and cars?" Corrie phrased the question like only a really silly person would get in the way of either.

Zeke mashed his face against the screened wooden door. "Cross my heart."

"Then, sure, why not? Last time I looked, this place is going to have your name on it one day. Might as well learn early what owning a big spread is about. Taking charge. Getting things done."

Zeke's eyes rounded. "And I can be a big cowboy like my dad!" He dashed down the steps, climbed onto the hitching-post rail across the way and brandished a pretend lasso over his head with his good arm.

By the time Corrie had the girls packed up, Jace was heading their way. "I'll let you two go over plans." Lizzie moved toward the equine barns west of the house. "You know where to find me if you need me."

Jace held up his watch. "Do we still have time to look things over before we meet the roofers?"

"Ten minutes is all I need. Would you like to look at things here or at the table?"

"Here's fine." He kicked off his boots at the door and settled alongside her on the couch.

"Can you see the screen?"

He inched closer… He'd been throwing straw. The scent of yellow straw and green hay clung to him.

"Coffee." Cookie came into the living room with to-go cups and set them on the coffee table. "I figured you might be needing some by roofer number two. And pretty sure your grandma doesn't stock cowboy blend."

"Thank you." She smiled up at him.

Jace acknowledged Cookie's statement with a wry look. "True enough. Thanks, Cookie."

The cook tipped one finger to his fishing hat. "No problem."

Focus on the computer. On your work. Ignore the hunky guy sitting right next to you.

"The first floor." She pointed out changes to him, updates that would bring some life back to the house. "I've moved your bedroom upstairs, and shifted your room to an office and this room to your sister's room. If that's all right with her."

He pulled out his phone and texted Justine right away. She answered with a quick thumbs-up emoji. "Done. That way I'm on the same floor as the girls."

"Exactly. Jace, what if this doesn't all get worked out legally? What if their mother comes back and takes them or the county doesn't let you have them?"

"A serious question that deserves a serious answer." He folded his hands in his lap and leaned forward. "It might take months to get things worked out. I expect the county will give us temporary permission to watch the girls when we ask, but in the meantime, I'm just figuring that the girls are visiting their uncle. And their uncle needs to have things ready for them."

"You don't worry that the county might take them away?"

He shook his head. "No, because for all of my grandmother's bluster, her money speaks around here. You see the mess she's made of things. But in their day the Hardaways helped a lot of people. If Gilda Hardaway claims these girls as her great-grandchildren, no one's going to argue, especially when a simple DNA test will bear her out. And if she asks her long-lost grandson to take care of them, no one will blink an eye at that, either. What Gilda says, goes."

"And their mother?"

He stared at her, confounded. "I don't know her. I know she's abandoned them once, and that Rosie and Harve Senior had concerns about her. I can't predict the future."

She nodded.

"But I can prepare for it the best I'm able. Either raising two precious little girls or putting up a new For Sale sign next spring."

"You don't worry?"

"Try not to," he told her. "My parents didn't believe in worrying. They believed God would provide. And that the rough roads of life built character. I always thought I took after them." He slanted a rueful look her way. "Oops."

"Nature might get things started but nurture adds the finishing touches." She flipped to the upstairs layout. "I don't know where we girls would be without Corrie. She's the only mother I've known. It didn't matter that she didn't birth us. It mattered that she loved us. And she's been right there with us, every step of the way, even when the money ran out."

"Selfless love."

"Yes."

"I like that you're going to put a full bath downstairs. It'll make life easier with kids."

"And it could make prospective buyers happy."

He stood quickly. Was it her changes that caused that

swift response? Or the thought of selling the family homestead? "Gotta grab that shower and hit the road."

"One more thing." She flipped to the home's exterior page, then held up the layout image for him to see.

His expression changed. He sat right back down. Then he reached out one finger and traced the outline of the stone-rimmed garden beneath the bedroom windows. "You can do this?"

His face was filled with love and longing and something indefinably sweet. "Yes."

"It's perfect." He indicated the picket fence separating the house from the road. "I should have kept that up better. I knew it. Then the weather bested me and I couldn't make it a priority."

"Now you can. We don't want the girls to get splinters."

"No, of course not. I—" He braced his hands together, then faced her. "I don't know how to thank you."

She started to shake her head, but she stopped when he laid one strong, calloused hand against her knee. "Don't shrug it off. When that Realtor started on me to change this and do that and fix the other thing, all I heard was take apart your whole life, throw it away and buy plastic."

She half smiled, half winced. "Ouch."

"I couldn't do it. It was like doing demo on our lives. But this." He faced her directly. "This is beautiful. My parents would have loved this. Simple beauty." He met her gaze and then, for long, drawn-out seconds, he kept meeting her gaze. As if wondering...

She was wondering the same thing, but she was only here temporarily. She hadn't come to take over the equine side of the ranch, like Lizzie had done. She wasn't here to make her mark on western Idaho. She was here to claim the stake her late uncle offered. A share of an enterprise. Then someone would buy her out, she'd return to civilization and continue her quest for a nationally renowned cable TV show.

She closed the laptop, stood and grabbed her coffee and her notebook bag. "I'll be in the truck when you're ready to go."

Her phone buzzed a text as she climbed into his truck a few minutes later. She opened it. Production company didn't just like the mock episode, Ezra informed her. They LOVED it. Time crunch is a problem. Call me.

So the production company loved it, but there was no getting around the time crunch. She was here for the coming year. Despite that, the news made her smile.

"Good news?" Jace asked as he took the driver's seat. He turned the key and thrust the truck into gear. It jerked, then stalled. He started it again, then scolded the engine. "Hang on until I get the first third of Mrs. Hardaway's money, okay? I'm not draining the savings account to save your sorry hide."

"Nice news, yes," she answered. She motioned to her car parked next to the three-stall garage. "I had no idea how expensive car repairs were until our family fell apart. Talk about a reality check. It's like a thousand here, a thousand there."

"I'm good around a lot of things, but new engines aren't one of them. Now, an old tractor like that one." He pointed to the big green rig near the sheep barn. "That's a tinker's dream. One part comes off. The other one goes on. With some coaxing along the way. Not a circuit board in sight."

"You like working on vehicles?"

"Winter work," he told her. "Your uncle heated the far barn so that we can overhaul equipment all winter, get it all ready for spring."

"I cannot even imagine what it would take to heat a place that size for the whole winter."

"Do that again."

She frowned. "Do what again?"

"The drawl."

She was tempted to go all Southern belle on him, but that would be stupid. And after having her last boyfriend walk out when he realized she was broke and in debt, she wasn't about to mess around.

Her goals didn't include life up north, so she refused the invitation to flirt. "I worked real hard to lose the drawl for mass-market appeal. The irony is that if I get my own TV show—" she faced him more squarely "—they're probably going to want the drawl. So the joke's on me."

He didn't respond.

He stared straight ahead while one finger tapped the steering wheel lightly.

He might not think much of her goals, but she'd grown used to that with her father and she knew one thing for certain. No way was she going to live in the shadow of someone's chronic disapproval ever again.

Chapter Seven

Jace's spine went stiff when she mentioned television. "The magazine stuff wasn't enough for you?"

"It made a great stepping stone. But TV was always the dream."

Her words hit him like a dash of ice water on a mid-July day. "Everyone should have a dream." He'd said the words, and mostly he believed them. But he'd been there before with a fame-loving woman and wasn't about to make that mistake again.

"Agreed."

He pulled into his grandmother's yard. The first roofer's truck had pulled in just ahead of him.

He hopped out and shook the man's hand, then introduced Melonie, and when they went up the steps, he let Melonie pick which side she'd go up...

And he chose the other with the roofer squarely in between. He'd been left cold once. He understood women and their weird mix of feelings and the lure of dreams. He might get it...but he was never going to let it affect him again. No matter how enticing the drawl was.

By the time they'd met with both roofers, it was

lunchtime. Gilda met them by what had once been an ascending garden. Now it was a heap of towering weeds and thin trees trying to stake a claim in the hillside soil. She came forward with a purposeful stride, the four-pronged cane smacking the ground with each step. "Are you hungry?"

He started to shake his head but Melonie replied first. "Starved. What's the plan?"

"I've got fresh bread and peanut butter and some of Sally Ann's good jam. She works down at the Carrington Ranch and she makes the best jam around, though no one says a word of that to Millie Gruber. She's a sensitive sort and folks worry about her feelings." She peered over her glasses at them. "Let's talk roofing."

Jace followed the two women, wondering what happened to the you-make-the-decisions-and-I'll-sign-the-checks mentality.

He didn't want to eat in the wretched house.

He didn't want to eat with this old woman who cast out children, then grandchildren, as if they were unwanted commodities. But he couldn't very well leave Melonie here, and she was already up the back steps.

A cat yowled.

He stopped dead, imagining cats on counters. On tables. Roaming around the sprawling house.

But then the cat dashed out from beneath a huge yucca plant, over toward the old barn.

The barn had a solid roof. He was just thinking how odd it was to reroof the empty barn and ignore the house when the door squeaked open. "Coming?"

He faced Melonie.

He wanted to back away. The combination of the

broken house and broken lives was too much. How one thing affected the next and then the next until a twisted network of lies and half-truths knotted itself. He was just about to say no when she held out a hand.

Just that.

Her expression stayed calm, but her eyes and that hand said she understood.

He moved forward when every fiber of his being wanted to go the other way, and when he climbed the four wide steps feeling grumpy and probably looking worse, she winked at him.

Not flirting.

Just…understanding.

The wink broke the mood.

If a formerly rich Kentucky girl could handle eating in the decaying mansion, he could, too.

He followed her inside.

"I forgot how to do fancy and nice a long time ago," said Gilda as she moved about the room with more comfort than she displayed outside. "But a clean sheet's as good as a tablecloth and the food's fresh."

She'd spread a bright floral sheet over the table. Jars of fresh peanut butter and homemade jam were placed like centerpieces. A loaf of bread sat to their right, and a pitcher of tea stood to the left. "This is lovely, Gilda," Melonie said.

The old woman rolled her eyes, but acknowledged the antique rose-covered pitcher. "I got the tea recipe from your magazine. I'm not much for trying new things, least I didn't used to be, but it looked good and tasted better. When I heard you were coming to town, and other things started falling apart, I realized maybe there's a reason for the tea recipe. And the magazine. Your sister's got a good heart," she went on as she handed them knives for the peanut butter and jam. "She didn't mind stopping by and sharing her ideas for getting things going. I didn't think much of it initially, of course."

Jace was pretty sure that was accurate.

"I like my own ideas in my own time…"

Another spot-on self-assessment.

"But when you don't necessarily have much time left, you start listening better. When I heard the preacher's words at Sean Fitzgerald's memorial service, I thought to myself 'Old woman! You'd best get going if you're ever going to make a difference in the world.' A good one, that is." Her hand paused. Her face shadowed. And for a brief moment, Jace almost felt sorry for her.

But not quite.

"So you decided to start fixing things?" Melonie asked. And then she did the nicest thing. She'd spread peanut butter across her slice of bread—peanut butter that managed to fill the kitchen with a familiar nutty fragrance—and she handed it to him.

He started to refuse it. "I can do my own, Melonie." But he stopped when she gave him that look again. A look that pushed him to go along with the kind gesture. "Actually, thank you. That's nice of you."

He spread jam onto the peanut butter, topped it with another slice of textured wheat bread, and when he took his first bite, the mix of flavors seemed like old times at his mother's table, feasting on PB&J.

"I didn't used to like simple." Gilda didn't put peanut butter on her bread. Just jam. "I thought too much of myself to even think simple, and that's the shame of it. I look back and shake a fist at myself, sayin', 'Gilda, what were you thinkin'?' And yet I know exactly what I was thinkin', being a woman who thought herself above others. That's the devil's own way of it," she told them, almost scolding. "No matter how your life goes, or what wonders come your way, you don't want to get caught in that kind of a cycle. It's wrong, and while a part of me knew it then, I kept right on. Now, your mother…" She pointed her bread at Jace with an adamant expression on her face. "Ivy Middleton was one of the best women I've ever met, and I should have told her that more often but we were afraid of gettin' up talk. Having folks figure things out. Because then you'd know things and the last thing she or your dad wanted was for you to be the talk of the town."

"So how exactly did they explain the sudden appearance of a one-year-old baby?" he asked point-blank. "Because if talk was what you wanted to avoid, handing over a baby in a small town probably wasn't the best way to do it."

"There's talk and then there's *talk*," she told him frankly. "She told folks that God had brought them the miracle they'd been praying for all along and folks loved her enough to let it go at that. Not being able to have children was a sorrow for so many, so when Justine came along six years later, that was quite the surprise and the joy, I'm sure."

He loved being Justine's big brother. He'd loved helping his dad with her when Mom was working.

"I'm not expecting you to love me, Jason."

He'd been about to eat the last corner of the sandwich.

He didn't.

"I don't expect anything of the kind from anyone, but

I have this vision," she told him, then included Melonie in her look. "Of this house bein' a home like it's never been before. Like it's never had a chance to be. With kids running up and down the hill. Playground stuff, too, like swings and slides and the stuff that childhood should be made of. Not stuffy gardens and fancy furniture like before, but a home. The way things should have been all along. I want to see it be that home before I die." She coughed then. Not too loud and not too long, but enough for Jace to understand.

"You wanted to discuss the roof," he said, changing the subject.

"I do not, I just figured it might be the only way to get you into the house and tell you my goals." She nailed him with a look. "You looked ready to jump ship. I don't have time or energy to chase you down, and there's no one else I want to do this job, so if you're having second thoughts, tell me now."

He sighed. Put his head in his hands for just a moment, then peered at her. "I was having second thoughts. But I gave my word, and a man's word is his bond. I won't let my reluctance mess this up. And I'll do a great job. But I can't just throw emotion away. I expect you know that."

"I do. Nor do I expect you to let bygones be bygones. It's too much to ask, of course."

It wasn't.

It was exactly what his faith told him to do. What kind of person would he be to ignore that?

"But I will be ever grateful for the help, Jason."

He wanted to correct her. He was named for his father, but everyone called him Jace. For as long as he could remember.

But oddly it sounded right from her. He stood. "Thank you for lunch."

"Thank you for staying."

"It was delightful." Melonie stood, too, but she reached over and hugged the old woman.

Jace didn't. He headed to the door. "I had another roofer appointment lined up for tomorrow, but I'm going to cancel it. Melonie and I both liked the second appointment today—"

"Western Idaho Roofing."

"Yes. Good prices, great reputation and quick start date."

"Do I need to leave the house?" Gilda asked.

Jace frowned.

Melonie got the gist more quickly. "You should be fine, but it will be noisy, Gilda. Why don't you come over to Pine Ridge during the day until it's done? It shouldn't take them more than a week. We'd be happy to have you."

"You can tell when someone's new in town, because not too many hand me invites these days," the old woman grumbled, but she looked less grumpy. "I might just do that. I don't do well with a lot of noise."

"Rosie might bring the girls by with Corrie. And her newborn baby. That can get real noisy."

"There's noise and then there's noise, young man, and while I can probably hold my own rockin' a baby, electric air hammers and drills aren't friendly to a woman my age." She faced Melonie more squarely. "I will accept your kind invitation, Melonie."

"Lovely. I'll let the others know." Melonie squeezed her hand gently. "And we'll have tea on the porch in the afternoon."

"Something to look forward to."

He looked Melonie's way when they'd climbed into the cab of his pickup truck. "You've got that sugar-coated, sweet-tea-offering Southern persona down well."

She frowned. "Excuse me?"

"Back there." He gestured as he turned the truck around. "Come to the ranch? Have tea on the porch? That's pure Kentucky, isn't it?"

"Or it's simple kindness to an infirm, elderly woman who's about to embrace a huge undertaking and trusts us to oversee it," she argued mildly. "She's grown old, seen the error of her ways and had a change of heart. Isn't that the basis for some of the best stories? The prodigal son. The woman in the street, about to be stoned. I love stories of redemption."

So did he. But not when the old person's solace came at the cost of his family's joy. How were he and Justine supposed to react to all of this, knowing their parents had woven a web of dishonesty around their lives? "Easy to say when it's not your life being affected."

She made a face, a kind of cute face of self-doubt. "You're right about that because if my father came to beg forgiveness for all his misdeeds, I'd be in a flux. A parent should only be allowed so much latitude. And then they lose the right to call themselves parents."

"Then the same holds true for grandparents."

She shook her head. Was she being intentionally obtuse? Or trying to fluster him? "Advanced age cuts them slack. They were raised in a different way. A different time. We have to be mindful of that. This forest is just gorgeous," she added, smoothly changing the subject.

"Like being in the Appalachians, but different, too. Not as many deciduous trees."

"Being this high and this far north changes what grows." He mulled her words as they headed for the lumberyard in McCall, unwilling to let the topic go. "You think the older the person, the more forgiving we should be."

She was tapping notes into her notebook. She paused as he rolled to a stop at a four-way and slanted him a look. "I think we should always be forgiving but I'm about the world's worst example so let's not go there. If I never saw my father again, I'd probably be okay with that, which means I've hardened my heart, mostly for self-preservation. But you." She closed the notebook and set it aside. "You had a wonderful life. A beautiful family. You're so skilled at all the trades your father loved. Ranching. Carpentry. Building. You said yourself that he kept you by his side all along."

He nodded as the home store came into view.

"Gilda might be the worst grandmother ever, but she made sure you had great opportunities. That can't be discounted."

He scowled. "Around these parts, we expect folks to do what they're supposed to do. All the time." He pulled into the parking lot and shoved the truck into Park before it was fully stopped, making it jerk.

She rolled her eyes. "If we need extra lumber we could always get it from that full-size chip on your shoulder." She slung her purse up, got out, then faced him as they rounded the truck.

"So is that whole sweet, Southern-woman image some kind of joke?" he asked. "Or do we only pull it out for grumpy old ladies?" He folded his arms and stared her down.

Looking up, she met his gaze without wavering and he wished he didn't like her panache. Yet he did. "Clearly you missed *Steel Magnolias* and *Fried Green Tomatoes*."

She folded her arms, too. "Let me tell you something. This Southern gal is going to help you get that house in order so that you can create a family with those perfectly adorable little girls. Be the father they would never have had if their mother stayed. A father like the one you had, Jace."

Her words hit the mark like a well-balanced nail gun.

She walked toward the store, head high.

A father like he had.

A blessed, wonderful man who showed goodness and kindness all of his days. Strong but loving and forgiving.

He hated that she was right. At some point he'd have to admit that.

He rubbed the nape of his neck as she cruised through that door, wishing she didn't look so good. The way she stood her ground with him made him almost look forward to sparring with her again.

If he wasn't careful he was going to find himself knee-deep in attraction with another unattainable woman, and that couldn't happen. But when he walked through the doors and caught her guarded expression, what he longed to do was make her smile again.

And that was a danger-laden emotion.

"You'll come with me to my bridal fitting tomorrow, won't you?" Lizzie asked Melonie that evening.

"If you can tear yourself away from Jace… I mean his project, of course."

Melonie purposely ignored her sister's intentional gaffe. "Yes, if you guys don't mind dropping me off at his place on the way back. As much fun as this all is—" she swept the busy ranch yard and house a quick look "—it's not quiet enough for me to design what I need for Gilda's place, and I've got two weeks to get my overall plan in order. By then, Jace should be done with his house and we can dive into the Hardaway place. But I'm going to need every minute of focus I can get."

"You think construction is quiet?"

Melonie laughed. "I can work upstairs while he's remodeling the first floor. The sound of tools won't bother me, but kids, people, doors banging, horses… I'd be distracted."

"I think you're going to be somewhat distracted at Jace's place, too, but what do I know?" Lizzie ducked away from the couch pillow Melonie flung at her, then grinned. "We'll be happy to drop you off after the fitting."

"Perfect." It wasn't exactly perfect because Lizzie was right. Avoiding Jace would be in her best interests, and yet…she didn't want to. And she was grown up enough to keep things under wraps because as cool as Pine Ridge Ranch was, it wasn't exactly quiet. Unless she hid out in the small apartment, and being that close to huge horses wasn't about to make the short list. "I can't wait to see you in the dress."

Lizzie sighed. "Me, either. Can you believe it? Us here and me about to be married to the love of my life?"

"I heard that, which means you want something." Heath braced himself with one arm on the side of the wooden screen door, then jerked his head. "Come walking with me. Let's see what that first full moon of summer holds."

"I'd walk in the moon's light with you anytime, cowboy."

Melonie stuck out her tongue at them. "Go, lovebirds. Some of us have work to do."

Heath opened the door. As Lizzie stepped through, he leaned down for a kiss...then took her hand, leading her into the moonlit yard looking so utterly in love that Melonie's heart wanted to break into a million little lonely pieces.

"Please tell me that angst isn't directed at me."

Jace's voice surprised her. He must have come down the back stairs. She dipped her chin toward the laptop, choking back emotion and biting back tears. "No angst. Just getting ideas down."

She felt him watching her.

She hoped he'd go outside or back to the kitchen. He'd been tucking the girls into bed with Corrie, and the whole process had taken a long time.

He didn't leave.

He moved her way. "Are the plan ideas giving you a rough time? I might be able to help." He took a seat across from her and when she drew her gaze up, he seemed genuinely concerned. "I'm no designer but I'm good at knowing what will and won't work if you've hit a bad spot."

"It's not the design aspects."

He frowned, then followed her gaze to where Lizzie and Heath had paused for yet another kiss. "Ah."

Her forehead knitted instantly. "Ah, nothing."

"Hey." He splayed his hands and shifted his eyebrows

up, intentionally dubious. "I find the whole thing annoying, too. Happy people, planning their lives. What is the matter with them?"

"Stop. You're not helping." He was, though. Laughing at the situation was way better than crying over being dumped by a ladder-climbing young executive back in Louisville.

"You're talking to a man who got left at the altar."

Now she stared at him because she couldn't begin to imagine that.

"True story. It was not my best day."

What a wretched thing to do to anyone, and the idea that it happened to him seemed outrageous. "Then the girl was clearly stupid and not meant for you, because what woman in their right mind would do that, Jace?"

He laughed. "My thoughts exactly, but she did and it took me months of embarrassment to figure out she did me a favor." He jutted his chin toward the ranch yard. "I watched Heath lose his wife and struggle with a newborn baby, a full-time job here on the ranch and grief. It wasn't pretty and there was nothing I could do to help my best friend. And when Camryn left me at the altar, he tried to help, but there's not much other folks can do. Except be patient. Be kind. And praying's never a bad choice."

"I'm getting closer to that whole did-me-a-favor mind-set," she confessed. "When my family's publishing company was closed down, my job was gone and I had a bunch of debt ascribed to me by the courts. My ex wanted no part of that."

"So he *did* do you a favor. He didn't deserve you."

"Well…"

"No arguing," he scoffed. "It's fact. If a man isn't smart enough to love you for yourself, who needs him?"

It sounded so right coming from him. "So we're the walking wounded?"

"My scars are healed, but I am most assuredly gun-shy," he said firmly. "Between your uncle's illness and the ranch, we've been so busy the past couple of years that it didn't much matter."

"The shortage of women might have made them easier to avoid," she noted, smiling.

"Shortage of people in general, which spurred lost job opportunities here." He stood and rolled his shoulders, easing kinks, and she tried to pretend he didn't look absolutely amazing when he did it. "Now with kids to raise, my focus needs to be on them."

"Agreed." She stood, too.

He stayed right there, looking at her.

She looked right back.

"So why is my focus longing to shift, Melonie?" He whispered the words as he gazed at her. Her lips. Then her eyes. Then her lips again.

A half step forward. That's all it would take to see... To test this attraction. It was a half step she didn't dare take. "Stop that."

He smiled. Raised one hand to her cheek. The feel of his palm, so strong. So tough. So rugged. As if she could nestle the curve of her face into his hand, his shoulder and stay there...forever?

Her phone rang.

She took that half step then, in the opposite direction. "You." She pointed at him, scolding. "I don't play games. Take your crazy cute cowboy self out of here so I can work." She tapped the phone to take the call, as if talking to her newly graduated veterinarian sister back in New York was vital. "Hi, yes, it's Melonie, may I put you on hold for just a moment?"

Jace left.

But he left whistling, his hands loose at his sides, as if Charlotte wasn't the only thing put on hold. Maybe she should hole up in the equine apartment to work, after all. "Char, thanks. I just had to finish a meeting with a client."

"You've been there a few days and already you have clients? Color me surprised."

"There are plenty of surprises out here, believe me. When are you coming?"

"Not for two weeks. I'm following up on a few horses here and my reciprocity paperwork should allow me to open my mobile veterinary practice there by mid-July."

"I know that's the plan, but there aren't a lot of people here," Melonie told her. "There might not be much actual work."

"Then I'll consider every little bit a blessing. I can't get large animal experience without hanging a shingle. How'd you snag a client so quickly?"

Melonie filled her in.

Charlotte sighed. "This whole crazy family dynamic seems to be epidemic, doesn't it? What's up with that?"

"I don't know." Melonie tucked her toes beneath a throw pillow as the evening temperatures dipped. "I see the mistakes in all of it, but Jace—he's the cowboy construction guy—ended up with the nicest family. Great parents. He loves his sister. So maybe she did him a favor, after all?"

Charlotte stayed quiet for a moment. Then she partially agreed. "Maybe. That's a fairly Pollyannaish outlook, isn't it?"

"I love Pollyanna."

Charlotte laughed. "I know you do. I just think that while it's nice to be optimistic, it's good to be on your guard, too. Like twenty-four/seven. Three hundred and sixty-five days."

"How'd you get so jaded for such a young person?"

"Twenty-six isn't all that young. And my plans for living a bucolic life in some posh Southern practice where little old ladies dote on their puppies have been dashed, so bear with me."

"You'd die of boredom and you know it. You're the adventurer among us. And you actually like big animals."

"Love 'em. So this crash course on an upstate New York big animal practice has been good for me. And downright dirty. Overalls and muck boots are my new wardrobe."

Melonie laughed as Jace came into view again. He and a couple of the men were talking in the yard, gesturing toward the hills, the hayfield, the pastures. When Lady came up alongside, seeking attention, Jace didn't think twice. He reached down, still talking, and gave the former stray dog a good petting.

"Just as well. The little old ladies out here are a breed apart."

Charlotte laughed. "That must make Corrie happy."

"Let's just say she's not one of a kind in the rugged north."

"Oops, gotta go—a call out from a farm and it's late here. Hope they've got decent lighting."

Melonie ended the call and set down the phone.

She needed to dive into the broad scheme for Mrs. Hardaway's house. She needed—

The men began walking away.

Jace spotted her watching. And for long, slow ticks of the living room clock, they locked eyes again.

Was his heart skipping beats like hers? Were his palms growing damp?

Stop this. You know better. You know your plans. You're leaving here as soon as you've secured your inheritance. His life is here. Yours isn't. And there are two baby girls to consider.

Her conscience delivered the wake-up call she needed. She wasn't here for a rebound romance. She was here to help the ranch and if the Good Lord saw fit to toss a possibly career-changing job into her lap, so be it. She'd had to leave her chance once. She wasn't going to mess it up a second time.

She shifted her attention back to the computer. She needed to keep things all business with Jace, and avoid those sweet baby girls, even if their big blue eyes and winsome smiles called to her.

They had Corrie and Rosie to mind them. And Jace. With a big job before her, she could keep the babies with the more experienced women. The hard part would be keeping all three of them—Jace and those little girls—at an emotional distance.

Chapter Eight

"Melonie gave you a list?" Heath grinned as Jace loaded garden tools into the bed of his pickup truck the next morning. When he tossed in two rolls of landscape fabric, Heath's smile stretched wider. "Pretty domestic for just meeting the girl, isn't it?"

"All part of the makeover," Jace replied smoothly. He aimed a stern look Heath's way. "Are you helping me demolish those two walls or not?"

"Getting to use a sledgehammer and wreck stuff?" Heath flexed. "I'm all in. And this is way more fun than I'd anticipated before a certain Fitzgerald sister rolled into town. Wearing silk, I might add."

Melonie and her fancy pants. No one around here wore fancy pants like that. He might actually hate them if she didn't look so good in them. "Do you think she even owns blue jeans?"

"Well, we know she's got leggings." Heath tipped his gaze to the three women, moving toward the ranch SUV parked next to Jace's truck.

Jace had tried not to notice, but when someone

looked as good as Melonie Fitzgerald, only a blind man would be immune. "You gals heading to Boise?"

"There's a shortage of wedding-gown seamstresses around here, so yes." It was Lizzie who answered. Melonie stayed quiet on the opposite side of the vehicle. "Mel said you guys are tearing down two walls today?"

Heath flexed again, making the women laugh. "We've got this. They dropped off the Dumpster yesterday afternoon. We're on a mission."

"You remember which two walls, right?" Melonie asked.

"I hope so," teased Jace. "You might want to stop by and mark them with an *X* so we don't mess this up."

She looked like she wanted to smile.

She didn't.

She gave a polite wave as she opened the car door. "I'll see you two in a few hours. And don't forget the garden stakes, okay?"

"In the bed of the truck as we speak."

"Perfect."

When he and Heath climbed into the truck, Heath laughed. "Man, have you got your work cut out for you."

Jace deliberately misunderstood. "Getting the Hardaway roof done is buying me time. Once my reno is complete, I can move the girls home. Then I tackle the monster-sized project." He waited until the women pulled away, then followed them up the long driveway.

"I was talking about your partner. The one tapping things into that notebook in the car up ahead. Does she ever stop working?"

She'd told him she was ambitious and nothing he'd seen so far negated that. "Doesn't look like it."

Heath studied the car ahead, then Jace, but he stayed

quiet. And by the time they'd gotten the two walls down
and the debris into the Dumpster, Jace was pretty sure
he'd just made the biggest mistake of his life. His mother's house—her lovely, historic home—was now filled
with plaster dust and gaping holes where walls had been.

Sure, he knew they'd fix it. But it still felt wrong.

"You men are amazing!" Lizzie's voice rang with
approval as she stepped in the back door just after one
o'clock.

"Oh, this will be a fine piece of work," Corrie chimed
in as she entered. Could they see beyond the mess to the
finished product? Right now he couldn't.

Melonie came in last. She didn't look at what they'd
demolished. The part of his past they'd just destroyed.

She looked at him. Just him. And when she gave him
a nod of approval, it helped. She set a big bag on the
counter and studied the newly opened layout. "With the
support beam here." She pointed up. "And the beautiful wainscoting, this will keep all the historic flavor
we want but open things up for the girls to see and be
seen." She turned her attention up to him and the sin-
cerity in her cloudy gray eyes did another number on
his pulse. "You guys did a great job."

Then she smiled. Not a flirting smile. A smile of
such understanding that he wanted to hug her. Thank
her. Because for a minute there, he was pretty sure he
was wrecking something precious. He wasn't. He was
changing things for something precious. Two some-
things. He moved to the wall nearest them. "I know
you wanted a closet here, but what about if we move
the closet there—" he pointed to the left "—and keep
this wall for kid pictures?"

"Kid pictures?" she asked, puzzled. "Won't you just put them all over?"

He shoved his hands into his pockets. Rocked back on his heels. "I thought it might be cool to keep putting pics up there. As they grow. To show all the changes in what they do. Who they are and who they turn out to be."

Her mouth formed a perfect O. "I love that idea. A wall-of-progress kind of thing—that's brilliant, Jace. What made you think of it?"

He shrugged and pulled his hands out of his pockets, almost nervous. But he never got nervous, so why would he be anxious now? "Just something I've thought of. Having a family someday. Seeing kids grow. Having all that cool stuff up on a wall."

"It is a wonderful idea, and it will be a beautiful balance of old and new," offered Corrie.

"Are you all set here?" Lizzie asked Heath. "If you need to stay, I can come back for you later."

"My part's done." Heath raised his hands in surrender. "The fixin' part is up to Jace. What are you two doing for lunch, though?" he asked Melonie and Jace. "There's no food here."

Melonie pointed to the counter. "We stopped by Shy Simon's in Council. I got us a Triple S pizza to share. I hope that's all right."

"A meat-lovin' cowboy's dream," he told her as Heath, Lizzie and Corrie headed out. He didn't want to smile at her, but he had to. She wasn't afraid to take charge. To make decisions. To move forward. He wasn't stupid, he knew that those same qualities would take her away next year, but what if she had reason to stay? What if staying became more important than leaving?

Dude. Been there. Done that. Disastrous results, remember?

She grabbed a bag and went upstairs quickly, the way she did most everything.

There was plenty to focus on without letting romantic nonsense mess him up. And there wasn't a place on an Idaho ranch for a woman who feared dirt. Dirt and hard work formed the backbone of Idaho. They went hand in hand.

He'd just convinced himself that Melonie's outfits put her completely out of the running when she dashed down the steps wearing loose capris, a faded T-shirt and a bandanna around the dark waves of her hair.

He stopped. Stared.

She looked at him, then herself, then back at him. "What's wrong? What did I do?"

He gestured. "The outfit."

She frowned. "Like it? Hate it? The yard won't care," she suggested with a quizzical expression. "I'm doing the front gardens today."

"*You're* doing them?" He couldn't hide his surprise because that was about the last thing he expected to hear. "I thought you were working on the Hardaway project and I'd get to the gardens as I could."

"I did work on the project," she told him. "All the way to Boise and back." The drawl crept back into her tone as she talked. The drawl that he found crazy attractive. "I wasn't about to waste valuable hours when I could make some significant progress…which I did," she added.

She walked over to the pizza, selected a slice and a paper towel, and went straight out that front door after she grabbed a hat that came right out of the pages of a

Southern ladies magazine. Then ate her slice of pizza while surveying the yard.

He wanted to go talk to her.

He didn't.

He'd unloaded the tools from the bed of the truck and lined them up beneath the cluster of catalpa trees his grandmother planted over forty years before. His adoptive grandmother, he realized.

He hated the new adjectives in his life. He'd been fine without them. Fine without knowing a truth that was kept from him. And fine with the house the way it was.

His phone chimed a text from Rosie. He opened the message and the picture she'd sent widened his grumpy old heart.

Annie and Ava, both standing, laughing, clutching the edge of Rosie's sofa and proud of their newfound freedom. The video clicked to life.

Annie shrieked in glee. Ava joined her. Then Annie released her death grip on the couch. She reached out and clutched her sister in a hug.

Ava hugged her back, and their faces…filled with laughter, the image of innocence, bright with joy.

He swallowed the lump of grouchiness that had taken hold a few days before. His parents weren't here to explain their choices, but that shouldn't matter. They were part of him. They'd raised him. Taught him. If they felt the need for privacy about the adoption, maybe it was for good reason.

"Jace? Do you have any old pictures of your mother's garden? In color?"

He was the worst person on the planet when it came to finding old stuff. "Probably in a bin somewhere."

She laughed.

His heart gentled. He strode forward and opened the door. "I could hunt them down," he told her as he took the three steps down to her level. "But maybe it would be nice to plant some new stuff. Create some new memories for the girls."

"A great idea." She focused on the shovel, then paused. "Then you're all right if I remove some things? I don't want to get rid of something cherished."

"We need to have a few roses," he told her. "Mom loved her roses but they'd get nasty every time we got a rainy stretch."

"We can plant a few disease-resistant varieties," she told him. "They don't get blighted easily. But I'd like to keep that climbing rose on the trellis," she continued. "If it gets too spotty, we can replace it next spring."

"Mom's favorite. She loved that grayish pink. Said it reminded her of old British novels." He reached over and lifted a shovel.

She turned, surprised. "I've got this. You've got inside work to do. I need to do something physical after being in the car. It clears my brain."

"It's supposed to rain tomorrow, so the more we get done out here today, the better. I'll start over here." He moved to one corner of the front garden. "How about you start at that end and we meet in the middle?"

"Sounds goods."

As they tossed old plants into the wheelbarrow, the clean smell of fresh dirt motivated him.

She didn't talk while she worked. Neither did he. He tried to ignore her, but when she started humming vintage dance tunes, she made it impossible.

Music.

He grabbed his phone and hit the music app.

She turned to him, surprised. "Nobody likes old music like that anymore. Except me."

"And me." He set the phone on the stack of black mulch chips. "Glenn Miller. Frank Sinatra. Nat King Cole."

"I used to pick old songs for my dance routines growing up," she told him as she worked his way. "The other kids thought I was crazy, but it got me two dance scholarships."

He whistled lightly. "You must be good."

"Well, it's like kittens. Or a litter of puppies," she continued. "If you have three orange kittens and one gray, the gray will get picked to go to a new home first. Because it's distinctive. Not better. Not worse. Different."

"Now you're negating the merit of your efforts." He frowned at her. "Don't do that. Nobody hands out scholarships because the music stands out, Melonie. They hand them out because the dancer stands out."

She looked at him.

He looked back. Suddenly Sinatra's "The Way You Look Tonight" started playing.

Jace put out his hand. She studied the hand, then him.

Then she laid hers in his.

It didn't matter that their hands were dirty. It didn't matter that hers were small and narrow and his were big and broad.

They fit.

And when he led her onto the short grass and spun her into a twirl...

She laughed, and it was about the prettiest sound he'd ever heard.

"You dance." She smiled up at him as he drew her back in.

"I love to dance. With the right person, of course." He slanted a knowing look her way.

She blushed and batted him on the shoulder. "No flirting allowed."

"But dancing's all right?" He laughed as he kept the moves in time with the music across the yard and around the thick-leafed catalpa trees. As the song drew to a close, he did a quick turn and dipped her. There she was, snug against his arm, head back. Her dark waves of hair cascaded over his arm.

"Dancing is always all right," she whispered, gazing up at him.

His heart caught, midbeat, because the feel of her there, in his arms, was so right. "You are beautiful, woman." He smiled down at her.

She smiled back.

Close. So close. Close enough to imagine leaning in for a kiss.

Was she wondering the same thing?

It didn't matter. They both knew better. And they had work to do.

He drew her back up until she was steady on her feet. "Thank you for the dance."

"My pleasure, sir."

Her slight curtsy made his heart tumble a little more.

Just then, his phone rang.

He crossed to answer it, then frowned. "We've got to go. Zeke and Annie have both come down with some kind of illness and they can't be around Rosie's baby. We'll have to keep the kids at the ranch house the next few days."

"Let's put the tools in the garage so they don't get mucked up in the rain."

Her suggestion surprised him. Why would a bunch of garden tools mean more than sick kids? He frowned. "No time. Let's roll. Or I'll send someone back here for you."

Nobody bossed Melonie around. Not now. Not ever again.

She waved a hand. "I'll stay here. You go tend the girls."

He stood still for just a moment. Then he climbed into his truck, backed it around and left.

The jerk.

Not for leaving for a sick kid, but for the Jekyll-and-Hyde maneuver.

She kept working, pulling plants and tossing them. Then smoothing the ground with the thick-forked rake.

She tried to draw up mental images of the Hardaway house as she worked, but mental images of Jace came up instead. The way he moved. The way he talked. The slow smile.

She didn't dare dwell on how the man danced, or that they loved the same old music.

A bedraggled clutch of coneflowers got to stay.

So did a daisylike flower near the porch, airy and pretty.

She deep-sixed almost everything else except for half-a-dozen primrose plants, long past flowering.

Once she'd laid and pinned the weed barrier, she sliced holes for the current plants, drawing them through. The bits of color popped now, as if they were happy.

A part of her wanted to call and see how the girls and Zeke were doing. Another part needed to maintain distance.

But that was already impossible. Spending a year here in Idaho, working with Jace, watching precious babies grow... That meant she'd have to try harder. When things fell apart, Melonie Fitzgerald simply tried harder. Besides, if something was seriously wrong, Lizzie would've contacted her.

An hour later, Melonie had just finished clearing the second small border garden when Corrie drove in.

"Child, you have your mother's touch with gardens, that's certain," she said once she'd parked the SUV.

"You think?"

Corrie put a hand to her heart as she crossed the yard. "Your sweet mama and I spent a lot of time in the gardens together. We both loved digging in the dirt and growing things. You are the only one to have the eye for this, and that is straight from your mama. It does my heart good to see it."

The thought that she was like the woman she couldn't remember seemed right and wrong. "I've always wished I could remember her."

"I know."

"You'd think that there'd be something, wouldn't you?"

"Memory is a funny thing." Corrie reached down to stroke a daisy blossom. "You might not consciously remember her, but those kindly feelings you shared, when she'd sing you to sleep, or dozed off with you in her arms, made you feel safe and secure. That security is part of who you are today, darling girl. And it started back then. In your mama's arms."

"How's Annie doing?"

"Fussy and feverish," Corrie reported. "I thought I'd come this way and see if I could give you a hand, though. They've got things covered there."

"But what if Ava gets it?"

"Well, that will make things busier."

"Let's not worry about this," Melonie told her. She stripped off the garden gloves and tucked the tools into the garage. "I can work on designs back at the ranch and help with kids if needed."

"You don't want to be getting sick with this big project coming up," Corrie said.

Right now that was the least of her worries. "I've got two weeks before the roofers get their part done, then nearly a year to see it through, Corrie." She closed the garage and slung an arm around Corrie's broad shoulders. "At this point I've got nothing but time, it seems. Let's go check those little ones."

"All right."

Corrie backed the SUV around and headed out the driveway, and by the time they parked alongside Jace's truck, Melonie's phone chimed a text from Lizzie. "Seems Ava's running a fever now, too."

"Then it's good we've got all hands on deck," Corrie told her. "We'll take turns rocking and singing, I expect."

"Like you and my mother did for me. For all of us."

Corrie blessed her with the smile she remembered growing up. The smile of a woman who loved her through thick and thin. "Just like that."

When she got inside, Heath was holding Ava and Zeke was curled up on the far sofa, sound asleep, dark lashes fanning against his milk-chocolate-toned cheeks.

Ava reached for Melonie.

That sweet baby half leaped out of Heath's big, strong arms the moment she spotted her, leaving her no choice.

"Hey, precious." Melonie curled the fussy little girl into her left arm as if she'd been doing this forever instead of scant days. "Hey, hey. I'm so sorry you don't feel good, darling."

"She doesn't want to rock. Or eat. And I just gave her medicine to bring the fever down," Heath told her.

"Well, then maybe a walk outside would be nice? Let's go breathe some lovely summer air, sweetness. I can walk with her out there just as easy as in here."

"That's a good idea. Jace is rocking Annie upstairs." She took Ava outside.

The change of scene seemed to brighten the baby's mood. She stuck her pacifier into her mouth, scowled, pulled it out, then stuck it in again.

Then she laid her head against Melonie's chest, subdued.

She walked back and forth, beneath the big spreading trees lining the driveway and around the ranch house, keeping the little one in the cool shade.

And when Jace came to get her a half hour later, she didn't want to let the baby go.

"I'm fine holding her," she whispered. Ava had finally dozed off against her shoulder. "I thought I'd sit in one of these porch rockers with her. If that's all right?"

"It's more than all right," he told her. He followed her up the steps, then drew the teakwood rocker farther from the wall. And when she settled into one, he took a seat in the other. "I'm sorry I ran out on you back at the house."

She arched one eyebrow in his direction.

"It wasn't my brightest move, I know. Five minutes wouldn't have made a difference, and the girls were in good hands. I'm not sure why I left like that."

"You did just become an instant daddy."

"And the county contacted me about filing for legal guardianship. When I told the social worker I'd like to adopt the girls, she said we either have to wait a long time for the courts to declare them abandoned, or get signed papers from Valencia that she's giving up her rights."

"Walking away and signing them away are two very different things." She patted the baby's back as she rocked.

"And no one knows where she is."

"Give Lizzie forty-eight hours and I expect she'd have an address for you. Probably less. She was an investigative reporter before she got pulled into a desk job at a ridiculously young age. She's got connections."

"But do we want to stir the pot?"

She understood the question. "Because she might want to come back and take over with the girls?"

Regret darkened his expression. "I'm not wishing their mother away. There's been enough heartache in this extended family to last a lifetime. But if she's in a bad frame of mind, would coming back help the girls? Or hurt them?"

"Will realizing their mother abandoned them help them or hurt them in the future?"

He winced slightly. "That will be a hard thing to face, I expect."

"That's one of the things your grandmother protected you from," she noted softly. "By pushing for a solid home for you, she gave you a normal life. From the sounds of things, if Barbara had kept you, your life would have been quite different."

"You want me to play nice with her."

She shook her head slightly. "I'm talking about understanding. Maybe putting three decades under the microscope and seeing why people made the choices they did. This isn't about her mean-spiritedness or a racist attitude toward a grandson. It's easy to look back and find fault with decisions people made years ago." She dropped her eyes to the sleeping baby in her arms. "It's much more difficult to make those decisions right now."

He drew a breath. Then he folded his hands. "I hear you. And if you asked me a week ago, I'd have said I was a fair man, schooled to think things through. Figure things out. Then decide accordingly. So maybe I need to do some serious praying about what I want to have happen and what should happen. Because it's a really muddy pond from where I'm sitting."

The promised rain began to fall. A summer rain, waking up the quiet dust of the graveled barnyard with each initial drop.

"We wait for the storm to pass, the skies to brighten. It always clears eventually."

"You're right."

She didn't mind hearing that at all because she was pretty sure he might have a different opinion when she showed him some of her ideas for Hardaway Ranch.

"I'm going to go check on Annie. You sure you don't want me to tuck Ava into bed?"

She shook her head. "Nope, we're good right here. What if she wakes up crying when we lay her down, wakes up her sister and then we've got two fretful babies? Peace and quiet is always better."

"Can't argue that. Tea?"

"Yes, thanks." She smiled up at him. "Sweet tea, a front porch rocker and a sleepin' baby. I might just imagine myself down South after all."

Chapter Nine

The sight of Melonie, cradling Ava, not worried about her time or her work…and he knew she cared a lot about both those things.

Yet here she was, comforting a small child she barely knew.

A gust of wind swept in with the rain.

He took a lap blanket from the glider and laid it around Ava and Melonie. "Those gusts have a chill in them."

"Thank you, Jace."

He went inside.

Zeke was still sleeping on the small sofa. Lizzie sat nearby. Heath had gone off to the fields to check on the sheep with a couple of hands. Rain didn't bother sheep. A bad storm might send them into a huddle, but normal rain was no big deal.

Annie slept on upstairs.

He felt superfluous all of a sudden. And restless.

Cookie was out back, grilling ribs for dinner. Corrie was working in the vegetable garden they'd created.

And here he was, with nothing to do when there was so very much to do.

"I suggest you take a minute to breathe." Lizzie came into the kitchen, grabbed a coffee pod and brewed herself a steaming mug.

"I'd have gotten that for you."

She shrugged. "Little guy is sound asleep, I need to get some wedding stuff done and the babies are both napping. I'm grabbing the minutes I can, same as Heath. I think this is how it's going to be," she warned him. "The minute you think you've got clear sailing, something goes wrong and a mad scramble ensues. Rosie said a few kids in town had a bug like this. It ran its course and was done in a couple of days."

"Shouldn't they see a doctor?"

"Corrie calls it the three-day rule," she told him. "If their fever doesn't come down with meds, call the doctor. If they get suddenly worse, call the doctor. Or if there's no change for the better by day three, call the doctor."

"So we wait?" Irritated, he scrubbed his hand along the nape of his neck. "I don't do waiting well."

She raised her coffee mug and clinked it against the glass of tea. "Welcome to parenthood. Maybe we can form a support group." She grinned, teasing. "Only new, uncertain parents need apply."

"Can I ask you something?"

"Sure."

"It's about your sister."

Lizzie lifted an eyebrow. "Don't ask me to divulge intense sister secrets, Jace. I value my life."

"The scar on her face. Backside of the left cheek. How'd she get that?"

"Not my story to tell. And not a topic she brings up. So good luck. But tread lightly. And most folks don't notice it now because of the way she wears her hair." She studied him. "But you did."

He was not about to mention dancing in the grass with Melonie. Dipping her. Then seeing the long curve of the scar just inside her hairline. "When we were working."

"Mmm-hmm." She sipped her coffee. Gazed at him. Then she smiled. "Work'll do it, Jace. Every time."

He flushed.

She wouldn't know it because the tint of his skin hid it, but the minute he did, Lizzie grinned.

Melonie had said she used to be an investigative reporter. He realized he wasn't getting much by the oldest Fitzgerald sister. "Melonie said that if I wanted to find Valencia, you might be able to help."

"Oh." Doubt changed her expression. "Are you sure you want to stir that up?"

"Not at all. But I need to have legal recourse with the girls. Gilda has already spoken with the county."

"A precipitous move on her part."

"Tell me about it. But we need to have things in place in case Valencia comes back. Except how do we keep a mother from her children?" He folded his arms, conflicted. "That seems so wrong."

"Speaking as the daughter of a runaway father, I can heartily say that it's never a black-and-white situation, Jace. But if we're looking after the safety of the children, then we have to look at any possible dangers to them. What if Valencia takes them and leaves them alone in some other place? Where there's no sweet uncle ready to open his doors and his heart? She's gone off and used false names before."

Gilda had said as much.

"Can we risk that?" she continued. "I can do a search," she went on as she moved back toward the living room. "I've got connections and it's pretty hard to hide these days. But you have to make sure it's what you really, truly want."

He didn't want it. He didn't know this sister, didn't know her story, her choices. Why would she take off now? Did something make her flee? Or did she simply abandon her babies? "I'll think about it." He'd set down Melonie's tea. He lifted it again. "Pray on it, too. I don't know what's right or wrong in all this."

Lizzie's face echoed that statement.

"But I know I want and need to do the right thing. Whatever that is."

He took Melonie's tea to the porch.

She'd dozed off with that sweet baby in her arms. Ava was nestled against Melonie's shoulder, and the pair of them sent a surge of protectiveness through him.

He set the tea down and put a firm check on his emotions.

He *should* want to protect these baby girls, his nieces.

He couldn't feel the same way about Melonie. They'd work together, help Gilda with her house. Then winter would sweep in and he'd spend the long, cold months running sheep. Counting lambs. Winter lambing was always much more labor intensive. The Middletons had run cattle. Not a huge operation, but a profitable one. They made do. But that had all ended when he was a boy. His father had dreamed of starting again. They'd envisioned running Angus together on the broad sweep of land that used to be Middleton property.

But then Sean Fitzgerald bought the land from his grandfather for a fair price. Once property values began to skyrocket the last decade, his father stopped talking about beginning again.

Then he was gone. They had the small stretch of land behind the house. Big enough to house the horses. Maybe a pig or two to put in the freezer. Not enough to stake a beginning. And with contracting jobs few and far between...

He'd finish this job. Do his best to make Gilda happy and bring Melonie's vision to life.

Then he'd go to Sun Valley next spring. As originally planned.

And Melonie would go back to her quest for success.

She shifted slightly. The small blanket slipped down.

He lifted it and gently settled it back where it had been.

He couldn't see the scar now. That side of her pretty face was obscured.

But having seen it made him wonder about her. The woman behind the classy clothes and strong work ethic. Seeing her in the dirt today, seeing that scar, he realized there was more to this woman than he first thought.

But she was cradling the very reason he couldn't explore that. His parents had always put their kids first.

He wouldn't be the man they raised him to be if he did any less.

"Now, that is a pleasant sight," Perched on the front porch railing, Melonie lifted her coffee mug in salute as Corrie walked the double stroller down the driveway toward Rosie's place three days later. "Two happy babies and one busy five-year-old, fully recovered."

Jace was standing just inside the screen door. He lifted his coffee in Corrie's direction, too, and agreed. "I'm glad they're better."

"Me, too. And we can be thankful for Corrie and Rosie, because now we can return to work."

She was glad when he kept their conversation work-related. "The supplies for my place are being delivered this morning. I'm heading over there to accept delivery, then I'm backtracking to Hardaway Ranch to check on the roofers. They're supposed to start today if the Dumpsters have been dropped off and…" He lifted his phone when it buzzed. "That's my cue that they've arrived and tear-off will commence within the hour. Listen, Melonie." He came through the door with a to-go cup in one hand and his phone in the other. "Why don't you work here where it's quiet?"

She slid her gaze from the busy sheep barn to the horse stables, then to the ranch house, where three hearty stockmen were having a quick bite of sausage, bacon, home fries, eggs, Texas toast and pancakes.

Then she brought her gaze back to his. "Your idea of quiet and mine are on opposite ends of the spectrum," she told him. "Gilda's due here anytime," she reminded him. "And while I'm sympathetic to her cause, I can't imagine getting a whole lot done if she's looking over my shoulder." She hesitated, then faced him directly. "Do you mind me working there?" she asked outright. "I figured on letting the morning sun dry up some of the rain so I'll work in your office at first, if that's all right." She lifted her laptop bag. "Then garden duty this afternoon."

"Shouldn't we hire someone to finish the rest of the garden?" he asked as he moved down the stairs.

"Except I enjoy it." He stopped when she said that. He didn't look back, but he paused, unmoving. "I like working in the dirt. Making things pretty. And seeing them stay pretty for years to come."

He hesitated for another moment, then continued down the stairs. "All right."

He drove off in his truck.

He didn't invite her to ride along.

That was okay. She'd need her own transportation later that day, but a part of her wished he'd offered her a ride.

He didn't, and when she got to the house a half hour later, the supplies were neatly stacked in the garage and his truck was gone. Off to Gilda's, she supposed.

He'd left the door unlocked. She moved through the newly opened living area, then past what remained of the bathroom.

When she heard him return less than an hour later, he didn't seek her out to say hi. Or check on progress.

The sound of his saw cut the morning quiet, followed by the pneumatic snap of a precise air hammer.

She stayed in his simple office space, the door shut, until she heard him call her name just before lunch.

She hit Save, got up and opened the door. Jace wasn't on the far side of the room like she expected.

He was there. Right there. And a trail of bright red blood marked the path behind him.

There was no time to think. Or swoon, which would have been her first choice.

She grabbed a towel from the adjacent linen closet. "How bad?"

"Nothing some salve and duct tape won't cure. But I can't do it one-handed."

Salve? Duct tape? "Please tell me you're kidding."

He looked positively perplexed.

"Anything that's bleeding that badly needs professional help, Jace."

"Or salve and duct tape. Seriously, if I could do it myself, I would, but I can't. Even if I tear the tape with my teeth."

She looked behind him, and sure enough, there were scraps of tape on the floor where the dolt had tried to treat himself. "I'll drive you to the ER."

His eyebrows arched. "All that time and money lost? Listen, my father used to say that if it bleeds well, bandage it. We'll know soon enough if it's not right."

She was not about to argue with his late father's advice. She motioned forward. "Kitchen."

He moved that way.

"Keep the pressure on."

"Got it."

Her stomach had risen right up into her throat at the sight of that blood, a leftover reaction from her childhood trauma. Since then she'd steered clear of anything blood-related, including rare meat.

She swallowed hard to gather her strength, turned the water on to a warm temperature and lifted the bottle of antibacterial soap. "Put your arm under here."

He did, letting the warm water sluice over the wound.

"Was this from your saw?" she asked as she finished scrubbing her hands.

"A piece of wood that bounced back."

"Equally unhygienic."

"Actually, it looked pretty good until I messed it up by bleeding on it."

"Jace." She didn't want to do this. She wasn't sure she *could* do this. But she also realized he might be right, that it wasn't necessarily an emergency-room injury. "I'll try not to hurt you."

"If you could see the scrub-brush techniques ER nurses use, you would not say those words. They're earnest," he told her, eyes wide on purpose.

He made her laugh.

She was laughing at his expression while cleaning a life-threatening wound. Well, maybe not life-threatening, she decided as she continued to flush the area. But not exactly minor, either.

"Are you sure you don't need stitches?"

"This only needs some Steri-Strips and a gauze pad under the duct tape to keep the duct tape from sticking to the gash. The first-aid box is right up there." He motioned to a shelf by the back door, and when she eyed the dust on it, he had the nerve to grin.

"That's why the case closes real tight," he told her. "To keep everything inside nice and clean."

Oh, brother.

"Those butterfly-shaped things. They're made to pull the sides of the cut together."

The last thing she wanted to think about was pulling sides together.

"Then maybe two of those gauze pads," he continued. "There's a fresh roll of duct tape right there alongside."

Yup. A thick roll of silvery gray industrial tape held a place of honor. "No medical tape? That nice, clean white stuff?"

"Doesn't stick," he answered. "Duct tape is made to stick. Gets me right back to work."

Inside the first-aid kit was a selection of bandages and pads, antibiotic salve and the duct tape right next to a clean bag containing tweezers, a needle and a tiny scalpel-like instrument that she refused to contemplate. "You have a personal ER right here," she muttered. "What are the super sharp scissors for?"

"Fish hooks," he told her. "They snap right through them, the normal-sized ones that is. We use them as needed."

Have mercy. She left his arm under the running water while she set things out and cut two lengths of tape. "If you get infected…"

"I'll go right over to the little clinic in Council and they'll put me on antibiotics. This isn't my first rodeo, Miss Mellie."

He said her name sweetly. It was funny, but kind, too, as if maybe he realized that binding wounds wasn't exactly her cup of tea. Of course, the expression of fear on her face might have given him a clue.

She pressed a clean towel to the area surrounding the wound, then applied the salve. Generously.

"Well, not much can hope to live through that," he told her. He grinned encouragement and approval. "Now the Steri-Strips. And then the pads."

"Thank you, doctor."

He cringed. "Sorry."

She applied the butterfly bandages, then followed with the pads and strips of tape. "These are going to hurt when you pull them off," she warned. "Duct tape is not meant to be used on arm hair."

He flexed his arm, then nodded. "It'll only hurt for a

minute. And look." He moved his arm back and forth. "Full mobility. You did great."

"Only because I didn't faint," she muttered as she cleaned up the area. "Are you at least going to rest a little? Give it a chance to bind?"

"And not work?" He stared at her in disbelief. "Then what would be the point of this? I want to be able to jump on Gilda's job when the roofing's complete, so there's no time to waste. And I can't bring the girls here until I've got this place done." He glanced around the house before he brought his attention back to her. "They need to come home, don't they?"

Sweet words from the man facing her. The kind of man who did what was needed, when needed.

She thought men like this only existed in stories. "You're right."

"If I need a hand putting things in place, are you available? I've got those last two-by-sixes ready to install."

"Yes, if only to keep you from killing yourself."

He sent her a lazy grin. "There's a comforting thought. But nice to know you can come through in the clutch, ma'am."

"Just don't sue me when you're fighting a major-league infection next week."

"On my honor. Grab hold of this here." They set the last two parts of the half wall together. She marveled at the precise moves of his hands, even with an injured forearm. He triggered the gun with his right hand as if it was nothing to do it one-handed.

She'd used air hammers before. They had a solid kick and buck.

Not in his hands. He nailed the supports like a skilled

craftsman, and when they finished with the framing lumber, she helped him with the wallboard. "Do you need me for the wainscoting?" she asked when the plasterboard was in place.

"No, I'm using the little gun. But thank you. This keeps me on schedule." Turning, he gave her an easy shoulder nudge. When she slanted her attention up, he nodded to the nearly renovated space. "I couldn't have gotten this far without you. Thank you, Melonie." Holding her gaze, he smiled.

She could get lost in those eyes, all velvety brown. Warm. Happy. Inviting.

This was an invitation she needed to turn down. "Simple teamwork, Jace. To get to project number two we must complete project number one."

His eyes lost the humor. He took a breath as if contemplating her words, then nodded. "That's the plan."

She went outside.

She'd squelched that light in his eyes on purpose, when it was about the last thing she wanted to do.

Are you that in love with the idea of your own show? Your chance to shine in the sun?

She wasn't, no. It wasn't about the show or the magazine or making a big deal of herself.

She stuck the small shovel into the ground pretty fiercely because it wasn't about her. She knew who she was. But in the back of her mind, lingering still, was the memory of the look of disappointment she saw in her father's face while she was lying in that hospital bed.

She'd failed him. She'd failed the horse, she'd failed the famed Fitzgerald name, she'd failed, pure and simple. Now she wanted to feel successful on her own terms. To show Tim Fitzgerald that even though she couldn't sit saddle like her sisters, she wasn't a failure.

Would he even know? her conscience argued. *Or care?*

Probably not. She knew that. But she'd carry the satisfaction with her. That would be enough.

She made a quick trip to the garden nursery in Council, and when she had two hanging baskets, three Knock Out rosebushes, wave petunias, wax begonias and eight different baby mum plants tucked into the car, she drove back to Jace's home.

He was gone.

She'd pre-dug the holes for the roses, and the begonias were an easy task. A stack of bagged black mulch stood at the driveway's edge.

It was quiet. Too quiet. It had been fun doing this with Jace a few days before. She took out her phone, hit a music app and when it started playing new country, she chose an oldies mix and started again.

Better, she decided when the strains of Glenn Miller's orchestra filled the yard.

She'd danced to "Moonlight Serenade" as a teen. And she'd boogied her way across the stage to "Pennsylvania 6-5000" a year later.

Corrie and her sisters had cheered her on. Corrie never made her feel like dancing wasn't as cool as show-riding. Neither had the girls. But her father, the man who sent roses to Charlotte and Lizzie when they brought home silver cups of victory, never once came to a recital. Never once brought or sent a bouquet. Corrie tried to cover for him after one performance. The roses had come, and she'd pretended she didn't know that Corrie had phoned the order in.

But when she thanked her father the next morning, his look of surprise gave it away.

"For I know the plans I have for you," says the Lord. "They are plans for good and not for disaster, to give you a future and a hope."

The uplifting verse from Jeremiah helped. That and a few other favorite scriptures, words of encouragement that helped show a true father's love. God's love.

By the time the new roses were set and watered, the trees offered sweet shade from the warm sun. She planted the smaller flowers quickly, and when she was done, she smiled.

She was just lifting her first bulky bag of mulch when Jace pulled in. He climbed out of the truck, tipped back his cowboy hat, lifted the heavy bag of mulch from her hands and whistled lightly. "You've done it."

"Do you like it?"

"Love it," he admitted. "My mom would have loved it, too. I don't know if she ever thought of black fabric to block weeds. And it works?"

"Like a charm. Between that and the mulch, keeping these gardens up should be a breeze."

He shouldered the mulch and strode across the sidewalk looking way too good for her not to notice. "Here?" He turned when he neared the porch and caught her look of appreciation.

He grinned.

She ignored him, and nodded. "Yes, thanks." *Play it cool. Maintain your distance.* "If you set it down, I'll open it and spread it."

"I'll dump them carefully, then you can maneuver it," he argued. "There is no reason for you to be lifting big, heavy bags like this."

She looked everywhere but at him. "Thank you."

"You're welcome. Got some sun today, eh?"

Setting one dusty hand to her cheek was a give-away. She'd thought it was the rising warmth heating her cheeks. Nope. "I forgot to put on sunscreen. Duh."

He winced. "I don't have any here. I'm not exactly the burn-and-freckle type."

Oh, he wasn't. He was absolutely the to-die-for tawny-skin type. "I know. You've got gorgeous skin."

Did she really just say that? Out loud?

She'd bent over to pat down the fabric around the second rosebush and if she could stay there forever, eyes down, she would.

Since that was impossible, she stood and dusted her hands against the sides of her old capris.

"Gorgeous, huh?"

Now it wasn't just the sun's rays heating her cheeks.

He stepped closer. And then he tucked one finger under her chin and lifted it gently. His voice went husky as he studied her face. Studied her. "I think you've got this confused, Melonie."

She raised her eyes to his. He gazed back at her with such a look of wonder that she was pretty sure her heart melted on the spot.

"You're the gorgeous one here." His hand touched her neck as if it was meant to be there. His voice, already deep, went deeper, and if her heart hadn't already gone soft, it did right then.

His gaze dropped from her eyes to her lips, then he touched his mouth to hers.

He smelled of sawdust and timber and fresh air, and when he deepened the kiss, she stretched up on tiptoe to ease the height difference between them.

"Melonie." He said her name like a summer night's whisper.

"I know." He'd pulled her in for a hug, a hug that felt like she was where she belonged. Of course, she wasn't. "We shouldn't be doing this."

"Whereas I was thinking we should be doing it on a regular basis," he teased. The scruff of his beard brushed her sunburned cheek, and when she winced, he drew back. "Ouch, sorry. I'll be sure to shave." He put his hand against her cheek—the scarred cheek—then met her gaze again. "I don't want to ever do anything that hurts you, Melonie."

She reached up her hand to cover his. "Then we need to wake up because this can't end well. We both know it."

He stepped back as if in full agreement. "You are absolutely right. We need to stop this. Right now."

That was about the last thing she wanted him to say, but it was the sensible thing, so she nodded. Even though she didn't really want to.

"We'll take it up again when we finish the gardens."

That wasn't what she meant, but he knew that. She went back to spreading the mulch while old-time music played in the background. Jace went through ten bags of mulch, then threw the empties into the construction dump. "I'm going to start on the bathroom."

"Wonderful." She didn't look up. "When we..." She stopped herself purposely. "When *you* get the girls to bed tonight, if all goes well, can I have you look at a few possible ideas for Gilda's place?"

"Absolutely. Meet you on the porch?"

He was teasing her.

She threw him a semi-scathing look. "In the well-lit

living room with chaperones, mister. I get that we're attracted to each other."

He tipped back the brim of his black hat and didn't grin. He just lifted an eyebrow slightly. And quirked his jaw.

"But we're like two trains, heading in opposite directions."

"Up here, in the Wild West, we know that a train might go in one direction…but it always comes back," he reminded her as he headed for the door. "Because it's a train, darlin'. And the track runs both ways. I don't see one sign saying beautiful women can't fix houses in Idaho. Not one anti-house statute that I know of."

He had to be kidding.

One look at his face said he wasn't. But when he read her doubtful expression, the smile left his face. "Not as big and grand, I expect."

What could she say? Gilda's job was the exception, not the norm. The area wasn't thriving. It was barely existing. A few rich ranches and a slate of empty houses and run-down farms. "Jace—"

"Gotta get back to it."

She'd hurt his feelings. She longed to go after him and apologize, but she'd pointed out a significant chasm. She wasn't ashamed of wanting to do well. It didn't define her. She wasn't foolish enough or pretentious enough to let that happen.

But doing a good job and having a career mattered to her and she refused to have to justify her choices anymore. Ever. She'd been given the magazine job because of who her father was. It wasn't like she was a well-known designer who'd earned her way up the ladder at twenty-eight years old. Nepotism had secured her job, then she'd had the guts and grit to prove she could do it.

Her father hadn't made her do that, and she knew why. He doubted her strength. Her capabilities. Her ambition.

Why do you need to prove anything to him? He's a cheat and a scoundrel. Why does this matter?

She spread mulch and realized it might take a team of therapists to reason that one out. She didn't owe her father anything. But just once in her life, just once, she'd like to think she'd done something to make him proud. He was the only biological parent she had…

And it shouldn't be too much to ask him to care.

She understood the reality, but the kid inside—the little girl she once was—was still waiting for that bunch of roses. A bouquet that he actually ordered and paid for. A bouquet that would never, ever come.

Chapter Ten

Not good enough.

Not rich enough.

Not opportunistic enough.

His hard-hit town, the town his family helped build, wasn't wealthy enough for Melonie.

You knew this. You knew it from the moment you set eyes on her, when she dismissed you with a single shrug of those pretty shoulders. You knew it and still you kissed her.

He knew better for a number of reasons, which meant applying the brakes one hundred percent.

He didn't want to. That kiss—that amazingly beautiful, wonderful kiss—had set his head to thinking and his pulse to jumping, but it wasn't just the kiss. It was seeing her with Ava, cuddled in that rocker. Seeing her pretend to nibble Ava's baby toes, and play peek-a-boo and laugh at the little blue-eyed blonde that seemed to think Melonie was pretty special.

What if the toddler got too attached? Would that mess her up when Melonie left next year?

He leveled the concrete and set the new tub about

the same time the electrician showed up to lay in additional wiring. He turned the bathroom over to him, and walked out back.

Bubba plodded his way. The old horse almost smiled, happy to see him. He wasn't used to Jace being gone so much, and in his advanced years, the gelding liked routine. He bobbed his head and when Jace laid out apple slices, Bubba accepted them greedily. And when Jace reached out to stroke his neck, the trusty mount leaned in like a faithful dog.

"I'm done out front."

He and the horse both turned toward Melonie's voice as Bonnie came their way from the opposite direction.

"I'm going to head back to Pine Ridge."

He nodded.

She indicated the horses with a look. "What will you do with them if you decide to move next spring?"

"Leave them."

She didn't look at him. Just them. His two old, loyal friends.

"I don't have the money to buy acreage in Sun Valley. It's much more upscale than this." He swept the broad, beautiful valley a long look. "But there's work there, so it's a trade-off."

She brushed her hands against her thighs. "Life's full of those, I suppose."

"How many trade-offs have you had to make, Melonie?"

He didn't mean to sound harsh, but he did and she jerked slightly. Then she leveled a cool look his way, and shrugged one shoulder. "Practically none." She walked away as Bonnie sidled up to the fence, looking for a handout.

He sliced another apple. They were from last year's crop and wilted now.

The horses didn't care.

They thought the less-than-perfect treats were wonderful.

Melonie's engine started as Bonnie lapped at his hand, happy with such a small thing. How he wished the woman walking away felt the same way.

By the time he got to the ranch, Corrie had walked the girls back up to the big house. As he climbed the porch steps, shrieks of joy and giggles came through the wooden screen door. Ava and Annie were in the living room. Baby toys were scattered across the floor.

Melonie wasn't inside. She wasn't on the porch, and although he didn't want to listen for her voice, he did.

Nothing.

"Hey, Papa Jace!" Lizzie had snagged a handful of cookies from the cookie jar. She handed him two. "Cookie said supper's an hour off because he had a slight kitchen emergency…"

"Emergency?" Jace had been working here for over a dozen years. Cookie had never so much as had a misstep, much less an emergency. "Is he all right?"

"Fine. But the first pot of stew might have cooked dry while he was up the drive, visiting the girls."

Cookie didn't go up the drive. He didn't lose focus. Ever. "He went up to Rosie's?"

"Thought he'd turned the pot down to simmer. Must have forgotten. He took cookies over to Corrie and Rosie."

To Corrie and Rosie…

Ah.

Jace raised his eyebrows. "So maybe it wasn't the babies snagging his attention," he mused softly.

"Miss Corrie Satterly may have found herself a beau!" Lizzie whispered, making sure no one was around to hear it. "You make sure to keep this to yourself, all right?"

"No one will hear it from me," he promised. He pretended not to notice that Melonie was heading their way from the direction of the horse stables. She had her computer bag with her. He averted his eyes intentionally, then got down on the floor to play with the girls. But when she didn't come in, he had to wonder where she'd gotten off to.

Then he heard Gilda's voice.

"So Gilda hung out here today?" he asked Lizzie from his spot on the floor.

"First she went to old Mr. Palmenteer's to take him some of Sally Ann's jam. They had a conversation worth having, according to Gilda. Then on to the Carrington Ranch to tell Sally how much folks loved her jams and jellies."

"The recluse is making the rounds," he mused.

Lizzie rolled a ball to Ava. Ava eyed the ball, then Lizzie, before deciding she didn't want to throw it back while sitting down. She crawled to the couch, grabbed hold and stood up. But then the ball was halfway across the room. She studied the ball, then the adults, trying to solve the problem.

"Then she came here with two more jars of jam and surprised us all by going up the drive, on her own, to visit the kids. And Zeke said she even sat down in the grass with the girls."

He didn't want to feel compassion for the old woman.

She'd made her choices. Years of them. Decades. So now she was trying to ingratiate herself to her neighbors and estranged family. Buying her ticket to heaven, he supposed. Except it didn't work that way, and he was pretty sure Gilda Hardaway knew that.

He couldn't hear Melonie's voice over the babies' babbles, but he heard Gilda's approving exclamations, which meant Melonie was showing her ideas.

He didn't want to intervene, or rain on their parade, but fancy designs didn't always work. Load-bearing walls and structural integrity were two things that some folks were willing to sacrifice in favor of a particular look. Too much sacrifice meant the roof might come down on your head.

He jutted his chin toward the porch. "Do you mind keeping an eye on these two while I butt into that porch discussion?"

"Not in the slightest."

Jace got up from the floor and headed to the porch, where Melonie and his grandmother sat. "Ladies."

Gilda looked up quickly when he came through the door. Her smile was more like a wince, but she aimed it straight at him. "I'm glad you're here, Jason. Melonie was just sharing some ideas with me and we wanted you in on the conversation."

"To see what's doable and what might need tweaking," said Melonie.

"I might have been able to save you both some time if I'd previewed the ideas." He made the comment lightly, but when Melonie lifted slow, gray eyes to his, he knew she caught the shielded reprimand.

"We're open to adjustments as needed," she said with candor, then poked Gilda's arm lightly. "But your grandmother knows this house far better than we do, so I thought I'd run some thoughts by her first."

"And I want it different." Insistence sharpened Gilda's response. "It never had the right feel the first go-around, so this one needs to be better. Done right," she insisted. "From top to bottom. And maybe not so walled-in here and there."

"We can open the first floor some, sure." Jace went around behind the ladies while Melonie brought up a new page. He pointed to the wall separating the kitchen from what must have been a grand living room at one time. "With a support beam here." He pointed to the current wall separating the two rooms. "And widening this here, we can keep the integrity of the structure and open things up."

"It's harder to keep secrets in a more open house." Gilda's voice softened.

Hairs stood up along Jace's neck.

He didn't want to hear about her secrets. He didn't care. The past and its pack of lies needed to be left there.

Just then, one of the babies shrieked in glee.

He started back for the door.

"You don't need to see any more?" Gilda asked. "No more advice?"

"At the moment there are two more important things to tend to," he told her. "This is my time with the girls. I was under the impression that consultation over the design layout of your house was going to take place later. Once they were in bed."

Gilda's mouth drew down.

Not in anger. But in sorrow. Because he sounded like a pretentious jerk after being a guardian for a matter of days.

"You go on, of course." She waved him off, apologetic. "I should be heading out now, anyway."

"I thought you said the roofers were working late." Melonie had the decency to look concerned while he acted like a dolt.

"A little noise and kabobble never hurt anyone." Gilda started to stand. Her dress snagged on the glider's edge. She began to tip slightly.

"Whoa." Jace grabbed hold of her arm quickly so she wouldn't fall.

"I'm fine."

"Of course you are." Melonie tucked the laptop aside and stood. "And you're not going anywhere except right here for supper and time with your great-granddaughters. They need that family time, it's the best thing for them. To have their Gee-Gee there—"

When Gilda looked blank, Melonie took Gilda's other arm and said, "Great-Grandma."

"I've never heard such a thing." Gilda frowned while Jace made sure they'd unsnagged the simple cotton dress she'd worn from the glider. "But I might like it."

"Down South there is a plethora of names for grandparents," Melonie told her as they moved toward the door. She must have showered since she'd returned because the scent of strawberries and something else— coconut, maybe—filled the air when she moved. "Meemaw, Mawmaw, Gammie, Mimi, Lovie, Neenee."

Gilda seemed shocked. "Not a soul your way just says Grandma?"

"Not too many, although my maternal grandmother was Nana. She and my father didn't get along and he made it very difficult for her to have any time with us."

"I am so sorry, my dear."

Jace opened the screened door as Gilda paused.

"Those family divisions are so wrong," she muttered,

as if scolding herself. Then she took a breath and sighed. "I only wish I'd known that as a younger woman."

Yup. A late harvester, just like they talked about in the Bible. How God paid all in equal amounts, even if they came late to the table of believers. As a working man, Jace understood the injustice in that. As a Christian, he understood the generosity God offered. Resolving the two…well, that was the problem, wasn't it?

The babies babbled when they moved into the living room. Ava had left the couch, and when she spotted Melonie she ducked her head and crawled as fast as those stocky little arms and legs allowed. Then she grabbed hold of Melonie's legs, and pulled herself up. "Bah!" she implored, then raised her hands up. Straight up, standing on her own. "Bah, bah!"

Melonie took a small step back. Then another, creating a span between her and the baby. Then she stooped low while the rest watched. "You want me, sweetie? Come get me."

Ava stared at her, then Jace and Gilda, as if questioning Melonie's right to move away.

Then she brought that blue-eyed gaze right back to Melonie. She stuck her two little arms out and waved them. "Bah! Bah! Bah!"

Melonie nodded, smiling, arms out. "I'm right here." She spoke in a voice laced with sweet encouragement and joy. "Come on, Ava. You can do this."

The baby squawked one more time, but seemed to size up the situation despite her vocal protest and then— with all of them watching, scarcely daring to breathe— she took a step.

Her expression changed.

She seemed a little bit frightened and very excited

all at once. She stood in place, bobbed up and down, almost dancing, then took a second step toward Melonie.

Oh, her smile!

A baby grin, from ear to ear as she chortled about her success before taking that final step, the one that brought her back to Melonie's very pretty legs. "Bah!" She screeched the word, laughing. "Bah!"

"You did it!" Melonie scooped her up, blew raspberry kisses along Ava's pudgy little neck and laughed with her. "You walked, schnookums! Good job!" She handed her right over to Jace. "Papa Jace is so proud of you, too."

His heart, which had gone sour earlier that day, unsoured right quick when Melonie handed him that baby so that he could share in the joy of those first steps. Sure, she'd gone to Melonie. Ava had developed a sweet spot for Melonie from day one. And it would have been so easy and natural to hog the moment.

She didn't.

He'd pretty much intimated that she grew up as a spoiled rich girl, yet who was it working on her knees in the dark Idaho soil earlier that afternoon?

Melonie.

And who handed over the beautiful child into his arms to share a milestone moment?

Melonie.

"They'll need baths today." Lizzie stood as Annie crawled toward Jace to see what all the excitement was about. "They had some fun outside earlier and since supper's going to be later than normal, should we bathe them now?"

"It makes sense," Gilda said. "I'm not as mobile as I used to be, but I can warm towels. I used to warm towels for your baths," she told Jace, as if there weren't thirty empty years yawning in between. "You were born just shy of Christmas and it was a long, cold winter. We had such good heat that I'd warm the towels while Barbara bathed you. Then I'd wrap that towel around you and you'd snuggle in, just so."

He wasn't sure what to say because he wanted to throw a million questions at her.

He couldn't. Not now. Maybe not ever. But the image of this old woman, as she might have been three decades back, wrapping him up in a warm towel and then snuggling him dry... He had to choke back emotion from his voice. "We can use the downstairs bathroom. I'll run the water."

He escaped into the bathroom long enough to recover his wits.

When she'd told him that the Middletons adopted him at a year old, he hadn't given much thought to the year prior. Only the years after.

Now she'd painted more of the picture. His father gone. And she and his mother, caring for him. Nurturing him.

It didn't compute.

How did you give away something you loved?

He started back to the living room and saw Gilda making funny faces at Ava. Yes, he could almost see her doing that with him, a long time ago.

Almost—but not quite.

"The mark's gone." Melonie swallowed hard as they finished bathing and diapering the babies about forty minutes later.

"The what?"

She looked from Jace to Lizzie and Gilda, then back. "The mark," she whispered. "To tell them apart."

"You marked them again?" Lizzie's voice was a mix of surprise and admiration. "I thought you were amazing because you could always tell them apart so I just followed along."

"Jace?"

He put up his hands. "No clue. Unless they're sleeping and we do the hand thing that Rosie suggested."

"There's got to be a way." Melonie stared at the girls.

"How about Corrie? Or Rosie?"

Corrie came into the room at that moment. "Sweet, clean babies! Just in time to have some mush, little darlings. Oh, you smell so good!" She got down and smooched both girls, then realized the four adults were watching her. "What's wrong?"

"Who are you kissing?"

Corrie's brow knitted. "Excuse me?"

"I mean the babies," Jace explained. "Which baby were you just kissing?"

Corrie looked from him, to the other adults, and then the twins. "You've gone and mixed up these sweet babies, and isn't that a bit of a pickle?" She stared up at their woebegone faces and burst out laughing. "You know twenty years ago this would be more difficult, but there is information at your fingertips every which way nowadays," she reminded them. "How were you telling them apart before?"

A sheepish expression darkened Jace's demeanor. "The colors. The pink and purple. I changed one at a time, so it wasn't a problem."

"Well, there are worse things in the world than being

called the wrong name for a spell, but there must be a way to distinguish them. Some little identifier," she reasoned.

"I'd marked them."

Corrie tipped her gaze to Melonie. "Say what, child?"

"With what was supposed to be a permanent marker," grumbled Melonie. "I've examined both feet. No dot," she explained as Heath and Zeke came through the back door. Heath kicked off his boots and the little guy followed suit.

"So now they're not dressed and there's no distinguishing mark because neither one has a birthmark or mole to help us out."

"Or a strawberry mark like you had," Gilda said to Jace. "Right at the back of your neck, where the hairline is. It went away in time, most do, but neither one of these little beauties has a mark."

They shared troubled looks while the babies giggled, free from the constraints of clothing while the adults tried to figure out what to do.

"I can always tell them apart," bragged Zeke once he'd lined his boots up alongside his father's. "It's easy, once you know the secret."

The hopeful look on Jace's face was almost amusing, but Melonie didn't dare laugh...at least not yet. "You can tell them apart?"

"Easy-peasy," said the boy, then he turned toward the babies. "Annie. Ava!" He didn't speak loud, he kept his voice calm and low, with just a hint of excitement.

One baby turned.

Zeke fist-punched the air. "That's Ava. I know because Ava always turns when I do that. Annie doesn't."

Annie doesn't.

He dashed off to the front room while the adults

faced one another. "What does that mean?" Jace asked. "Does Ava turn because she's trying to hear what's going on? Or does Annie not turn because she doesn't hear what's going on?" He lifted Ava while Corrie picked up Annie. "Could one of them be deaf?" he asked, and the sorrow in his voice highlighted the depth of emotion for two babies he'd only met a week before.

"They can do hearing tests, Jace."

"On babies?"

Heath nodded as he reached out a hand to Ava's still damp wisps of hair. "Then we'll know."

Jace hugged Ava to his chest until she squawked to get free. He took her out to the big front room, and when she wriggled to get down, he set her on the floor with a tender touch.

Then he watched as Corrie slipped a pink-and-yellow paisley romper onto Annie while Melonie did the same with a lilac version for Ava.

The supper bell clanged.

Heath and Lizzie slipped away with Zeke. Corrie lifted Annie. "I've got their supper ready and waiting and I expect that bath invigorated them."

"May I feed one of them?" Gilda hadn't said a word, but her face registered concern. "I'm not strong enough to carry one into the kitchen, but I can still lift a spoon and wipe a pretty little face."

"Of course you can," Melonie told her. "You're their great-grandma."

Jace stayed quiet, and when Melonie came back from the kitchen, he'd moved to the porch. She hung at the door for long, drawn seconds before she pushed it open.

He was standing at the rail, hands braced, chin down.

She wanted to go to him. Tell him it would be all right, but would it?

She approached the rail, turned to lean her back against it, then stood beside him, silent. Praying.

"I didn't notice," he said finally. "I've been with these babies for over a week, and it took a five-year-old to point out the obvious. That one of the girls doesn't react to her name. Or overreacts to it, straining to hear. What kind of a person am I? What kind of dad will I be to them?" he went on, gruffly. "If I don't notice a big thing like that, how can I pretend to be the right person to do this? I don't know anything about babies. About raising kids. What kind of person has to go online and order three books about parenting because he doesn't have a clue how to do the right thing or even know what the right thing is?"

She stayed quiet as the sun set lower in the Western sky. Filtered through feathered bands of cirrus clouds, the oblique rays splayed coral and orange through the green-leafed trees, like an inspirational painting. And when he finally turned her way, she asked one simple question. "Do you love them?"

He didn't hesitate at all. "Absolutely. It would be impossible not to love them. They're adorable."

"Then you do exactly what your parents did with you at the very same age," she whispered.

That got his attention. He swallowed hard as reality set in.

"You love them. You stumble along, learning as you go like all new parents do, but as long as you're bound by that love, you'll do just fine, Jace. And if one of the girls has a hearing problem, then who better to be her champion than a big, rugged cowboy who knows how to wrestle cattle, birth lambs and wrangle a whole mess of hay under cover when rain threatens the outcome? If I were that little girl, either of them." She aimed a pointed look inside. "I'd pick you every time. And those two girls will grow up knowing they're blessed to have you on their side. And that's the truth of it, Jace. Even though you do have a grumpy side from time to time." She couldn't resist adding that last bit, mostly because it was true on occasion.

He still gazed out. But then he slanted his gaze her way. "I'm not grumpy."

She made a face, doubtful. "Of course not, my bad." When he growled lightly, she smiled. "It's not that you haven't had a few things to grumble about. It's that there's so much more to be grateful for, Jace. Your health. Your sister. Your faith, your home, even those two old horses you love so well." She folded her arms as the temperature dipped lower. "And this brand-new family you didn't know you had. I'd say your cup is overflowing." She crossed to the glider and lifted her laptop. "Go enjoy your time with the girls. I'm going to make some adjustments to my plan. We can go over them tomorrow. All right?"

She didn't really give him a choice because she moved toward the westward-facing porch stairs as she spoke.

"Melonie."

She turned at the top of the stairs.

He sighed and kept it simple, cowboy-style. "Thank you."

She dipped her chin slightly. Then she raised one finger and pretended to touch the brim of a nonexistent cowboy hat. "'Til tomorrow."

Chapter Eleven

Jace left a message for the pediatrician's office, then drove to the Hardaway Ranch to check on the roofing progress.

"Jace." The foreman moved his way and pointed out how far they'd come. "We're getting there."

"I'll say." The uppermost roof was done and the side wing was being retooled by a crew of four. "It's amazing how a good roof finishes the look of a place, isn't it?"

"In this case, it couldn't hurt," the foreman told him. "I've got two guys who can help you with demolition inside if you want. I can spare them for two days once this job is done. That would save them from a lull no one wants or can afford."

"Are they solid workers?"

"Wouldn't offer them if they weren't. Those of us sticking around for the long haul know how important it is to have good help. Frankly, I'm amazed that the old lady is tackling this." His expression appeared more disparaging than amazed. "It's kind of scary but cool, all at once. I mean, what's the point?"

Funny.

Jace didn't have a whole lot of respect for his biological grandmother, but hearing someone else call her "the old lady" bothered him. "She's my grandmother, Art. And no matter how eccentric she may be, she's hired us to do a job and deserves respect."

The foreman looked from Jace to the house and back. "You're messing with me, right? Because I knew your parents. Remember?"

"My parents adopted me. Gilda is my biological grandmother."

"Well, that's one for the local news, isn't it?" Art folded his arms and braced his legs. "You never knew?"

"Nope."

"In a town that's not known for keeping the lid on anything, folks sure managed to do a good job keeping quiet on this." Art didn't hide his surprise. "Any more surprises up your sleeve, Jace?"

"Two, but nothing you'd believe so we'll leave that for another day. Let's see what you've got." Art showed him around the buildings. They decided to wait on new gutters until painting was done, and just as Jace was about to head back to his place, Gilda came out the front door wearing another simple cotton dress, the kind with a little white collar and a cinched waist. It was a dress that seemed to come from a long-gone era. "Why are you still here?" He moved forward, concerned because the noise level couldn't be good for an elderly person.

"I had a few things to attend to, and five cats to feed," she told him. She indicated her worn car. "But now I'm ready to go over to Pine Ridge. I'm going to show Corrie how to put up sour cherry jam. It's not something they did in Kentucky, I guess."

"I love sour cherry jam," he said. He wasn't sure why

an old-fashioned jam kind of connected him to her, but it did. "It's always been a favorite of mine."

"I gave your mother my recipe a long, long time ago," Gilda told him as she moved toward her car. "She liked learning things and she especially liked learning things about you. Knowing you loved jam and bread from the time you were just a little tyke made her feel like she'd been part of that first year, and that's a good feeling for any mother."

"Except mine." He put the words out there and let them hang. Art had gone back to work and Gilda paused, her hand on the car door, her eyes down.

"Barbara loved you," she said finally. "As much as she could love anyone, Jason, and I don't know if that's because we failed her or she failed us, and when you get to this age you realize it doesn't really matter and never did. What I do know is that if God offers the chance and time to fix it, you jump on board and do what you can. She didn't have to have you, you know. The law had opened up choices and she could have ended the whole thing and no one would have been the wiser."

Jace stood stock-still as her implication came clear.

"Especially when Lionel shrugged his shoulders and walked off."

The thought of a father turning away from a child was incomprehensible to Jace and the very opposite of how he was raised. "He didn't want me."

"He didn't want much of anything except to be respected but then he had a hard time doing anything respectable so that became a problem." She pressed her lips into a thin line. "He wasn't a terrible person, but he wasn't a strong person, and when your grandfather offered him money to go away, he took it. I'm not saying it was a bad thing to do, but it broke Barbara's heart, thinking he could be bought. She took her college money out of the funds we set up for her and decided she didn't have one drop of interest in being a mother... And that's when I thought of Ivy and Jason." She sighed softly, gazing out, then brought her eyes back to his. "They wanted a baby so badly and thirty years ago there weren't all these specialized clinics to help folks who couldn't have children, so year after year they waited. Hoping. Praying. They'd put in for adoption but babies were scarce." She winced. "When Barbara decided she wanted her freedom, placing you with Ivy and Jason seemed like the right thing to do. I had exactly what they wanted." She said those words softly. So softly.

But Jace heard the truth behind the words. "A dark-skinned baby that wouldn't fit the Hardaway image."

She turned toward him with a look of anguish. Not just everyday sorrow, but true grief. "You always fit my image, Jason. From the very first day. But I will confess that I married a man who wasn't the kindest or best or a believer in anything other than himself and money, so in that way you're correct. You didn't fit *that* Hardaway image. But don't you ever think for one solitary moment that you didn't fit mine. Because you did."

She opened the car door, climbed in and pulled it shut behind her. Then she backed out, leaving him to consider what she'd said.

Easy words now. To pretend she'd cared, that she'd loved him. That she'd gone the distance for him, but the former opulence of the grand old house said that appearances had been important, at least back then.

He moved to the classic barn, climbed up to the loft for a better view and paused.

Idyllic beauty rolled along fields tipping away from the house. From the ground, two decades of growth obscured the view of the land that made up the Hardaway acreage. From here, the rolling fields opened wide with opportunity. Gilda must have rented some of the land out, a smart move. Two mammoth hay fields stretched across the valley. A series of broad paddocks meant for cattle linked far pastures to the nearest barn, but there were twin barns forming an L at the far end of the second paddock. From here he could see the gravel drive, hidden from the road by long years of brush growth, where trailers must have pulled in to load market calves.

The place must have thrived in its day.

A tiny seed of what-if stirred inside him.

Could this place be brought back to life? Could the ranch be restarted?

Does it matter? It's not yours to speculate on.

It wasn't, thought Jace as he snapped a series of pictures with his phone, but he wasn't a fool. He'd sat at Grandpa Middleton's feet when the old man talked about Middleton land. Middleton horses. The Middleton Ranch, gone before Jace was born, but something to aspire to. A few bad years had put the ranch on the market a long time ago, and Jace understood the truth in that. A farming enterprise could sustain some ups and downs, but too many bad years spelled disaster.

But this—

This spread must have been unbelievable in its day, and still Gilda had let the whole thing go to wrack and ruin once her husband died.

A call from the pediatrician's office interrupted his

musings. And when he explained why he needed both girls to be seen and evaluated, the nurse offered him an appointment in four days.

He gripped the phone tight. "Four days? You can't get them in sooner?"

"Are they ill, sir?"

"No, they're fine."

"No fever, no injury, nothing out of sorts?"

"Well, if you can conclude that a possible hearing loss isn't out of sorts, then no. I guess not." He sounded snippy. He felt snippy, as if this should be taken much more seriously by the medical community.

She moved the appointment up a day and apologized, which made him feel like a jerk. "Mr. Middleton, we've got to get the records transferred from the clinic so we can see what the twins have had in the way of immunizations and care. To be able to properly assess what's going on, we need to do physicals and bring them up to date in our practice. It's not that Mountain View Pediatrics doesn't share your concern, but we'd be remiss to jump the gun before we have all the facts, and because you've got twins, I need to block out sufficient time for each baby."

He hated that it made perfect sense, and when she gave him a twelve-thirty Thursday appointment time, he realized someone would be missing their lunch break because he'd thrown a mini-fit. "Actually, go back to the Friday date," he told her. "You're right, I'm new at this and more than a little nervous. And let me add that I hate admitting that," he finished.

"If you're sure?"

"Yes. Friday at nine thirty is fine."

He pocketed the phone before he climbed down the

loft ladder, then pulled it back out when he reached the ground floor and hit Rosie's number on speed dial. "How are the girls doing?"

She laughed. "So well! Miss Ava has taken a few more steps today, but mostly is crawling and trying to make her way to off-limits places like the stove and the bathroom, while Annie is quite content to amuse herself and watch her sister's antics from a distance."

"How can they be so different?" he asked as he moved to his truck. "They're genetically identical. This makes no sense."

"The body may appear the same, but the soul is unique, is it not?"

He hadn't thought of that. It made perfect sense. "Well, of course they couldn't have the same soul."

"Exactly the truth, which is why science can only do so much. For the rest, we trust in God."

"Thank you, Rosie. I'm heading back to my place to work on the bathroom. Call me if you need me."

"Of course."

He drove back to his parents' house—his house now, his and Justine's—quickly. There was a lot to do in the next week because once they began interior demolition on Gilda's house, he'd be tied there for several months. Even working with a crew of one or two, he wouldn't be setting any speed records, and how would the folks at Pine Ridge hold up if Gilda became a regular visitor?

He cringed but decided to cross that bridge when he came to it. He spotted Melonie's car as he crested the hill a few minutes later. His pulse jumped.

He tamped it right back down. She'd made her position clear, but the moment he spotted her sitting in the shade of the catalpa trees, wearing that ridiculously big hat and tapping away on her laptop, his heart leaped again.

She looked up. Smiled. And when she did, something stirred inside him, an urge to keep right on inspiring those smiles. He crossed the yard as she stood. "Were you able to set something up for the girls?" she asked right off.

His heart thwarted his lame attempts to tamp it down the moment she asked the question. While their job at Hardaway Ranch was huge, nothing mattered more than those babies' well-being. "Friday morning."

"That's the soonest they could see them?" She looked as surprised as he'd felt, but when he explained the nurse's reasoning, she nodded. "That makes sense," she agreed when he was done. Then she indicated the laptop. "I think I've grown too accustomed to instant gratification and quick-moving programs. I have to say that's one of the perks of being up here in the country. Things aren't moving at a breakneck pace."

She turned away to get the laptop. "You found Kentucky to be fast-paced?" The South wasn't exactly known for moving quickly.

She burst out laughing and turned back.

So pretty, with her hair pulled off to one side, just enough to hide that scar. So bright and engaging. A great smile. The inviting laugh. And skin so soft…so touchable…

He reached a hand to her cheek.

Yes, he'd promised himself to steer clear, but there was no keeping clear of this woman. Her warmth and joy urged him closer, even when common sense scolded him to keep away. "Melonie." He didn't mean for his voice to go all deep and husky. But it did, the moment he felt the warmth of her skin beneath his hand.

She didn't move. She gazed up at him with a softer smile now, but a look that offered permission. Permission he couldn't refuse.

He kissed her. He kissed her long and slow. And she kissed him right back. He held her close, her head tucked against his big, old cowboy-beatin' heart. "I know we're not supposed to do this."

"So why do you suppose we keep right on doing it?" she whispered, but there was amusement in her tone. "Because I'm not going to pretend I don't like it, Jace."

He smiled, his cheek pressed against her hair. "I'd say we like to tempt fate, but we don't."

She shook her head, agreeing.

"Or maybe it's that we're thrown together and proximity is the guiding factor."

"I've been in proximity to a lot of men over the years, and I can't remember anything remotely like this." She leaned her head back and caught his gaze, which got her kissed again.

"Then maybe it's just meant to be, Melonie. Maybe we'd be downright foolish to fight it."

He felt her smile against the thin cotton of his shirt. "Now, that's a solid pick-up line."

"Or a solemn pledge," he whispered. But then he stepped back firmly. "However, we've got work to do, and I need to read up on kids' hearing disorders later, so what've you got for me? And I promise not to shoot it down too quickly."

She picked up the laptop and set it onto her lap as he settled onto the bench beside her. She showed him a photo of the front of Gilda's house. "We'll keep this the same except for adding this eight-foot window unit here. It's a shame to have a view like that and not exploit it from the house."

He'd noticed that, too. "So we add on this window bay. For both stories?" he asked, surprised, and she nodded.

"It will balance the lines of the house and that way whoever has the master bedroom on the second floor can share the view that we'll have in the living room."

"It's beautiful. And functional," he added.

"Function first, but there's nothing wrong with dolling it up," she told him. She was looking down and when she did, she pushed the hank of hair from her left shoulder, revealing the scar.

He reached up gently. Then ran his finger along the inverted C of the mark.

She turned sharply, and there was no missing the deer-in-the-headlights look she gave him. "Stop that."

He dropped his hand but not his attention. "What happened?"

She huffed a breath, went back to the computer and ignored his question.

Jace Middleton didn't hold well with being ignored. "Tell me." He left the words hanging for a few seconds before he whispered, "Please."

She stared down.

Her jaw went tight, and for just a moment she resembled her uncle when he'd had about enough of people's nonsense. But then she breathed in and out. She lifted the shoulder closest to him in a half shrug. "I went a few rounds with a very big horse when I was eight years old. The horse won."

He leaned forward to catch her eye. "I'm so sorry."

The thought of a small child being injured by a huge horse wasn't something he'd ever had to worry about. Now he would.

She looked the other way.

"Hey, don't do that." He reached around and turned her gently. "I didn't mean to put you on the spot."

"Yet, you did."

"Yes." He waited for her to turn. She didn't. "I asked Lizzie and she said it wasn't her story to tell."

"Old news, Jace. I'd prefer to talk about the future, not the past."

If sadness had a name, it was written in her eyes. Her expression. He recognized that emotion in her face right now, and he longed to make it disappear. "We don't have to say any more about it. Not now. Not ever. But if you ever want to talk, Melonie?" He stroked her cheek, staying clear of the scar. "I'm here."

For just a moment he thought she might give in. Open up.

She didn't. Gazing down, she went to the next page of her prospective designs. "I appreciate the offer."

Give her space. Give her time. Give yourself time to feel your way through all of this.

"When is your sister coming in?"

It was a good change of subject. He'd had some time to get used to this strange turn of events. Justine would be coming face-to-face with the babies and the reality that he wasn't biologically related to her. "Friday night. Then she catches a flight back on Sunday afternoon."

"Well, let's get cracking here. If you can have the girls over here, then Justine has time to absorb all of this without the entire Fitzgerald clan hovering around."

"It is a whole lot busier and noisier than it used to

be," he teased, but it was the simple truth. Since Lizzie and Corrie had come to town, the ranch had courted visitors of all kinds, held a beautiful memorial service for Sean Fitzgerald and stirred up emotions in a place that most thought was dead.

Shepherd's Crossing wasn't dead.

Sleeping, maybe, but the Fitzgerald women didn't seem too keen on letting things lay low or stay quiet and he was beginning to think they were just what the town needed.

Chapter Twelve

The paint crew arrived at Jace's house at dawn Thursday morning. They had the house and trim done just in time for a local service to install gleaming white gutters, but when Melonie asked about moving the girls into the house, Jace put her off.

"I'm going to wait until Justine heads back to Seattle," he told her Friday morning as he and Corrie fed the girls.

"Why?" she asked as she sipped her coffee. If she stayed on this side of the wall, maybe the longing to jump in and feed those babies—care for those little girls and their handsome guardian—could be kept in submission.

That worked for about five seconds, and then Ava spotted her and clapped her hands, slopping morning mush all over herself, Jace and the high-chair tray. "Bah!" She reached her arms right out toward Melonie. "Abba abba bah!" And despite Jace's best efforts to keep feeding her, Ava was insistent. She wanted Melonie and that left Melonie no choice. She wet a clean washcloth from the stack Cookie kept on the nearby counter and crossed to the extended table. "You're a mess, schnookums."

Ava grinned and slapped her gooey hand against the tray, splattering all of them again. "Nee Nee!"

"A new word has been added to our extensive vocabulary." Jace swiped goo from his arm and cheek, then kept feeding Annie, who didn't seem nearly as excited to see Melonie.

"I think she's saying your name," Corrie remarked as she helped wipe down a whole list of things that bore the splatter of Ava's enthusiasm. "Melonie. Nee Nee."

"Bah! Nee Nee!" Ava grinned at Melonie, so precious and funny and sweet. Corrie had set the spoon on the tray.

Ava picked it up, stuck it in her mouth, then grinned like a little clown.

"Oh, you are going to be a handful, darling girl." Melonie took Corrie's spot, a seat that brought her right next to Jace, the very man she'd tried to avoid for forty-eight hours—only when you're working a major project with a person, necessity brought proximity, so how on earth was she going to table this attraction?

"Jace?"

They both looked up as Lizzie approached. She held a printout in her right hand. "I've got information on Valencia. Where she is right now, at least."

His jaw tightened, but he nodded. "Thank you. One way or another we've got to make things legal. It would be great if she would sign rights over without issue, but either way we can't leave these babies in limbo. That leaves them with no legal protection if she comes back, and the sheriff said she could be arrested for abandonment if she returns." He took the paper from Lizzie while she made coffee. "I don't want to make a bad situation worse than it already is, but we've got to put the girls' safety first."

He scanned the paper quickly.

Melonie wanted to ask what it said.

She didn't have to.

He held it out to her. "She's in Oregon right now. Near Bend. Should I ask you how you got this information?" He posed the question to Lizzie once she brewed her coffee.

"Probably not."

"I've got the girls' doctor's appointments this morning, then Justine's due to arrive this evening." He drew his eyebrows down. "Who'd have ever thought I'd have to ignore one sister to help the other?"

"Well, Justine's making the effort to be here. To spend time with you and meet her nieces." Melonie stayed practical. "If Lizzie tracked Valencia down once, she'll do it again."

"And who knows? She may stay put there for a while. There are a bunch of hotels there looking for housekeeping help. She's experienced and has a decent track record with her former employer," Lizzie noted.

"The amount of information that comes to your fingertips is mind-boggling and possibly frightening." Melonie handed Ava her sippy cup.

Disenchanted with the option, the baby tossed it to the floor and burst out laughing.

Melonie retrieved it and handed it back.

Ava grinned…and tossed it down again. She was having her own personal game of fetch and Melonie was the pup-in-training.

"You're done." Melonie slipped off the tray, handed it

to Corrie and lifted the baby out of the seat. "We don't throw things," she scolded as she re-swabbed Ava's face with a clean, wet cloth. "That's naughty."

Ava's eyes went round.

Her lower lip thrust out and she stared up at Melonie in disbelief, as if her beloved Nee Nee had just delivered a crushing blow.

Then she started crying. Big, breath-shaking tears, about as cute and over-the-top as she could get.

"I made her cry." Melonie looked from Jace to Corrie and back, distressed because this was the last thing she expected. "What do I do? I just made an itty-bitty girl start crying. I didn't mean to," she went on.

"She'll be fine in two minutes," counseled Lizzie. "Show her a shiny object. It will help. I promise."

"Better they cry now than you cry later," added Corrie. "Being naughty might be cute at this age. It is not amusing when babies grow. There is no time like the present to begin that lesson."

"Lessons? They're not even a year old." Jace looked as surprised as Melonie felt.

"Lessons begin the moment they start reaching for the stove. Or a sharp object. Or a doorknob. We begin teaching to keep them safe. We keep teaching so they learn to love knowledge."

"That settles it." Jace grinned at Annie as she blew raspberries through her last bite of Corrie's mush. "I'm taking Corrie home with me. I need her counsel and wisdom to get me through this. At least the first year," he added. "Corrie, what do I have to do to tempt you away from all this?"

"Marry one of my girls," she shot back, and never even looked over her shoulder. "I am an officially retired nanny," she went on as she rinsed baby dishes in the sink. "But I will never retire from being their mama or a grandma. That's the only way to get my services these days, I'm afraid." The older woman aimed a knowing look at Jace. "But I appreciate the compliment."

"It could be worth it," Lizzie teased. "Like a two-for-one sale at the grocery."

"We'll have to see if Charlotte's available when she arrives." Melonie shot her sister a stern look as she grabbed a handful of tissues. Ava's sobs lessened to whimpers against her shoulder. "I'm taking little Miss Ava to get changed."

Jace's phone rang as she went to the living room. They'd set up a changing station there. Diapers, wipes, onesies and rompers. Jace came into the room as she finished dressing Ava. She stepped away from the changing table and set Ava on the floor. "Your turn."

The first day it had taken him a long time to change the wriggling babies. Not anymore. He got Annie cleaned and dressed in record time, then set her near her sister. "Gilda wants to come to the doctor's office with me."

"It's kind of nice that she wants to be involved, isn't it?" she asked. Then she read his face. "How is that bad?"

He made a face. "Not bad. Awkward. I don't know what to say to her. What not to say. And I still feel like lashing out irrationally when she harps on the past."

"Perhaps for her it's not harping, but asking forgiveness. And understanding."

"What if I can't understand why they did what they did?"

"That's a self-directed question if ever there was one."

He frowned as the rumble of Gilda's tires crunched across the barnyard gravel. "Why does everything have to get talked to death? Maybe that's a better question. Listen." He put his hand over hers. "I know you've got work to do, but if I absolutely leave you alone to work this afternoon, will you come with us? To the doctor's appointment? Not just because of my grandmother, I'm pretty sure I can handle her, but I could really use your help."

"You don't need me there, Jace." She knew it, and she was pretty sure he knew it, too. Including her in family things like this would only make things harder and, frankly, they were hard enough already.

She stood to go.

Ava grabbed her ankle. And her heart. "Nee?" She grabbed hold of Melonie's other leg and stared up, imploring. "Nee?"

"She is saying your name." Jace looked at Ava with such a look of pride that Melonie's heart went soft all over again. "How cute is that?"

"Nee." Ava patted Melonie's leg, then raised her arms up.

"We both want you to come, Melonie."

How could she resist that? Maybe she was foolish to tie all her dreams to a what-if life down South. What if she dared to transfer her hopes and dreams to the forest-rimmed valley of western Idaho?

Ava leaned her head against Melonie's leg, as if hugging her. She lifted the baby and kissed her soft cheek. "If you promise to give me work time this afternoon..."

Jace smiled. "My word of honor."

What a delight that she could actually trust his word. She lifted the diaper bag he'd packed earlier.

He had Annie in one arm.

She held Ava.

And when he reached over to take the bag from her shoulder, a new thought blossomed. Of raising these two girls together. Here, in the mountain-rimmed valley.

Are you crazy?

She felt a little crazy when she looked up at Jace and matched his smile. And when his deepened, her heart quickened, a ridiculous and absolutely marvelous reaction.

"Best get going." Gilda was at the base of the porch stairs, impatient. "We don't want to keep the doctor waiting."

"You're right," said Jace. "We don't want to be rude."

"Are they warm enough?" Gilda's voice lost a grain of harshness when she talked about the babies.

Melonie answered as she wrestled Ava into her seat. "If not, she will be," she muttered. "The struggle is real."

"And little Annie goes right in." Gilda seemed surprised, and Melonie couldn't blame her.

"The same but different, right?"

"I guess." Gilda seemed flustered. She eyed the vehicle, then her car.

"You ride with Jace. I'll follow along."

"You don't mind? I don't go driving into the city much."

"Happy to do it."

She opened the door for Gilda. The old woman climbed in and pulled her seat belt into place.

She didn't dare look at Jace.

She could have had Gilda ride with her, but learning

to be family around these girls was part of the point, wasn't it?

Her phone rang as she followed them out of the driveway. She hit the Bluetooth connection when she recognized the name of her former coworker. "Ezra, hey. How are things going? Have you found a job yet?" Ezra Jones had been her photographer and site director for the magazine. He'd staged the looks, taken the shots and organized the production of her *Shoestring Southern Charm* pilot videos six months ago. When the magazine folded, so did his job.

"Possibly. I might have found *us* a job."

She'd pulled out of the driveway but paused. "Us?"

"I'll give you the details. I'm heading your way."

"You're coming here?"

"Kentucky is blazing hot and I wanted to go over a few things with you. Get your opinion. You don't mind, do you?"

Ezra had been her friend for years. "Of course not. Come on up and bring your cameras. There is a wild and rustic beauty up here. Not low-key, sweet-tea serenity like we have in the South. But beautiful."

"I'll let you know when I get close."

"You're going to leave me hanging?" she asked as she navigated the next turn.

"Temporarily. I'm working out details. Car phone connections are amazing things."

"Talk to you soon." She disconnected the call, but there wasn't a lot of time to ponder his meaning. Ezra thought outside the box, 24/7. He was a concept guy, who looked beyond the everyday, and he'd end up somewhere, doing great things. She knew that because he had the talent and the drive to see it through. They'd made a great team.

A job for us...

And yet he knew she had to be here for a year.

She reviewed her options for Gilda's house. Her palms itched as she considered the magnitude of this project. She'd have Ezra grab pictures of the "before." She'd sent him a few when she and Jace made the agreement with Gilda, and he'd sent back a one-word answer. *Wow.*

Wow was right, but as she'd gotten to know Gilda, and sensed the longing to make things right, the house design became more than a massive makeover.

It became a mission.

Chapter Thirteen

Annie didn't need help.

Ava did.

"I'm going to send you to a specialist near Boise," the pediatrician told them midmorning. "My guess is they'll recommend putting tubes in Ava's ears."

"Tubes for what?" Gilda drew her eyebrows tight, and when she did that, the word *formidable* came to Jace's mind. "What do tubes do and why does she need them?"

The doctor didn't take offense. Jace guessed she'd worked with frightened grandparents before. She pulled out a chart while the twins batted small plastic balls around the carpeted floor of a small meeting room. "She's got fluid buildup in her right ear. I looked at the clinic records and saw she'd been treated for three ear infections in five months."

"Her caregiver told us that she's had recurring colds and light fevers."

"So it's even possible that she's had a couple of un-diagnosed issues. For some kids, it's no big deal. For others, like Ava, the chronic ear infections leave a fluid buildup and dull hearing. It is usually reversible with the tubes and maturation, but I'll let the ENT doctor go into that detail. We'll set up the appointment for next week, and they'll take it from here."

"Should we do both?" asked Gilda. Melonie stayed quiet. She'd taken a seat on the floor and let the girls crawl all over her, keeping them happy while Jace, Gilda and the physician talked.

"It's always curious when identical twins show differences like this, isn't it?"

Gilda nodded.

"Annie's not showing any signs of problems, and her newborn screening and this hearing screening are both normal. I'd chalk this up to normal variances. When you're talking babies and narrow passageways, growth is often our best friend. A more open passage allows the body to get rid of bacteria and viruses faster. Faster healing, fewer problems."

"They don't have insurance," Gilda spouted. "But I'll pay for what needs doing."

"Wonderful." The doctor smiled at her, and Gilda seemed to physically relax. "You're the great-grandmother, correct?"

She nodded.

"And you're the uncle seeking guardianship?"

"I am."

The doctor leaned forward. "Something for you to consider. If the specialist's office questions guardianship, they probably have to refuse treatment."

Jace wasn't just surprised by that. He was shocked. In the local towns, no one refused Gilda Hardaway anything. It simply wasn't done. "What?"

The doctor explained her meaning in a matter-of-fact manner. "They'll need parental signatures to proceed.

Or, if the girls become wards of the state, then they'll need the Human Services office to okay the surgical procedure."

"I have the means to pay," Gilda insisted. "And my great-granddaughters aren't wards of anything. They're family!"

The doctor sent her a sympathetic look. "And they're blessed to have so many people invested in their outcome, but the specialist will need to have a legal guardian approve treatment."

"What if we had an emergency and needed treatment?" Jace asked. He'd never considered they might refuse to help the girls.

"In an emergency situation, the need to treat outweighs everything. But it's still a sticking point that should be rectified ASAP. Will your guardianship be approved soon?"

Jace scrubbed his hand against the nape of his neck. "That's uncertain."

"Well, my advice is to get that done quickly," she said, standing. "They'll ask, and you don't want to be falsifying records. It's not about who's caring for the kids," she assured Jace in a kind voice. "It's about legal recourse, and hospitals are pretty picky about it. You might want to get the legal ends tied up quickly."

There was no quick way to fix this unless Valencia signed off. "I'll get right on it."

"Good." She shook his hand and referred them to the front desk, where an efficient office manager took care of setting up the appointment for the specialist in two weeks. Which meant he needed to get to Bend with legal papers and get Valencia to sign off before then.

What if she didn't?

He didn't dare think that way, because when Annie clutched his neck and blew raspberry kisses along his cheek, her laughter clinched the deal. How could he not take a chance on them? And did his sister care?

There was only one way to find out.

They tucked the girls into the car seats and he placed a call to Mack Grayson. Mack was a cowboy by birth and a lawyer by education, the perfect guy to help local ranchers and business owners. He left Mack a voice mail, then headed back toward Shepherd's Crossing.

A few weeks ago he'd been lamenting too much time on his hands. That wasn't the problem any longer. Now he'd have to figure out getting to Bend, finishing his house, working with the demolition crew on Gilda's place, caring for two children and having time with Justine over the next couple of days.

"Do you want me to go to Oregon? I can take the train over."

Gilda's raspy voice interrupted his running thoughts.

"To see Valencia?" That might be the worst idea ever. Or the best. How would he know? But Gilda wasn't in great health, so he nixed the idea. He spoke gently because he didn't want to hurt the old woman's feelings. "I appreciate the offer, but I'd prefer to go myself. What I'd really like, if you have the time—" he angled a quick glance her way "—is if you'd help with the babies while I'm gone. It's a lot for Rosie to handle and I'd feel better knowing they're having some Gee Gee time. I want them to know their family, as silly as that might sound at their age."

"Not silly at all." She didn't sound so raspy right now. "You knew your mom and me real well, Jason. By this age you'd figured out how to wrap me right around your finger with those big brown eyes and that beautiful smile." Eyes down, she fiddled with her purse strap as she spoke. Her voice had gone soft, talking about him. Now it hiked up once more, as if she was excited about the girls. "Getting to know these two will be an absolute pleasure."

She sounded genuinely excited.

And yet when his mother abandoned ship, his grandmother didn't step in to raise him. Why?

Try as he would, he couldn't understand her decision. He couldn't imagine giving the twins away to someone or walking away from them. And that only made him wonder how parents justified such a choice?

A return call from Mack interrupted his thoughts. "Mack, I need some legal help and I need it fast. Can I come by today?"

"I'm making a house call to Carrington Acres in about an hour," Mack told him. "How about if I swing by your place after that?"

That would give him enough time to get the girls back to Rosie's and make the short drive to his house. "That works. See you shortly." He hung up as he turned down the Pine Ridge Ranch driveway.

"Is Grayson that young lawyer from Council?" Gilda asked.

"That's him."

"His daddy was one of those Grayson boys from up in the hills."

Jace wondered if there was a point to the statement. There usually was…eventually.

"I knew his grandfather. We kept company for a while when we were young."

Well, that was a surprise. "You and Mack's grand-father?"

She pressed her lips into a thin line. "I was young. My parents owned the original mercantile on Main Street and then bought a couple of other businesses as well."

He'd known the town had a rich history, but the sadness of losing the Middleton Ranch had made Shepherd's Crossing history verboten in their house. So he knew *of* it, but not much about it.

"I never did without, and I thought that was the reason I was happy." She rolled her eyes as they drew up to Rosie's turnoff. "The foolishness of youth, I guess. So when Richard Hardaway showed interest, I showed interest right back because he was already on his way to a bright future and I knew I'd want for nothing." She twisted her fingers, restless. "Life might have been very different if I'd made other choices, but then I wouldn't have you. Or these precious girls. So maybe things work out in their own way after all."

He had no idea what she meant, and she did like to ramble, but if she was talking regret, then, yeah. He had a few. But more joy than regret overall. Even with the craziness of this new family situation.

He dropped Gilda and the girls off at Pine Ridge, then hurried back to his house. Justine would be arriving that evening. He wanted to spend time with her, but with the doctor's news, maybe he didn't have that time to spare.

Melonie had texted him that she was going straight to his house to work, but when he pulled into the drive, she wasn't there.

He started to text her when her SUV rolled into the short driveway. She parked next to him, climbed out and handed him a deli bag. "Sandwiches. And more of that cowboy blend coffee. I saw you were getting low and figured I'd grab some while we were in the city."

He didn't need more reasons to fall for this woman, but thoughtfulness and kindness added to the growing list. Food and coffee. So simple, but crazy appreciated.

She saw. She acted. Those were great assets in business, but he realized they were also wonderful in everyday life. That get-it-done mind-set his parents had embraced.

Camryn hadn't been like that. He realized that after she dumped him, that her life wasn't structured around others. It revolved around her. In retrospect she'd done him a favor, leaving him.

Melonie was an amazing woman with her own list of hopes and dreams. Did he dare take the risk, knowing her plans?

One look at her face told him it was already too late. He grabbed a pair of sodas from the fridge and brought them to the table. "Can I leave the girls at the ranch while I track down their mother in Oregon?"

"Of course. I just assumed that's what we'd do." She unwrapped her sandwich, then surprised him by reaching for his hand to say grace. Head bowed, she talked to God like they were old friends.

"Lord, we thank You for this food. Simple fare, the best kind there is. And, Lord, we ask You to bless Jace with wisdom about the babies, about their mother. He's in an unexpected place, God, and he could use Your guiding hand. Amen."

"That was sweet, Mel."

She focused on food, not compliments. Then she waved toward the laptop. "I've got a huge amount of work to do the next five days, and you're almost done here, which keeps you on track. But you weren't planning on spending a couple of days in Bend, I expect."

"I wasn't," he admitted. "But I can't leave this hanging, and if we sue for abandonment, then she's got some kind of official record to her name. I don't want to make trouble for anyone. But I need to make things right. And keep the girls safe."

A knock sounded on the door, but Mack didn't wait for an invitation. He walked right in, spotted Melonie and swiped his hat off mighty quick. And if the look of appreciation in his eyes got any brighter, Jace might have to knock some sense into him, and that would be a shame because they'd been friends a long time. "Mack, you hungry? Melonie grabbed sandwiches and there's plenty."

"I just ate, thanks, and you must be Melonie Fitzgerald." Mack extended his hand. "I'm the one who sent you the copy of your uncle's will."

"I remember. Thank you." She stood and shook his hand. "I'm going to use the office for work while you two sort out the contract and the relinquishment papers."

Mack made himself coffee while Jason talked, and when he got done, Mack was stirring half the sugar bowl into his cup. He tasted it, then brought it to the table. "The relinquishment papers are a simple draw-up. That's ironic, right?" He asked Jace. "I can polish those a whole lot faster than the house contract and that's a sorry commentary of today's world. Giving over custodial rights is a clear and simple matter. I'll have that to you by tomorrow morning. The house contract can go either way," he went on as he retrieved a notepad from his Western-tooled leather case. "We keep it precise and notate every little thing, or we keep it more general and you work within boundaries."

"The latter. I don't think my grandmother knows what she wants, but she sure knows what she doesn't want. A mess of a house and yard anymore."

"I'll have the house papers to you midweek. Does that give you time to start demolition? You don't want to jump into that until the contract is ready and signed."

"By Wednesday, yes. I can be done here and back from Bend."

"Then I'll make sure you have them by Tuesday so all parties are covered before you go all out."

Jace stood and shook Mack's hand. "Thank you. I'm grateful."

"The house looks great, Jace." Mack slipped the notepad into the bag once he stood. "The exterior, the gardens, the yard."

"It took two babies to light a fire under me to update. I don't know what I was waiting for, but it's nearly done now."

"And a huge project awaits." Mack faced him when they got outdoors. He glanced toward the house. "Is she up for it?" he asked.

"Over-the-moon to be able to show her stuff."

"What about you?" Mack's expression turned serious. "This had to hit hard, Jace. We've been friends a long time. But hey, if you don't want to talk about it—"

He didn't. And he did. He grimaced. "A lot to get used to, but then I look around and realize that drama follows lots of families. I just never associated it with mine."

"I know. Your mom and dad were the best. They were sure good to me." He clapped a hand on Jace's shoulder. "I'm out. I'll see you Tuesday."

"Thanks, Mack."

Mack offered a no-thanks-needed wave as he climbed into his car. By the time Justine pulled into the driveway later that afternoon, the bathroom was complete and the floor was ready for refinishing. The interior paint crew would come by on Monday to freshen up the living areas with fresh coats of cream-colored paint.

Melonie had gone back to the ranch. When he asked her to stay, she'd gripped his hand gently. "You need time to talk to your sister alone. Then bring her over. Don't make it too late or the girls will be cranky and tired. Cookie's got barbecue going and Corrie's made a bunch of sides to feed us through the weekend. That way we can relax with the girls while you're gone."

She was stepping up to the plate big-time. He knew she needed time to plot out rooms. The Hardaway house wasn't a typical box-style home. The architectural integrity of it needed to be respected, even when changed.

"Corrie has assured me that I'll have time to work."

"Did I look that worried?" He wasn't a worrier by nature. But then, he'd never been a parent before.

"Concerned," she told him. She grabbed her bag and hurried toward the door. "I'm expecting a phone call on some materials and it's easier to pick it up uninterrupted in the car. See you tonight."

He worked nonstop until he heard the crunch of Justine's tires in the driveway.

He didn't wait for her to come in.

He walked out to meet her, and when she climbed out of the car, she took one look around the beautifully reclaimed gardens and burst into tears.

And when Jace pulled his little sister into his arms— and felt her sob against his chest—emotions put a stranglehold on him, too. They'd cried at two graves in the past five years, but they had each other. They still did… and now, so much more.

Justine Middleton wasn't just lovely, Melonie realized when Jace and his sister pulled into the ranch later that day.

She carried herself with a quiet dignity, like her big brother. And when she climbed out of her car and spotted the girls in the double stroller, she went straight down to their level instantly. "Oh, my word, Jace, they're beautiful. And they really are babies!"

Jace aimed a dumbfounded look down. "I may have mentioned that. And I sent pictures, sis." He shifted his attention to Melonie and Corrie, behind the stroller. "So this is my sister, Justine, aka Captain Obvious."

"Hey." She looked up at Melonie and Corrie, smiling. "He sent pictures, yes, but the reality is a thousand times better." She stood and stepped back when Ava stuck out a quivering lower lip, but extended her hand. "It's so nice to meet you both, and thank you for helping Jace figure all this out."

"Well, it's mostly me," growled a distinctly male voice from the porch.

Justine spun around, laughed and dashed up the steps. "Heath!"

"Hey, kid." Heath hugged her, and when he stopped, he kept an arm draped loosely around her shoulders. "Glad you could sneak away for the weekend. Welcome home, brat. We want to hear your plans while you're here. What's in store for little Justine Middleton when the internship ends?"

She gazed up, indecisive. "I don't know," she told

him. She directed a sincere smile toward the stroller. "I thought I did, but this is a game-changer."

"It's not," said Jace from his spot in the driveway. "I've got this. You've got a career to build and a life to lead, Jus. Don't make me go all big-brother on you."

She laughed, and Melonie liked her more because of it. "As if. We've got lots to sort out and I'm taking time to do it," she told him. "I'm putting it in God's hands and I intend to get to know these babies all weekend. If that's all right?" She looked from Heath to Melonie and back. "Jace explained that he's leaving to track down their mother."

"It's more than all right," Heath told her. "We've never had the pleasure of this much female company on the ranch. It's been real nice for us cowboys."

"True words." Jace tipped that black cowboy hat slightly, but when Annie started to fuss, he called Justine back down. "Let's take the girls for a walk. We'll hear the bell when Cookie rings it."

Melonie began to back off.

Jace didn't let her. "I meant all of us."

"Except me," Corrie told them. "I'm needed in the kitchen." She climbed the stairs quickly. "Miss Justine, I'm Corrie Satterly."

Justine's eyes lit up when she heard the distinct Southern accent.

"It's a pleasure to make your acquaintance."

"And yours." Justine came back down the stairs.

"And I'm Melonie Fitzgerald," Melonie added as they began strolling.

"The one who redesigned our house?"

Please don't let her hate me for changing things...

Melonie winced slightly. "That's me. I know it was a surprise to come home to. *Another* surprise," she added.

"I love it."

Melonie's heart began beating again.

"Jace didn't want to change a thing, and once you get to know him you realize that he's rock solid in a lot of ways, and not embracing change is only one of many. But Mom had put some changes on hold to help pay for my education. In a way, you guys have made her dreams come true. I love the new open layout. And the updated bathroom is a huge plus," she laughed.

"I've been handed my share of changes lately," Jace reminded her.

"And you're adjusting brilliantly," Justine teased. "Uh-oh. Someone's unhappy."

Melonie peeked around front of the stroller. Ava was sitting back, content, watching the world.

Annie needed a clean diaper. "Bad timing, little one." They paused the stroller and she lifted Annie out. "I'll walk her back and change her. By then it should be suppertime."

"We'll turn around shortly. Or now," he decided when the porch bell sang out.

"I've always loved this place. This town." Justine smiled at Annie, then Melonie, and when the baby smiled back at her, she posed a question. "Is it normal for them to be this easygoing with so many people?"

Jace shrugged. "Maybe easygoing natures. Maybe being cared for by multiple people. And—" He stopped as Gilda came out of the house. She posted a hand to her forehead, looking for them.

"That's your grandmother."

Jace hated that Justine used words he wouldn't use

himself, but it would sound crazy to say so. "Mrs. Hard-away. Well, Gilda now. Since we're working together."

His sister sent him a sharp look. "I hope you're not playing judge and jury on whatever went on back then, Jason."

He frowned deliberately. At the name? Or her words?

"I've studied enough science to understand that human nature isn't dictated by science but by emotion. She had the guts to come to you, explain everything and beg for help. That couldn't have been easy for a proud woman like her."

"Pride goeth before the fall," he muttered.

Justine rolled her eyes. "And that could mean that lack of pride in one's endeavors brought the fall."

"Or that a prideful spirit is destined to fail."

"Will she be here this weekend?"

"Yes." Melonie kept her voice soft as they drew closer. "They're doing her roofs right now, a complete tear-off and replacement, and that's far too much noise and confusion for an elderly person."

"And she wants to help with the girls. She's surprisingly good at it," he added.

"Then we'll get to know one another over the next couple of days."

"Melonie." Gilda moved to the edge of the porch steps as they climbed up from below. "I know you're busy, and I know you've got a lot on your plate, but I want you to go to Oregon with Jace."

"Except I need to be here to help with the girls and work on your house plans."

"Corrie and I will be here, Rosie's available as needed and while Lizzie is busy with horses this weekend, we can call her on backup. And if Jason's sister is here, I think we've got this covered." She paused, as if picking her words. "To the best of my knowledge, Valencia knows nothing of Jason. I don't think her adoptive mother knew about him, and there was no one to fill her in."

Jace had been lifting Ava out of the stroller. He paused with her in his arms. "You think I'll make her nervous."

"Not nervous. But will she believe you, Jason? Even with my letter?" Gilda frowned in concern. "If we had time to get everything checked out to prove things, that would be one thing."

"You mean like DNA testing." Justine looked from Gilda to Jace. "I'm Justine, Mrs. Hardaway. Jace's sister."

Then Gilda did something out of character. She reached right out and hugged Jace's sister. "It is a pleasure to meet Ivy Middleton's other child," she whispered. "Your mother and father were very dear to me. Very dear."

"They were special people. Jace." She turned toward Jace as he climbed the porch stairs. "I think Mrs. Hardaway is right."

"That I need someone else there? To lessen the blow of a dark-skinned brother?"

"I don't think that will be a blow at all," Gilda argued, and now he stopped again, confused. "But she hasn't met you. It's not like Rosie showing up, or Harve or Heath. She knew all those people. You're a virtual stranger, and I'd suggest Rosie or me going, but Rosie's got a nursing baby and I'm not up for a trip like that. I won't push it," she finished and folded her hands. "I simply think it would be a good idea."

Chapter Fourteen

He hated that his grandmother was right, Jace realized the next day.

He'd never thought about how things might appear to Valencia, because he had the birth certificate and the letter from Gilda explaining things. But why would Valencia willingly sign over her daughters to a stranger, even if that stranger was her half brother? No one in their right mind would do that. Having Melonie along provided a buffer and an opportunity to know her better. That would work except she was busily developing ideas for the old mansion for most of the trip they embarked on the next day.

"Are we close?" she asked as he took a turnoff toward Bend.

"Yes. Do you want to eat first? Or go straight to the inn where she's been working?"

"The inn," she told him. "I'm not sure how this will all go down and I'm way too nervous to eat."

"And yet you've been working straight through."

"Nerves can't stop production," she told him as she closed the notebook. "My grandpa taught me that. He said there were many times when you did what you had to do, hating it all the while, but you just hunker down and do it. It made sense. And besides, this was the attic rooms and the second floor. Not much scope for the imagination there, but good clean lines to make the building inspector happy."

He spotted the inn's name up ahead. His heart beat louder in his chest, as he pulled into the inn's parking lot. "We're here."

Lizzie hadn't found an address for Valencia. Just a workplace. And he didn't want to do anything to get her fired from her job. But the thought of little Ava, needing medical help and unable to get it, spurred him forward.

He approached the front desk. The clerk looked up, met his gaze and smiled. But when he withdrew a picture of Valencia that Rosie had taken two months before, the smile disappeared and the clerk drew back slightly. "Sir, I'm sorry. I can't answer questions of a personal nature about anyone."

Undeterred, he still proffered the photograph. "This is my sister. She's not in any trouble, I just wanted to connect with her. We were told she works here."

The desk clerk stared him down and reiterated her statement. "I am not allowed to answer questions of a personal nature about anyone. Guest or employee."

Melonie moved forward. "I actually commend you on following the rules," she said. When the woman still appeared suspicious, Melonie withdrew paper from her bag and began to write. "Too many people disregard rules." She spoke as she scribbled a quick note. "They think they know better, but some rules exist to keep people safe." She folded the paper in quarters. "We're here on family business and I honestly don't know how much she'd be comfortable sharing. The name we know her by is Valencia Garcia. Some folks call her Val or Valerie. If she's here, please pass this on to her. We're in town briefly and it's important or we wouldn't have made the six-hour drive. Do you have grandparents?" she asked.

The clerk nodded.

Melonie added a copy of Gilda's note to the folded letter. "This is from the biological grandmother she never knew. She's not in the best of health and we offered to make this trip on her behalf."

She turned and started walking away.

Jace hesitated, torn. They'd come all this way to leave a couple of notes on a desk? Right now he figured the US Postal Service would have been a lot quicker and easier.

He caught up with Melonie just outside the door. "We're leaving?"

"We're going across the road to have coffee. And lunch. I'm starving, aren't you?"

"Now you're hungry?"

She leaned against the door. "For a patient man, you sure are impatient right now. Give her time to get the note. Read it. Think about it. Have you ever had to work a job like this? Tucked in a building all day, away from the sunshine and the breeze, cleaning rooms and scrubbing toilets?"

Of course he hadn't.

"Let's not cost her the job she's found. Let's wait and see what she says. If she comes over on her lunch break."

"You told her we'd be across the street?"

"I did. What I didn't tell her is that we've got rooms booked in this hotel for tonight."

He'd done that in case they couldn't see her. Or if she wasn't there. "She might not be here. I mean here, as in Bend. She might have moved on."

"Then we keep looking. But Lizzie seemed pretty sure of herself, and I've learned to never second-guess things with my sister."

They drove across the street, ordered coffee and lunch and twenty minutes later, Valencia Garcia walked in the door.

She glanced around the room, puzzled.

Jace got up and started toward her. "Valencia?"

His appearance only deepened her look of question.

He stopped shy of her and extended his hand. He'd come here, unsure what to say.

When he met her eyes, his heart softened. He'd seen lost puppies look more trusting than this woman. "I'm your brother. Jason Middleton. I was adopted by one family and you were adopted by another."

She stared at him, then shot a glance to Melonie.

Melonie put her hands up in surrender. "I'm just moral support. Although I am totally in love with your daughters. Who are both fine, by the way. Mostly."

"Mostly?" Valencia looked from her to Jace quickly. "Is something wrong with them? What is it?"

"Do you have time to sit a minute? Have lunch with us?"

"No, my break is short and I'm new here. I don't want to mess this up, they've been very good to me. It probably doesn't seem like much of a job to most, but I do it well. And that means something."

"Of course it does. Coffee?"

"Yes, thanks." She took a seat while Melonie ordered the coffee from the café side of the restaurant. Once she sat, she faced Jace. "Are they all right? The girls?"

"Yes and no. Ava's got a hearing problem from so many ear infections and they're going to put tiny tubes in her ears. But the doctor told me they won't let me sign off because I'm not a legal guardian."

Valencia put her head in her hands. "How are you involved in this? I thought that Rosie or maybe Heath would feel sorry for the girls and take them. They're such good people, I knew they'd never let them go."

"Except that's what they'd have to do, and what we'll have to do if you don't relinquish custody of them. No court is going to award their great-grandmother custody at her age, your mother has moved to Florida and I'm not technically part of the family. It's a legal mess that can get cleared up easily with a few official papers."

She winced. Because she needed to let them go? Or because the girls were in danger of becoming wards of the state? He didn't know.

"Gilda approached me a few weeks ago. Right after you left."

"The woman who says she's my grandmother." She lifted Gilda's note.

"Her story checks out, and she asked for my help."

"You're a cowboy. How's a cowboy going to raise two little girls? This wasn't what I wanted to happen. This is wrong. All wrong."

He gave her a minute to compose herself before he spoke. "Their great-grandmother asked me to raise them. She was the one who found my parents for me, my adoptive parents. She's got a good eye for people who love children, but more importantly, she sees all the mistakes of the past and wants to help fix them."

"Is she the skinny old woman who wears her hair up all the time? Kind of frail and bossy?"

He couldn't have described her better. "That's her."

"She came to Rosie's a few times. I saw her there."

"She knew who you were. You didn't know her."

"Why didn't she help then? Why couldn't she have coughed up some of that old money and given me a handout? Or a hand up? She couldn't be bothered then, when I was on my last dime and my mother was trash-talking my name all over the place. Maybe then—" She ducked her chin. Eyes down, her hands clenched. She looked angry and lost and forgotten...

But then she took a breath. A deep one. And her hand came up to a small silver cross hanging from a chain around her neck. And when she took another deep breath, she raised her gaze to his. "I'm sorry."

He waited, unsure what to say.

"I know I'm not right for them." She fingered the cross, restive. "I've known it for a while. I get mad too easy. Frustrated with things, when they don't go my way, and then I don't think straight. I'm trying to do better, but I can't seem to focus on keeping myself calm and taking care of two little girls who need constant attention. They shouldn't be with someone who resents spending time with them. They should be with someone like Rosie, who dotes on children. Maybe mother-hood's not my deal—"

"But you had them, Valencia." Melonie interrupted her with that poignant fact. "You had other choices. It takes a woman of courage to make the choice you did."

"I didn't feel all that brave," she admitted. "Mostly

sick. And tired. And when the clinic gave me options, I walked right out. I was the only chance the girls had. Babies get a one-shot deal, right?"

Melonie and Jace both nodded.

"So the old lady didn't offer to help, and that was probably because she was right about me. About me not being best for the girls, but I already knew that. So why shouldn't she be right about you?"

Jace read the pain in her eyes.

"She wants to help." When Valencia frowned, he pressed on. "She sent along a check for you." He set Gilda's check on the table.

"To buy me off?"

He shook his head instantly. "No. To assuage the guilt of not acknowledging her family when she had the chance. She's old and not in the greatest health and would love to hear from you. But I understand how that's not the easiest thing to do right now." He slid the check toward her and was glad when she slipped it into her pocket. "It's up to you what you do with it, but she sends it with a sincere heart, Valencia."

"Val. Please. I like Val better." She gazed down for long, drawn seconds as if the weight of the world hung on her shoulders. Then she raised her head and extended her hand. "Do you have the necessary papers with you?"

He withdrew the legal forms from the side of Melonie's computer satchel and handed them over. "A local lawyer drew them up."

She didn't read them.

She scanned them, then signed where indicated. And when she was done, she stood and faced them. "I've got to get back to work."

She turned to leave. Then she paused. Her hand was

on the back of the chair. The knuckles strained white against the honey maple wood.

Jace stood, too. "Do you want me to keep you updated, Val? Send you pictures? Keep you in the loop?"

The tight hand said more than her short words. It said how hard it was to let go of something so wonderfully precious...even for their own good. "No." She stood there, facing away, silent. Then she turned slightly and her words hit home with Jace. "Not because I don't love them," she said softly. "But because I do."

She left without a backward glance, and when she cleared the door, Melonie put in a call to cancel their hotel reservations.

Five minutes later they were back in his car, heading east, with the signed papers tucked in her bag.

The girls would be safe. Val would bear no legal problems because of her decision to leave them at Rosie's.

And he...

He swallowed hard because up to this point it had all seemed a little surreal.

He had just become a father.

While driving back to Shepherd's Crossing, Jace called Mack to file for a court hearing to approve the change of guardianship legally and file adoption papers.

Then he called Justine.

Next was Gilda, letting her know how things went. Despite the slight quiver in her voice, she sounded strong, as if getting things done was having a positive effect.

Melonie dozed off on the way back. He let her sleep, thinking how sweet she looked. How lovely. Wondering what it would be like to have her share this crazy new life with him. With those girls. Sure, she had big plans and dreams, but maybe he and the girls could become her plan. Her dream. She fit with him. Not just as a designer and a builder who would love to run a working ranch, like his grandfather before him. Both grandfathers, he realized.

Melonie inspired him to reach higher. Try harder. Go the distance.

To be a better man.

She touched his heart and soul in a way that had never happened before. So maybe...

He pulled into the Pine Ridge Ranch driveway as he made plans.

Melonie stirred and stretched, then she saw the house and the time and her eyes went wide. "I slept for two hours?"

"You did. And you didn't snore once."

She smiled at him and that smile set his heart tripping over itself to beat harder. Faster. "Good to know. I—" She paused as a figure stepped down the house steps. Then she laughed, undid her seat belt and was out of the car like a shot. "Ezra!"

The man—a little older than Jace, and square-built—grabbed her in a hug and spun her around. "We got it!" he said, over and over. "I knew we would if we found the right people, Mel, and I wasn't going to stop trying, because you deserve this. All that hard work, all that effort, I wasn't about to let that fall apart for a little thing like geography. You are now the soon-to-be star of *Shoestring Charm*. Just what you always wanted. And I was glad to be the guy who delivered it to you!"

Melonie gave this Ezra guy a kiss on the cheek, and

almost squealed for joy. "I can't believe you managed to pull this off." Then she hugged the guy—really hugged him—and the happiness in her face when she turned Jace's way shined the light of truth.

He had no right to steal her hopes. Her dreams. Whoever this guy was, he'd gone the distance for her. He'd done whatever it took to give her the shot she wanted.

Jace didn't have that ability.

He didn't care about renovation shows or fame or fortune. Simple country cowboy was his claim to fame, meager as that was.

He faked a smile, shook the guy's hand, then went inside to tuck the girls into bed. He'd already been away from them too long.

He settled the twins with Corrie and Justine's help, and when they were sound asleep, Corrie poured tall glasses of sweet tea for both Middletons. In a motherly fashion, she shooed them onto the porch. "I'll clean up the toys in here. You two, go. Talk. Figure things out." And when he and Justine settled onto one of the porch swings, he could make out the faint outline of Melonie and her friend, walking and talking in the fading light.

His family was here and that's where he belonged. He knew it. And he was pretty sure Melonie knew it, too.

And it didn't seem to matter nearly as much to her as it did to him.

Chapter Fifteen

"I thought I'd be in time to help get the girls ready for church, but you guys are a step ahead of me," Melonie said as she smiled at Justine and Jace the next morning. "They look wonderful. Do you want me to ride with you? Help with them?" She turned toward Jace.

He didn't look up. Didn't acknowledge her presence at all, actually. He shook his head. "We've got it, thanks. And thanks for the ride-along yesterday, Mel. I really appreciated it."

He said it like you'd thank anyone, not someone you'd kissed several times in the past week.

He said it like she was a casual friend. Worth a nod. Nothing more.

Ava turned her way, arms up, imploring Melonie to cuddle her.

Jace intercepted her smoothly. "Gotta go, little one." He strode through the living room, through the door and down the steps without a backward glance.

Justine reached for Annie and she went willingly, babbling baby sounds. So sweet. So dear.

They settled the twins into the car, then Jace drove

off, toward town. The little church had no pastor right now, so area folks took turns leading services. It was a sweet thing to do in a bind.

But Jace's attitude, seeing him drive off without even a backward glance, put her back up. She was done with not being good enough. Done trying to impress the men in her life and falling short.

Standing there, she realized that she wasn't the one falling short.

It was them. And between Uncle Sean's generosity and Ezra's industry, she didn't have to impress anyone anymore, because Ezra's good news proved she already had.

In church, she sat with her family. Prayed with them. And when folks were exclaiming to Jace and Justine about the girls after the service, she quietly left the church and headed back to the ranch.

No one got to brush her off. Not now. Not ever again.

She buried herself in the stable apartment, working on the first-floor plans for Gilda's house, and when Ezra came by midday, she took him to the Hardaway house so he could meet Gilda and ask permission to film there.

If Gilda refused, it would be a blow, but not a crushing blow because Shepherd's Crossing was ripe with makeover opportunities. She'd had one crushing blow already that day, when Jace shrugged her off as unimportant.

Anything else would be easy, compared to that.

Jace didn't have to worry about how to keep his distance from Melonie.

She did it for him, and that was an unexpected burr beneath his saddle for the following week. Justine had gone back to the West Coast and he felt more assured about his guardian status since the trip to Bend, but his personal status had crashed and burned. That's what he needed, right? To create distance from a woman bound for cable TV glory?

He might need it, but he hated every single minute of the estrangement.

The painters dolled up the first floor of his house on Monday. By Tuesday, he was ready to furnish the first-floor rooms. When boxes and crates arrived on schedule, he wanted Melonie there with him. Opening things, laughing over this and that.

But Melonie wasn't there.

Silence claimed the little house.

Birdsong filled the air outside, but inside, where her laughter had once brought life back to a place of sorrow, the quiet grew thick around him.

He put together two cribs with no help.

He laid the pretty oval rug on the girls' floor, then had the two delivery guys position the white dressers where Melonie had indicated on her design.

Double toy shelves.

A play table.

Two cribs.

They'd given the girls the biggest bedroom, but by the time he was done, the room seemed full. Yet empty. Because Melonie wasn't sharing the joy of preparation with him.

Gilda had given Melonie's friend permission to film some of the renovation.

They hadn't asked him.

Just as well.

He'd have offered his opinion and messed things up

even more than they already were. By the time he and the guys tackled demolition on Thursday, he was regretting his decision to step away.

He grabbed a sledgehammer and began demo on the Hardaway home interior with three hired hands. For the next week he'd be buried in breaking things down, shoring them up and putting structural beams into place. And moving the girls into the Middleton house.

There wasn't time to think of anything else, including Melonie, but he couldn't seem to think of anything *but* Melonie—and that was a whole other problem.

"You guys are amazing. I can't believe how much you've gotten done." Melonie came through the front door of the Hardaway house on Saturday and gave the four-man crew a thumbs-up. "You guys don't mess around, do you?"

"Jace doesn't let us up for air, but he keeps having pizza and sandwiches delivered," one man offered.

"And muscle cream and ibuprofen," laughed another man.

"So that takes the edge off," added Spike Bennett, an older carpenter who lived in town. "Food, coffee and pain relief."

"He's a considerate guy." She didn't look at Jace when she said it. He was considerate. When he wanted to be. But no matter how much she missed their time together, she wasn't anyone's casual acquaintance. Especially when there wasn't one thing casual about those kisses.

She turned to Jace, pretending she didn't care. "I've got a favor to ask you."

"Sure."

"I've got to get some final quiet work done before we have the building inspector look at these plans, and Pine Ridge Ranch is anything but quiet right now with wedding plans, people and babies. Can I spend Monday at your place?"

"Yes, of course."

"Perfect. Thank you." It wasn't perfect. Perfect would be having his arm around her shoulders. Drawing her in. Laughing at Ava's attitude and Annie's questioning looks. Cuddling on a sofa. Tucking the girls into bed.

Ezra called her name from the door. "I got some great demo and clean-up shots this morning. Can I get a few of you guys interacting amid the rubble?"

"Sure." She complimented the guys again, this time for the camera. And when she asked Jace about working at his house, he answered in a cool, polite tone as if the whole thing was a bother.

That made her all the more determined to put the polish on this project. Not to show him up. But to show her stuff because no one would ever get to consider her a bother again.

Jace motioned toward the darkening sky midday on Monday. "It looks like the forecasters got it right this time," he told Spike. He'd hired the older man to double-team the Hardaway project, and no one knew carpentry and construction better than Spike. "That's a mean-looking sky heading our way."

"It's fierce, for certain. Makes you glad the roofs are done. And we've got this place just about ready to renovate, but I think we need to sit down with Melonie and go over those design plans. I work better with a clear picture. Tonight, maybe?" Spike had mentioned this before and he'd put him off.

"Should work." Chin down, Jace pried nails out of the hardwood flooring. He'd deliberately delayed going over the plans with Melonie, but he'd have to prioritize it now. Spike shouldn't have to ask. He should have set the meeting in stone. What if they needed to make extensive alterations to her ideas?

He'd been able to cut the other two men loose after Saturday's work. Now it was him and Spike to complete the renovation, guided by Melonie's vision and her camera-hugging friend.

Thunder rumbled. They'd been dry for two weeks, not unusual for Idaho summers, but when things got too dry, wildfires became a concern. And things dried out real quick in a mountain summer.

Another flash of lightning commanded his attention as the threatening sky pitched their way. He put aside the flash of concern. The girls were safe and sound. Gilda was at Pine Ridge making jam with Corrie. Melonie?

Nope. Not his concern, but he had to shove the niggle of worry aside with mental force. She was at his house, and from the looks of the sky, the storm was rolling in north of his place. She'd be fine.

Focusing on demolition details, he ignored the growing tumult. There was work to do and one way or another, he meant to do it.

Chapter Sixteen

Melonie glanced outside as the light dimmed. Dark clouds skirted north of her, rolling across the valley like a well-done movie shot. She hadn't bothered checking the weather report that morning, but when her phone indicated a storm alert, she frowned. It looked like the storm would narrowly miss Jace's house, but Pine Ridge Ranch was in its path. The brewing storm was definitely going to make the folks over there sit up and take notice.

A sharp crackle of lightning split the air, followed by a swift, harsh crash of thunder. No rain, but the busy side of the storm had found her.

Lightning struck close again, almost sizzling, and when the thunder followed quickly, a gust of welcome, cool wind filled the kitchen.

The horses whinnied. One? Both? She wasn't sure, and the sound was muffled, like it came from the barn.

Lightning cracked again, with a distinctive *snap!*

Thunder followed instantly.

Her pulse quickened. Her heart beat a little harder in her chest.

To the south, the sky was deceptively clear. The town of Council was getting glorious sun.

But to the north, Mother Nature was unleashing her fury. Melonie's visibility was obscured by the intense storm, even though the rain didn't reach Jace's place.

Were the girls all right at Rosie's little house? Was Zeke there, or at the big house with Lizzie?

She started pacing the room, fighting nerves. She'd been in storms before, but the wide-open valley gave her a better vantage point, and this storm was raging over people she loved. Still, it was just a thunderstorm. She was being silly.

She moved back toward the computer.

The wind blew again, shifting the ruffled topper she'd put on the kitchen window. And with the wind came smoke.

Not just the scent of a distant campfire.

Smoke blew into the newly renovated house, a thick cloud of it, smelling foul and rancid.

She slammed the window shut, grabbed her phone and dashed outside, where her heart managed to jump straight into her throat.

The barn, a scant hundred feet from the house, was on fire. And Jace's two horses were inside, crying in piteous equine voices.

Her heart raced. Her palms went hot and damp.

She hit 911 and spoke quickly as she tried to open the gate. When the gate gave her trouble, she scaled the fence and landed with a thud on the other side. "Barn fire, 1727 Crossing Corners Road. Lightning strike, spreading quickly."

"Are there people in the building?"

She ran across the paddock. "No. Two horses."

"We've got Engine Company Two responding."

She pocketed the phone.

Bubba and Bonnie Lass didn't have time to wait for fire engines and big, brawny men.

They had her, and she knew how badly horses hated fire. And how much she feared horses.

Her gut seized. Her breath went shallow.

She stared at the barn as the raging fire swept from north to south along the back wall. Stacks of dried hay and straw fed the flames. To her right were the horse stalls, but the horses hadn't been closed in that morning. They'd been walking the paddock when she arrived. So they weren't closed in the stalls but they were in the barn, and they weren't wearing halters.

God, give me courage. And don't let me fail.

She whispered the prayer as she grabbed a lead rope from the hooks inside the broad, open doors, and didn't think. She didn't dare think, because if she did, she'd be useless and she couldn't afford to be useless now.

Bubba stood in front of Bonnie Lass as if sheltering her, and when she slipped the noose around his neck, he came right along, outside. She prayed Bonnie Lass would follow the old guy's lead, and when she got Bubba upwind of the fire, she tied him to a fence post, then ran back to the barn.

The north end was fully engulfed now. Bonnie Lass was at the other end, near the closed doors. If those doors would open, bringing Bonnie out might not be all that hard.

She ran that way, but when she tried the doors, they wouldn't budge.

Heart racing, she went back to the west-facing entrance, grabbed another lead line and hurried in.

Bonnie Lass backed up farther. She pushed herself into the far corner and stared at Melonie with frightened eyes.

Then she whinnied, only it was more like a scream.

"Easy. Easy, girl."

Bonnie Lass wanted no part of her easy talk. Smoke was pushing their way, and the crackle of fire grew louder. She felt the temperature rising, and still she reached for the horse's face.

Bonnie Lass rose up on her back legs.

Melonie's heart slammed.

Memories grabbed hold of her, of another horse. Another time, only that time it was Melonie in the corner, with no escape. And the horse was big...so big. And so very angry.

Don't think about that now.

This isn't Sweet Red Wine. This is Jace's horse, and she's nice. But scared. Think, Melonie. Think!

"Whoa. Whoa. Whoa." She slipped her hand up Bonnie Lass's face, toward her ears. "There we go, there we go. Good girl."

Her words seemed to help. The words themselves or the tone?

She didn't know and didn't care. She stroked the horse's face again. Would she let her slip on the rope? Should she take time for a halter?

The rising noise of the wind-fed fire nixed that idea and Melonie didn't have to look back to know that her escape route would be cut off soon. "Here, girlie." She'd heard Jace use that term before. "Come on, girlie, let's get out of this place. We've got fresh air waiting for us, right through that door."

She slipped the rope halter up, over Bonnie Lass's ears. The horse shied back.

Melonie hung tight. "Gotta go, girlie. Gotta go." She thought she whispered the words, but maybe not, because the horse shied again.

Smoke billowed up, then at them.

The flames were licking closer. There wasn't time for sweet talk or coaxing. Bonnie Lass either came now or would be left behind.

Melonie put more pressure on the rope as she turned away. "Come along. Come along."

Bonnie Lass rose up. Up. Up.

Don't think about it. Don't remember. Just keep walking.

Melonie didn't turn. She couldn't. The sight of those hooves raised high in the air might undo her and she couldn't afford to be undone now. "Come along, girlie. We've got this."

She didn't have it. The horse came down with a thud, and when she tried to shy away, Melonie tugged the other way, almost to the door. Close to safety. So close. "We've got this."

"We sure do." Strong hands closed above hers on the rope. "Mel, get out there. I'll draw her out. If I can."

Jace.

There, with her, with a pair of strong hands to help. But she wasn't about to leave now, with the wide opening so close behind them. "On three." She quick-counted to three and with both of them pulling at the same moment, Bonnie Lass stuttered along those last few steps, then cleared the door.

She let go then.

Fire engines were racing their way. Sirens blared, and as they came around the corner, the sight of them...

And the horse's fear...

And the noise...

Brought back all she'd forgotten about that horrible day twenty years before.

The small fire.

The horse.

Being trapped.

And then...

Her heart chugged to a full stop, remembering the sound of the single shot that brought the horse down. And her father, the anger and the disappointment she saw on his face as the prize filly was lying on one side of the barn's corner...

And his brutalized daughter was lying on the other.

"Come on." Jace grabbed hold of Melonie and led her through the gate. "Come out front, we'll be out of the way."

She let herself be led as a myriad of thoughts vied for attention.

"Is your laptop in the house?"

His voice jerked her back to the present. "Yes."

Looking up, she realized the house was in danger unless the fire company could keep the flames from spreading. "On the kitchen table. I closed the window."

He stared at her, then brought a cool, soothing hand to her hot face. Her cheek. "Thank you, darlin'. I appreciate it." He ran through the front door, ignoring the scoldings of the first responders, and came back out with her laptop, purse and an armful of family pictures that they'd just rehung on the living room walls.

"Got the important stuff," he told the fire chief as he came his way. "Just in case." He set the pictures in his truck with her computer, then started to guide her to the trees as a rescue vehicle pulled in.

She turned back and tugged him that way. "We've got to move the horses, in case they get free. They might go back to the barn. They do that, you know. Sometimes."

"I'll see to that right now," he told her.

"You can't do it alone." She slipped from his hand and started to hurry toward the open end of the paddock. "I couldn't get the gate open." She was talking fast, as if trying to explain why Bubba was still in proximity to the barn. "It jammed and there wasn't time—"

"I'll help him, Melonie." Heath's voice made her turn. "Lizzie's here. You go sit with her where it's cool, okay?" He locked eyes with her and spoke slow and firm. "You did real good, Mel. It's our turn now."

She blinked up at him.

Then Jace.

She nodded.

But tears were slipping down her cheeks, fast and furious, and there was no way Jace could leave her like that.

"I've got the horses," Heath said. "And here's Ty Carrington. We'll move them to the next section. Ty?"

"I'm in." A tall, broad man strode their way, and he and Heath went to draw the horses to a safer area.

"Hey, hey. Don't cry, Melonie." Jace drew her into his chest. Into his heart as her tears soaked the front of his plain white cotton T-shirt.

"I couldn't get away."

He frowned, not understanding, but not willing to break in, either.

"There was a fire, not a big one like this, a small one, and it wasn't even that close. I went to look and when I turned around, she charged me. She was big, Jace." She drew back as if trying to convince him. "So big. And all I could see was her anger and her fear and those hooves. And then I couldn't get away, I was boxed in, and she just kept kicking me. It seemed to last forever and no matter what I did, or how small I got, she wouldn't stop hurting me."

The scar on her face.

His chest went tight. "She hurt you?"

Her breath caught, then softened. And for several seconds, she breathed in and out as if calming herself. The maneuver seemed to work, and that probably meant it was well practiced. "She pummeled my head. Broke several ribs. Bruised my whole body. And mangled my cheek. My jaw was wired shut for weeks and I had multiple surgeries to put things back together."

He prayed mentally.

For her strength, for her well-being, for her peace. No wonder she steered clear of horses and barns. And he'd been willing to believe she was just a spoiled little rich girl who never had to prove herself in anything. Or to anyone.

"I knew I was going to die," she said softly. "I heard voices, screaming and yelling, but they couldn't pull her away. They couldn't get her off and the alley was blocked. And then I heard the gunshot."

Help her, Lord. Please help her.

She kept her face pressed against his shirt, against his chest and he held her there, wishing he could do something—anything—to make this better. "I'd forgotten so much of this," she went on. "The details of it.

They said it was because of the concussion. That I might never remember, and I didn't care because who wants to remember that? But then, today." She drew back as the firefighters surrounded the barn and house, pumping water through thick, heavy hoses. "I could see it in my head. I had to tell myself that Bonnie Lass wasn't Sweet Red Wine, that she was a nice horse. A good horse. She had to be because she was yours and you wouldn't keep a bad animal on the farm."

"Never."

"And then I remembered the shot. And my father's face, so angry. So disappointed. So sorry to have to put that beautiful animal down because a little girl went where she wasn't supposed to go."

Jace gripped her shoulders. "Is that what you think? That he was angry about putting down a rogue horse?"

She looked up at him. Confusion drew her eyebrows down. "He was angry about it. That horse was worth a quarter-million dollars. Anyone would be angry about it."

"Did your father hesitate, Melonie?"

She knew he didn't because she heard his voice, screaming…and then the shot. She shook her head.

"He wasn't mad or disappointed in you. I'm going to guess he was absolutely furious with the horse."

He was wrong, of course, but Lizzie came to her side at that moment. "Jace is right." She had a cool, wet cloth in her hand. Reaching out, she applied it to Melonie's right cheek. The chill of the cloth soothed the heated skin. "Dad has a laundry list of faults, we all know that, but he wasn't ever mad at you, Melonie. It was the horse. He bought her, thinking they could gentle her. They couldn't, she was a crazy girl, and I don't think he ever got over blaming himself for what happened. He made everyone promise not to talk about it unless you brought it up."

Was Lizzie right? Had Melonie spent two decades carrying around guilt about something that was never her fault?

The fact that it was a distinct possibility shamed her. "And I never brought it up."

Lizzie acknowledged that with a sad smile and a warm hug. "Who would, sweetie? I never dreamed you blamed yourself for what happened. I just figured the trauma was enough to make you go off horses and barns forever, and it wasn't like Dad was about to win any Father of the Year awards. And yet today—" She shifted her gaze to where Heath and Ty Carrington were putting a firm fence between the horses and the fire. "You were a true hero. I honestly can't imagine how you did it, Mel. But you did, and I'm proud of you."

So was Jace. Proud and grateful. She'd faced her greatest fears for him, after he'd been acting like a first-class jerk to her.

The EMT came alongside them right then. "Let's have a look here, missy." The older woman pointed to the rescue wagon. "I want to check your breathing and vitals. Then you can go back to hugging your boyfriend."

"I'll be right there with her," Jace promised.

"But the fire—"

He kept his arm looped around her shoulders as he led her to the waiting ambulance. "It's only a building. As long as you're okay, nothing else matters, Mel."

And he hoped she'd give him the chance to prove that he meant it.

Chapter Seventeen

The sting in Melonie's cheek had eased by Wednesday. A surface burn, like a moderate sunburn, and nothing more.

"Rosie's got a doctor's appointment for Jo Jo today, so we're keeping the girls here." Corrie washed up Annie and then Ava when the girls had finished breakfast. Lizzie had taken advantage of the early morning sun and was giving Zeke a ride on Honey Bunny, one of the ranch stock horses. "Do you have to get to Gilda's?"

"No. Supplies are scheduled to be delivered today and the men will start rebuilding the upstairs tomorrow. Jace is moving sheep right now."

"Well, I wonder if these two would like a nice walk in that big, fancy stroller we've got out there. Maybe see what their cowboy daddy is doing?"

Melonie laughed.

The stroller was big, all right, but not one bit fancy. Rosie had found it at a garage sale the previous year when she first started watching the twins. It was bulky, but the thick tires worked on farm lanes, and that meant everything around here. "I'll take them. I could use a walk myself. We can go see Jace in action and maybe meet some sheep."

They fastened the girls into their seats. Ava might have beaten Annie at walking, but Annie was part monkey when it came to climbing. She'd wiggle her way out of that stroller seat in a heartbeat without the safety buckle firmly fastened.

"I've got to get that cake in the oven," Corrie reminded her. "Are you okay on your own with them?"

"They're way smaller than the horse I tackled a few days ago. I think we're okay."

Corrie laughed, then hugged her. "My brave girl! See you when you get back."

Ezra was editing video in the first-floor equine-barn office. He'd gotten some great preliminary shots and a short but poignant one-on-one interview with Gilda— an interview he wouldn't let anyone see, which meant it was good. Real good.

She pushed the stroller forward.

June had started out with kelly green grass rolling across the hills, like the Irish countryside pictures her grandmother had always loved. As the end of the month closed in, the green had deepened. Dandelions nodded yellow heads all around the farmyard. Clumps of perennials were grouped in random spots, not yet blooming.

It was a beautiful place. Different than Kentucky, more rugged. Less pristine, yes. But it called to her like it was meant to be. Like she belonged there. But how hard would it be to be here, day after day, watching Jace raise these babies from afar? When he'd held her a few days ago, she'd sensed his caring emotion.

But between the fire's aftermath, smoke damage to the bedroom wing of the house and the final bits of teardown at Gilda's, she'd barely seen him. Now he was moving sheep for Heath, making ready for the next round of lambs, which were due soon.

He was at the far side of the nearest pasture when they approached. He sat tall in the saddle on a Pine Ridge Ranch horse, and the straight lines of his back, his easy hands and the tilt of his black cowboy hat made him look like an ad in a Western magazine.

He saw them. He raised a hand in a salute, then headed their way, taking care to not disturb the ewe and lamb groupings.

He pulled up in front of them and looked down, smiling.

He shouldn't be so handsome. So strong. So good and nice.

He climbed down off the horse, let it graze, then crossed the last few feet to them. He was on one side of the sheep fence.

She was on the other.

He fixed that by jumping the fence as if it was nothing. "You gals out for a midday stroll?" He smiled at her, then the girls.

Ava babbled, waving both hands, then she shrieked at the sheep like a little banshee.

Annie looked up at him and simply grinned. Her whole face lit up, without needing to make a scene about it.

Melonie nodded while the girls flirted with him in their distinct ways. "It was too nice to stay inside, but Ava doesn't like the feel of grass under her feet."

"A trait she'll need to lose to be happy on a ranch," Jace teased the baby, and Ava giggled as if sharing the joke.

"And Annie said she wanted to come see her daddy. So I said sure."

"You did?"

She'd been looking down at the girls.

The husky note in his voice made her look up. And when she did, she didn't want to look away from those warm, brown eyes. "Well, sure, it's wonderful for them to see what you do. What it takes to build a place or herd sheep or cut hay."

He leaned closer. "Do I dare hope that you like coming to see me, too? Maybe a little bit?"

Her heart stutter-stepped.

Like coming to see him? Love was more like it. "I believe you've known that all along, Jace. But then you started acting like a jerk, and—"

He kissed her.

He didn't wait, didn't ask, just wrapped those big arms around her and drew her in. And when he was done kissing, her, he kissed her all over again. "I'm sorry I was a jerk. I saw you and Ezra and knew you had dreams and goals that went way beyond an old six-room house in western Idaho. I didn't want to face the thought of you leaving. So I pulled back."

She leaned back against his arm and poked him. "Did it ever occur to you to ask me?"

"You'd already told me how you wanted to do your show, showing off your skills. And that drawl you tried so hard to lose. I find that drawl to be a mighty pretty thing, Melonie Fitzgerald," he added, sending a look her way that set her pulse humming.

"Why, cowboy…" She batted her eyelashes to match the Southern drawl. "You flatter me."

His grin widened. "Woman, you talk like that and I will be at your beck and call. I'm pretty sure I'm going to be at your beck and call anyway, Melonie. And if that means following you to Kentucky—"

"You would follow me to Kentucky?" She didn't even try to mask her surprise.

He didn't hesitate at all. "Anywhere, Mel. Just as long as you don't mind being a carpenter's wife and a mother to two little girls. I hear Kentucky gets a little hot for a northern guy like me, but I can adjust. Given a little time and encouragement," he added another kiss, and when he finally eased back, she laid her head against his chest.

"What about staying with me right here in Shepherd's Crossing?"

He pulled back and lifted a brow. "I don't get it."

"What if the producers were so in love with the pilot that they're interested in doing the show with a Western twang instead of a Southern drawl? That I get to stay here with you and raise two little Western girls?"

"You're staying?"

"I believe I just said that."

He picked her up and whirled her around, then set her down when Annie burst into tears. "Sorry, darlin', sorry. Daddy's just a little excited, I didn't mean to scare you." He unclasped her safety belt and withdrew the crying baby from the stroller.

Melonie reached down, unclipped Ava's seat belt and did the same with her. Then she reached into her pocket now that Annie had calmed, pulled out her phone and stretched her hand out and up. "All right, you guys. Our first family selfie. Say 'cheese.'"

The word activated the camera function, and when she held out the image for Jace to see, he put an arm around her shoulders and tugged her close. Ava was in her right arm. Annie was perched on his left hip. And they were the absolute image of a happy couple.

"I love it, Melonie. And—" he eased around and

rubbed his forehead against hers, gently "—I love you. And despite the fact that you've already kind of asked me, will you marry me, Melonie? Be my wife? And help me raise these precious little girls?"

"I will," she assured him. "Oh, I absolutely will! But we have to wait because I don't want to mess up Lizzie's wedding plans."

"What if the last thing I wanted to do was wait?" he asked then. "And what if we shared their wedding?"

"Say what?"

"What if we have a double wedding with Heath and Lizzie and we all do that happily-ever-after thing?"

Was he joking?

One look at his face said he wasn't.

"Just so you know, I already ran it by them and they were fine with the idea."

She wasn't sure if she should kiss him or smack him.

She'd spent a lifetime longing to be loved and cherished not for what she was, a rich man's daughter, but for who she was.

And she'd found that right here in the rugged hills and valleys of western Idaho in the arms of the best man she'd ever known.

She reached up and pressed her lips to his mouth. "I love you, Jace. Just in case we get too busy with these two and I forget to tell you."

He grinned down at her. "I know you do, darlin'. But it's sure sweet hearing you say it out loud."

A sheep baaed in the background. Then another one joined in. He eyed the pasture, then her as he tucked Annie back into her side of the stroller. "Duty calls, but I'll look forward to more of that kissin'-and-huggin' stuff tonight. And you little gals be good for your mama, all right?"

More sheep began blatting. A border collie loped his way, as if wondering what was taking so long.

He hopped back over the fence while she settled Ava into her seat. And when he rode uphill, he paused midway, deliberate and slow. Then he turned the horse slightly and gave the brim of his cowboy hat a tip with one finger.

A cowboy salute.

She laughed, waved and aimed the stroller back toward the house, wondering how life had turned around so completely in the last few weeks and so incredibly glad it did.

A home. A soon-to-be husband. Jobs for both of them, and the promise of rebuilding Hardaway Ranch into a Middleton home.

And two baby girls, needing someone to love them and care for them and raise them. Just like the Middletons had done for Jace.

Her world had changed in a matter of weeks. From doubt had sprung faith.

What if she hadn't taken Uncle Sean's challenge to move here for a year? She'd have missed God's plans for her. For these girls. For Jace, her beloved.

A rooster crowed from the chicken coop west of her. He crowed again, and she laughed.

It wasn't their highfalutin' Kentucky horse farm.

It was better.

And she was here, with a bright new chance at faith, hope and love. And, of course, the greatest of these...

She leaned down and kissed the twins' soft, sweet cheeks...

Was love.

Epilogue

Melonie rolled over, spotted the clock and flew out of bed. She threw on clothes and rushed downstairs. How had she overslept on today of all days? With so much to do?

She dashed into the empty kitchen.

The rich smell of cowboy blend coffee filled the air, but the little house was quiet.

Too quiet.

Then she caught a glimpse of the front yard.

Balloons bobbed and weaved everywhere. Dozens of bright primary-colored helium balloons were tied to every post and open branch and even the chair handles. Color filled the yard, and as she moved through the front door, Jace looked up.

He grinned and her heart just about melted on the spot. "You did all this? Why didn't you get me up, Jace?"

The girls were running their miniature scooters on the driveway. Back and forth, laughing and giggling.

He cupped her cheeks and kissed her. Long and slow and when he stopped, she leaned in for just a little more.

"You worked so hard to get everything ready for today. For their birthday. I wanted you to get some rest so when I heard them chattering, we moved the crazy outside and began filling balloons."

"It looks amazing."

He looped an arm around her shoulders. "So do you, darlin'. And that coffee smells mighty good. I wouldn't mind if a cup found its way out here. I had one earlier but I didn't want to leave the girls alone to go brew another one."

"I'm on it. And I'll bring out the tablecloths."

Bubba nickered from the far pasture. A lean-to shed gave the pair cover for now. They'd have to see about building a replacement barn before winter set in.

But that wasn't a concern today.

Today their soon-to-be adopted daughters turned one year old, and they'd invited friends and family to come have a day of barbecue, babies and children. A celebration of life and love.

"Jace?"

He'd grasped another bunch of balloons and turned, looking absolutely amazing and adorable.

She smiled at him.

He smiled back.

And then she went to make him coffee.

She hadn't had to say a word. He knew. He understood her emotions. Her joy. Because he felt the exact same way.

She brought him out a steaming mug.

He'd tied the balloons to the mailbox post, marking the entrance. A neighbor had loaned them a bounce house for the day, and Gilda had ordered a waterslide.

The twins were too small to appreciate it, but everyone else would love it.

He crossed to her, set the coffee aside, then hit a button on his phone.

The music of Glenn Miller filled the air.

He took her into his arms.

The twins giggled and bobbed up and down, their own way of dancing to the music.

And when Jace began leading her across the lawn to the sweet old tune, Melonie followed, step for step. And when the first song wound down, she leaned up, batted her eyelashes against his cheek and made him laugh. Then sigh.

"I am looking forward to spending the rest of my life doing this—" she indicated the yard, the kids and the handsome cowboy with a wave of her hand "—forever. I couldn't ask for anything more, Jace. Except…"

He lifted one eyebrow.

"Another dance? Please."

He smiled. And then began dancing her across the lawn again, as if there weren't a million things to do to get ready for the party.

Because nothing was more important than dancing with his wife.

And she loved that most of all.

* * * * *

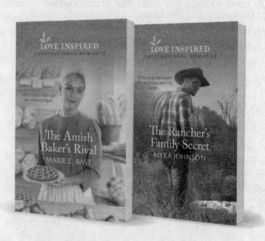

SPECIAL EXCERPT FROM

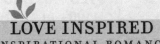

LOVE INSPIRED
INSPIRATIONAL ROMANCE

*When Susannah Peachy returns to her grandfather's
potato farm to help out after her grandmother is injured,
she's not ready to face Peter Lambright—the Amish
bachelor who broke her heart. But she doesn't know his
true reason for ending things…and it could make all the
difference for their future.*

Read on for a sneak peek at
An Unexpected Amish Harvest *by Carrie Lighte.*

"Time to get back to work," Marshall ordered, and the other men pushed their
chairs back and started filing out the door.

"But, *Groossdaadi*, Peter's not done with his pie yet," Susannah pointed
out. "And that's practically the main course of this meal."

Marshall glowered, but as he put his hat on, he told Peter, "We'll be in the
north field."

"I'll be right out," Peter said, shoveling another bite into his mouth and
triggering a coughing spasm.

"Take your time," Lydia told him once Marshall exited the house. "Sweet
things are meant to be savored."

Susannah was still seated beside him and Peter thought he noticed her
shake her head at her stepgrandmother, but maybe he'd imagined it. "This does
taste *gut*," he agreed.

"*Jah*. But it's not as gut as the pies your *mamm* used to make," Susannah
commented. "I mean, I really appreciate that Almeda made pies for us. But
your *mamm*'s were extraordinarily *appenditlich*. Especially her *blohbier* pies."

"*Jah*. I remember that time you traded me your entire lunch for a second
piece of her pie." Peter hadn't considered what he was disclosing until Susannah
knocked her knee against his beneath the table. It was too late. Lydia's ears had
already perked up.

"When was that?" she asked.

"It was on a *Sunndaag* last summer when some of us went on a picnic after
kurrich," Susannah immediately said. Which was true, although "some of us"
really meant "the two of us." Peter and Susannah had never picnicked with
anyone else when they were courting; Sundays had been the only chance they

had to be alone. Dorcas, the only person they'd told about their courtship, had frequently dropped off Susannah at the gorge, where Peter would be waiting for her.

"Ah, that's right. You and Dorcas loved going out to the gorge on *Sunndaag*," Lydia recalled. "I didn't realize you'd gone with a group."

Susannah started coughing into her napkin. Or was she trying not to laugh? Peter couldn't tell. *How could I have been so* dumm *as to blurt out something like that?* he lamented.

After Lydia excused herself, Peter mumbled quietly to Susannah, "Sorry about that. It just slipped out."

"It's okay. Sometimes things spring to my mind, too, and I say them without really thinking them through."

It felt strange to be sitting side by side with her, with no one else on the other side of the table. No one else in the room. It reminded Peter of when they'd sit on a rock by the creek in the gorge, dangling their feet into the water and chatting as they ate their sandwiches. And instead of pushing the romantic memory from his mind, Peter deliberately indulged it, lingering over his pie even though he knew Marshall would have something to say about his delay when he returned to the fields.

Susannah didn't seem in any hurry to get up, either. She was silent while he whittled his pie down to the last two bites. Then she asked, "How is your *mamm*? At the frolic, someone mentioned she's been…under the weather."

I'm sure they did, Peter thought, and instantly the nostalgic connection he felt with Susannah was replaced by insecurity about whatever rumors she'd heard about his mother. Peter could bear it if Marshall thought ill of him, but he didn't want Susannah to think his mother was lazy. "She's okay," he said and abruptly stood up, even as he was scooping the last bite of pie into his mouth. "I'd better get going or your *groossdaddi* won't let me take any more lunch breaks after this."

He'd only been half joking about Marshall, but Susannah replied, "Don't worry. Lydia would never let that happen." Standing, she caught his eye and added, "And neither would I."

Peering into her earnest golden-brown eyes, Peter was overcome with affection. *"Denki,"* he said and then forced himself to leave the house while his legs could still carry him out to the fields.

Don't miss
An Unexpected Amish Harvest *by Carrie Lighte,*
available September 2021 wherever
Love Inspired *books and ebooks are sold.*

LoveInspired.com